They were there.

Luke froze, lying under the pitted steel belly of the speeder. Listening.

No sound.

But they were there, watching him. He knew it. Even through the silent trumpets of the Force in the deep stillness of the wastelands, he could sense their presence.

The invisible watchers.

The planet's unseen original inhabitants.

Luke lowered his eyelids, trying to call the shape of them within the Force. But such was the interference of the Force on this world, the sheer magnitude of its presence in alien guise, that he could get no clear picture of those invisible ones. Maybe, he thought, that was the point of the interference to begin with.

Nor could he tell exactly when they had begun to dog him, or feel whether their interest was beneficent, malicious, or merely inquiring.

They were only there.

"Who are you?" he called out, aware of his vulnerability. "I mean you no harm. You don't need to be afraid to show yourself to me. *Can* you show yourselves to me?"

Their presence drew closer—or something drew closer, a distinct awareness of their awareness of him. He wondered how he knew it was *they* and not *he, she,* or *it.*

STAR WARS™
PLANET OF TWILIGHT

Barbara Hambly

BANTAM BOOKS
TORONTO · NEW YORK · LONDON · SYDNEY · AUCKLAND

This edition contains the complete text of the original hardcover edition.
NOT ONE WORD HAS BEEN OMITTED.

STAR WARS: PLANET OF TWILIGHT
A BANTAM BOOK : 0 553 50529 7

Originally published in Great Britain by Bantam Press,
a division of Transworld Publishers Ltd

PRINTING HISTORY .
Bantam Press edition published 1997
Bantam paperback edition published 1998

Bantam Books are published by Transworld Publishers
61–63 Uxbridge Road, London W5 5SA,
a division of The Random House Group Ltd,
in Australia by Random House Australia (Pty) Ltd,
20 Alfred Stret, Milsons Point, Sydney, NSW 2061, Australia,
in New Zealand by Random House New Zealand Ltd,
18 Poland Road, Glenfield, Auckland 10, New Zealand
and in South Africa by Random House (Pty) Ltd,
Endulini, 5a Jubilee Road, Parkton 2193, South Africa

Reproduced, printed and bound in Great Britain by
Cox & Wyman Ltd, Reading, Berkshire.

For Ole and Nedra

1

The first to die was a midshipman named Koth Barak.

One of his fellow crewmembers on the New Republic escort cruiser *Adamantine* found him slumped across the table in the deck-nine break room, where he'd repaired half an hour previously for a cup of coffeine. Twenty minutes after Barak should have been back to post, Gunnery Sergeant Gallie Wover went looking for him, exasperatedly certain that he'd clicked into the infolog banks "just to see if anybody mentions the mission."

Of course, nobody was going to mention the mission. Though accompanied by the *Adamantine*, Chief of State Leia Organa Solo's journey to the Meridian sector was an entirely unofficial one. The Rights of Sentience Party would have argued—quite correctly—that Seti Ashgad, the man she was to meet at the rendezvous point just outside the Chorios systems, held no official position on his homeworld of Nam Chorios. To arrange an official conference would be to give tacit approval of his, and the Rationalist Party's, demands.

Which was, when it came down to it, the reason for the talks.

When she entered the deck-nine break room, Sergeant Wover's first sight was of the palely flickering blue on blue of the infolog screen. "Blast it, Koth, I told you . . ."

Then she saw the young man stretched unmoving on the far side of the screen, head on the break table, eyes shut. Even at a distance of three meters Wover didn't like the way he was breathing.

"Koth!" She rounded the table in two strides, sending the other chairs clattering into a corner. She thought his eyelids moved a little when she yelled his name. "Koth!"

Wover hit the emergency call almost without conscious decision. In the few moments before the med droids arrived she sniffed the coffeine in the gray plastene cup a few centimeters from his limp fingers. It wasn't even cold. A thin film of it adhered to the peach fuzz beginnings of what Koth optimistically referred to as his mustache. The stuff in the cup smelled okay—at least as okay as fleet coffeine ever smelled—and there was no question of alcohol or drugs. Not on a Republic escort. Not where Koth was concerned. He was a good kid.

Wover was an engine room regular who'd done fifteen years in merchant planet-hoppers rather than stay in the regular fleet after Palpatine's goons gained power: She looked after "her" midshipmen as if they were the sons she'd lost to the Rebellion. She would have known if there had been trouble with booze or spice or giggle-dust.

Disease?

It was any longtime spacer's nightmare. But the "good-faith" team that had come onboard yesterday from Seti Ashgad's small vessel had passed through the medical scan; and in any case, the planet Nam Chorios had been on the books for four centuries without any mention of an endemic planetary virus. Everyone on the *Light of Reason* had come straight from the planet.

Still, Wover pecked the Commander's code on the wall panel.

"Sir? Wover here. One of the midshipmen's down. The meds haven't gotten here yet but . . ." Behind her the break room door *swooshed* open. She glanced over her shoulder to see a couple of Two-Onebees enter with a table, which was already unfurling scanners and life-support lines like a monster in a bad holovid. "It looks serious. No, sir, I don't know what it is, but you might want to check with Her Excellency's flagship, and the *Light,* and let them know. Okay, okay," she added, turning as a Two-Onebee posted itself politely in front of her. "My heart is yours," she declared jocularly, and the droid paused for a moment, data bytes cascading with a faint *clickety-click* as it laboriously assembled the eighty-five percent probability that the remark was a jest.

"Many thanks, Sergeant Wover," it said politely, "but the organ itself will not be necessary. A function reading will suffice."

The next instant Wover turned, aghast, as the remaining Two-Onebee shifted Barak onto the table and hooked him up. Every line of the readouts plunged, and soft, tinny alarms began to sound. "Festering groats!" Wover yanked free of her examiner to stride to the boy's side. "What in the name of daylight . . . ?"

Barak's face had gone a waxen gray. The table was already pumping stimulants and antishock into the boy's veins, and the Two-Onebee plugged into the other side had the blank-eyed look of a droid transmitting to other stations within the ship. Wover could see the initial diagnostic lines on the screens that ringed the antigrav personnel transport unit's sides.

No virus. No bacteria. No poison.

No foreign material in Koth Barak's body at all.

The lines dipped steadily toward zero, then went flat.

"We have a complicated situation on Nam Chorios, Your Excellency." Seti Ashgad turned from the four-meter bubble of the observation viewport, to regard the woman who sat, slender and coolly watchful, in one of the lounge's gray leather chairs.

"*We* meaning whom, Master Ashgad?" Leia Organa Solo, Chief of State of the New Republic, had a surprising voice, deeper than one might expect. A petite, almost fragile-looking woman, her relative youth would have surprised anyone who didn't know that from the age of seventeen she'd been heavily involved in the Rebellion spearheaded by her father and the great stateswoman Mon Mothma: With her father's death, she was virtually its core. She'd commanded troops, dodged death, and fled halfway across the galaxy with a price on her head before she was twenty-three. She was thirty-one now and didn't look it, except for her eyes. "The inhabitants of Nam Chorios? Or only some of them?"

"All of them." Ashgad strode back to her, standing too close, trying to dominate her with his height and the fact that he was standing and she remained in her chair. But she looked up at him with an expression in her brown eyes that told him she knew exactly what he was doing, or trying to do, and he stepped back. "All of us," he corrected himself. "Newcomers and Therans alike."

Leia folded her hands on her knee, the wide velvet sleeves and voluminous skirt of her crimson ceremonial robe picking up the soft sheen of the hidden lamps over-head and of the distant stars hanging in darkness beyond the curved bubble of the port. Even five years ago she would have remarked tartly on the fact that he was omitting mention of the largest segment of the planet's population, those who were neither the technological post–Imperial Newcomers nor the ragged Theran cultists who haunted the cold and waterless wastes, but ordinary farmers. Now she gave him silence, waiting to see what else he would say.

"I should explain," Ashgad went on, in the rich baritone that so closely resembled the recordings she had heard of his father's, "that Nam Chorios is a barren and hostile world. Without massive technology it is literally not possible to make a living there."

"The prisoners sent to Nam Chorios by the Grissmath Dynasty seem to have managed for the past seven hundred years."

The man looked momentarily nonplussed. Then he smiled, big and wide and white. "Ah, I see Your Excellency has studied the history of the sector." He tried to sound pleased about it.

"Enough to know the background of the situation," replied Leia pleasantly. "I know that the Grissmaths shipped their political prisoners there, in the hopes that they'd starve to death, and set automated gun stations all over the planet to keep them from being rescued. I know that the prisoners not only didn't oblige them by dying but that their descendants—and the descendants of the guards—are still farming the water seams while the Grissmath homeworld of Meridian itself is just a ball of charred radioactive waste."

There was, in fact, very little else in the Registry concerning Nam Chorios. The place had been an absolute backwater for centuries. The only reason Leia had ever heard of it at all before the current crisis was that her father had once observed that the old Emperor Palpatine seemed to be using Nam Chorios for its original purpose: as a prison world. Forty years ago it had been rumored

that the elder Seti Ashgad had been kidnapped and
stranded on that isolated and unapproachable planet by
agents of his political foe, the then-Senator Palpatine.
Those rumors had remained unproven until this second
Ashgad, like a black-haired duplicate of the graying old
power broker who had disappeared, had made contact
with the Council in the wake of the squabbling on the
planet and asked to be heard.

Though there was no reason, Leia thought, to make
this man aware of how little she or anyone knew about
the planet or the situation.

Do not meet with Ashgad, the message had said, that had
reached her, literally as she was preparing to board the
shuttle to take her to her flagship. *Do not trust him or accede
to any demand that he makes. Above all, do not go to the Meridian
sector.*

"Very good!" He passed the compliment like a kidney
stone, though he managed a droll and completely automatic little chuckle as a chaser. "But the situation isn't as
simple as that, of course."

From a corner of the lounge, where a dark-leaved
dyanthis vine shadowed the area near the observation
port, a soft voice whispered, "They never are, are they?"

"Well, I was given to understand that the only inhabitants of the planet before colonization recommenced after
the fall of the Empire were descendants of the original
Meridian prisoners and guards."

In the shadow of the vine, Ashgad's secretary, Dzym,
smiled.

Leia wasn't sure what to make of her irrational aversion to Dzym. There were alien species whom the humans of the galaxy—the Corellians, Alderaanians, and
others—found repulsive, usually for reasons involving
subliminal cues like pheromones or subconscious cultural programming. But the native Chorians—Oldtim-

ers, they were called, whether they belonged to the Theran cult or not—were descended from the same human rootstock. She wondered whether her aversion had to do with something simple like diet. She was not conscious of any odd smell about the small, brown-skinned man with his black hair drawn up into a smooth topknot. But she knew that frequently one wasn't conscious of such things. It was quite possible that there could be a pheromonic reaction below the level of consciousness, perhaps the result of inbreeding on a world where communities were widely scattered and had never been large. Or it might be an individual thing, something about the looseness of that neutral, unexceptional mouth or having to do with the flattened-looking tan eyes that never seemed to blink.

"Are you one of the original Chorians, Master Dzym?"

He was without gesture. Leia realized she had subconsciously been expecting him to move in an unpleasing, perhaps a shocking, way. He didn't nod, but only said, "My ancestors were among those sent to Nam Chorios by the Grissmaths, yes, Your Excellency." Something changed in his eyes, not quite glazing over but becoming preoccupied, as if all his attention were suddenly directed elsewhere.

Ashgad went on hastily, as if covering the other man's lapse, "The problem is, Your Excellency, that seven hundred and fifty years of complete isolation has made the Oldtimer population of Nam Chorios into, if you will excuse my frankness, the most iron-bound set of fanatical conservatives this side of an academic licensing board. They're dirt farmers—I understand. They've had centuries of minimal technology and impossibly difficult weather and soil conditions, and you and I both know how that makes for conservatism and, to put it bluntly, superstition. One of the things my father tried to institute on the planet was a modern clinic in Hweg Shul. The place can't make enough to keep the med droids up and running. The farmers would rather take their sick to some Theran cult Listener to be healed with 'power sucked down out of the air.'" His hands fluttered in a sarcastic, hocus-pocus mime.

He took a seat in the other gray leather chair, a blocky man in a very plain brown tunic and trousers obviously cut and fitted by a standard patterning-droid and dressed up with add-ons—gold collar pin, gold-buckled belt, pectoral chain—that Leia had seen in old holos of his father. He leaned his elbows on his knees, bent forward confidingly.

"It isn't only the Newcomers that the Rationalist Party is trying to help, Your Excellency," he said. "It's the farmers themselves. The Oldtimers who aren't Therans, who just want to survive. Unless something is done to wrest control of the old gun stations away from the Theran cultists, who forbid any kind of interplanetary trade, these people are going to continue to live like . . . like the agricultural slaves they once were. There's a strong Rationalist Party on Nam Chorios, and it's growing stronger. We want planetary trade with the New Republic. We want technology and proper exploitation of the planet's resources. Is that so harmful?"

"The majority of the planet's inhabitants think it is."

Ashgad gestured furiously. "The majority of the planet's inhabitants have been brainwashed by half a dozen lunatics who get loaded on brachniel root and wander around the wasteland having conversations with rocks! If they want their crops to fail and their children to die because they refuse to come into the modern world, that's their business, I suppose, though it breaks my heart to see it. But they're forbidding Newcomers entrance into the modern world as well!"

Though she knew that Dzym would undoubtedly back up anything Ashgad said—as the man's secretary he could scarcely do otherwise—Leia turned to the Chorian. He was still sitting without a word, staring into space, as if concentrating on some other matter entirely, though now and then he would glance at the chronometer on the wall. Beside him, the port offered a spectacular view of the ice green and lavender curve of Brachnis Chorios, the farthest-flung planet of the several systems that went by that name, whose largest moon had been designated as the orbital rendezvous of the secret meeting.

The escort cruiser *Adamantine* was just visible at the edge of the view, a blunt-nosed silvery shape, unreal in the starlight. Below it, close to the bright triangle of colored stars that were the primaries of Brachnis, Nam, and Pedducis Chorii and pathetically tiny against the cruiser's bulk, hung the cluster of linked bronze hulls that was Seti Ashgad's vessel, the *Light of Reason.* Even Leia's flagship, the *Borealis,* dwarfed it. Assembled of such small craft as could slip singly through the watchful screens of Nam Chorios's ancient defensive installations, the *Light* would barely have served as a planet-hopper; it could never have taken a hyperspace jump.

Hence, thought Leia uneasily, this mission. Even before she'd had the surreptitious message, their distance from the nearest bases of the New Republic's power on Durren and their proximity to the onetime Imperial satrapy of the Antemeridian sector, made her nervous.

Was that all that note had meant? Or was there something more?

"The Theran cultists are not anyone into whose hands I would be willing to place my destiny, Your Excellency," murmured Dzym. He seemed to draw himself back into the conversation with an effort, folding his small hands in their violet leather gloves. "They hold an astonishing amount of power in the Oldtimer settlements along the water seams. How could it be otherwise when they are armed, mobile, and have for generations been the only source of healing that these people have known?"

Beyond the dyanthis leaves that masked the edges of the observation port, Leia's eye was caught by a flickering of the lights along the *Adamantine*'s gleaming sides. She saw that in the rear quarter of the escort ship, a number of them had blinked out.

"What do you mean, you can't get through?" Commander Zoalin turned, harried, from the comm board, which had blazed into life like a festival lamp, to stab yet another flashing switch. "Are you not getting an answer from the *Borealis*, or what?"

"It seems to be a simple signal block, sir." Communications Chief Oran touched her forehead in a nervous salute. "Legassi is running a scan for it."

In the small screen, Oran turned in her chair, granting the Commander a glimpse of the comm center, on whose main board a huge readout of the *Adamantine*'s comm circuits was illuminated in glowing yellow lines. Red lights flowed along them, synaptic testing for a blockage or interference in the power transmission, easy enough to find and correct under ordinary circumstances.

But the circumstances had gone from ordinary to hideous in just under ten minutes. And by the red lights flaring all over his comm board; by the hastily gasped message from the infirmary; and by the sudden absence of anyone replying or reporting from maintenance, shuttles, power, and several other ship sections, things were plunging from bad to worse with the speed of a decaying orbit.

"Legassi?" Oran rose from her chair. Zoalin saw past her that the chair he had thought empty in front of the scan console was, in fact, occupied. Yeoman Legassi had collapsed forward over his console, squamous salmon-colored hands clutching the edge of the board spasmodically, in time to the dreadful shudders that ran like waves through his frame.

Zoalin thought, *Calamari aren't supposed to be affected by human viruses* . . .

If this was a virus.

Neither, of course, were Sullustans or Nalroni, both of which species were represented by crewmembers who had reported ill in the past five minutes. Zoalin seemed to recall from his xenobiology courses that Nalroni and Mon Calamari were a textbook example of mutually exclusive immune systems. What a Nalroni could get, a Calamari literally couldn't.

"Legassi?" Oran bent over the Mon Calamari's shivering body. "Legassi, what . . . ?" She staggered a little, almost as if she had been struck, and put a hand to her chest. Groping, as if trying to massage away some numbness or pain.

"Commander Zoalin," stated the calm voice of Two-Onebee, the head of the infirmary section, on the channel that he had left open, "I regret to report that bacta tank therapy appears to accelerate rather than retard dissolution of subjects, by a factor of nearly thirty-five percent, as far as can be analyzed."

With the measured tones sounding in his earclip, Zoalin flicked the central console screen from image to image, keying through to corridors where the search teams in quest of the signal block device turned toward the infirmary as first one, then another of their number would stop, lean against the wall, knead and rub at the chest or head or side. The view cut to sick bay, where the calm and tireless droids operated mechanical lifts to re-move Sergeant Wover's lifeless, dripping body from the bacta tank; to the shuttle bay control room where the last yeoman on duty lay dying alone in a corner by the door.

Fifteen minutes, thought Zoalin blankly. *Fifteen minutes since Wover signaled from the deck-nine break room.*

He hadn't even severed the connection when the other calls had started pouring in. Midshipman Gasto down. Engineering Chief Cho P'qun down. *Sir, we can't get any signal from maintenance . . .*

"Foursi." He clicked through a channel to the Central Computer's Operating Signal Division—Division 4C. "Emergency reprogramming request. All maintenance droids of the . . ." His head was aching—his chest, too. He found it difficult to breathe. *Stress,* he told himself. *And no wonder.* He had to find the signal block, had to get in touch with the Chief of State's flagship. Had to get a signal out to the Sector Medical Facility on Nim Drovis.

"All maintenance droids of the See-Three category. Search for nonstandard equipment in . . ." *What color would the lines be, that a signal blocker would be cut into?* "Non-standard equipment in the green lines." He hoped that was right. His head was throbbing. "Implement immediately."

Not that it would do much good, he thought. Droids were systematic. Their method of hunting for nonstandard equipment would be to start at the *Adamantine*'s nose and work to the stern, investigating every hatch and relay, rather than checking the most obvious places first, the places where some member of Seti Ashgad's small good-faith party might have made a few moments for himself alone.

Not that it had to be Ashgad. A signal blocker could have been set with a timer. The thing could have been planted in the *Adamantine* before their inconspicuous departure from Hesperidium.

Zoalin found that without thinking about it, he had slumped back into his chair. His hands and feet felt cold. He cut into the image of the flagship *Borealis,* distant against the blackness of the stars. So close, but kilometers away in the palely shimmering green glow of the planet beneath.

Had this, whatever it was, broken out there, too? Was Captain Ioa trying to reach *him*?

He leaned his head back. *Twenty minutes,* he thought. *Twenty minutes.* He felt as if he were in a turbolift, plunging into long darkness.

"I realize there's been a great deal of ill said about the Rationalist Party over the past few years." Seti Ashgad had risen from his chair as if the sheer importance of his cause drove him to his feet, and paced restlessly back and forth behind it. "But I assure you, Your Excellency, that we're not the—the strip-mining capitalists we've been portrayed. The Newcomers went to Nam Chorios in the hopes of opening new frontiers. Individual entrepreneurs can't get a foothold in Pedducis Chorios. Places like Nim Drovis and Budpock and Ampliquen have their own civilizations, settled up and locked in. Given the presence of the heavy industry in the Antemeridian sector, the trading opportunities alone should have made the entire colonizing of Nam Chorios self-sufficient!

"But it isn't just that the Newcomers are forbidden to bring in any ships larger than a personal flitter—or to let any out. The Theran habit of opening fire on *any* vessel over a certain size means that when equipment wears out, it can't be replaced except for an exorbitant fee. It means there's no export to support anything but the barest subsistence livelihood. It means we have to pay smugglers' prices for everything. It means that because the Registry didn't give sufficient information about conditions, these people have condemned themselves to exile in a cultural backwater. You can't pretend that's fair."

"No, I can't," said Leia slowly. "But isn't that what colonization is about? Gambling on what conditions are going to be when you get there? I'm not saying that the Therans are right," she added, holding up a hand as the man before her drew breath for an indignant protest. "What I am saying is that they are supported by the majority of the population of the planet."

"Who are kept as their slaves by superstition and lies!"

That isn't the Republic's business. Leia straightened her shoulders under the velvet weight of her robe, seeing, in the flare of Ashgad's anger, the reflection of what her own reactions would have been at eighteen. *But it shouldn't be that way!* She remembered crying to her father, when after a complicated and emotional court case concerning vampiric Garhoons and their prey, the prey had elected to return to their vampires. It had taken her a long time to understand and respect her father's decision to pursue the matter no further.

"Nam Chorios is not a part of the Republic. Legally, we have no right to interfere in their affairs."

"Not even to protect the rights of the colonists? The rights of men and women who . . . ?"

"Who left the Republic," said Leia, "to go live on a world that was not part of it. Who decided to take a chance on a world about which they knew almost nothing. Everyone knows the deficiencies in the Registry's information. And the Empire 'protected the rights' of Alzoc III, of Garnib, of Trosh."

Ashgad's broad face reddened. "The cases are nothing alike! We certainly aren't asking you to enslave a native population! Just to ensure those who wish it the right to a decent livelihood."

"The majority of Nam Chorios's population voted not to affiliate with the Republic," said Leia. "And that, the colonists *did* know. We have no right to disregard the wishes of the majority. I have no wish to sound hard-hearted, Master Ashgad, but the Newcomers are not being constrained in any fashion that I have heard of."

"Except that their lives are there. All their assets, which with the gun stations in operation they can't even take with them should they leave. Their stake in the future is on that planet."

"So is the stake of the original inhabitants, Master Ashgad."

The big man stood for a moment, one hand on his hip, the other on the back of his chair, head down, one dark lock of his thick hair hanging over a forehead furrowed with frustration and thought. Among the dusky leaves of his miniature bower, Dzym had fallen silent again, gloved hands folded, a small frown of concentration furrowing his smooth forehead. He hadn't, as far as Leia could discover, even made secretarial notes to himself in a hide-out mike to supplement a recorded transcript of the interview.

"What I will do is this," said Leia, after a moment's silence. "When I return to Coruscant, I'll authorize an investigation team to see what's really going on down on the planet and to explore other options, if possible. We may be able to negotiate with the Therans who control the gun stations."

"No one negotiates with the Therans." Fierce bitterness flashed like a dagger in Ashgad's voice and glinted in his green eyes. "They're fanatical lunatics who've had that entire population of credulous fools under their spell for generations."

There was a small movement among the dyanthis leaves. Leia glanced quickly across at Dzym, in time to see the secretary sit back, strangely misshapen-looking in his granite-colored robes, an expression of satiated ecstasy flowing across his face. He sighed deeply, savoringly, and was still.

"I had hoped to convince you to come to our aid, Your Excellency." Ashgad's voice again drew her mind away from the curiously nonworking secretary. "And I very much appreciate your sending a commission. I'll certainly use all the influence I possess in the Newcomer community to help them with their findings."

Leia rose, and extended her hand. "I know you will." She spoke with genuine warmth, though the cynical rebel who still lived in the back of her mind added, *I just bet you will.*

Ashgad bowed low over her hand, an old-fashioned courtesy she hadn't encountered since she'd left Palpatine's court. The man seemed completely sincere, and Leia's own instinct to help and protect embattled minorities sympathized with his frustration. From having contended with such factions as the Agro-Militants and the United Separatists, she did genuinely wish that she could do something for modern, intelligent people struggling to free themselves from irrational tyranny.

If that was what was actually going on.

"See that Master Ashgad finds his way back to the shuttle bay all right, would you, Ssyrmik?"

Leia's small honor guard sprang to their feet as the Chief of State and her guests stepped through the doors to the conference chamber's anteroom. The lieutenant bowed, and shouldered her sleek white-and-silver ceremonial blaster rifle. "This way, Master Ashgad, Master Dzym."

Looking at the youthful faces and earnest demeanor of

those half dozen young graduates of the New Republic's Space Academy made Leia feel a hundred years old.

The trio of bodyguards Ashgad had brought with him bowed to her as well: Handsome androgynes in close-fitting, light blue uniforms with the oddly dead-looking hair of very expensive dolls.

As she watched the bronze-embossed doors of the corridor shut behind them, Leia heard a soft, gravelly whisper behind her say, "Those three smell wrong, Lady. They are no living flesh."

Leia glanced behind her at the four small, gray, wrinkled humanoids who seemed to have melted from the antechamber's walls. The smallest, who barely topped Leia's elbow, regarded the bronze doors with narrowed yellow eyes.

Several years had passed since, in the face of mounting pressure from the Council, Leia had eliminated her bodyguard of Noghri hunter-killers. Leia understood it; even before the unfortunate incident of the Barabel ambassador, there were those who said it ill behooved her to wield a weapon that had been Palpatine's. Bringing them on this mission had been a terrible risk.

Do not trust Ashgad, the message had said.

She had sent for them, secretly, just before departure. There were some risks greater than schism in the Council.

"Technically, it *is* living flesh, though," said Leia thoughtfully. "They're synthdroids, Ezrakh. I've seen them in the pleasure domes on Hesperidium and Carosi. Sculpted synthflesh over metal armatures. They have only minimal internal computers; their actions are centrally controlled, probably from Ashgad's ship, because I don't know of any technology that would transmit from as far away as Chorios itself."

She folded her arms, and a small dark line appeared

between the sharp brushstrokes of her brow. "And as far as I know, they're very, *very* expensive. Would you just make sure for me that they *do* get on their vessel?"

The Noghri inclined his head, but not before she saw the twinkle of amused comprehension in his eyes. "Gshkaath already sees to it, Lady."

Maybe the message she had received had prejudiced her, she thought, shaking her head. It was something she tried daily to guard herself against, but personal prejudice could never entirely be discounted.

The Noghri started to withdraw—they tended to keep themselves separate from the Academy honor guard, who were among the few even aware of their presence on the ship—but Leia raised her hand impulsively. "What about Master Dzym?" she asked. "How does he smell to you?"

Ezrakh hesitated a moment, weighing the question, the folds of his leathery gray face tightening. Then he made a sign of negation. "His smell is a human smell. I do not like him either, Lady—I do not like his eyes—but he smells as other humans do."

Leia nodded, a little comforted. "Will you come with me?" she asked. "And you, Marcopius, if you would." She smiled to one of the young Academy guards. It wasn't their fault, she knew, that the hunter-killers of Honoghr could slice a potential assassin to pieces before a human—particularly these youths—could unlimber a blaster rifle, nor was it the fault of the Academy guards that she could not risk any possibility of threat while on this mission. Throughout the trip she had been very careful to keep the Academy guards in their usual position at her side, and to emphasize to them that the Noghri were only a backup, a holdout weapon against unexpected catastrophe.

And as Luke would say, there was no way of telling which group might be her salvation in a crisis.

At the turbolifts she touched the summon switch, and when she and her two guards were within the car, toggled the controls for the shuttlecraft hangar deck.

2

Do not meet with Ashgad.

Down on the *Borealis* shuttle deck, Luke Skywalker turned the slip of flimsiplast over in his hands.

It was small, about the length and width of two fingers, the semitransparent stuff used for packing and wrapping delicate objects for shipping. It had been carefully but unevenly torn from a larger piece and wadded tight in the innards of a cheap music box in fact. The words were written in graphite marker, such as his uncle had used to mark rocks and scrap metal out in the field.

The tune the box played was an old one, a song about a beleaguered queen and her three magical birds.

The handwriting was Callista's.

> *Do not trust him or accede to any demand that he makes. Above all, do not go to the Meridian sector.*
>
> *Callista*

His heart was a slow battering ram against the inside of his ribs.

He barely heard the quick, soft beeping at his side as

the astromech droid Artoo-Detoo emerged from around the airfoil of the modified B-wing that rose like a suspended wall in the rear corner of the deck-six shuttlecraft bay. See-Threepio, protocol droid extraordinaire, followed close behind, golden carapace shining in the soft light. "According to Artoo, all systems appear to be in flying order, Master Luke," stated the protocol droid in his prissy mechanical tenor. "But personally, I should be much happier were you to take a larger craft with greater oxygen capacity."

Luke nodded absently, "Thanks, Threepio." But in fact his attention never left the slip of plast in his hand, the bold, firm, slightly old-fashioned writing across its face.

He was seeing the snows of Hoth, and the way Callista's lightsaber had vied with the ice planet's dim sunlight for brightness. Seeing the ruined bunker there and how the ice had glittered in the smoke-brown tousle of her hair. Remembering what it had been to fight at her side, more a part of him than his own hand or arm; knowing which way she'd turn, or lunge, or drive the snow monsters into his blade.

With the memories of the snow were the warm scents of night on Yavin Four, and of lying in each other's arms on the hillside above the jungles, counting stars. Callista had explained to him with great solemnity why it had seemed so logical for her and two other Jedi apprentices, thirty-three years ago—in another body, another life— to try to concoct the illusions of ghosts haunting an old drift station on Bespin to puzzle their Master and why this had turned out to be not such a good idea after all.

He hurt with wanting her. Missing her. Needing her.

I realized I could not come back to you. I'm sorry, Luke.

The blazing glare of the monster ship, the *Knight Hammer,* and all the hopes of the renegade Admiral Daala's fleet, crashing in flames . . .

His own voice crying Callista's name.

I have my own odyssey . . .

The warm, boyish, husky voice coming to him from the recording, the gray eyes in the ghostly oval of her face.

I'm sorry, Luke . . .

The shuttle deck of the *Borealis* was quiet. Only a few security officers stood around the antiquated Seinar system brig that had brought Seti Ashgad over from the *Light of Reason,* talking with the brig's graying, downtrodden-looking pilot, their white-and-silver ceremonial blaster rifles slung on their backs. Ashgad had arrived with only his secretary, his pilot, and three synthdroids; and Luke could have reassured his sister's guards that it was not physically possible for a Seinar brig to carry more than six humans. Seinar brigs—particularly the old H-10s like that one—were the staple of smallsystem personnel transport. Luke had taken apart and put together enough of them in his youth on Tatooine to know there wasn't a compartment big enough to tuck a Ranat into, let alone anything human or human size.

The vessel was in good shape, but the metal was patched, pitted, and old. If Seti Ashgad, who according to Leia was one of the wealthiest men on Nam Chorios, could obtain no better, it was little wonder he was willing to join up with the Rationalist Party to try to better conditions on the planet.

He turned the message in his fingers again.

The music box, a cheap and ingenious mechanical contraption without a chip in it, had been forwarded from Atraken, but analysis of the peculiar crystalline dust beneath the nailheads securing the panel behind which the message had been found had revealed that it had been put together on Nam Chorios.

Callista was on Nam Chorios.

Or had been, when she sent the message.

Artoo tweeped again, more quietly. Artoo-Deetoo was the only droid Luke had ever encountered who seemed to be able to sense human moods. See-Threepio would catch on eventually if the problem were translated into binary and jacked at full-blast into his receptors—and would then feel and express genuine sympathy—but Artoo just seemed to know.

Luke sighed and patted the little droid's domed cap, as if it were a pittin's head. Through the gaping maw of the magnetically shielded shuttle port, the violet-white speck that was Nam Chorios's primary glimmered against the powdery banners of starlight and galactic dust.

There was something about it. A curious tingling in the Force that Luke could feel even at this distance. What it might be, he didn't know.

Do not meet with Ashgad.

Do not go to the Meridian sector.

"Can I be of any further assistance, Master Luke?" Threepio's voice was diffident. Luke made himself smile, and shook his head.

"No. Thanks."

"According to my internal chronometers, Her Excellency's meeting with Master Ashgad should be concluding now. Normal departure protocols occupy on the average twenty minutes, and you did express a desire to be away from the *Borealis* before Master Ashgad returns to the shuttle bay."

Luke glanced at the chronometer on the wall, an automatic gesture, since he knew Threepio's internals were accurate to two or three beats of atomic vibration. "Right. Thank you. Both of you." He hesitated, then slid the plast into the pocket of his gray flightsuit.

"Good luck, Master Luke," said Threepio. He hesitated a moment, then added, "Given an estimated population of less than one million humans, and no indigenous life forms on Nam Chorios, chances of locating Lady Callista within a standard year should be well within the seventeenth percentile."

Luke made himself smile again. "Thanks." And the seventeenth percentile—in a year—wasn't bad. Not when you considered how vast even the known portion of the galaxy was. It had been a year already, since the *Knight Hammer* had plunged blazing into the atmosphere of Yavin 4.

At least he had it narrowed down to one planet.

If she were still there.

Why Nam Chorios?

He was turning toward the ladder that led up to the B-wing's hatch when the main bay doors opened. His sister entered, golden boot tips flashing beneath her figured gown and the great state robe of ruby velvet spreading behind her like a thranta's wings with the speed of her stride. The young Academy midshipman who accompanied her everywhere fell back and stood near the door; as Luke held out his hands to her he glimpsed the Noghri Ezrakh, lurking almost unseen in the shadows. "So, did he whip out an ion cannon and try to murder you?"

Leia grinned, but the smile was a wan one and disappeared almost at once as she shook her head. "There's just—I don't know. Maybe it's because he looks so much like the holos I've seen of his father. I sympathize with his cause—him and the Newcomers on that planet. But it's out of our jurisdiction." She looked over at the brig and did a double take. "He came in *that*?"

"He's not kidding about those gun stations." Luke gestured to the long char on the brig's side. "A B-wing should be just small enough to get past the screens."

There was a moment's silence, awkward, neither

knowing quite what to say. To break it, Luke fished in his pocket for Callista's message. "You need this for anything? Analysis?"

"Keep it." She put her hands on his shoulders, drew him down to kiss his cheek. "We've got all we can out of it. It may tell you something about where to find her, once you get down there."

There was silence. Then, "She's got to come back," said Luke softly. "She'll stand a better chance of regaining the ability to use the Force at the Jedi academy than she will on her own. We have all the records that are still in existence, all the training aids you found on Belsavis. The Jedi power has to be still within her somewhere. Cray had it. It isn't as if Callista's mind went into the body of a non-Jedi. And the Academy needs her."

Leia was silent.

"*I* need her."

"You'll find her." Still she held his hands, willing him to feel a reassurance she did not share. She had never seen her brother happier than during the time he'd spent with that quirky, silent, gentle lady: A Jedi Knight reincarnated without her powers. A woman who had been a ghost and lived again.

But she'd been with Callista on Belsavis, when she'd realized that her ability to use and touch the Force had not carried over into the body that Dr. Cray Mingla had bequeathed to her. She'd watched the woman's grief, frustration, and slow-growing despair; had talked to her about things that could not be said by either one to Luke.

Luke would find her, Leia thought sadly. Somehow she knew that much. But to what end?

"You'd better go," she said. "Luke—When you're down there, look around, will you? According to Ashgad, the Theran cultists who control the gun stations use coercion and superstition to rule the Oldtimer population."

As Leia spoke, she followed Luke to the corner, where he'd stacked the supplies he'd take with him: a water bottle, a small medkit, food tablets. They'd chosen a B-wing over the smaller X-wing fighter partly because of the nearness of the pirate-nests on Pedducis Chorios, but partly because of Callista's warning. The three systems had been scanned repeatedly, and reported clear. But Leia still felt uneasy. A B-wing could take on a much larger ship in a fight, but it was perilously close to the estimated automatic target mass of the gun stations.

"Now, if it's just superstition, there's nothing we can do about that," she went on. "It's their free choice, and they voted overwhelmingly to keep the original trade restrictions in force. But if there's coercion involved, that may change the Rationalists' case. We may be able to negotiate. Moff Getelles still rules the Antemeridian sector 'in the name of the Emperor,' and it isn't that far away."

That had been yet another reason for choosing a B-wing.

"If fighting breaks out between the Newcomers and the Therans, he may try to interfere. We've got a pretty strong force at the Durren orbital base, but I'd rather not have to use it."

Luke nodded. She stood below, looking up as Luke climbed the long, fragile ladder up the side of the airfoil and began working the bottles and packets into every spare cranny of the cockpit. In the days of the Rebellion, and during the long mopping up of sporadic warfare with the various Moffs and Governors and self-proclaimed Grand Admirals of the Empire, he'd participated in space battles and dogfights without number. Given the presence of Imperial Warlords and a sizable

Imperial fleet still under the control of those who longed for the old regime, he supposed he'd take part in hundreds more. But more and more, in the back of his mind, was a growing regret, and a terrible sense of waste.

"I'll keep an eye out," he said. He climbed back down to her, and zipped up the light, tough fabric of his suit. "Being incognito should help." He glanced across at the brig, its pilot still in conversation with the guards. The dispatch of an escort vessel would rouse very little curiosity, given the proximity of Pedducis Chorios.

"Just the fact that Callista would send that message, would come out of hiding to send it, means there's something going on. The fact that she didn't think it could go subspace means it's serious."

Leia shook her head, the gold finials and cabochon gems of her hairpins flashing. "It could be. . . . That's something else I wanted to ask you." She leaned her shoulder against the airfoil, which rocked just slightly in its antigrav cradle, and lowered her voice. "It isn't generally known, Luke, but there's some kind of leak in the Council. Information's getting out to Admiral Pellaeon and to the Imperial Moffs like Getelles and Shargael over in I-sector. Minister of State Rieekan thinks it may be through someone in the Rationalist Party—maybe even Q-Varx himself, though I think the man's honest. They have adherents both in the Republic and in nearly every piece of the Empire still big enough to field a fleet."

She hesitated a moment, her mouth wry and her brown eyes suddenly older than her years. Luke saw in her eyes the years of bitter wrangling, the betrayals: Mon Mothma poisoned, the Council split by factions, Admiral Ackbar betrayed, discredited, hounded . . .

"Myself," she said softly, "I think it could be almost anyone. But Callista knows something about it."

"I'll keep my ear to the ground." He checked the seals

on his flightsuit and the helmet tubes of the emergency systems—not that any system would save anyone's life in a true emergency in vacuum. "Leia . . ." He reached out a hand for hers, not entirely certain what it was he wanted to say.

Her eyes met his. He understood the look in them. Before she was twenty she had seen her family, her world, everything she knew, casually wiped out as a demonstration of the Empire's might. Before he had ever met her, she had lost some essential part of herself.

But that weary hardness in her eyes, that look of steeling herself so as never to be surprised by even the worst . . .

And she knew it. She felt what she was becoming.

He said, not knowing that he was going to say it, "Keep up with your lightsaber practice. Kyp or Tionne should be able to help you. They're the best, the most centered in the Force. You need it. I'm speaking as your teacher now, Leia."

Surprise wiped the defensiveness from her eyes, but she looked quickly away. When she looked back it was with a quick grin, to cover her uneasiness. "To hear is to obey, Master." Turning his seriousness aside.

But in the meeting of their eyes he saw in hers, *Please understand*. Although he knew she didn't understand herself the false note in her voice or the intention, momentarily seen and as quickly buried, to let the turmoil in the Grand Council, the massive investigation of Loronar Corporation's abuses in the Gantho system, the Galactic Court trial of Tervig Bandie-slavers, the education of her children—anything and everything—divert her from the Jedi training she knew in her heart that she needed.

He didn't press her. "You kiss the kids for me." He drew her close for a quick, warm kiss on the cheek, awkward around the helmet, tubes, wires. "Tell the guys at the Academy I'll be back."

"I wish you could take at least Artoo with you."

He climbed a few rungs of the ladder up the airfoil. "So do I. But even if I took him apart and tucked the pieces into every corner and under the seat of this thing, there wouldn't be room."

She drew back, and watched as he climbed the rest of that long ladder, settled himself into the B-wing's cockpit. "I'll subspace you from Hweg Shul when I need to be picked up," he said, his voice tinny through the helmet comm as he fastened himself in. "Probably before that, if I can find a transmitter strong enough that'll take the code."

"I'll be waiting." She reached out with her mind, through the glowing inner net of the Force, and touched his spirit like the warm clasp of a hand. Felt his thanks for that final reassurance.

Then she and the droids retreated, and at her signal the security guard, the shuttle's pilot, and Marcopius joined her at the bay doors. Ezrakh had already faded into the corridor's shadows. The great leaves of dull gray metal slid open to let them out. Her last sight of the bay showed her Luke's B-wing turning with weightless grace to face the black, star-spattered rectangle of the magnetic portal and the steady-burning violet eye of the distant world where Callista had taken her refuge.

The doors slid shut.

Keep up with your lightsaber practice.

Why had she felt that guilty flinch when he'd said that? *You need it.*

Why did she feel in her chest that slight sensation of

panic, like a woman deathly sick who fears to ask the doctor what she has?

She knew she needed it.

The comm light was flashing in her stateroom when she reached it, but when she pressed the toggle and said, "Organa Solo," there was only the faint hum of an open channel. She frowned, annoyed and a little worried, and kicked the heavy train of her robe aside as she settled into the chair before the station.

"If you have no further requirements, Your Excellency," said Threepio, "Artoo and I will take this opportunity to repower."

She looked up quickly—she found she had been staring reflectively at the blinking comm light—and said, "Oh, okay. Fine. Thank you." She punched through an alternate comm number, and again, got only tone.

It happened, of course. Usually it meant that the comm watch was in the break room. As a girl she'd had the annoying habit of coding and recoding comm numbers every few seconds until she got results. It had taken her years to break herself of it, to relax for a few moments, do something else, then try again like a normal person.

But the situation wasn't normal. Though the Meridian sector included a number of Republic planets and two major fleet strongholds at the Durren orbital base and on Cybloc XII, Moff Getelles's satrapy in the Antemeridian sector wasn't all that far away. And whereas she doubted he or his admirals would try anything in the face of the combined firepower of the *Borealis* and the *Adamantine*, the fact remained that her mission to the Chorios systems wasn't widely known. If there was trouble, response time would be slow.

The bright-faced boys and girls of the Academy guard leapt to their feet as she re-entered the anteroom, bringing their weapons to the present. Leia returned the salute with a grave lifting of her hand. "Marcopius, would you do me a favor? I know this sounds really paranoid, but I've got a message light and I can't raise anyone in Comm. Could I get you to go down there and see if it's anything urgent?"

"Of course, Your Excellency." He slung his weapon, bowed, and departed like an advertisement for the Academy before she could get her thanks out of her mouth. As Leia returned to her private parlor she smiled a little in reflection. Several members of the Council—notably Q-Varx, who like most Rationalists was enchanted by gadgetry—had moved to purchase an executive honor guard of the new synthdroids, arguing that, in addition to eliminating any further need to use the Noghri, it would be cheaper to maintain in the long run and provide more uniform security with less chance of betrayal or individual error.

Her desk—neatly arranged by See-Threepio, who had taken it on himself periodically to pass through her stateroom like a golden hurricane of tidiness—contained a very nicely produced ad-cube from the Loronar Corporation's synthdroid division concerning the aesthetic quality, utter reliability, high performance standards, and low cost (*Hah!* thought Leia) of the new droids. "Hardly droids at all," the pleasant voice of the obviously synthdroid announcer had lauded before Leia muted the sound. She had to hand it to Loronar ("All the finest, all the first"): The cube had been in her stateroom since the start of this mission and as far as she could tell hadn't repeated itself yet.

Centrally Controlled Independent Replicant technology could allegedly reproduce the watchfulness and defensive capabilities of the Noghri, though she didn't believe it and wasn't sure she wanted something like that on the open market. She had to admit, seeing Ashgad's three, that they were nice looking, undoubtedly efficient, less aesthetically intrusive than droids, and certainly less unsettling than Noghri. Freed of standard droid memory system requirements, for all intents and purposes they looked like human beings, if human beings were what you wanted.

She shook her head and sat down at the comm station again, suddenly overwhelmed with fatigue. Members of Daysong, a splinter group of the Rights of Sentience Party, claimed that an honor guard was a form of servile humiliation and should be replaced by droids *(Hadn't these people ever heard of magnetic flux disruptors?)*. But Leia didn't consider either Ezrakh or Yeoman Shreel, for instance, either humiliated or servile. In his off-duty moments—not that a Noghri was ever completely off duty—the little hunter-killer would tell Leia tales of his childhood on Honoghr, of his wife and children there, the same way Yeoman Shreel or Yeoman Marcopius would show her holos of their brothers and sisters and pets at home.

The Daysong folks objected violently to the synth-droids too, of course, on the grounds that synthflesh was living and had rights as well.

The Theran Listeners, wandering around the desert holding conversations with rocks, couldn't possibly be crazier.

Leia leaned her head against the back of the chair, tired beyond words. Tired, she thought suddenly, as her hands and feet grew cold, beyond what she should be. It didn't exactly hurt her to breathe, but every breath was an effort. The hand she raised, or tried to raise, to rub the ache behind her sternum felt as if she'd been mana-cled with lead.

This is ridiculous, she thought. Every member of Seti Ashgad's party and yesterday's good-faith inspection of the vessel had been scanned. Of course they'd been scanned. No virus, no microbe, no poison . . . nothing had been detected.

Dizziness swamped her. She reached across the table for the comm button, but collapsed halfway and slid to the floor in a great sigh of velvet robe.

"Your Excellency?" The door *swished* open. "Your Excellency, I have been attempting to monitor fleet communications, and . . . Your Excellency!"

Threepio toddled into the stateroom, golden hands flying up in a singularly human gesture of alarm. "Your Excellency, whatever is the matter?"

Artoo-Detoo, close on the protocol droid's shining metal heels, rolled up to Leia's side and directed a scanner beam over her. He tweeped informatively.

"I know she's not well, you stupid bucket of bolts! And don't you go quoting heart-rate readings to me." He was already at the wall comm unit. "Infirmary? Infirmary? There's no answer!" He turned dramatically to his counterpart. "Something terrible is going on! I attempted to get in touch with the *Adamantine* just now to check on our departure for the rendezvous point and there was no answer! We must . . ."

The stateroom door slid open, framing in its tall rectangle the slumped, small form of Dzym.

"Oh, Master Dzym!" cried Threepio. "Something terrible has happened! You must inform the emergency services . . ."

The man only stepped clear of the opener beam of the doorway and walked to Leia's side. He seemed a trifle unsteady on his feet, as if drunk or drugged. His colorless eyes half-shut, he wore on his face an expression Threepio—never truly good at interpretation of human facial expression despite the most advanced of pattern-recognition software—could not define or even guess at:

ecstasy, concentration, dreamy pain. He stood beside Leia for a time, looking down at her. Then he half-knelt and began to pull off his violet leather gloves.

The door swished open behind him. "Dzym!" cried Ashgad, striding through as his secretary slewed around.

Dzym got quickly to his feet, pulling his glove on once again. Ashgad dropped to one knee at Leia's side.

"Oh, Master Ashgad . . ." began Threepio, starting forward.

Ashgad said briefly, "Push him aside," and one of the fair-haired, androgynous synthdroids stepped through the door after him, and shoved Threepio hard across the room. The synthdroid had the startling strength of cable and hydraulic joints, and Threepio, for all his excellent construction, was only middling well balanced. He went crashing down in the corner, flailing and struggling to get up.

"Stop it," said Ashgad, looking up at Dzym, holding his gaze: Meaning, obscure to any onlooker, passed between them that they both understood. "Release her."

"My lord, she may revive before . . ."

"Release her! Now!"

Dzym's mouth turned pettishly down for a moment. He shut his eyes in momentary concentration. Then he drew a little breath, and said, "Very well. The action is stopped."

Ashgad turned back to Leia. Artoo-Detoo, standing over her with his single little clamper-arm extended downward as if to try to rouse her, swung back to his upright mode and backed hastily.

"Wait!" cried Threepio. "No!" For the first time, he had an almost human intuition that this man had not the smallest intention of taking the Chief of State to the infirmary. "Artoo, stop them!"

But Ashgad was human, and Artoo, though he had a

certain defensive capability with his electronic welder, could no more have attacked him than he could have danced on a tightrope. It was something that normally programmed droids simply could not do.

Ashgad got to his feet, with Leia limp in his arms, the red velvet of her robes hanging nearly to the floor. To the synthdroid, Ashgad began to say, "You're to wait until the brig is . . . Yes, Liegeus?"

The thin, tired-looking man whom Threepio recognized as the brig's pilot stepped in as the door swished open once more. "It's finished," the pilot said. "I've launched the slave relay with the time-delayed projections of final reports for both vessels. I used scrap from the active files of both onboard computers. The messages should be indistinguishable from real transmissions."

His face was white in the dark, graying tousle of his hair, and there was a tautness to his mouth, as if he had just finished being sick. "Everyone on board both ships appears to be dead or incapacitated."

He glanced over at Dzym, whose eyes had gone dreamy again. Dzym smiled and murmured, "Yes. Oh, yes."

The man Liegeus looked away from him, pain and loathing in his eyes. "The synthdroids have taken one of the shuttles over to the escort ship. They should have no trouble boarding."

"Very good." Ashgad glanced at the wall chronometer. "It should take about thirty minutes for us to return to the *Light of Reason* and take her far enough from these ships for safety."

The door opened as they turned to enter the anteroom. Through it, Threepio could glimpse Noghri Ezrakh, sprawled on the floor across the threshold, still moving feebly but his face livid with the pallor of approaching death. Ashgad, with Leia in his arms, stepped over him, and over the others, human and Noghri, lying on the floor beyond, the crimson velvet dragging over their faces. Dzym knelt for a moment at Ezrakh's side, passed his gloved hands lightly across the dying bodyguard's face and throat, his face suffused with pleasure; Liegeus averted his eyes and avoided touching him as he passed.

The closing door cut off the sight of them, and whatever Ashgad said next.

"Oh, *do* something!" cried Threepio, and tried to get to his feet. Artoo rolled over to him and extended his welder as a sort of lever arm to help him up. "Why didn't you do something, you ignorant little adding machine! We have to stop them! Guards! Guards! They're kidnapping the Chief of State!"

The anteroom door swooshed wide at Threepio's touch. The protocol droid hesitated over the body of Ezrakh, dead now, eyes staring in horror, then turned helplessly away. With the opening of the door into the corridor he stopped in alarm. Two other Noghri lay on the floor, one still breathing with slow, harsh, stertorous gasps, the other utterly still. They bore no marks of violence or struggle.

"Shuttle bay!" cried Threepio, punching the code on the wall comm. "Shuttle bay! They have to be stopped!"

There was no answer but the whine of a signal blocker somewhere in the system.

He hastened after Artoo, who hadn't even paused, trundling down the corridor and making a little detour around the dead guards. "What can have caused it? Symptomatic analysis indicates . . ."

Artoo stopped, with such suddenness that Threepio nearly cannonaded into him, over the body of a third Academy guard. He extended his gripper arm to prod the young man's shoulder, and Threepio saw that this one, the bodyguard Marcopius, bore on the side of his head the mark of a heavy blow.

"Yeoman Marcopius, Master Ashgad has kidnapped Her Excellency!" cried Threepio, at the first sign of reviving consciousness.

Sitting up, the youth said a word that Threepio knew in close to a million languages but was programmed never to utter in any of them. "The whole ship's been poisoned!" He rolled to his feet with a nimbleness that caused the droid a momentary flash of envy.

"I beg your pardon, sir, but the symptoms are less those of poison than of disease," reported Threepio worriedly. "Specifically, my databanks show a ninety percent correlation with the Death Seed plague of seven centuries ago. But how such a thing came to pass . . ."

"Whatever it is, they're panicking down in the infirmary." The boy scooped up his ceremonial weapon and strode so quickly along the corridor as he spoke that the two droids could barely keep pace. "The engine crew sealed themselves off. I caught that pilot of Ashgad's—if he *is* a pilot—doing something with the transmission records . . ."

"They're going to do something to both vessels, something to destroy them!" said Threepio. "They said they had to get their own ship out of range. We're doomed!"

"Not if we can get to one of the scout boats, we're not."

Beyond the vast portal of the magnetic hatch, the stars were already moving when Yeoman Marcopius and the two droids reached the shuttle bay floor. The shuttle brig was already gone, a dwindling gray flake in the blackness. The three bay guards lay dead on the floor, unmarked and peaceful. Far off the *Light of Reason* was a tiny berry, a cluster of minute bronze, black, and silver minihulls, and farther still the silver arrowhead of the *Adamantine* could be seen moving, too.

"Where are they going?" cried Threepio, stopping dead in his tracks to watch. He thought he saw something move in the shadows, something tiny scuttling along the wall, and turned his head in an attempt at visual tracking. "There isn't anyone alive on that ship, I heard them say so . . ."

Marcopius grabbed his arm and dragged him up the small scout craft's ramp. "They're taking it out of the vicinity of the Chorios systems," said the boy, slamming shut the scout boat's hatch behind them and dropping into the chair behind the bridge controls. "If Ashgad kidnapped Lady Solo—if he found some way to poison the crews on both ships, or whatever he did—he's not going to want record of either ship disappearing too soon after the rendezvous." He was jerking over levers, checking readouts, activating the emergency relays to open the magnetic portal once again, while beyond the portal the stars glided quicker and quicker as the tiny dots of the Chorios systems fell behind.

"He's going to want to say, *Oh, they were all fine when they pulled out of here.* Look at this." He cut into the coded deep-space Net channel. Its screen flashed an image of the two Republic cruisers making their serene way toward the standard Coruscant jump point on the far side of the Chorios systems. Immediately afterward the image of Leia's face appeared, reporting the conference successfully concluded.

Brassy lights flared over Marcopius's dark frown, and the cool, neutral voice of an emergency recording began to announce monotonously, "This vessel is in stage two of hyperspace sequence. Taking a scout craft out at this time is extremely dangerous. Contact the main bridge and review your instructions. This vessel is in stage two of hyperspace sequence . . ."

"Hyperspace!" wailed Threepio. "Who could be taking it into . . ."

"One of the synthdroids. No one else is alive." Marcopius delicately lifted the scout boat from its moorings and swung its nose weightlessly toward the black rectangle of the portal. "Can't you shut that thing up?"

"I'm terribly sorry, Yeoman Marcopius, but my program forbids me to tamper with safety equipment of any kind."

The young man made a final sequence of adjustments, lip between his teeth, sweat glistening on his forehead, while the warning voice repeated over and over that it was extremely dangerous to take out a scout craft of any kind. Ahead of them, through the portal, they saw the *Adamantine* flash bright as it turned, accelerating, then vanished in a spangle of hyperblue light.

"Where can they be going?" nattered Threepio. "That's nowhere near the hyperspace jump point for Coruscant. If we can somehow extrapolate from the jump point to learn where they're going . . ."

"They're not going anywhere." Marcopius was breathing hard now, setting the controls. On the decoder screen before them the digitalized images of the flagship and its escort continued to float among the empty, lifeless worlds that comprised most of the sector. "They're just taking the ships into hyperspace, period. Don't you see? The whole point has to be that Her Excellency vanishes, without a trace, *after* she's seen to leave the rendezvous safely. They must have one turbo-powered holo faker working for them." He put his hand to his chest, as if to massage away some deep, troubling ache. "Hang on."

He eased forward on the levers, sweat sparkling in the

cropped suede of his hair in the doubled glare of amber and scarlet warning lights. The small, boxlike craft slid through the magnetic portal and flipped immediately down, around, avoiding the *Borealis*'s stabilizers, picking up speed while interacting with a far larger vessel, which was ripping along at thousands of kilometers per second.

Threepio clutched at the back of the empty navigator's station, circuits momentarily jammed with alarm. Artoo let out a long, trilling wail as the scout boat whipped by inches from the bigger ship's secondary tanks. The wake of the flagship's magnetic field tossed and dragged the little craft like a chip in a riptide. Marcopius's dark hands flickered and danced from levers to joystick to toggles as huge sheets of metal and rivets rocketed past the observation ports, alternating with slabs of interstellar blackness already shimmering with the light-shift effects of hyperspace sequence. Then the scout boat plunged away, spinning dizzily, stars and ships and planets reeling in a disorienting tumble past the ports. There was a blinding flash, far too near for comfort, as the *Borealis* plunged into the glimmering void of quasi-reality that was called "hyperspace" for lack of any better term.

Far to starboard, as Marcopius stabilized the spinning scout boat, the *Light of Reason* had left orbit as well, streaking toward the Nam Chorios primary like an incandescent teardrop.

"Shall we go after them?"

"And do what?" The young yeoman's hands were trembling where they lay on the console. "Throw spitballs at them? This is a scout boat, not an E-wing. Besides, we're too big to make it past those gun stations they were talking about."

He nodded toward the viewport, where the *Light of Reason* was diminishing into the stars. "Just looking at that ship I'd guess it comes apart and goes down to the planet in self-powered sections, leaving the main reactor in orbit. It's the only way they could get enough bulk for even limited hyperspace capability."

He guided the scout boat in a long loop, began setting coordinates, an expression of grim sorrow aging his face. "What do you know about Pedducis Chorios? That's the nearest civilization."

"Well, it can't really be called civilized," said Threepio judiciously. "The local Warlords have taken on so-called advisers—ex-smugglers, Imperial renegades, Corporate sector mercenaries, fugitives from both Imperial and Republican justice. I shudder to think what would happen to us if we went there, or to Her Excellency if anyone there discovered the predicament she was in."

Marcopius nodded, and made another adjustment. "It has to be the fleet orbital base at Durren, then." He paused, trying to draw breath, his face gray around the lips. "Are either of you programmed to handle one of these once we get out of hyperspace?"

Artoo, who had released himself from his takeoff cradle, let out an optimistic trill, and Threepio said firmly, "Oh, no, sir. Upon the single occasion that we tried any sort of piloting at all, the results were most unsatisfactory. Certainly the more modern craft are entirely beyond our programming capacity. I'm a protocol droid, as you know, and though Artoo is quite a competent astromech, I'm afraid he has his limitations in other areas."

The young man nodded again, leaning his forehead on his fist, his breath going out in a long sigh. Threepio could see he was still shivering: With shock or exertion, the droid supposed sympathetically. Some humans were simply not as resilient as others.

Encouragingly, Threepio ventured, "It isn't that far to Durren, sir. The ship should run well enough until we have to make orbit. If you wish to lie down and rest, I can certainly wake you when you're required to pilot the ship into base."

For a long time Yeoman Marcopius didn't answer. Then he murmured, "Yeah. I guess that's how it'll have to be."

He got to his feet, staggering and catching himself on Artoo's stubby bulk. The astromech rolled beside him, to help him to the narrow bunk in an alcove just beyond the control room door. The young man groped blindly for the blanket—Artoo extended his gripper arm and pulled it up over him, and emitted a gentle trill of comfort and farewell as he rolled from the room.

Thirty minutes later, when Threepio returned to ask the youth how long it would be before they could subspace the Durren base, he found Marcopius dead.

3

The Force was everywhere, palpable, warming her like sunlight.

Lying—on a divan? On the toothed, fist-size crystals that carpeted the old sea floor plains as far as vision could descry?—Leia Organa Solo basked in the warmth of the Force. So much warmer than the heatless fingernail of the sun, she absorbed it through her skin, as if her body had been rendered transparent like the amoebic Plasmars of dark Y'nybeth.

Someone was saying something to her, but she was deeply asleep and could not make out the words.

She dreamed.

She was in her father's palace in Aldera. His study was a garden room, looking through a double line of smooth, snow-white pillars to a small lawn beyond whose curved railing the blue waters of the lake could be seen, the endless plains of wind-combed grass beyond. The intoxicating smell of the grass blew through on the warm winds, and she could hear the muted whisper of the wind chimes among the pillars and the soft cooing and twittering of the cairokas, the sounds of her childhood. Her father was there. She was presenting her children to him, Jacen and Jaina and Anakin grown to teenagers, wearing the faces she knew they would one day wear.

"You've done well, daughter." Bail Organa extended a hand to touch Jaina's heavy chestnut hair. The gold ring on his finger gleamed like a fragment of the world's final sunset. "What have you taught them, these young Jedi of the House of Organa?"

"I've taught them to love justice, as you loved justice, Father." Leia's own voice sounded deep and quiet in the chamber's gentle twilight. "I've taught them to respect the rights of all living things. I've taught them that the Law is above any single being's will."

"But we know better." Anakin spoke in the breaking treble of an adolescent, and there was an unfamiliar, ugly grin on his face as he stepped forward, and a light in his crystal-blue eyes that Leia had never seen in waking life. "We're Jedi Knights. We have the Power." His lightsaber licked out crimson from the shadow and slashed her father in half.

Leia sprang back from the toppling pieces of the corpse, screaming—Why couldn't she scream through the clogging weight of sleep? Her father's body lay in pieces in the shadow, cauterized where the blade had severed thorax from pelvis, only a trickle of brownish fluid worming across the marble floor toward her feet. She cried something, she didn't know what. Anakin, Jacen, and Jaina all turned to gaze at her.

All three had drawn lightsabers. Three blades gleamed, red and shining columns of power, the light making six red flames in three pairs of demon eyes.

"We're Jedi, Mother," Jaina said. "There's no Law for us. We can do whatever we want."

Anakin said, "That's your gift to us. We're Jedi because you're Jedi, too. We are what you are." He turned to look back at the pieces of Bail Organa's body, the eyes open and staring in shock, the outstretched hand with its golden ring. "And anyway he wasn't really your father."

Leia screamed "No! *No!*"

The images blurred to darkness and she heard Luke's voice. "Learn to use the Force, Leia. You have to."

"Never!"

You have to.

She couldn't swear then that it was Luke's voice. The warmth of the Force touched her, comforting, but it seemed that she could see it only through a viewport or a doorway. She lay in shadow, and the shadow was cold.

She heard movement behind her head, and opened her eyes.

For a time there'd been a man named Greglik who'd piloted a reconditioned ore hauler for the Rebel forces, back when they'd been moving from planet to planet ahead of Admiral Piett's fleet. Greglik had been a good pilot but an addict, whose addictions had deepened until he'd gotten himself and seventeen Rebel fighters killed in a stupid collision with an asteroid.

She remembered him now. One night in a temporary HQ on Kidron, when they were watching for an attack, he'd told her about being an addict, about mixing drugs to achieve the exact rainbow of mental damage to match any mood he sought to erase.

"Glitterstim's all right if you're blue," he had said, his brown eyes dreamy, like a man recalling the great love of his life. "Everything takes on a rise, a buzz, a life, as if your whole body had been made new and your whole future with it. And for those nights when you've got an itchy anger in your soul against all the people who've robbed you or jeered at you, there's pyrepenol. Two shots of pyrep and you'll spit on the Fates that spin your life thread. When you're hurting for the girl who could have saved you *if-only*, Santherian tenho-root extract's your poison: gentle, gentle, like the sun breaking clouds at the end of day."

He'd smiled, and Leia's contempt for the man had transmuted to pity, as she comprehended for the first time all that he had done himself out of for the sake of those easy illusions. He had been a handsome man, bronzed and fair like a charming god, but sexless, as most addicts quickly became, and without the courage to face a relationship or hold an opinion of his own.

"But sometimes there's nothing that'll do it but sweetblossom. It's a good thing the blossom's not addictive," he'd added with a grin. "It could grind galactic civilization to a halt in a week flat."

"It's that deadly?" Leia had asked.

Greglik had laughed. "My darling child, few drugs are that deadly. It's what they get you to do to yourself that destroys you. Blossom is exactly like sleep. A little of it— two drops, maybe—and it's like you've just woken up, before your mind is in gear to do anything: You just sit around in your pajamas saying, *I'll take care of business when I'm feeling a bit more the thing.* But, of course, you never do. Five drops is good for endless sitting, curled up, comfortable, thinking nothing, watching addercops spin webs or dust motes make patterns. Your mind is perfectly clear, you understand, but the starter won't engage. Seven or eight drops and you're paralyzed. Awake, but unmoving, unable to move, like those mornings when you open your eyes but your entire body's still asleep. A good way to get through—oh—days when things are happening to you that you'd rather not feel."

Leia had thought at the time, *Like seeing your world destroyed, and the deaths of everyone you know?* She'd dealt with that one by helping Luke and Han escape with the Death Star plans, by setting in motion the events that had blasted Grand Moff Tarkin and the Emperor's cherished superweapon into stellar dust.

She'd changed the subject, and a few weeks later, Greglik had been killed. She hadn't thought of him, or that conversation, in years.

But his words came back to her as she heard the soft *snick* of the door lock unbolting and the rustle of clothing just beyond the line of her sight. She tried in panic to turn her head and couldn't.

She couldn't move at all.

Blossom, she thought.

Panic flooded her.

Someone was definitely approaching the divan on which she lay. The heavy velvet robe of state she'd worn to her meeting with Ashgad still wrapped her like a shroud of molded lead. There was a doorway or a long transparisteel panel in the wall opposite her feet, and the end of the trapezoid of blanched sunlight that fell through it touched her knees, heating them uncomfortably under the velvet's folds. The wall around the doorway was poured permacrete, lead colored and unplastered; beyond she could see a paved terrace and a low permacrete wall and a hugeness of air imbued with hard-edged, sugary light.

Clothing rustled again. She felt the vibration of someone grasping the carved headboard of the divan.

Its legs scraped softly on the permacrete floor as the divan was drawn backward, away from the rectangle of sunlight, into the deeper shadows of the room.

Every atom of Leia's body screamed and thrashed and struggled to rise, to fight—at least to turn her head. And every atom of the sweetblossom in her system laughed at her and held her still.

The dragging stopped.

Get up, get up, get up!

Dzym came around the head of the divan. He stood gazing down at Leia with his large, utterly colorless eyes—(*They were brown on the ship. I know they were brown on the ship.*)—and Leia saw that the skin of his throat, where it was revealed by the open neck of his loose gray robe, was purplish brown, shiny, and ever so slightly articulated. Chitenous, not like human skin at all. When he sat on the divan beside her and took her hands in his, she saw between the cuffs of his gloves and those of his robe that his wrists were the same.

He saw she was looking at him and smiled, running a very long, very pointed tongue over sharp brown teeth. While his eyes held hers he turned his shoulder to her, so that she could not see his hands, and drew off his gloves. She felt him lay them over her arm. Then he took her left hand between both of his.

The terrible sinking, the slow ache in her chest were as they had been in her stateroom on the *Borealis*. A growing, spreading coldness. The seeping away of her breath.

I'm dying, thought Leia, as she had then. She saw the secretary's thin, dark lips part in what might have been a smile or only a satiated sigh. Ecstatic, as he had been on the ship.

He stood and walked around behind her. Lifting aside her hair, he put his hands to the sides of her neck. Something sliced her that wasn't pain and wasn't cold, more terrifying than either.

She thought, *Please, no more.*

She thought, *Han* . . .

She thought, *You'd better finish me off, you squalid parasite, because if you don't, by my father's hand I swear I'll break your stinking neck.*

She sank into drowning darkness.

·   ·   ·

Voices cried out through the Force.

Hundreds of them—Luke felt their terror and despair. Dying, he thought. . . . He thought also, in that first cold lance of panic, that Leia's was one of them, terrified and alone. But in the clamor he couldn't be sure.

His hand flashed to the comm panel, calling up the far-off images of the *Borealis* and its escort. Readouts showed them on their way to the Coruscant jump point; a long-distance visual confirmed. Luke debated for a moment trying to contact them—he had a scrambler in the B-wing's comm system—but the possibility of being overheard by Getelles's agents, or by those other, nameless threats, held his hand. Instead he cut into the pickup channel, and heard Leia's voice dimly making her report to Rieekan and Ackbar: ". . . successful conclusion to our enterprise. We're on our way home."

Trouble elsewhere? he wondered. On Pedducis Chorios, perhaps? Or some other world in the vicinity? Sometimes it was difficult to tell, with the Force. It picked up and magnified some alterations in the life-tides of the universe, distorted others. Even now, the tugging grief, the cold panic, he felt had faded; he wasn't even sure exactly where it had come from.

He turned his eyes toward the growing violet star that was Chorios II, Nam Chorios's primary. That speck of piercing white beside it should be the planet itself.

A singing surge of the Force washed over him, filled him, sieved the tiny craft like gamma rays. Like coming in to Dagobah that first time, looking at the seething life readings of that strange world, he felt now in the presence of a vastness he could not understand.

No wonder Callista was drawn to this place.

He touched the levers, accelerated into high orbit.

Now the planet was clearly visible. Wastes of slate, smooth and hard as rollerball floors, stretched kilometer after kilometer. Zones of broken rock surrounded them, wall after brittle wall of toothed mountains uneroded by rain or the roots of growing plants. In other places the dry sea floors were covered for thousands of miles in faceted, quartzine gravel that glared as if the world were one great cut-glass gem. Crystal mountains flashed a bleached and broken reflection in the wan light of the tiny, faded whitish sun, chains of them petering out into lines of solitary crystal-rock chimneys, like widely spaced sentinels, far into the shimmering, twilight wastes.

Light and glass, dizzying alien cloudless heights, and among it all, tiny zones of green.

Luke's hands played fast through the orbital checks, then returned to the subspace, signaling back to the *Adamantine,* the *Borealis.*

Nothing. They'd gone into hyperspace by this time, heading back to Coruscant.

Death, his memory whispered. He had felt death, massive death, he thought. His recollection of it was dim and dreamlike, and he could not be sure where, or when, or from what direction the sensation had come.

But Leia was alive. Somewhere, wherever she was, she was alive.

He flipped his scanners to their widest range, but saw only the yellow speck that would be Seti Ashgad's pieced-together planet-hopper, blinking along at max sublight, heading for home.

His single B-wing should be too small to register on its scanners at this distance, he thought. But it would be best to disappear into the planet's magnetic field before Ashgad got any closer.

Do not meet with Ashgad.

Why?

Do not go to the Meridian sector.

Luke studied the scan again. This close to Antemeridian, it paid to be cautious, though by all accounts Moff Getelles didn't have the firepower to bump heads with the fleet at Durren, or the guts to try. And indeed, no sign of any deep-space vessels disturbed the provincial calm of this portion of the Meridian. Just the occasional orange flicker of planet-hoppers, small traders, light cargo haulers going about their petty businesses between the stars.

What did Callista know about Seti Ashgad?

He edged the B-wing into a lower temporary orbit and brought up the coordinates for the town of Hweg Shul.

He would find her, he thought. He would see her again.

The long-range laser cannon took out his rear deflector shield and nicked the stabilizer before he was even out of sight of blackness and stars.

It was only luck it didn't destroy the craft entirely, luck and probably the difficulty in homing on a vessel at the bottom end of its target mass. Luke flipped at once into evasive action, twisting, zagging, plunging toward that vast glittering eternity of dimness and crystal through a flaming howl of atmosphere. A second bolt clipped the B-wing's airfoil; and as he fought to pull out of the crazy spin, Luke saw the white lances of light slash upward from the ragged line of slate-gray foothills.

So much for Seti Ashgad's information about the minimum mass needed to activate the gun stations, thought Luke grimly. *Was that what Callista had meant about not trusting the man?*

But Ashgad hadn't known Luke would even be on Leia's mission, let alone that he'd be going to Hweg Shul. Nobody but Han and Chewie had known that. He twisted the controls, trying to avoid sliding straight into one of those white lances of killing light. The ground rushed upward, radiant, burning with wan, reflected sun.

Blast, thought Luke, as the joystick lurched under his hands, *don't quit on me now.*

There was enough play in the remaining stabilizer to land without killing himself—just. The antigrav cradles were still okay. But when he leveled off he'd be a better target. He zagged right, left, dropped instinctively as a beam slicked over his head. Those were live gunners, they had to be. No autostation had that kind of response flexibility. Live gunners who knew what they were doing.

Huge cliffs; mountains; towering, terrifying, bare monuments of basalt and crystals yawned fathomless below him. He plunged the big fighter down among them, veered through narrowing chasms as a laser bolt splintered a black column of rock a thousand feet high to his left and rained the craft with fragments. The steady, howling winds of the higher atmosphere turned to random hurricanes that smote him from every canyon and crevice. With its long ventral airfoil the B-wing was almost impossible to control. Luke pulled into a level slide, barely avoiding another bolt and a toothed crag of what looked like gray striated quartz, the glare of the sunlight from a million million mirrors nearly blinding.

He was out of range of the gun stations, hidden in the mountains, plunging down a long, scintillated canyon toward the wasteland beyond. The stabilizer went, and Luke forced the controls over, reached out with his mind to touch the Force, nudge the crazily plunging craft away from the rock walls, past the jutting towers and razor-ridged hogbacks of stone, heading for the blue notch of the canyon mouth.

Too low. No altitude. He'd never . . .

He put out all his will, all the strength of the Force, to lift the B-wing over the last ridge of rose-gold shining glass, edge it down, down . . .

Wind slapped him like a monster hand. The B-wing

veered wildly, then the airfoil scraped and tore on the pebbled wilderness beyond the canyon. Rocks and dust and fragments of crystal enveloped him in a whirlwind of heat. Shaken nearly out of his bones, Luke held the controls steady, fighting to see, hoping there was nothing ahead of him but more level gravel.

There was. A transparent boulder the size of a speeder caught what was left of the airfoil. The whole craft slewed sideways, rolled, the delicate S-foils buckling and snapping. Luke feared for one heart-tearing second that his seat restraint would give way, and he'd break his neck on the console. The belts held—there was an explosion of sealant and crash foam—the B-wing rolled twice more, like a barrel, and came to a stop up against something that sent up another splintering cloud of fragments and dust.

Then stillness, the moaning of the wind, and the dying pitter of pebbles raining down on the laser-cracked hull.

"Here, Your Excellency."

Strong hands helped Leia sit up, put a cup into hers, held it steady while she drank. "How are you feeling?"

She blinked. The divan had been moved out onto the terrace. Weak, strangely colored sunlight lay in mosaics of glassy brightness across the cinder-colored permacrete walls of the house that loomed over them, glinted on the treeless lunacy of the heaped stone ridges, columns, pinnacles, and buttresses that dwarfed the house on three sides and framed, on the fourth, eternities of flashing gravel, as if the sea had sunk away long ago and left its foam solidified into salt and glass.

It must be the crystals that pick up and reflect the sunlight, thought Leia, looking around at the huge outcrops of them embedded everywhere in the rocks of the mountains. The small sun gave only thready light in cobalt oceans of sky. Dim stars shone even in the presence of its glow. Because of the light thrown back by the rocks, there seemed to be no shadows anywhere, or a confusing multiplicity of watered ones. The dry air tightened her face, as it had not in the moister mini-climate of the house.

She turned from those bizarre distances to meet the anxious dark eyes of the man who sat on the divan at her side.

It was Seti Ashgad's pilot.

A nice man, she thought at once. He reminded her a little of the pilot Greglik for some reason, though the physical appearance could not have been more dissimilar. Of medium height and slender build, this man had a sort of saturnine darkness to him in utter contrast with the Rebel pilot's flamboyant good looks. Maybe it was the nose—an elegant aquiline—or the battered, deeply woven wrinkles around the eyes that spoke of a life lived very hard.

More probably, she thought, *it was something in the expression of the eyes.* Odd again, to think of the daredevil Greglik. This man's eyes were the eyes of one who wouldn't harm so much as an insect or stand up to someone who was taking shameless advantage of him for fear of hurt feelings. *An escaper,* she thought. Not escape into drugs—he hadn't Greglik's unhealthy complexion—but escape by simply not being there if he could manage to get away.

But nice.

"I'm fine. I think I'm fine." Had Dzym been a dream? The slicing pain in the sides of her neck, the hands that drew life from her, exactly as the sickness had on the ship. The horrible impression she had had of some other being under his clothing, some vile movement, tucked away where it didn't show. "Where am I? What happened?" Her thoughts felt as if she'd dropped them, and they'd rolled to the far ends of the room, and exhaustion prevented her from gathering them up again.

"I'm afraid I can't tell you where you are, Your Excellency." He sounded genuinely sorry about it. "You understand, it's better if you don't know. My name is Liegeus Sarpaetius Vorn."

"Vorn . . ." With the greatest of difficulty, as if she were laboriously constructing a house of cards by means of waldoes, Leia put things together in her mind. "Liegeus Vorn—You were Seti Ashgad's pilot, weren't you? And Dzym . . . Dzym was here. Is this Nam Chorios?"

"Dzym was here?" He held the vessel away from her reaching hands, his dark brows knotting. "I think you've had enough of this, Your Excellency. I'll get you some water."

He emptied the cup—which Leia thought *had* contained water—over the low wall at the edge of the terrace. She sat up, watching it fall, the droplets flashing and dwindling as they tumbled in slow motion past the walls of the house, past the rocks of the bluff on which it stood, down to the broken tumble of slate and scree and adamant two hundred meters below.

"Stay here in the sunshine," he urged gently. His voice was very soft, almost inaudible, but deep and one of the most beautiful she had ever heard. "I won't be a moment."

Leia remained where she was, not because he had told her to, but because the warmth was pleasant on her face, like the slow return of health after a terrible coldness.

The Borealis, she thought. *What happened on board the* Borealis?

She'd been ill. The memory of cold returned, the slow

dimming down of every system in her body. Or had that been later, when Dzym had come into the room there?

Ashgad had apparently taken her off the ship, brought her to this place. She recalled nothing about it. Had Captain Ioa thought she was dead? But in that case, they'd have brought her body to Coruscant, not here.

Han, she thought. *Han will be worried sick. The children* . . .

Other things were leaking back into her consciousness.

The blinking message light on the comm that no one had been there to answer.

Yeoman Marcopius darting away down the corridor.

Admiral Ackbar saying, *It looks as if there was an information leak at Council level,* and Representative Q-Varx tapping the malachite tabletop in her private conference chamber with a stubby brown finger and saying, *All arrangements have been made for the secret meeting with Ashgad, Your Excellency. Though he has no official position on the planet, this conference could be the key to the entire policy of beneficial usage of untapped planetary resources.*

Do not meet with Ashgad.

Do not go to the Meridian sector.

What had happened to the Noghri?

The thought wended its way leisurely across her mind. She wondered, if she were to go into the room behind her and try the door, whether it would open. *But, of course,* she thought, *locked or unlocked makes little difference.* The house itself seemed to be situated in an utterly deserted wasteland of sawtoothed mountains and glaring, jeweled plain.

Voices rose to her from somewhere below. She recognized Seti Ashgad's: "We'll just have to go over Larm's head and talk to Dymurra. Larm's an idiot anyway. He still has no concept of what we need to complete the *Reliant.* Has any word come in on the subspace?"

The beautiful baritone carried strongly in the thin, dry air. *Larm*, thought Leia. Moff Getelles had an admiral named Larm. She'd met him at the diplomatic reception on Coruscant to celebrate Getelles's elevation to the position, one of the last she'd attended at the Palace. Larm was of the flat-backed, by-the-book, spit-and-polish, boot-kissing school of soldiering, toadying Getelles and every other Moff and Governor without ever relaxing his tough-warrior manner. He'd come up through the fleet as Getelles's stringer, a dark-visaged and sternly efficient foil to the new Moff's hail-fellow-well-met fairness and had been duly promoted over the heads of several better-qualified candidates when Getelles had been made Moff of Antemeridian.

Who Dymurra was she had no idea, though the name was familiar to her.

She couldn't make out the words murmured in reply, but the purring voice pierced her, an arrow of cold under her solar plexus. Dzym. She looked down at her hand again.

Soreness lingered on the sides of her neck, over the main arteries, but she lacked the strength to put her hands up to feel. The cold of death lingered in her mind, and something else, the aftertaste of nightmare.

That was why she felt so weak.

No, she thought. *I feel weak because there was sweetblossom in the water.*

"I suppose you're right." Ashgad's voice was quieter, but just as penetrant. "Three synthdroids! When I think about how much even one of those things costs . . ."

Dzym's voice was a little louder now. Knowing Ashgad's habit of pacing, Leia assumed he was farther from his secretary than he had been a few moments before. "It could not be helped, my lord. Synthdroids were the only way we could bring the Death Seed on board the vessels undetected."

The Death Seed! Leia's breath left her, as if with physical shock.

Seven hundred years ago that plague had wiped out millions. Whole sectors had relapsed into primitive subsistence, as those who understood machinery and spaceflight had perished wholesale . . .

It was the casualness of Dzym's tone that galvanized Leia into action. She rose from the divan, pulled the cloaklike folds of her robe more closely around her—the sunlight held no heat—and made her way shakily to the far end of the terrace. Perhaps twenty-five meters below her, just above where the walls of the great, rambling house merged into the harsh basalt of the bluff itself, another terrace ran the length of that side of the building and curved around the face of the cliff. Heavy hedges of brachniel and loak grew from planters of imported soil as windbreaks around two sides, brilliant and alien green against the gray permacrete. A sort of gazebo stood at one end of the terrace, the shade densely black within. A complex system of mist jets and pipes mitigated somewhat the dryness of the air. By the way Ashgad turned, Leia guessed that Dzym sat within the gazebo's shade.

There was a third being on the terrace, stretched out on a black-and-orange air-duvet under a veritable rainshower of air misters, and Leia flinched with revulsion at the sight of it, and the sound of its gluey, tuba bass.

"Dzym's right." It rolled over, flexed its gelid length—at roughly twelve meters, it was the longest Hutt Leia had ever seen. It was massive, without Jabba's obesity; like a young Hutt in its agility and speed but grown to the size of an old one. "You couldn't have gotten past the medical scans without them. And only droids would have taken the vessels into hyperspace without a second jump coordinate."

Hyperspace!

Marcopius. Ezrakh. Captain Ioa. Those poor children of her honor guard . . . Threepio and Artoo.

Sickness and horror swept her, replaced a moment later by a burning rage.

"Yes, but at a hundred thousand credits apiece!"

"Cheap at the price." The Hutt shrugged. "Dymurra thought it was worth the expenditure. I agree with him. It wasn't enough to have Liegeus put through that 'Mission accomplished, we're leaving for Coruscant' message, or even the faked transmissions from the jump point. We couldn't bring those vessels here. We couldn't destroy them without the risk of telltale debris. And what do you care, anyway? Dymurra paid for the synthdroids, not you."

"And that makes it all right?" Ashgad turned impatiently from the railing to face the huge, reclining shape. "With an attitude like that, it's no wonder you're no longer ruling this territory, Beldorion."

"Anyway," rumbled Beldorion cryptically, "the price is about to come down on them, isn't it? And what's three hundred thousand credits, if you can get rid of all evidence of where Her Excellency is and what became of her? Once Rieekan goes into a coma, the Council's going to be chasing its tail for days, each member trying to keep the next from being named successor."

He swelled up a little and produced a burp of cosmic proportions, leaking green drool from his mouth and releasing a vast breath of gases that Leia could smell from the terrace above. He rolled a little and delved with one tiny, muscular hand into a washtub-size porcelain bowl of some kind of pink-and-orange snack food that rested on the duvet at his side. Even Ashgad turned his face aside in disgust.

"And don't speak to me about not ruling this Force-benighted planet anymore," the Hutt added, around a mouthful of small, squirming things. "No one forced me—*me,* Beldorion the Splendid, Beldorion of the Ruby Eyes—to retire. I ruled this world longer than your petty Empire existed, and I ruled it well."

He shoved another handful of whatever it was into his enormous mouth. Some of it escaped and made it nearly to the edge of his duvet before he tongued it up. "So don't tell me I was too wasteful or too lazy to know what I'm talking about." He extended one hand, and Leia felt it.

The Force.

A silver cup, probably kept in some kind of cooling bowl under the gazebo's black shade, floated into sight and drifted across toward the stubby, outstretched yellow fingers with their golden rings.

And all around her, Leia felt the air change, as if the iridescent sunlight had thickened or changed its composition: Itchy, swirling, angry.

Beldorion the Hutt had been trained as a Jedi.

And against his use of the Force, there was a stirring, a reaction, a movement in the Force itself that Leia, though only marginally adept with her Jedi powers, felt like sandpaper on the inside of her skull.

Leia's knees felt weak, and she retreated to the divan again, catching the head of it for balance, shivering within the garnet weight of the state robe.

The *Borealis,* sent into hyperspace blind and unprogrammed, never to emerge . . . But if what Dzym said was true, if the Death Seed plague had been on board, that was just as well.

She had had the Death Seed. She shook her head. It

was impossible, according to the records no one recovered.

And Minister Rieekan, her second-in-command in the Council . . . *When Rieekan goes into his coma . . .*

I have to warn him. I have to warn someone . . .

She dropped onto the divan, shaking in every limb with weakness and shock. Panic and rage struggled against the thickness of the sweetblossom that clogged her brain, a fury to escape, to outwit them.

And the drug whispered its reply, *Of course you should. But not just now.*

Something in the pocket of her robe pressed into her thigh, hard and uncomfortable. Leia frowned, trying to recall what she'd carried with her in the garment's bulky folds to the meeting with Ashgad. The answer was, of course, *Nothing.* The velvet garment of state was sufficiently heavy without adding weight to it.

But in that case, who could have put something there, and when?

She fished and fumbled around until she found the pocket in the lining, originally designed to carry a recording device or, depending on who the wearer planned to meet, a hold-out blaster.

Clumsy with the effects of the sweetblossom, her fingers closed on metal.

It was her lightsaber.

4

She brought it out, stared at it in a kind of shock. Touched the switch, the quivering laser blade humming faintly, pale blue and nearly invisible in the odd, moiréd light.

Luke's voice came to her, *Keep up with your lightsaber practice. You need it.*

And like an echo, the voice of the Anakin she had never heard, *We have the Power* . . .

She pushed the ugly dream from her mind. But she couldn't push from her the knowledge of what they were: The grandchildren of Darth Vader, with only the teaching of Law and Justice between the New Republic and that terrible dream. She remembered all the efforts that had been made to kidnap them, to use them, to twist them into tools for greed or obsession. And all the while people assumed that she would teach them better, teach them not to use their powers for selfishness or impulse, while she watched the jackals of the broken Empire and the members of her own Council squabble and snatch and waste time and lives.

And Luke kept urging *her* to take up that personal,

frightening power: the power of Palpatine. The power to have it all her own way.

She touched the switch again. The shining blade was gone.

Artoo. Dimly she remembered Threepio's despairing wails into the comm, and as she slid toward cold darkness, the soft *clickety-whirr* of the astromech's servos near her. *Artoo knew I was in danger. He helped me the only way he could.*

She closed her eyes, fighting tears.

I will kill them, she thought, the cold fury breaking through the sluggishness of the drug. *Ashgad, and Dzym, and that foul Hutt, and Liegeus with his drugged drinks and phony concern. Whatever they're up to, I'll destroy them.*

Before Liegeus came back, she thought, she'd better check out her room for whatever escape she could find.

The air was softer indoors, subtly modified to escape the piercing dryness. That meant magnetic shields on the doors and windows—not cheap—and some kind of mist generators in the ceilings. Away from the jewellike refractions of the sunlight the shadows were thick, and the massive walls sheltered a sour muskiness that no air-conditioning could disperse.

Anyplace a Hutt occupied smelled of Hutt, of course. Nobody ever liked that heavy, rotted odor. On Tatooine, Leia had learned to hate it, though her experience of living in Jabba's palace had served her well during her negotiations with Durga the Hutt on Nal Hutta. She was one of the few diplomats who could deal with highly odorous species like Hutts and Vordums unjudgmentally and relatively unflinchingly. One couldn't, she knew, discredit their intelligence just because their digestive enzymes were set up to deal with everything from tree roots to petroleum by-products.

There were bugs, too. She saw them, tiny and purplish brown, skittering along the densest shadows at the base of the wall and under the small, roughly constructed chest of drawers that was the room's single other piece of furniture. Most storage was in wall niches, natural in a world where only intensive agriculture on the part of its unwilling inhabitants centuries ago had been able to eventually produce woody plants large enough to make furniture out of. The niche doors and the old-fashioned manual outer door of the room were high-impact plastic. There were bugs in most of the niches, fleeing even the muted indoor light.

Leia shivered with distaste as she shut the doors again.

In the end she tore strips from the heavy interfacing between the velvet of the robe and its silken lining to bind the lightsaber to the small of her back under her long, billowing red-and-bronze figured gown. Liegeus Vorn had worn a sort of loose tunic, trousers, and vest, probably standard in an economy poorly supplied with raw materials or the leisure for frivolity in fashionable fit. At a guess, whatever clothing they gave her to wear would be too big. Every hand-me-down she'd ever gotten from the Rebel pilots during the years on the run had been so.

Moving around the room to search had cleared her mind a little. *Luke*, she thought. Luke getting into the B-wing, sliding the cockpit closed—Luke's spirit thanking her for the final touch of farewell.

She had no idea where Ashgad's house was in relation to the city of Hweg Shul, which according to the Registry was the only large settlement on the planet. Even given fairly primitive transportation they could be hundreds of thousands of kilometers away. If Ashgad had ships of at least planet-hopper capability—not to speak of synth-droids—he probably had landspeeders as well.

She scratched the back of her wrist, where a small red bug bite showed her that whatever those little bugs were, they were pests. The sleepy temptation still lay heavy on her, to return to the divan on the sunlit terrace, to sit blinking out over that endless nothingness of glittering gravel, contemplating its colors: grayish whites, pinks, dusky blues, and green like unpolished tourmaline, an endless bed from which the sun glare winked like a leaden kaleidoscope.

I can't, she thought, shaking straight her gown again and pulling on the velvet robe. *When the drug wears off a little more I'll have to put out a call to Luke.*

If Luke hadn't contracted the plague on the ship. If his B-wing hadn't smashed into the planet with his dead or dying body aboard.

She leaned her forehead against the handleless corridor door. *I got out of the Termination Block of the Death Star,* she thought grimly. *I can get out of here.*

"You're to leave her alone!" Ashgad's voice, muffled and distant, came to her through the door.

Dzym's reply, soft though it was, sounded shockingly near. The secretary must have been less than a meter from the door. "What can you mean, my lord?"

"I mean Liegeus told me you'd visited her." Ashgad's voice grew louder, even though he was keeping his tone down. The tap of his boots brought him to where Dzym must be standing. She could almost see him, towering over the smaller man. "Stay away from her."

"She is a Jedi, Lord," murmured Dzym, and there was a note in his voice, a dreamy greediness, that twisted Leia's stomach with nauseated panic. "I was only seeking to keep her under control."

"I know what you were seeking to do," replied Ashgad shortly. "The sweetblossom will keep her under control without help from you. You're not to go near her, understand? Skywalker's her brother. He'll know if she dies."

"Here, Lord?" Dzym's voice sank to a whisper. "On this world?"

"We can't take the chance of the Council naming a successor. Until everything is accomplished, let her alone."

His boots began to retreat. There was no sound from Dzym. He hadn't budged, standing next to the door. She heard Ashgad stop, probably looking back. Still in arm's-reach of her, Dzym murmured, "And then?" She could almost see him rubbing his gloved hands.

There was a long silence.

"And then we'll see."

Luke hung for several minutes in the seat restraint, getting his breath. Part of his mind he kept stretched out to the Force, manipulating the power of fusion and heat to keep the small impulse fuel reserves from exploding; part he extended, listening, probing across the harsh landscape for signs of danger.

People were on their way.

His mind picked up the radiant buzz of hostility. Theran fanatics, almost certainly. He hung at a forty-five-degree angle above the jagged jumble of what was left of the control board, seat, and flooring; the tiny space stank of leaked coolants and crash-foam. Huge gaps in the hull where the metal had buckled on final impact let through slabs of thin, fragmented-looking light. Sand and pebbles had come through, too, and lay in tiny dunes and pools among the wreckage. Dust made a shimmering scrim in the air.

Luke wound his left arm in the straps, twisted his body so that his right hand could reach the snap locks on his harness. Swinging down and bracing his feet on the wrecked console, he experienced a moment of surprise that he was still alive, much less relatively unhurt, barring a wrenched shoulder, strap bruises, and the general sense of having gone over the side of Beggar's Canyon in a not very well constructed barrel.

The locker where he'd stowed food, water, a blaster, and spare power batteries was well and truly jammed shut.

And judging by the angry vibration in the Force, company would be arriving in five minutes or less.

Luke had used the kinetic displacement of the Force on occasion to open locks, but the door itself was jammed. He pushed up his right sleeve; shifted the relative strength of his robotic right hand to its highest; and, bracing the heel of his hand against the crumpled metal of the locker door, bent the least-solidly stuck corner inward until the triangular gap was large enough for him to reach through and fish out the water flask, with the intention of getting the weapon next because he could already hear the hum of badly tuned speeder engines and the clashing crunch of padded hooves on gravel.

He couldn't get purchase on the blaster in time to free it before the weight of springing bodies rocked the fighter. Shadows fell across the gaps in the buckled hull as Luke snaked his arm free empty-handed, sprang to his feet, and slithered through the smaller split in the other side of the tiny cockpit moments before the crashing racket of expanding-gas percussive weapons echoed like thunder in the tiny space, and a shower of high-velocity stone pellets spattered the space where he had been.

There were a lot of attackers: Twenty or twenty-five, Luke estimated, dropping to the gravel in a long roll to get back under the shelter of the broken S-foil. Men and women both, as far as he was able to tell, for in the sharp cold they were wrapped in thick vests and jackets, sometimes covered by ragged burnooses, their heads further protected by veils or wide-brimmed hats. In addition to the scatterguns they had bows—both autobows and primitive longbows—as well as short javelins, and they surrounded the wrecked B-wing completely.

Luke didn't want to have anything to do with any of them.

There are a thousand ways to use the Force in a fight, Callista's old master, Djinn, had told her. *And a thousand and one ways to use the Force to avoid a fight.* Luke now used something Djinn had taught her, and she him, so simple a use of kinetic displacement that he was embarrassed not to have thought of it himself years ago. His mind jarred at the gravel underfoot, and the gravel coughed forth dust.

A *lot* of dust.

The problem with that trick was that you had to be ready for it yourself. Luke had already picked his line of retreat through the closing ring of Therans and was dragging up the neck of his flightsuit to cover his nose and mouth, squinting his eyes for what protection he could find, even as he launched himself out of the shelter of the B-wing. He'd always had a good sense of direction, and Yoda had drummed into him an almost supernatural ability to orient himself in an emergency. He knew in which direction the Theran speeders and riding-beasts lay and made for them amid a roar of gunfire and a rain of projectiles, half-seen ghostly bodies rushing about in all directions in the sudden gray-white obscurity of suspended grit.

The field effect of the dust was an extremely localized one, rapidly dispersing in the remains of the dying wind. The Theran speeders lay outside its plumy, smoking ring, as grubby a collection of fifth-hand makeshift junkers as Luke had seen this side of the Rebellion's worst days: aged Void-Spiders, XP-291s, and something that looked like the offspring of a Mobquet Floater and a packing crate engineered by a gene splicer who'd had too much glitterstim. Among them a dozen cu-pas were prancing and yammering, the brightly hued, hot-weather cousins of tauntuans whose pea-sized intellectual powers made the snow lizards appear to be candidates for sentient status—and doctoral degrees—by comparison.

Mindful of the water he carried, and the unknown distance he'd have to travel before he reached civilization, Luke flung himself into the best-looking of the speeders, checked the fuel gauge, reached back to slash the lines of the two cu-pas tied to the stern, rolled out the other side, and dashed to the next-best one he could find, a raddled XP-38A. That one had more juice in its batteries. He cut loose the cu-pas attached to that one, too—they immediately made tracks for the horizon, gronching and wibbling like enormous pink-and-blue rubber toys—and slammed the speeder into gear, driving his mind and the Force against the ground again like an enormous, stamping foot.

More dust bellied up, engulfing the Therans who rushed from the first dust cloud in his direction and sprayed him with gun pellets and curses. The speeder slashed out of the dust cloud, and Luke put it into a long turn, heading back into the nearest canyon of the monstrous, glittering massif through which the B-wing had descended. The shadows swallowed him in a winding maze of dry wadis, chasms, and cracks.

He could tell when he got too far from the wreckage to hold the heat fusion of the fuel tanks in stasis by the power of the Force. The explosion boomed out over the empty plain, bounced through the dirty jewels of the hills like a flat, heavy word of thunder.

Luke hoped the Therans—if those people were, in fact, the fanatic cultists of whom Leia had spoken—had gotten away from the craft before it blew.

Later, in the shelter of a fantastically splintered notch somewhere near the top of the ridge, Luke saw the white flicker of a laser cannon firing skyward again, like threads of perfectly straight lightning pointed into the dull navy blue of the jeweled, arid sky. In time, their target came into view, weaving and dodging in what was clearly an extremely complex preprogrammed pattern: One of the small bronze mini-hulls of the *Light of Reason,* detached in orbit and making its way separately into the atmosphere.

Shading his eyes against the shimmering brilliance that radiated from the iridescent gravel, Luke knew when ground control cut in to guide the fragment. Every civilian Luke had ever talked to—Leia included, for years—claimed that a program was as good as a live operator, but he didn't know a single pilot who couldn't distinguish the difference. Not one who'd survived more than a few firefights, anyway.

The mini-hull came in under the lowest point of the gun station's attitude, leveled off parallel to the rolling adamant of the plain, and streaked away to the north. Far away Luke could descry another threadlike flash of laser brightness in the sky.

He got to his feet, scrambled up the shining slabs to the top of the ridge. The ceaseless wind flattened his flightsuit to his body, whined softly among the rocks. Five or six kilometers away on the plain below the glassy hogback he saw what looked like the outline of ruined walls, and against the translucent rose and purple of the surrounding ground, the startlingly green splotches of what he had not yet seen in all this world: vegetation.

He raised to his eyes the macrobinoculars he'd found under the speeder's seat—much-mended manuals and probably older than he was, but they worked. They showed him wind-scoured foundations, long stripped of everything usable. At a guess it was one of the old prisons that had formed the original colonies on this world. He traced the treble walls, the placement of blockhouses designed to defend against an attack from within rather than without.

Still, there was water down there somewhere. The harsh projections of faceted stone cut his hands as he picked his way back down to the speeder, and he shivered a little in the chill as he put the craft into gear and headed down the canyons toward the ruin.

With clumsy dignity, See-Threepio arranged the body of Yeoman Marcopius in the scout boat's small specimen-freeze chamber. The craft contained only emergency medical kits, not even a class-3 med droid, much less a stasis box, and though Threepio hooked the boy immediately into life supports and diagnostics, nothing had been able to save him. The diagnostics faithfully reported no anomalous conditions, no poison, no disease, no bacteria, and no virus on one screen, while the other cataloged the absence of oxygen absorption or brain function.

There was nothing wrong with him. He'd just died.

The protocol droid coaxed the young man's limbs into the most dignified position possible in a chamber slightly more than a meter square, then straightened himself up, made a few little human warm-up noises, and proceeded to produce the standard Service for the Departed, complete with music.

Artoo tweeped a worried inquiry. Threepio paused in mid-fugue and said, "Well, of course I'm playing the Service for the Departed on full-speed fast-forward! We'll be coming out of hyperspace soon—*if* poor Yeoman Marcopius's computations were correct. And I don't scruple to tell you, Artoo, that I'm very worried that he might already have been feeling ill when he input the calculations to the computer. It takes so little to disarrange an organic brain. Really, only a temperature variation of half a dozen degrees. Who knows where we might emerge from hyperspace? Or if anyone will be within hailing distance to pilot the ship into port?"

The astromech wibbled another comment.

"Oh, you've checked? We are on the proper course to emerge within hailing distance of the Durren orbital base? Why didn't you say so before? Now don't keep interrupting me. It isn't respectful."

He turned back to the young man in the white uniform—the young man who had been their primary hope of a swift and successful planetfall at Durren—assumed a pose of reverent mourning, and whipped through the two-hour service in one seven-second lightspeed burst.

"There." He slid the freeze chamber lid shut and turned the locking ring. "The unit is certified to contain any form of communicable disease in the Registry. Once we've alerted Fleet authorities as to Master Ashgad's appalling treachery, poor Yeoman Marcopius's family can be notified. . . . Good heavens!" His gold head snapped a quick thirty degrees as a light went up over the infirmary door. "That's the warning signal. We'd better immobilize to come out of hyperspace."

The amber light blinked faster as the two droids ascended the lift to the bridge. Though the scout boat was set for an automatic deceleration and would have emerged from hyperspace whether or not anyone was at the controls, Threepio felt vaguely safer as he stepped into one of the several immobilization niches near the lift door of the bridge. Beyond the vacant chairs of captain and co-pilot, the line of readouts appeared normal. No warning lights shone beneath the great viewports with their swirling lights and darks of mutated starlight and bent gravitational fields. Artoo settled himself in the niche nearest the consoles and extruded an input jack to the dataport at the near end of the board. He tweeped reassuringly as the lockdown lights flowed from their flutter of blinking into steady, burning gold.

"I know we're coming out at the far edge of Durren planetary space," retorted Threepio crossly. "Durren is a major port. Only an idiot would set an automatic deceleration sequence for anywhere that there would be the slightest possibility of encountering another ship."

The lights on the bridge shifted and brightened. The gravity field surged as regular power cut in. The weird, mottled-silk patterns of stretched starlight flexed, lined, and gave way suddenly to the blackness of normal space, barely seen behind the small Republic gunship that occupied eighty-five percent of the front viewscreen and toward which the scout boat was barreling full-blast.

Threepio said, "Oh, dear!" and Artoo let out a screaming whistle of alarm. There was a flash and a glare, then the whole screen washed out in an actinic blaze of blue-white as the gunship blew up—it must have taken a direct hit in the tanks—instants before the scout boat plunged through the surging whirl of debris where it had been.

The scout boat lurched, heaved, and cartwheeled under the slamming shock waves and pounding debris. Threepio cried, "Oh, dear!" again as the viewscreens cleared and the vast blue disk of Durren appeared, the space between dotted with sparkling clouds of dissipating debris, silver flashes of E-wings and various small craft that looked like planet-hoppers and armored traders spitting laser fire at one another in battle and, farther off, the sprawling, angular, black-and-silver bulk of the Durren orbital base surrounded by a cloud of attacking ships.

"Great heavens, Artoo, what can possibly be going on? I know the orbital base is being attacked," he added irritably, in response to his friend's immediate reply. "But who would do such a thing?"

Artoo, still jacked into the main computer, plastered the readouts below the viewscreen with stats.

"They're all converted trading vessels." Threepio pushed the stabilizer bars from the front of his niche and toddled to the console for a better look. Though vessel identification had not been part of his original programming, several years with the fugitive Rebel fleet had augmented his databanks in that area by a factor of three.

"Look at that. Even orbital shuttles have been converted into fighter craft. But why isn't the Durren base responding with anything larger than an E-wing?"

Artoo twiddled.

"Oh, yes. Of course. I was about to do that." The protocol droid toggled the comm and keyed through to Durren frequencies. His stiff golden fingers navigated the board, switching from channel to channel through the curses of squad commanders, base commanders barking out orders and contravening them in the next breath, and a spate of intelligence and reconnaissance from the planet itself.

"It's a rebellion!" said Threepio, shocked. "A factional revolt against the Durren Central Planetary Council! The insurgent coalition has repudiated the Planetary Council's agreements with the Republic and is even now attacking the main government centers!"

Artoo beeped a question.

"Yesterday, it seems, after the *Caelus* and the *Corbantis* left the base to deal with reports of pirate attack on Ampliquen. The major attack on the government center began last night, and they began the assault on the base only hours later."

He tilted his head, listening again. Between them and

the planet, a Kaloth Y-9 trader maneuvered itself out of orbit and headed away out of the system.

"With attacks being made on all major ports, interplanetary trade is being turned away. Artoo, this is terrible! No ships are able to come in! There's no effective ground control! But someone will have to come out and get us. Listen . . ."

He stabbed the comm toggle. "Durren base, this is the scout boat from the Republic flagship *Borealis*! Come in, Durren base! Something terrible has happened!"

Static growled and whined at him, broken fragments of someone's voice jarring out of the comm and then being drowned again.

"But Her Excellency has been kidnapped! There was an ambush, a plague . . ."

Artoo swiveled on his axis, all lights flashing, and let loose a shrill barrage of twiddles, whoops, and beeps. The taller droid turned his horrified attention from the blue curve of the planet, which had grown slowly larger at the top of the screen but was now sliding toward its edge as the scout boat's trajectory began to carry it past Durren and out toward the empty starriness of space.

"Don't be ridiculous, Artoo. Even if there is a traitor in the Council, *all* communications can't be monitored!" He turned back to the comm. "You have to listen to us . . . !"

But only static replied.

On the screen before them, the bulky but heavily armed traders of the partisan forces opened fire on the E-wing squadrons that were evidently all the orbital base had to send against them. The smaller, lighter ships scattered like silvery flak in the planet's reflected light.

"Chief of State Organa Solo has been kidnapped!" Threepio tried again. "She's being held captive on Nam Chorios! We're not getting through." He made a few tentative stabs at the controls, but nothing happened. The blue disk of Durren slipped to the edge of the screen, then vanished.

Only space lay before them. Space and eternity, empty and dark as the abyss of a tomb.

Threepio toggled the comm again. "Help!" His faint, despairing cry reached vainly out toward a welter of broken receivers and beings who were in no mood to pay attention. "Can anyone out there hear us? Help!"

5

As Luke maneuvered it down the canyon, the XP-38A sagged lower and lower toward the ground. Either an antigrav cell was giving out or the fuel that powered the cell's modulator coil was running low. It was impossible to tell which from the defunct and sand-blasted gauges. Luke muttered sotto voce imprecations against those who would let a good piece of machinery like this get into such a condition, and reached out with the Force to boost the vehicle's rusty belly over a line of palely gleaming transparent rocks—blanched violet, jade green, white blues, all rinsed-out hues like glacier ice.

At the last moment he decided not to use the Force after all and applied the brakes instead. The speeder wibbled to a halt in a way that made Luke think there was a problem with the stabilizers as well. After a moment, like a tired bantha, the small craft settled to the slanted rocks of the canyon floor.

The silence was huge, like the desert silences of Tatooine. Like the desert silence, it breathed.

Then behind him he heard a soft, deadly crackling, and felt the lance of electricity stab the air. Turning, he saw flickering snakes of lightning racing down the face of the cliffs, like skeletal hands, or the wide-flung root systems of a thorn plant, a zone of fast-moving coruscation close to half a mile broad and heading his way.

For an instant he watched it, fascinated. It poured down the face of the cliffs, raced over the jagged rocks at the bottom, sparking and leaping brighter as it raced over the slabs and projections of giant crystals that seemed to grow out of the darker rock. As it came closer he put forth his mind into the Force and raised the speeder in which he sat a few feet above the ground. The ground lightning poured past under it, flowing at the same time along the canyon walls to both sides; he felt the bolts of it that leapt up and struck the bottom of the speeder, jarring him even through its insulation with mild jolts of pain. At the same time he could feel the Force, like a roaring in his mind or hot wind blowing across his face, could almost see it as a sort of ghostly light reflecting back from the clusters and facets of crystals that glowed all around him in the shadows.

The storm, whatever it was, flowed by under him for perhaps five minutes. When it had gone past him he let the speeder ease to the ground and stood up on it, watching the sparkling flood race down the rocks to the open plain, pale in the wan sun. It washed through the edge of the prison colony ruins, flowed along the jeweled ground beyond, vanishing at last in the direction of the line of spiky crystal rock chimneys that stretched away into the wastelands.

Even in the stillness it left, the Force was everywhere. Luke could feel it, like a radiation penetrating his skin.

The planet is dead, he thought. *Completely without life, except for the tiny enclaves of human habitation.*

But the Force was here.

It comes from Life, Yoda had said. *Binding you, me, all life together* . . .

And Callista had come here seeking it. Seeking the key to the frustration, the fear, the terrible forces that had driven her from him.

There is life here, thought Luke, suddenly aware of it, sure of it. *Life somewhere*. He wondered if the ruins he'd seen contained some clue as to why no mention had ever been made, in any survey of the planet ever taken.

Luke could have raised the speeder with his mind and floated it down to the ruins at the canyon's foot. By the same token, he understood, Yoda himself could have flown wherever he wanted to travel or could have built himself a palatial dwelling of rock instead of the mud hovel in Dagobah's swamps. Ben Kenobi could have ruled a small planet.

Wars do not make one great, the little Master had said.

And neither did the ability to tote a mass of metal where one could just as easily walk.

Luke dug his canteen from the speeder, checked the lightsaber at his belt and the blaster he'd found with the macrobinoculars under the seat, and started down the canyon on foot.

Little remained of the Grissmath prison colony after some seven centuries. It had been situated above a ground water seam but evidently the hidden moisture had proved insufficient when terraforming had gone beyond crom and the simple gomex mosses that broke down the minerals of unyielding rock into soil that such plants as balcrabbian and brachniel could use. Without careful cultivation, most of the intermediate growths of the artificial ecosystems had died before they'd reached the stage of being self-sufficient. Lichens and podhoy still grew everywhere around the walls, as if the entire place had been dunked in a vat of crimson mud that had left a rough scum; close to the broken pump housing, a little soil remained, where hardy balcrabbian plants spread their leaves.

Luke sensed a human presence there moments before his danger-trained eye picked out the dull metal of another speeder concealed in the shadows of a broken foundation. He drew around himself the aura of advanced inconspicuousness that Yoda had spoken about and that later Callista, recalling her own training, had taught him: Beyond a doubt the same means by which old Ben had wandered around the Death Star utterly unnoticed by the most highly trained troops of the Empire.

The owner of the speeder sat in the dappled shade of the balcrabbian, protected from the wind, where the long-ruptured pump dribbled a series of tiny pools among the broken pavement. A young man, six or seven years junior to Luke, Corellian or maybe Alderaan stock, to judge by the brown hair, the medium build. He reminded Luke of any of the dozens of young farmers he'd known on Tatooine, trying to wrest a living from an inhospitable world. The duranex of his jumpsuit, though one of the toughest fabrics known, was patched and frayed, and the leather of the utility belt and satchel he wore much mended. He looked up quickly when Luke deliberately scraped the side of his boot on a lump of old-style permacrete. The young man's hand flashed to the long, primitive pellet gun at his side, but something about Luke seemed to convince him that this wasn't the danger he'd been fearing. He put the weapon down again and raised his hand with a grin.

"Where'd you drop out of, brother? Don't tell me you were on that B-wing they brought down."

Luke grinned back ingenuously. "I just want the name of the guy who said B-wings were too small to draw their fire, that's all. Owen Lars," he introduced himself, holding out his hand.

The young man rose. "Arvid Scraf. Were you modified for cargo? Trying to make Hweg Shul? Something the size of a B-wing usually *can* get through the automatics. Smugglers use them sometimes, but I've heard they're tricky. The Therans must have been in the base itself when the sensors picked you up. They can take them off auto and fire themselves, if they want."

Luke knelt by the water, dipped his half-empty canteen. The harsh dryness of the air, chilly as it was, filled him with a curious sense of having come home.

"That's my luck. I once picked up half a crate of glitterstim for twenty-five hundred credits, only the guy who sold it to me forgot to tell me he'd stolen it and it had sensor relays in it. I hadn't even cleared the atmosphere when I had fourteen revenue cruisers around me like buzz flies on a ripe fruit." It hadn't happened to him, but it had to Han, and it gave him credentials of a sort, and a persona. More than that, it let him size up Arvid Scraf for a few moments more.

"I heard the Therans were savages—the ones who tried to put holes in me sure looked like them. My cargo must have upped the ship's mass reading. They can run a gun station?"

"Don't sell them short." Scraf picked up his own canteen. Water splotched his sand-beaten orange sleeves, and down the front of his suit. "Where'd you come down? The Therans will have finished by now. I'll help you haul whatever's left into Ruby Gulch. You can get cash for it there."

A childhood on Tatooine had made Luke familiar with the economics of salvage. They'd been severe enough on the desert world, which had an open trade of sorts through Mos Eisley. On a planet with virtually no natural resources and little access to imported goods, that much metal and microchips would make him a wealthy man.

"Who are they, anyway?" he asked, settling himself on the rough wooden bench that served Arvid Scraf's landspeeder as a seat. The speeder was a crumbling Aratech 74-Z Jawas wouldn't have touched. The starboard buoyancy tanks were so low that the deck canted sharply, and Arvid had built up a second deck on planks, with posts to level it up. He'd rigged a retractable limb underneath as well, with a wheel to keep the whole thing steady if too heavily laden. It gave the speeder the appearance of a badly misshapen mushroom, balanced on a single stem that did not quite touch the ground.

"She don't look like much, but she covers ground," the young man said, half-proud and half-defensive, when Luke did a double-take. With Luke on the bench, Arvid had had to shift the gravel sack ballast to compensate for his weight.

But she did, in fact, cover ground. Like the *Millennium Falcon,* there was marginally more to her than met the eye.

Now Arvid said, "Who, the Therans? There's little villages of 'em up the canyons, or in caves, anyplace they can find a spring or an old pump still working. But most of 'em just come out of the farms. Half the Oldtimers were Therans at some time in their lives. Kids go out of the settlements and ride with the bands for a couple-three seasons. They sniff the smoke, they hear the voices, they dream the dreams, and they meet people they wouldn't have met if they'd stayed around home, I guess. Then they come back and get married and have kids of their own. Sometimes they ride out again later, but mostly once seems to be enough."

He shrugged, clinging like a bantha-buster to the

struggling levers, his eyes moving constantly between the sand-scored gauges and the eroded jags and zigs of the rising ground as the Aratech labored through the narrowing steepness of those light-laden crystal rocks, to where Luke had left his appropriated XP-38A.

"That's why we can't make headway against 'em," Arvid Scraf went on. "Their Listeners tell 'em anything coming in or going out is bad, tell 'em in their sleep, in their dreams. Then it's part of their dreams for all time. It gets stuck in their heads so bad you can't make 'em see different. They can't see what this world could be, if we could get any kind of trade going. 'We don't want that,' they'll say, and you can talk to the edge of anoxia, and they just look at you with those eyes and say, 'We don't want that.' *We.* Like they know what all the other Old-timers think. Weird."

He shook his head. His big hands on the levers were calloused and stained with grease, as Luke's own had been, he remembered, back in his days of trying to wring a living from a world not intended to support human life.

The two of them wrestled the XP-38A up wholesale and lashed it to the -74's bed. Luke knew the reasoning well. In a world without native metal, without timber, without imports, a rusty bucket was treasure.

The anemic sun was sinking fast, and harsh wind pounded them out of the west, making the repulsorlift vehicle jerk and wobble. As they were wrassling the ropes, Luke caught the leg of his flightsuit on one of the -74's makeshift struts, scratching the flesh underneath. Reaching down to feel the scrape, his fingers encountered what felt like a droplet of plastic, hard and smooth, on his flesh, and when he pulled up the fabric and stripped the placket, he saw on his calf a very small swelling, like a minute hill in the flesh. In its center bulged a tiny dome of hard, purple-brown chiten, unmistakably the shell of some sort of pinhead-size insect, which vanished into the flesh even as he watched.

With an exclamation of disgusted alarm, Luke pinched the flesh around the swelling, forcing the thing back and out again. The swelling bubble of blood-dark shell elongated into a repellent abdomen perhaps a centimeter long, that ended in a hard little head and a ring of tiny, wriggling, thorn-tipped legs. It immediately turned between his thumb and forefinger and tried to dig into the ball of his thumb. Luke flicked it away hard, and heard it strike the flat facet of a nearby rock. It bounced down to the slippery canyon floor and scuttered fast for the shadows of the nearest stone.

Luke said, "Yuck!" and pulled his pant leg up farther. His calf was dotted with tiny, reddened swellings, or fading pink patches where the bugs were already burrowing down into the flesh.

"Don't waste your time on 'em," advised Arvid, from the other side of the speeder. He tied down a final knot and clambered over the tailfins to Luke's side. "You probably picked 'em up in the shade around the water." He pulled up his own sleeve to show at least four swellings on his forearm, one of them with the hard little insect tail just vanishing into the flesh. Casually he pinched the thing free and flicked it away against the deck, grinding it to a little purple blotch with the heel of his boot when it began to crawl toward his foot again.

"They're kind of gross but they just die and get absorbed. There's stories of crystal hunters who run out of food in the barrens and stick their hands into holes so they can absorb enough drochs to get energy to make it to a settlement. Not something I'd care to do myself."

He made a face.

"Drochs?"

Arvid nodded. "They're everywhere on this planet, and I mean *everywhere*. Their reproductive rate makes sand bunnies look like Elamposnian monks. Everybody has bites. Sunlight kills 'em. You just keep as clean as you can and don't worry about it."

Reflecting on some of the more loathsome—but quite harmless—denizens of Dagobah who'd scavenged crumbs in the corners of Yoda's dwelling, Luke supposed Arvid had a point.

Fifteen or twenty minutes later, as the piggyback speeders turned from the eye-aching crystal mazes to the plain where the burn marks of Luke's crash landing could be seen, Luke pulled up his sleeve again. Only a few pinkish splotches remained. He pinched the flesh around one carefully, feeling for the hardness of a foreign body, and found nothing. With his mind—with the techniques of the Force—he probed at the molecules, water, life energy of the muscle tissue itself, and found only the few vanishing traces of an alien energy field, which dissolved even as he observed them, becoming first identical with his own body, then a part of it.

Virtually nothing remained of the B-wing. Scuffmarks, charring, a huge slick of fused gravel where the reactor core had ruptured—even the massive cylinder of the reactor itself was gone. What Luke thought of as the "soft parts" of the ship were scattered broadcast over the harsh ground: the upholstery of the seats, some fragmented plastic from broken couplers, insulation that had been cooked brittle by the crash itself. Everything else had been taken.

"Didn't think we'd find much." Arvid scuffed with his toe at the cracked corner of what had been a console housing, and held it up. Even the screws were gone. "They use everything. Why not? Everybody does." A dry twist of wind flipped his brown hair across his eyes. "I'm really sorry, Owen."

The sun was sinking. Everywhere the orange and rose and cinnabar of its changing lights glanced and glared off the gravel, rocks, the towering crystal chimneys, so that Luke felt as if he were trapped in the midst of a limitless, heatless lava flow that stretched to the ends of the world. The wind had swelled to a torrent, and the temperature was plunging fast.

"At least you got one of their speeders. That's something." Arvid lowered his voice. "Uh—you didn't owe anything on that cargo, did you?" He worked his fingers into clumsy hand-knitted gloves, and tossed Luke a disreputable coat he'd pulled from beneath the speeder's seat. His breath was already a cloud of mist. "That was on your craft? I mean, to people who'd make trouble for you?"

Luke was about to disclaim further interest in his fictitious cargo, but another thought crossed his mind. He lowered his voice also, although it was patently obvious there was no one and nothing to hear them for hundreds of kilometers, and said, "Well, I'd sure rather a couple of individuals thought I bought it in the crash until I can come up with a little working capital again, if you know what I mean."

Arvid nodded, with a prompt understanding that made Luke wonder how often smugglers made landfall on this planet. With Pedducis Chorios so close it made sense.

"You can put up with me at my aunt's in Ruby Gulch tonight," Arvid said. "You'll freeze, out of doors. Aunt Gin'll give you top price for the speeder, too, if you want to sell, and that should be enough to get you a launch offplanet when you get to Hweg Shul."

"Thank you," said Luke, and pulled closer about him the ragged, too-big jacket. "I appreciate it."

"Well, we don't get a lot of strangers." Arvid looked a little shy as they clambered back into the Aratech. "The Oldtimers are all each others' cousins, but those of us who've come here in the last ten years or so, we sort of like to hear how things are going, back toward the Core. You know?"

Luke knew. For the next hour and a half, while Arvid fought the evening wind across the sea floor plains by the light of a couple of wavery chemical lamps, he entertained the young man with smuggler stories gleaned secondhand from Mara and Han and Lando, with tales of the Rebellion edited together from his own adventures and those of Leia and Winter and Wedge. To these he added news and gossip and hints enough to imply that he was a minor-league planet-hopper making his living as best he could in the chaos without giving allegiance to either side, much as Han had been, once upon a time.

And, as he himself would have been, ten or twelve years and several lifetimes ago, Arvid was enchanted.

The young man had gone many hours out of his way to help Luke. Though Luke was tired and would rather have dozed, or asked questions about this eerie world of light and ungiving glass, he knew that such entertainment as he could provide was payment for Arvid's trouble. There would be time later, he thought, to learn what he had come here to learn.

Against the darkness, far-off light speared the sky.

"What the . . . ?"

"That'll be the gun station!" Arvid braced his feet against a ballast bag and threw his weight on the steering lever. "Big one—over by Bleak Point . . ."

The speeder sagged heavily, the hot flares of its lamp-light sparkling on the facets below them. The wind had fallen with full darkness, and in the stillness the cold deepened until Luke's ears and teeth ached. "There's a couple blaster rifles under the seat, Owen, if you'd be so kind."

Luke fished out a Seinar proton blaster and a venerable Merr-Sonn Standard Four.

"You take the proton," offered Arvid generously, as he tromped the accelerator and the scattered boulders and chimneys flashed and whirled past them with horrifying speed. "The Four's got her ways—I better handle her."

"Uh—you probably better." Luke checked out the Seinar. The geriatric weapon had been refitted repeatedly, like every other piece of equipment he'd seen on the planet, but it was spotlessly clean and the charges were topped. "What's going on?" The fitful blasts of light ahead were coming from ground level, not pointed at the sky. Luke balanced himself on a stanchion and stood up, wind slapping his gray flightsuit, focusing his mind through the darkness, reaching toward the source of the intermittent glare.

Anger. Violence. A great, swirling turmoil in the Force.

"It isn't that—that ground lightning I saw earlier, is it?"

Braced against the seat, Arvid shook his head. "Looks like an attack on the station."

The gun station was a squat, dark complex of permacrete shapes seemingly fused into the black shoulder bones of the hills. By the flare and smolder of laser light, Luke made out the massive cylinder of the outer wall, featureless and scuffed by time and sand storms: No gate, no postern, no door, no windows. The upperworks of the station, where the cannon's gleaming black snout pointed at the sky, were crowned with a ragged, thorny palisade of projecting buttonwood poles, planks, and what looked like the whole twisted trunks of scrub-loaks, pointing like spears in all directions and strung with catwalks, bridges, and crow's nests from which the defenders could fire on those below. Tiny lights were entangled in the overhanging masses—lanterns, sodium flares, and here and there an occasional string of jerry-built worklights against whose sulfurous glare Luke saw moving figures darting among the jackstraw shadows. Arvid brought the speeder to a halt on the crest of a ridge above the little box canyon in which the gun station stood, perhaps a hundred meters from the walls. From this vantage point Luke watched the little band of attackers run back and forth along the curving bastion, firing up into the superstructure with hard, clear bursts of proton light.

"Yep, that's Gerney Caslo." Arvid had the macrobinoculars indispensable to any frontier dweller to his eyes, adjusting them as he followed this figure or that. "Gerney's one of the biggest water sellers between here and Hweg Shul. Without him we'd never have gotten those old pump stations going again. The Oldtimers just let 'em rot, except for the ones in their villages. See that gal there with the white hair? That's Umolly Darm. She ships out Spook crystals, the long green-and-violet kind you find in clusters up in the deep hills. They make some kind of cross-eyed optical equipment that's supposed to make flowers grow better on worlds with K-class suns or something. She works for an outfit in Hweg Shul—three suborbitals and they can pretty much ask their own price on whatever they can slip past the gun stations."

He lowered the macrobinoculars, clearly in no particular hurry to join the attack, though Luke noticed he kept the Merr-Sonn Four propped where he could lay hands on it at seconds' notice. "She'll be the one to ask about getting yourself on a ship." His breath plumed in a diamond cloud. "Her or Seti Ashgad, in Hweg Shul itself. She can wire through for information to the head office in town, if you'd like."

Below them a faint cheer went up. A small group of what looked like armed farmers and townspeople scrambled onto a speeder that had been backed up to the wall itself. Even without macrobinoculars, Luke could see the extra buoyancy tanks strapped underneath the speeder's hull. The attackers must have waited until the evening winds died to use antigrav transport at such a distance from the ground.

There must have been some kind of primitive deflector shield on it as well, for the rocks and lances hurled down from above missed it with a suspicious persistency. One of the crouching figures did something to a stripped-down control console, and the speeder began to rise straight up along the wall.

Luke wondered if the defenders were sufficiently wise in the ways of deflector shields to lower a man on a rope below the rising speeder's level. "You think Mistress Darm might be able to trace an incoming passenger for me?"

"Don't see why she wouldn't. Just about everybody who comes in, comes through Hweg Shul."

From the jackdaw mess of timbers overhead a rope extended. Like a plumb bob on a line, a single lankily graceful figure in grubby crimson, tattered leather, and what appeared to be pieces of very old stormtrooper armor rappelled casually down the permacrete face, far enough from the speeder with its little gang of attackers so that the curve of the wall offered a shadow of protection against laser bolts. Only a perfect shot could have struck the solitary defender, and none of those on the speeder was that good. The bolts seared wild off the hard black wall, leaving long dirty scars but no chips. The Grissmaths had built well.

At precisely the right moment the defender wrapped an extra bight or two of line around one arm and, hefting a beltful of grenades in the other hand, kicked away from the wall in a long, flying parabola, coming pendulum like close to the underside of the makeshift assault platform. The men on the platform fired wildly down at the bloodred form swinging toward them through the darkness, but the rail of the speeder impeded their aim.

The timing was flawless. The lone defender hurled the belt of grenades up into the speeder's undercarriage, with an expert flick that tangled it with the emergency balance gear, then struck the wall and kicked off again, swooping on the end of the line back into darkness. The line was already shortening, those hidden in the superstructure pulling the grenade thrower in. The platform headed groundward, seconds ticking away—the crew bailed at eight meters, jumping outward, and the speeder exploded in a rain of red-hot shrapnel two meters above where the attackers' heads would have been had anyone still been standing underneath.

Searchlights flowed out over the gravel from the direction of the open plain. Lances and arrows glittered in flight, and a smattering of red laser fire stitched the night, accompanied by the flat snaps of pellet guns. Focusing his mind through the Force to pierce the darkness, Luke saw a ragged agglomerate of men and women approaching in speeders and on speeder bikes, more poorly dressed than the assault forces—whom he presumed to be Newcomers—but without the raffish tatters of the Therans.

They were far more numerous than either of the other groups, however, well over a hundred strong. The

Newcomers turned, yelling and brandishing their weapons, and Luke could make out curses and accusations on the harsh night air. Very few shots were fired once the two sides joined. It seemed more like an enormous brawl, men and women pulling and pushing, hitting with clubs or wrenches or hoes, grappling and punching and pulling hair—enemies, he thought, but enemies who know they'll be meeting one another in the same food store tomorrow morning.

"Are those the Oldtimers?" he guessed, and Arvid nodded sourly.

"Cheesebrained idiots," muttered the younger man. "What business is it of theirs if we bring in ships or not? If we trade our crops for pumps and processors and transport? They can live like animals if they want to, but why make us do it?"

Disgusted, he shoved over the levers, backed the speeder, and headed down the ridge. Luke thought, *Maybe because it's their planet?*

Over his shoulder he saw forms standing among the struts and timbers of the gun station's superstructure, silhouetted against the glare of the lights: the thin, gawky, graceful form of the crimson warrior and the lean, tiny shape of what looked like a youngish man with long, braided hair. Behind them, a thin lance of cold green light stabbed straight upward from the station's main gun, losing itself in the sheer distance of the night overhead.

A moment later a second light shot up from far over the hills. Tiny in the infinite distance above, a bright pin of fire burst in the sky.

"Sithspawn," whispered Arvid, with a quick glance over his shoulder, as quickly reverting to the ground ahead. "Somethin' coming in."

The attackers around the wall ceased to shove and

curse. They, and the Oldtimers who had taken them from the rear, only stood in sullen groups, panting like dragons in the cold. They glared upward as the gun station's cannon flared again.

"Got one of 'em," muttered Arvid, braking to a halt at the foot of the ridge. "Didn't get 'em all, though. Gerney'll know what stuff came in and what they'll be charging for it."

Seti Ashgad's ship, thought Luke. Beyond a doubt the attack on the gun station had been coordinated—in who knew how many places?—to better the populist leader's chances of a safe return.

With the tiny explosion above the atmosphere, the erstwhile attackers began to curse and threaten again, striking out for no purpose now, but out of frustration and anger. Arvid shoved the accelerator again in bitter silence, and Luke's eyes were drawn back to the little braided-haired man on the wall and the tall, thin form beside him, before the jutting boulders and crystal chimneys hid the gun station from sight.

Where the last, scattered lines of rocks gave way to the emptiness of the starlit sea bottoms, Arvid's speeder overtook the retreating clumps of combatants, men and women in sand-scoured orange or yellow or green worksuits, rifles over their shoulders or blasters hanging at the utility belts that were the hallmark of frontier dwellers throughout the Outer Rim. Now and then speeders or bikes carrying Oldtimers would pass them and the Newcomers would curse and shake their fists, but no further hostilities occurred.

Some distance from the gun station, Luke saw a line of immobilized speeders drawn up, most of them in little better shape than Arvid's Aratech. The Newcomers were clambering into them. One man called out, "That you, Arvid?" and a woman's voice added, "Where have you been, child?" It was an elderly lady who reminded Luke a little bit of his aunt Beru, with Beru's weather-worn complexion and air of quiet competence. "And where'd you get that speeder? She badly stove up?"

"Belongs to Owen here, Aunt Gin." Arvid waved at Luke. "He—uh—took it in trade for an injury."

Aunt Gin guided her clapped-out swoop over to pace Arvid's vehicle, smiled slowly as her expert eye, even in the intermittent wobbling glare of the sodium lamps, identified the probable origins of the craft strapped onto the cargo deck. "Did he indeed? And what do you do, Owen?"

"I'm a speeder mechanic, on my way through to Hweg Shul." Luke stowed Arvid's proton blaster back under the seat. "Arvid was kind enough to offer me a lift out of the hills when her tanks packed up." He tucked his gloved hands under his armpits against the cold.

"Owen'll be staying with us the night, that okay, Gin?" asked the young man, with every sign of the kind of casual friendship Luke had never managed to achieve with his own guardians. "I thought I'd take him on to Hweg Shul in the morning."

"Sounds dandy," agreed Gin. "Always provided he doesn't want to stick around and work awhile. We can't pay much," she added to Luke, "but with your board found, you can save a little for the city. We can use the help."

"We coulda used the help an hour ago," grumbled a thickset man with a beard like a bantha in molt, coming up on the other side in an antediluvian SoroSuub Skimmer.

Under the jarring movement of the speeders' lights, Luke was aware that the ground had changed. He felt the shift in the air first, the easing of the bitter dryness. Now the gravel gave place to thin, dusty soil, and he glimpsed the hardy plants familiar to colonial terraformers: Bolter, snigvine, and the ubiquitous clumps of balcrabbian. Ahead of him, against the dim, ambient light of a settlement, a line of scrubby buttonwood trees reared their tattered crowns; and beyond those the weird, floating shadows of tethered antigrav balls, bristling with smoor, brope, and what smelled like majie. After the silence of the wastelands, the soft grunts of blerds and the burble of grazers sounded weirdly loud; the droning of mikkets and the harsh, clattering flight of nocturnal nafen.

Great, thought Luke. *Drochs* and *nafen.* He wondered if there was a planet in the galaxy that those bad-tempered brown pests hadn't managed to colonize, growing from minuscule juveniles hiding in packing-material and necessitating inevitable rounds of inoculations, since they always picked up *some* kind of local disease, mutated it, and fed it back to colonists and indigenous ecosystems with their bites.

"What was that all about?" he asked ingenuously, wondering how much power Ashgad actually had.

The heavyset man made an angry gesture. "We just got sick and tired, that's all. We got word a planet-hopper was sending in a shipment of chips and droid parts, and them motherless Therans were out to blast 'em because that braidy-haired Listener of theirs told 'em droids were against nature or something. Blast it, if they got a problem with droids, we'll import Bandies—they're tough enough to do the work of droids, if you keep 'em fed, and just smart enough to pick and haul but don't make trouble. I hear we can ship 'em in cheap from Antemeridian."

"Oh, come on, Gerney," interrupted Gin irritably. "If the Listeners don't like droids, you bet they'll object to slaves!"

"Bandies aren't slaves!" flared Gerney Caslo. "That's

like calling a cu-pa a slave! You're as bad as my cousin Booldrum! Bandies breed like sand bunnies, work like droids, and they're better off with somebody taking care of 'em."

"That's a matter of opinion."

"Oh, just 'cause some bleeding-heart rigged a big-deal Sentience Test . . ."

"Bandies are sentient," said Luke quietly. "They may not be terribly bright, but that's their privilege. I've met humans who weren't terribly bright, either. They deserve better than slavery."

"And who're you?" Gerney glared belligerently across at the slight, beard-stubbled form sitting relaxed on the speeder bench in the near darkness. His voice turned heavily sarcastic. "You another one going to lecture us on the motherless rights of motherless sentience the motherless galaxy over?"

"Anyway, that wasn't all of it," put in Aunt Gin quickly. She looked up at Luke, "You come in off the hills, pilgrim? You didn't happen to meet Therans, did you? See them up to anything?"

"Besides stripping my ship of everything but the space tape, you mean?" He grinned, understanding her attempt to head off a quarrel, and she grinned back. Silver space tape was a standing joke among colonists, as it had been among the Rebels: Everything was held together with it, from household appliances to—allegedly—the Imperial Palace on Coruscant.

"No, it's serious." The woman Arvid had pointed out as Umolly Darm moved over carefully to the side of Caslo's skimmer, small and trim and pretty with an ion cannon slung casually on her shoulder. She must have muscles like a rancor, thought Luke. "About six hours before the attack there was a . . . I don't know what. I've heard the Oldtimers talk about Force storms, and this must have been one of them. Weirdest thing I've ever seen. Every tool came flying off the bench, whirling around the room like a cyclone. Boxes of crystals heaving and scattering rocks and jumping off the shelves. Down the street at the grocery it was like somebody hit the shelves with a dirtmover. Tinnin Droo and Nap Socker were working at their smelter; it leapt up like a live thing, they say. . . . They don't think Socker's going to pull through, he was burned so bad."

Her blue eyes narrowed, troubled and darkly angry. "They always did say the Listeners had some kind of special power. I never heard of this kind of thing, never. They—the Oldtimers—say there used to be these Force storms, a hundred, two hundred years ago."

"The Oldtimers say," said Gerney Caslo with a sneer. "Like they say their Healers can cure a man of everything from petal fever to a broken leg just by laying hands on him." He looked Luke up and down again. "When'd you meet these Therans, friend? And what was they up to?"

Luke shook his head. "They attacked me with lances and pellet rifles when my ship came down, that's all," he said. "I escaped."

Six hours before the attack on the gun station.

At the very hour when he had used the Force to get himself away.

I knew it. The all-encompassing presence of the Force, the terrible strength of it, moving like wind around him, imbuing the very air.

He had caused the Force storm.

Yoda's voice came back to him, the rough green fingers pinching his arm. *Its energy surrounds us and binds us. . . . You must feel the Force around you, between you and the tree, the rock, everywhere.*

The old Jedi must have known. Callista must have known. He had thought he would be able to track her through the Force with his mind, but now he wasn't sure. He wasn't sure he could track anyone or anything on this world, with the Force like an intensity of light blinding his mind.

"Well, what's done is done," said Gin philosophically. "Talking won't better it."

"We can festering better it by breaking a couple of heads," snarled Caslo, and pulled the skimmer away, the blue-white glare of the Aratech's lights flashing across the shiny black housings of his blaster rifle. "They better be festering careful in the future, that's all I can say. When Ashgad gets back from this conference of his . . ."

"Gerney's mouth's always been the biggest thing he's got," explained Gin, swerving her bike to avoid the tether of an antigrav ball the size of a small house. Dark vines hung down from it, ravelly clouds of nisemia thread blossoming from them like tiny clouds.

They were close to the lights of Ruby Gulch now and the crops that supported the town were everywhere in evidence, stunted bott and smoor making a dark patchwork of vegetation across the coarse, thin soil of the Oldtimer farms, and spiky towers of branswed and topato protecting the more fragile, higher-yielding plants of the Newcomers from whatever blights and diseases might inhabit the soil. The antigrav balls worked better still but, Luke suspected, were expensive. All the balls rode high, their tethers extended with the dropping of the wind.

"The rest of his family are decent folk, though. His cousin Booldrum's got the biggest library in Hweg Shul, bigger than Master Ashgad's, even. The offer's still open, to stay and work at my place awhile."

Luke shook his head. "Thank you. If Mistress Darm can help me with finding a friend who might have come in through Hweg Shul, I'll be on my way."

"As you please." She nodded toward the two clusters

of lights that marked the town, the tidy lines of the Newcomer dwellings set high on buttonwood pilings, and the dimmer, lower clumps of brightness that showed where the Oldtimers had their humbler abodes. "I got stew and beer back at the house, unless the pair of you want to go on to the Flowering Bott Pub with the rest of those louts and grouse about how this place would be paradise if only we could get trade in. It ain't never going to be paradise, you know, no matter what Seti Ashgad works out with whomever he made such a big deal of getting to talk with him." She glanced across at Luke again. "No place ever is, if you're not restful in your heart."

She swung her bike in a long loop, heading toward the high-standing Newcomer houses with their bright lamps.

She was right, of course, thought Luke. But he doubted her opinion was that of the majority of Newcomers, nor should it be. They had a right to live in comfort, to have their children grow up with proper medical attention, to avoid the grinding, horrible labor of primitive agriculture and stagnant economy.

They were a minority on the planet, the majority of whose population did not want their world to become part of the Republic. Nothing Seti Ashgad said to the Republic's representatives would alter that.

But while their speeders were tinkered together from scrap and their clothing consisted of makeshifts and hand-me-downs, somebody, Luke noticed, had thought it worth his while to provide *every single one* of those Newcomers with the very latest in blasters, rifles, and ion cannons.

6

```
INCOMING - 77532 - CCNP-XTTN-5057943,QQ7 to RRNP-XXY79
SCRAMBLE CODE 9 RT. HON. EXLCY LEIA ORGANA SOLO
EXTREMELY URGENT - RESPOND AT ONCE

INCOMING - 77539 - CCNP-XTTN-5057943,QQ7 to RRNP-XXY79
SCRAMBLE CODE 9 RT. HON. EXLCY LEIA ORGANA SOLO
EXTREMELY URGENT - RESPOND AT ONCE

INCOMING - 77601 - CCNP-XTTN-5057943,QQ7 to RRNP-XXY79
SCRAMBLE CODE 9 RT. HON. EXLCY LEIA ORGANA SOLO
EXTREMELY URGENT - RESPOND AT ONCE

INCOMING - 77610 - CCNP-XTTN-5057943,QQ7 to RRNP-XXY79
SCRAMBLE CODE 9 RT. HON. EXLCY LEIA ORGANA SOLO
CRITICAL - IMMEDIATE RESPONSE IMPERATIVE
```

"Son of a . . ." Han Solo tapped back to the beginning of the message queue and scanned it again. Twelve
scramble 9s. He punched into the first of them, though
he knew the comm screen would give him nothing but
gibberish, and he was right.

"Where's Goldenrod when you need him?"

At the far end of the terrace, Chewbacca groaned a question.

"Nothing." Solo paged through the queue again, as if he thought a message would manifest itself saying, DON'T WORRY ABOUT A THING, WE'RE 50 HOURS LATE BECAUSE THE ENTIRE DIPLOMATIC MISSION JUST STOPPED OFF ON CYBLOC XII SO I COULD BUY MYSELF A PAIR OF SHOES. HOME SOON. LOVE, L.

In my dreams, thought Han.

He glanced at the chronometer. It was a few hours after noon, the bright, misty daylight of the resort moon Hesperidium already losing its strength. Above the dark-leaved trees with their neon-bright clusters of gold and scarlet fruit, the sky was fading to its characteristic rosy lavender, the dark edges pricked already by the more prominent stars.

There was no possible way he could continue to deceive himself. Even taking into account the worst imaginable outcome of the conference with this Ashgad character, even taking into account an emergency detour to Coruscant, even taking into account an unscheduled Council session *and* a harangue by Councillor Q-Varx of the Rationalist sympathies and inexhaustible rhetoric—and why wouldn't she have at least sent a message to that effect?—Leia was late.

Very, very late.

Chewbacca hauled himself out of the terrace pool and shook, spattering water in all directions. Behind him among the realistically engineered rocks, Winter glided fishlike with the giggling twins in the mild water while Anakin patted solemnly all around the pinkly glowing field of his confinement bubble. Jaina had lately become fascinated with knotting and braiding, and the long feathering of the Wookiee's mane and arms bore random macramés of her efforts. Dripping, Chewbacca padded to

Han's side. He growled another query, his voice low, for the twins understood Wookiee almost as fluently as did their father.

"I can't even do that," replied Han softly. "That was part of the cover. She's supposed to be here with us, not in the middle of the Meridian sector meeting with a guy who isn't even the elected representative of his planet."

Chewie asked something else, tilting his great head, blue eyes glittering worriedly under the overhang of his brow.

"What would Ackbar be able to tell me?" Han spread his hands. "If he knew anything he'd have contacted me already. With a leak someplace in the Council, and the Rationalists and the Rights of Sentience Party ready to split the Council in half, he can't go through regular channels any more than we can."

The Wookiee rumbled deep in his chest.

"I know." Han closed his fist, brought it down with surprising restraint—softly, a slow-motion blow—on the thick glassite of the tabletop beside which he stood.

The small villa that had housed a succession of the Emperor Palpatine's concubines—one of several retained by the government of the New Republic to shelter diplomats it wanted to impress—had been thoroughly swept for listening devices before Leia and her family went to stay there for an ostensible vacation on what was arguably the most beautiful moon of the Coruscant system, but Han still felt easier talking on the terrace. The gurgle of the fountains among mossy stones and the soft singing of the warbleflowers, would have baffled even a long-range directional listening device.

"She should have listened to Callista," he said. "She should have listened."

In his heart, of course, he knew that Leia couldn't have heeded the warning. The Rationalist Party had spent too many months setting up the secret meeting with Ashgad—and had too much influence both in the New Republic and in the various fragments of the old Empire—for the whole matter to be jettisoned at the last minute on the strength of an anonymous note. Q-Varx, the Calamari Senator who headed up the party on that watery planet, had pointed out that, on the one hand, the case of the Newcomer minority on Nam Chorios could very well turn into a test case for the whole issue of planetary self-determination and, on the other, though Moff Getelles of Antemeridian was in no position militarily to go against the Republic fleet in the Meridian sector, it was too much to hope that he would not find some way of turning disaffection on that world to his advantage.

That was the problem, reflected Han, with power.

Even before he'd come into contact with actual power, he'd concluded that people who wanted to rule the galaxy—or even some weedpatch township on Duroon—were idiots. As Lando Calrissian had discovered on Bespin, power tied you down. You could no longer follow your instincts or act on the spur of the moment.

All Leia could do, when Callista's message had reached her, was include her Noghri bodyguard in the party and run the risk of the hideous scandal that would result if they were discovered. Every precaution that could be taken had already been taken.

She should have run. Han touched the keypad again, and watched the long parade of scramble 9s—there were fifteen of them now—scroll past.

The face of Luke's beloved—the soft oval contours, the strong chin and full, decisive lips, the rain-colored eyes that were at once so old and so innocent—returned to his mind. The light, husky alto voice that was like a teenage boy's and the gawky grace of her long-boned body.

She'd disappeared almost a year ago. She knew Luke would go after her, thought Han. She wouldn't resurface lightly.

All that, Leia had known.

And had gotten on the *Borealis* shuttle anyway.

It was a kind of courage Han frankly wasn't sure he possessed.

He said again, out loud this time, "She should have run."

The screen blinked again. Another scramble 9. From Coruscant, this time, a long block of text, in the purple lettering that meant *very, very urgent*. At the same time a green light went up over the fancifully carved, moss-padded stone doorway that led from the terrace to the house, and in what looked like an antique stone niche a decorative statue revolved to admit a round TT-8L droid on the end of its jointed limb.

The bronze lid blinked as the blue glass optical adjusted to read who was on the terrace. Then a very pleasant voice announced, "Two visitors in the vestibule, Captain Solo. They have declined to present credentials. Would you like them to be admitted or would you prefer an observation first?"

"Admit 'em." Han hated spying on his guests. If they came out the door shooting, he and Chewie could probably deal with the situation.

"It will be my pleasure."

Chewie grumbled something and shook his mane. He disliked vestibule observation as much as Han did, and disliked tattletale droids, if possible, even more. Han laughed, and agreed, "Yeah, can't you just see all his little diodes sparkling with sheer delight?"

The laughter wiped from his face a moment later as

the automatic door slid quietly back into its quasi-stone slot, and he saw who his visitor was.

He had a bad feeling about all this.

"Well, well." The door of the airlock slipped open. "What have we got here?"

See-Threepio, who had advanced with hands extended in near-ecstatic welcome, pulled up short at the question. "As I explained over the viewscreen," he reiterated, "this is a scout vessel detached from a . . . a major disaster, and we are on our way to the fleet base at Cybloc XII." As he spoke he was analyzing the broad-shouldered, fair-haired man with the scar on his lip who stood in the doorway, the man who, half an hour previously, had identified himself on the viewscreen as Captain Bortrek of the *Pure Sabacc.*

"Our pilot is unfortunately deceased . . ." He followed Captain Bortrek down the corridor to the bridge, the young man swaggering ahead, looking around him thoughtfully and whistling a little through his teeth.

"He the only crew?" Bortrek paused in the doorway of the tiny lab, where Yeoman Marcopius lay cramped into the stasis box.

"Of course. Had there been anyone else to navigate us into the Durren roads, we could have . . . ."

"What'd he die of? Anything catching?"

"I believe so, yes, sir, but the stasis box is certified for full-spectrum biological security." Though scrupulously programmed to have no personal opinions about humans whatsoever, Threepio could not help comparing this young man to Captain Solo as he had been when Threepio and Artoo had first encountered him in company with Master Luke. This man seemed to have a far more casual attitude about things, however, and to walk with more of a swagger, aside from dressing in a fashion that Threepio recognized as both flashy and not in the best of taste. "Eighty percent of the crew had perished by the time we were able to . . . Here, sir, what are you doing?"

"What's it look like I'm doing?" demanded Captain Bortrek irritably, pausing in the midst of ripping the stasis box's connectors free of the walls. "Gimme a hand getting this to the other airlock, Goldie—over there, you stupid hunk of junk! Antigrav lifters!"

Threepio automatically filled in—as he was programmed to do—the context and gesture to mean, *Bring me those antigrav lifters under the cabinet.* He could not but compare the man's tone to Master Luke's—and Her Excellency's—invariable use of polite nonessential grammatical elements such as *Please* and *Thank you*—not that any protocol droid worthy of his battery packs would take offense at being referred to as a hunk of junk or even by the patently untrue epithet *stupid.* Threepio knew quite well that he was not stupid.

But it was contrary to his programming to correct the man's deeply inaccurate estimate of his mental capacity, as it would have been for him to object to Bortrek's manhandling of the stasis box onto the antigrav lifters and shoving it out into the corridor with the patent intention of dispatching Yeoman Marcopius's mortal remains into the outer vacuum, box and all. Captain Bortrek was a human.

Thus Threepio kept his reflections to himself, as he assisted the captain in maneuvering the detached box into the smaller, secondary airlock. Marcopius had been a loyal retainer of Her Excellency's, a good pilot, and, as far as Threepio was capable of judging, an admirable young man. Though Threepio personally saw no reason why human remains should not simply be jettisoned, burned, or for that matter stewed and eaten by other humans in an emergency (provided they were certified free of harmful bacteria first and, if possible, aesthetically prepared), he was acutely aware that neither Her Excellency, the young man's family, nor the deceased himself would have considered this send-off at all respectful. Respect and custom being the foundation stone of protocol, Threepio was deeply offended.

Not nearly as offended as he later became, however.

"Nice ship," remarked Bortrek again, turning from the airlock door before the cycle had even cleared.

"My counterpart informs me that it is a top-of-the-line scouting vessel designed for short-range deep-space travel and limited hyperdrive," replied Threepio helpfully. "It has ten-point-two engines and a hull capacity of thirty-five hundred cubic meters."

"What," grunted Bortrek, "you trying to sell it to me?" He passed a hand close to an auxiliary door on the way down the passage, nodded with approval of the opening speed without going in. "Sure beats hell out of the old *Sabacc*. Pity it's not bigger."

Having seen the *Pure Sabacc* as the large, ramshackle Y164 had maneuvered into docking position on the scout, Threepio was inclined to agree, though he knew his own judgment on such matters was limited. Artoo had checked the *Sabacc* by scanner and had confirmed the opinion: The other vessel's power output ratios were all far lower, and though clearly a long-distance hyperdrive vessel, she appeared to be less maneuverable as well.

"The engines of this vessel were seriously damaged by collision with debris during the recent battle," Threepio went on, still trailing Bortrek as the man made his way around the little ship, flicking readouts to life, tapping walls, bending to look into access hatches. "It is imperative that my counterpart and I obtain passage to the fleet installation on Cybloc XII. Although I have no official clearance, I can assure you of a high probability of reward, to be forwarded to you after our arrival on Coruscant at whatever address you wish to give."

Bortrek halted in the middle of the bridge, looking from Threepio to Artoo-Detoo, who was still linked into the main navicomputer, absorbing readings and information whose echoes flashed across the screens all around him. Though, as Threepio had said, the guidance systems of the scout vessel had been damaged by collision with debris—rendering drift into interplanetary space almost inevitable had not Bortrek picked up their distress signal—the comm lines were still open. Artoo tweeped a string of information that made Threepio exclaim, "Good heavens!"

"What's he say?" Bortrek was tallying up the burned-out consoles with a knowing eye.

"There are reports of revolt from Ampliquen and King's Galquek, and according to Artoo, plague has broken out on the Durren base as well. This is terrible!"

"Terrible enough for me to get my tail out of here, anyway, Goldie." Bortrek crossed to where Artoo stood and rapped with speculative knuckles on the little droid's domed cap. "What model R2 is he, Goldie? Dee?"

"A dee, yes. They're quite good models, and extremely versatile, though sometimes a little erratic. For any type of sheerly astromechanical or stellar navigation, one cannot better the records of the R2 series in general, and the dee models in particular—or so I'm told."

Bortrek knelt and flipped open Artoo's back panel, reaching in with an extractor he'd produced from the pocket of his reptile-leather vest. "So you are told that, are you?" Artoo emitted a little squeak, then withdrew his data jack from the port. "Well, Goldie, I been told that, too. So I'll tell you what. You and him just head on back to the primary lock and wait for me on the bridge of the *Sabacc*. I'll be over in a while."

"We really are very fortunate, you know," Threepio said, as he and Artoo crossed through the narrow neck of the port-to-port tunnel that linked the two ships. "With trade being turned away and rebellion on the planet, and now plague as well, no ships of hyperspace capability are going to be leaving the Durren system for quite some time. The Meridian sector is very thinly inhabited and well out of most trade routes. We could have drifted for years—centuries, perhaps—before we were discovered. By that time, goodness knows what might have befallen Her Excellency."

Artoo vouchsafed no reply. Threepio guessed that Captain Bortrek had disabled a portion of the little astromech's motivator, a wise precaution, perhaps. Artoo was unaccountable sometimes and might have refused to abandon the patently useless scout.

"Once we reach Cybloc XII, we can notify the proper authorities of Her Excellency's whereabouts. I doubt it would be safe to do so from this ship or in fact to let Captain Bortrek know of the matter at all. Grateful as I am for the rescue, one cannot be sure of such a man's loyalties. But I'm sure that we can put in a voucher to the Central Council to make ample remuneration to him for his trouble . . ."

He broke off, leaving his speculation unfinished, as they emerged from the *Pure Sabacc*'s lock into her main holding bay. Strongboxes were stacked casually against the walls—one of them, open, showed bundles of bearer-bonds and a considerable quantity of gold coins. Another was filled beyond closing point with platinum and electrum cast into shapes that Threepio immediately identified as sacred to four of the six main faiths currently fashionable on the planet Durren: Reliquaries, monstrances, jeweled prayer-wheels tumbled at random and bent to accommodate the confines of the chest. Items too large for easy storage—statues and pieces of furniture clearly valuable for their workmanship and materials— were tumbled and shoved in corners, along with roughly tied masses of embroidered velvets and precious stohl fur, and more sacks that had the unmistakable shape of coinage.

"Good heavens!" Threepio exclaimed in surprise. "Judging from the latest market valuation statistics of gold and platinum, there must be several million credits in this hold alone! Whatever is a man like Captain Bortrek—who does not appear to be of the more prosperous classes, nor is he even a native of the planet Durren— doing with all this wealth?"

"Taking it on commission, my friend."

Threepio turned, and Artoo swiveled his cap to align his visual receptors with the scar-lipped captain as he emerged from the airlock at their heels. He carried a huge square of plastic casing that had been a console housing, filled to overflowing with components and wire, and had a thick black remote unit in one hand.

"Commission, sir?"

He grinned a slow grin, reminding Threepio, who was not fanciful, of some semisentient species less developed from its hunting ancestors than standard humankind. "For absent owners and their—uh—heirs. There's a lot of unrest back there in Durren. Partisans coming in out of the countryside, riots in the streets. Lots of houses being burned, lots of people getting the hell away before things get worse. Some of 'em decide now's a good time to clean out their closets, get rid of all that excess gold and platinum they got lyin' around. You."

He gestured with the remote unit at Artoo. "I burned out my main navicomputer after a little difference of opinion with the Port Authorities, pox eat their lyin' hearts. I'm gonna need you."

Artoo hesitated and let out another protesting wail that caused Bortrek to point the remote in his direction and Threepio to admonish, "Artoo, behave yourself! If Captain Bortrek is being so good as to transport us to Cybloc XII, it's only right that we assist him with his ship by any means in our power."

The astromech wavered, rocking on his wheels, but Captain Bortrek had quite clearly disabled the upper level of motivators. After a despairing little meep, Artoo followed Bortrek through the door. Threepio started after them, saying, "Now, Captain Bortrek, once we reach Cybloc XII it is imperative that we get in touch with Admiral Ackbar of the Republic fleet . . ."

The door shut in his face. After a considerable period of time, during which he amused himself by pricing the contents of the hold at somewhere between twenty-three and twenty-eight million credits (allowing for an inflation index as a result of the unrest in the sector and fluctuations in the average price of Durren artwork), Threepio's auditory sensors picked up the scraping and rocking of the port-to-port tunnel being retracted. Calling up a readout on the pad near the storage hold's door—the binary language was a very simple one—Threepio ascertained that the *Pure Sabacc* was being put into pretravel mode.

"How very curious," the droid remarked to himself. "I quite distinctly heard Captain Bortrek say that his navigational computer was nonfunctional."

He addressed a few further remarks to the computer core, which when phrased in quite standard codes caused the mechanism to blurt everything it knew on any number of subjects in a succession of high-speed bursts. It took Threepio a few seconds to download the bursts from his temporary holding memory and process the information into existing systemic memory, but when he did, he felt as close to outrage as a well-programmed protocol droid is capable of being.

"Why, that course that's being laid in is nowhere near Cybloc XII!" he exclaimed. "The man is a thief! We're being stolen!"

"The entire mission has disappeared." Mon Mothma, guiding spirit of the Rebellion and former Chief of State of the Provisional Government, held her wasted hands close to the semicircular iron fender of the hearth, and the flame outlined her fingers in threads of amber light.

Han Solo, though he'd come to know the tall, beautiful woman well over the past several years, still felt in awe of her. Her picture was everywhere, in histories of the Rebellion and of the last days of the Empire. It was like sitting across the fire from a god of ancient legend, or finding oneself in the same room with smashball center guard Rip "Iron One" Calkin who'd made seven hundred last season.

"Disappeared?" Something within the cage of his ribs went still and cold.

Winter had taken the children to the nursery, a vine-hung tower room at the top of a long flight of steps. The small parlor was dim, the lamps cached in discreet niches casting warm patterns of light on the painted ceilings with a wavery gleam indistinguishable from that of combustible fuel. The fire that played over the lumps of coal and wood on the hearth's white sand was genuine, though it issued from a buried gas pipe, and Han remembered with a sudden pang making love to Leia on the rug of milk-white stohl fur, the night before her departure.

"We're keeping the news quiet for as long as we can."

Mon Mothma straightened up a little, luminous dark eyes catching the firelight. She looked a million times better than she had the last time Han had seen her, lying in the hospital after yet another round of bacta-tank therapy to combat the wasting effects of an attempted poisoning, and a million times worse than the woman he had first met in the ragged chaos of some temporary headquarters of the Rebel fleet. She had never lost the gaunt look of death, and the skin hung loose under jawbone and wrists. Her hair, dark through the horrors and vicissitudes of the fight against Palpatine, had begun to gray with the poisoning and was white now, and she still walked with two canes when she was not on public view. She was still beautiful.

"The matter is complicated by the fact that Minister of State Rieekan has fallen gravely ill. At first we were afraid it might be related to the plague that has been reported in the Meridian sector, but . . ."

"Plague?" demanded Han, and cold touched him again. *Not Leia . . .*

"Reports are too fragmentary to be sure," she said, in a tone that told Han that she was darn sure. "When it broke out on the Durren orbital base it was suspected to be poison, but there's no evidence of that. No evidence of an actual illness, either. No bacteria, no virus, no polyphagous microorganisms. . . . Nothing. Only men and women dying. We can't get med teams in because of the revolt that has broken out on Durren itself. Local factions have the base under siege . . ."

"Siege?" said Han. "With two cruisers there?"

"The cruisers were—are—out, investigating what is either a pirate attack on Ampliquen or what might be a rupture of the truce between Budpock and Ampliquen. We haven't heard. Nor have we heard anything of Leia's flagship or its escort after they reported the meeting 'acceptably' concluded and entered hyperspace at the scheduled jump point."

An R-10 trundled in, dispatched by the house timer with a glass of beer for Han and cocoa for Mon Mothma. Like everything else in the house, the little droid was designed to fit in with the rustic fantasy, hand-crafted in patinated wood and old green bronze. If the Emperor still owned the house, reflected Han, the droid would probably have been replaced by a synthdroid, which according to the ads could be shaped to exactly resemble any sentient or semisentient life form in the Registry. Han wasn't sure how comfortable he'd have been with them around, in the unlikely event that Leia's salary would even cover the cost of such a thing.

"Have you checked Ashgad's part in this?"

She nodded, and sipped her cocoa, setting the cup down on the droid's worn-looking bronze top. "Final report from the *Borealis* includes sensor readings from Ashgad's vessel, which indicate nothing unusual. The captains of both the flagship and the escort reported no other vessels closer than Pedducis Chorios, and Leia herself said that Ashgad seemed content with the outcome of the meeting. We've sent a message to Ashgad . . ."

"Which means nothing if he's in on it."

"Maybe." She rubbed her arms, and Chewbacca picked up one of Winter's shawls, whose pattern and colors changed kaleidoscope-like every few minutes, and draped it over the former Chief's shoulders. She looked her thanks to him with a smile.

"Now, I know an Interdictor can extract a ship from hyperspace. . . ."

"It can," said Han. "But Intelligence has been keeping a pretty close eye on everybody who's *got* Interdictors—everybody that we know about. As far as I know we haven't heard a peep. I mean, yeah, they can pull a ship out of hyperspace, but then they've got a ship on their hands that has to be explained. We've been watching for that one."

"As you said," murmured Mon Mothma, "you can only watch those you know about. Might someone alter a jump point by remote? Re-route them?"

"Not possible," said Han. "I mean, I'm not a scientist or anything, but those navicomputers are shielded like a Valorsian harem against every kind of solar flare and gamma particle for just that reason, but when I was in the game there were always rumors about either the Imps or some one of the big smuggler chiefs figuring out a way to do that."

The chill behind his sternum seemed to tighten as he said it. All his life he'd played tag with the black hollows of eternity, and he knew just how immense were the spaces between stars. Anything could be out there. It was every deep-spacer's nightmare to be somehow disoriented in the interstellar gulfs. It was why he had labored to memorize hundreds of starfields, why he still kept reams of hardcopy starcharts on the *Millennium Falcon* in spite of the teasing he got about it from Lando and his other smuggler buddies of years past.

Just the thought that someone might be able to alter a jump point by remote was enough to scare the pants off him.

It was something else. It had to be something else.

Angrily, he said, "So whose great idea was it for the Council to select a pro tem successor if both the Chief of State and the First Minister bought it? The minute they know she's missing they're gonna deadlock, and then you won't be able to do anything."

"We can't do anything now."

"What about a hologram?" asked Han. "We could get some holo faker to splice together recent footage . . ."

"That," said Mon Mothma coldly, "has already been tried. Once by the Daysong Party, who have heard rumors of the disappearance . . ."

"From whom? Where?"

She shook her head. "Rumors are already beginning to fly, Han. Admiral Ackbar has put the Council on a twelve-hour hiatus to prevent violence between Senator Typia of the Daysong Party and Senator Arastide of Gantho. The second faked hologram we haven't been able to trace, though we suspect the Tervigs, since it declared that trade in Bandie slaves from Tervissis was acceptable. In any case, it was so badly put together that it obviates any connection with the original disappearance.

"And no matter what the circumstances," she went on, measuring her words with arctic exactness, "substitution of a holographic fake for the Chief of State of the Republic is not a precedent I wish to see set. Nor, I think you would agree, does Leia."

Han felt like he'd been caught with his hand in the cookie jar. "No. I guess not."

Another reason, he reflected, not to rule the galaxy.

"What about Luke?" he asked into the silence that followed.

"Luke?"

"He was on the *Borealis*. He was here to see her off. Then she got a message at the last minute from Callista—saying for Leia not to trust Ashgad as far as she could throw him—and Luke went along. He planned to take a small craft down to the surface past the gun stations, to see if Callista was on Nam Chorios."

"Ashgad," said Mon Mothma softly. "I didn't know that. We've been trying to reach Luke on the moon of Yavin. His students thought he might have returned and gone into the jungle to meditate."

Han grunted. Then the silence returned, save for the wickering of the fire, and the murmur of the fountain in the corner of the parlor. Firelight caught in Chewbacca's eyes, twin blue glimmers beneath the shadow of his brows. Beyond the tall, magnetically guarded opening that made up the room's southern wall, the magic skies of the Coruscant system shimmered with ropes and veils and spilled treasures of prodigal starlight.

"I'll need to get in touch with Lando," he said at length.

Mon Mothma nodded. She seemed to have read his mind from the first. He reflected that it was probably part of the Chief of State's job description.

"He'll have his own ship for the search. We have to keep this small—we'll probably never know who originally blabbed, among the crews of the *Borealis* and the *Adamantine*. Any objections to Mara Jade knowing? She knows how to quarter a sector."

Mothma nodded. "Anyone else?"

"Kyp Durron, from the Academy. Wedge Antilles, if he can be spared. Kyp'll need a ship. Nothing that'll get noticed, but it has to be fast."

"It's done," said Mon Mothma. She held out to him a red plast cube. "These are the final reports from Leia, Commander Zoalin, and Captain Ioa, and the sensor readings on Ashgad's ship and on all the surrounding five parsecs. You'll also find the coordinates for the jump point where they disappeared."

"Doesn't matter where they went in," said Han. "If someone found a way to alter the jump, they could have come out anywhere from here to the backside of last week." He stood up, and helped her to her feet. It was an indication of her ease with him—her trust in him—that she had brought her canes with her. She took them from him with a smile, and Han felt curiously honored. For her to let him see her walking with the canes meant that she regarded him as her friend.

"How long can you hold off the Council?"

"A few days," she said. "Maybe a week." The house was equipped with NL-6 courtesy droids, but Han escorted Mon Mothma to the vestibule himself. "We're still trying to get a medical support team out to Durren, or escorts to take teams in from the Medical Research Facility on Nim Drovis. As I said, the reports are fragmentary, but it doesn't sound good."

"Unknown?" said Han, looking across at her in the reflected fire glow.

She hesitated, and in her eyes he saw that it was known. She just didn't want to admit what it might be.

The vestibule doors slid open before them. Mon Mothma's courtesy guard-cum-footman got to his feet, a gloomy looking, sandy-haired young man whose expression never seemed to alter no matter what was done or said around him.

"You be careful."

Han gave her a grin. "Your Excellency, the day I start being careful is the day I buy myself a foot warmer and a rocking chair. I'll find her."

But when the door closed behind her and her bodyguard, Han stood for a long time in the vestibule, the little red hunk of plast closed in his fist, staring at nothing. Thinking about hyperspace. Thinking about interstellar space.

Thinking about Leia.

Five years since they'd married. Thirteen since they'd met, in the Death Star's corridors with blaster fire zapping around them. If he couldn't find her . . .

There was no conclusion to that sentence. No conclusion to the thought. Only a darkness as deep as the nightmare of disorientation in realtime space, with no starcharts, no navicomputer, no spectroscope, no clue as to which of those tiny, infinitely distant lights to aim for.

His hand tightened around the datacube, and he turned back toward the firelight of the parlor, to tell Chewie to get the *Falcon* into preflight. They would head out just before dawn.

7

"Sir, I must protest!" The bridge doors of the *Pure Sabacc* slid open before Threepio's determined advance—a considerable improvement over those of the storage hold in which he had been incarcerated for the past 2.6 hours while the vessel jolted into hyperspace—and the protocol droid marched through to behold Captain Bortrek ensconced at the main console, picking his teeth with a laser extractor. "Artoo-Detoo and I are duly registered to Her Excellency Leia Organa Solo, and misappropriation of any duly registered droid is contrary to Sections Seven, Twelve, and Two Hundred and Forty-Three A of the New Republic Universal Galactic . . . Artoo-Detoo!" Threepio exclaimed in astonishment, as he cleared the doorway and got a better view of the bridge.

The astromech droid made a sorry little sound.

As well he might, See-Threepio reflected. All of his access hatches had been bodily removed, some to admit sinewy snakes of data cables, some to accommodate blocky add-on patches of machinery, which themselves connected into at least three of the bridge stations. An enormous switch box had been screwed into the little droid's domed cap, connected to what Threepio vaguely recognized as the navigational computer; another housing had been affixed to his side with silver space tape, to pipe information to and from the vessel's central core station. His sturdy legs had been unscrewed and lay in a corner, the connecting hydraulic cables dangling sadly at his sides. The general impression was that of a small life form half-absorbed within a carnivorous flower, streaked with grease and glinting with green and orange lights.

"What in the name of goodness happened to you?"

"A little creative reprogramming, that's all." Captain Bortrek set down his laser extractor. "And I don't give a Ranat's sneeze who you're duly registered to, Goldie. You're mine now, like your little friend . . ." He jerked a grimy thumb at Artoo. "And I didn't call you here from the hold to quote me some pox-festering regulation, either, you understand? A good See-Three unit's worth a pile even without provenance, but don't think I couldn't get almost as much for your chips and wiring."

Threepio considered the matter. "Actually, sir, See-Three units with specialized programming like myself sell for a minimum, used, at forty-three thousand standard credits, Blue Registry prices. The aggregate of my components would only bring in five thousand at the very most . . ."

"Shut up!"

"Yes, sir."

"And come with me down to the hold. I want you to give me a valuation on every piece of that garbage so I know Sandro the Hook isn't going to cheat me once we get to Celanon City."

"Are we going to Celanon, sir? A most pleasant planet, I've been told. It isn't necessary to return to the hold, you know. While incarcerated there I took the opportunity to price your acquisitions to the best of my knowledge—which was updated only last week from the Coruscant Index—and the information is still in my memory."

"No lie?" Captain Bortrek tongued his scarred lip, and studied the golden droid speculatively. In the background, Artoo-Detoo made soft whirring noises indicative of intensive activity, and the ship's core computer flashed and burbled replies. "I tell you what, then, Goldie. You come with me and we'll get that stuff sorted out, and maybe when we get to Celanon I won't sell you to a travel agent for your programming."

He stood up, and pulled from a pocket of his embroidered leather vest a small flat silver flask, from which he took a drink. By his exhalation, as he walked past Threepio and preceded him out the door, the fluid within consisted of equal parts grain alcohol, synthetic gylocal stimulant, and hyperdrive coolant.

This was, Threepio learned, a constant in Captain Bortrek's life. Over the next several hours, while Threepio shifted the booty in the ship's three holds into some semblance of order and Captain Bortrek made notes about market value, the human had frequent recourse to the flask, his speech becoming both increasingly slurred and increasingly scatological as the level of his blood alcohol rose.

The universe, it appeared, had never been kind to Captain Bortrek, conspiring against him in a fashion that Threepio privately considered unlikely given the man's relative unimportance. Knowing what he did about the Alderaan social structure, shipping regulations, the psychology of law enforcement agents, and the statistical behavior patterns of human females, Threepio was much inclined to doubt that so many hundreds of people would spend that much time thinking up ways to thwart and injure a small-time free-trader who was, by his own assertion, only trying to make a living.

Still, it was not for droids to contradict humans unless requested to do so for informational purposes, so he moved gold reliquaries, and held his peace.

"Now, is it likely—you tell me, Goldie—is it likely that the festering Rim Patrol would come after me the minute I showed up—the very festering minute!—without provocation—if they hadn't been tipped off by that festering witch-hag ex-wife of mine back on Algar, hunh? Is it? I swear she . . . What the stinkin' stang's goin' on with the stinkin' lights, fester it?"

They had dimmed for perhaps the fifth time in an hour, one of several small fluctuations of power that Threepio had been aware of. Most of them—alterations in the temperature and mix of the atmosphere and shifts in the thrum of the *Pure Sabacc*'s engines—had been below the level of human perception.

"I suspect, sir, that those are readjustments of the system as it accommodates Artoo-Detoo's presence as a central memory capacitor."

Captain Bortrek pettishly hurled a necklace of priceless flame opals against the opposite wall. "Festerin' droids," he muttered. "Blasted hunks of machinery. I was hopin' I'd run across one of them new droids, them synthdroids, on Durren. A hundred thousand credits they bring, and I wouldn't sell. You seen 'em, Goldie? Beat you by a kilometer."

He wagged an owlish finger at his unwilling assistant. His fair hair hung sweatily over his eyes now, and he had unlaced his red-and-gold leather doublet to expose an expanse of gold chains and chest hair. "Centrally programmed. They do this crystal attunement stunt— CCIR—Centrally Controlled Independent Replicant." He pronounced the words with great care, as if afraid of tripping over them. "None of this wired-brain stuff you got goin'. They leave their brain back in some central location and do what you festerin' tell 'em—six, eight, ten of 'em, however many of 'em you want. Central brain. You tell that brain what each of 'em should do, and they go do it without givin' you any festerin' lip about it, y'unnerstan'?"

"Yes, sir," agreed Threepio.

"Brain processes it all. Huge distances—you can leave the brain on your festerin' ship and go down to a planet with six or ten or however many of 'em, and you tell 'em, fetch me that, or paste that guy, and they do it. They figure out how to do it without none of this, 'Oh, and how do I do that, sir?' " His whiny voice took on a sarcastic inflection, imitating precise droid speech.

"*And* they can make 'em like a man or a woman or whatever. Doesn't matter. They got steel skeleton, they grow synthflesh over top of it, and as long as they got that little hunk of crystal in their skulls, that can listen to the Central Controller, they're yours. And boy, wouldn't I like to have one shaped like Amber Jevanche." He named the newest holo star popular on Coruscant, a woman of whom Threepio had also heard Captain Solo speak highly, though to his knowledge Captain Solo had never met the young lady.

He proceeded to describe, in great anatomical detail, exactly what acts of sexual congress he would have such a synthdroid perform, though Threepio was somewhat at a loss as to why any human would wish to couple with a machine, and went on to expound his philosophy of Man's Needs and Man's Rights—meaning, Threepio gathered, his own immediate desires irrespective of the wishes of the other party. His speech was deteriorating in both form and content all the while, but it wasn't until the man pitched forward onto his face that Threepio thought to take a sample of the cabin atmosphere, to discover that it consisted of nearly 12 percent carbon dioxide and not much oxygen at all.

"Good heavens!" he cried, and hastened to the comm port on the wall. "Artoo! Artoo!"

A quick series of bleeps answered him. Threepio immediately obeyed, hurrying to the door and up the corridor toward the bridge. He had gone four or five steps when the door, which had closed automatically behind him as usual, emitted an ominous clank. The noise stopped the protocol droid in his tracks; then he sought the nearest comm port and flicked the toggle. "Artoo, now the doors of the hold have locked!"

A soothing warble. "Well, if you're sure it's all right," replied Threepio doubtfully, and continued his steps to the bridge.

He found Artoo still enmeshed in the console boards, the entire core system ablaze with lights like a Midwinter Festival tree and fluttering with the soft chatter of new systems being installed or altered. "Artoo, you really must do something about the cabin atmosphere in that hold!" said Threepio. "Humans do not do at all well in environments containing under twenty percent oxygen. Oh, you've taken care of it? Well, it was very, very careless of you to permit the core system to make that alteration in the ventilation feeds. But if you've done that already, why ever did you request my presence on the bridge?"

Artoo explained. Rather typically of Artoo's explanations, it did not elaborate much.

"The toolkit? Oh . . . Under which hatch? I see." As he crossed back to his friend and opened the requested access cover, he added, "But I'm very sure Captain Bortrek would be much handier with this than I am. Oh, very well. Which activation switch? Oh, I see. A simple

backup/overwrite of original motivator settings. I still
don't see why Captain Bortrek couldn't reset your motivators. He's the one who altered them in the first place,
you know."

Artoo tweeped apologetically. There were a few minutes of whirring while the motivator circuits reset, then
the whole core system console began to wink and flash
again as Artoo did something—it looked to Threepio like
he was again rerouting instructional paths for data and
commands.

"He's going to be very angry at being locked in the
hold, you know," added Threepio. "You simply must
learn to be more careful, Artoo. We aren't designed to
. . . detach what? What switching box? Oh, that one
. . . I'm sure Captain Bortrek would not approve."

Another line of wibbles and beeps.

"Well, on your head be it, but it appears to me he
went to a great deal of trouble to adapt you as part of the
central core. I'm doing it, I'm doing it," he added pee-
vishly, bending awkwardly down and grasping the sonic
extractor with gold fingers never designed for delicate
manual work. "At least I think I'm doing it. I really think
you ought to let Captain Bortrek out of the hold first,
though. We're going to reach the hyperspace target point
in an hour, and we need him to take us out and navigate
us into Celanon."

He obeyed another string of commands and unfastened the cable lines from the gray switching box space
taped to Artoo's side. "What do you mean, we're not
going to Celanon? Of course we're going to Celanon."

A pause for more instructions. The central core chat-
tered and shifted data in waves of green and yellow
lights.

"Nim Drovis? I'm sure he has no intention of returning to the Meridian sector. And no, I can't see the

switches you're talking about. Of course I'm looking!" He bent and squinched sideways as best he could, studying the switching box. "I don't see anything of the kind. How should I know what a DINN looks like? The only DINN I know about is the Horansi past participle of the verb *ad'n*, 'to clean one's toenails'; the Nalros word for 'small hard-shelled insects'; the Gamorrean adjective meaning 'inclined to drool excessively'; Gacerian for 'one who is always getting married and divorced'; Algar for. . . . Well, if you can't describe it any better than that I'm afraid that switching box is going to stay where it is."

Amid considerable bickering, the protocol droid laboriously followed Artoo's instructions for detaching him from the consoles, resetting certain switches in the consoles, and reattaching Artoo's legs. Granted the astromech retained several extraneous parts like the switching box, which See-Threepio couldn't manage to disconnect, but at least, Threepio thought huffily, he hadn't left any bits of Artoo in the consoles.

"It's all very well to reroute your motivators through the central core to get around Captain Bortrek's commands," Threepio said when he was done. "You know perfectly well he's just going to hook you up again."

Experimentally, Artoo leaned forward on his third leg, and trundled, albeit with less than his customary speed and accuracy, toward the door.

Threepio followed. "You'll have to let him out, you know, if we're ever going to get out of hyperspace. What?" Artoo had paused in the doorway to tweep a command. "Oh, very well." Threepio went back for the toolkit. "It's not going to do you the slightest bit of good, you know. We're prisoners of a thief and a criminal and will end up peddled to spice-processing factories or cannibalized for spare parts the moment we reach Celanon. There's nothing else that can be done with black market stolen droids." He clanked down the corridor in the wire-trailing wake of his newly asymmetrical friend. "We're in the hands of cruel fate. We cannot escape it."

Artoo made no reply. Instead he made his way to the smaller of the two airlocks, where he issued a whole new string of commands to Threepio involving the removal of another access hatch and the reattachment—by temporary clips, this time—of his data couplers and ports to the main trunkline of the central core.

"Artoo, what are you doing?" demanded Threepio irritably. "This is really outside of enough! Captain Bortrek will be awake by this time, if you restored the oxygen to his hold, and will be most displeased! I shouldn't be surprised if he sold you by the pound for scrap."

Still no reply, except the heavy clank of the outer airlock door locking. The small comm screen flickered, displaying a view of the empty bridge. "Really, the ideas you get in your head . . ." Threepio turned away, and tried the door. "What?" he demanded irritably, to Artoo's imperative beep. "Come back to the screen? If as you say you've let Captain Bortrek out, why would you need me to . . ."

On the main bridge, visible through the viewscreen, Captain Bortrek came slamming through the doors in a violently disagreeable mood. At the sight of the patched-up wires and systems where Artoo had been he began to curse, with great vehemence and little imagination and continued to curse until, at Artoo's urging, Threepio called his name four or five times.

Swiveling where he stood, Bortrek faced the screen with eyes red and bulging with rage. "You stinkin' little garbage can!" he screamed. "You don't think I can see where you are? I'm gonna come there and . . ."

He strode to the door and almost broke his nose on it when it would not open.

"Artoo!" cried Threepio. "Tell the core system to open that door for him at once!"

Artoo-Detoo made an apologetic noise, then issued another set of instructions.

"You want me to say *what*?"

It took quite some time to get Captain Bortrek's attention; even more, to wait until he ran out of breath and ceased his wholly anthropomorphic remarks on the droids' parentage, ancestry, reproductive proclivities, and ultimate destination, in terms impossible to apply to droids and probably not even to the human-appearing synthdroids of which he had seemed so fond.

"Captain Bortrek, I am terribly, terribly sorry," said Threepio. "I apologize wholeheartedly for my counterpart here, and I am overcome with embarrassment at his behavior. But he requests that when we emerge from hyperspace, you . . ." He hesitated, knowing that the words would evoke yet another spate of furious imprecations. "He requests that when we emerge from hyperspace you proceed by the most direct route to Nim Drovis, and there land and let us out."

Threepio found he was absolutely right about the effect of his words, though he felt that Captain Bortrek's commentary on himself was hardly fair, considering he was only Artoo's translator. A certain allowance should be made, of course, for the disinhibiting effects of alcohol, gylocal, and hyperdrive coolant on the human system.

"I'm terribly sorry, sir," he said, when the irritated captain had once again shouted himself breathless. "I simply don't know what's gotten into him. He says that if you do not comply, the moment we are clear of hyperspace he will flood the entire ship with carbon dioxide again and, when you are unconscious, send out a distress signal to the Galactic Patrol. Those are his words, not mine," Threepio added, in the face of more unfair adjurations and implications. "None of this was my idea at all."

"You stinkin' hunks of scrap metal!" screamed Captain Bortrek, whose face had returned to the rather livid hue of cyanosis despite the 20.78 percent oxygen present in the cabin. "You think you're gonna get the better of me? I can rewire this crate in twenty-five minutes and pull the two of you out of there . . ."

"I'm sure you could, sir," said Threepio diffidently. "But according to the chronometer on the wall immediately to your left, the ship will reach the hyperspace target zone in less than four minutes, and though I am myself not a pilot, I believe that if you miss the zone you will condemn us all to drifting forever in hyperspace—a fate that would be fatal to you long before either one of us would even suffer boredom. And your last remark," he added, finally stung, "is not only untrue but physiologically impossible for any nonorganic life form."

As if for emphasis, Artoo-Detoo did something that caused the lights to dim and the faint *thrum* of the central core readjusting itself to penetrate even to the secondary airlock, and a small puff of pink gas swirled out of the ventilator on the bridge. Captain Bortrek swung around, terror in his eyes at the sight of it. Then he veered back, screamed curses at both droids in the safety of their airlock for a few moments more, and threw himself into the pilot's seat to begin the procedures to take the ship out of hyperspace on target.

He did not cease to blaspheme, however, and though he repeated himself frequently and never emerged from the realm of purely mundane and unimaginative scatology, he continued to relieve his emotions at the top of his lungs throughout the journey to Nim Drovis, during planetfall at a small smugglers' pad in the bayous south of the Bagsho spaceport, and was still cursing when Artoo-Detoo jammed the airlock open on a timer, See-Threepio quickly disattached the temporary wiring, and the two droids hastened down the ramp. Extrapolating from statistical probability, Threepio assumed that Captain Bortrek was still cursing when the *Pure Sabacc* lifted off.

With the fading of the *Sabacc*'s launch engines in the gluey warmth of the night, darkness settled around the two errant droids. In every direction around the wide, smoke-stained permacrete rectangle of the pad, hillocks of brush-furred mud alternated with forests of reeds whose thin heads rose no more than a few centimeters above the ambient water, a desolation of marsh-gunnies, gulpers, and the blinking green eyes of wadie-platts like ghost lights among the sedge. Against the dark hem of the sky, a sprinkling of lights marked Bagsho, largest of the planet's free ports, settled largely by Alderaan colonists but transformed in the past five years into a major crossroad between the New Republic and the neutral systems of the Meridian sector.

Had he been capable of doing so, See-Threepio would have heaved a sigh. As it was he turned from the glimmer of the lights to regard his comrade and said, "Well, I hope you know what you've gotten us into."

Artoo whistled a sorry little whistle, dropped himself forward onto his roller-leg, and snapped on his headlamp. A trifle unsteadily—because of the switching box still space-taped to one side and the clusters of wires looped up from a jack on his back that hadn't been there before—he led the way across the permacrete pad to the narrow ribbon of trail that led toward the city, Threepio clanking resignedly in his wake.

·   ·   ·

"There," said Umolly Darm, sitting back in her chair and pecking through a save command on the ramshackle keyboard. "Eight and a half months ago, on Buwon Neb's run in from Durren. One human passenger, female, hundred and seventy-five centimeters tall—she's the only human female that height all year. Cleared port authority under the name Cray Mingla."

"That's her," Luke said in a breath. His whole body felt strange, tingling with pain and grief and joy. He was almost afraid to speak, in case the grimy orange lettering should be swallowed into the monitor's dark again. "Thank you."

"No occupation listed," went on Darm. Her violet eyes flicked kindly to his face, then away; she kept her voice matter-of-fact. "Though in Hweg Shul . . . drat!" The screen fuzzed out. Luke felt as if he'd been knifed through the heart; a moment later, he was aware of the prickling lift of the hair at his nape and turning quickly toward the window, saw the racing blue tentacles of ground lightning pouring across the gravel, writhing between the pylons of the Newcomer houses, crawling up the cable tethers of the antigrav balls and the battered, pitted metal columns supporting towers where branswed and topato grew.

"Not a big one." Darm got up and crossed to the open door. "It'll pass in about ten minutes."

They stood together in the doorway, watching the electricity race and chitter under the pilings of the house, the light of it splashing like water up over their faces from the faceted gravel. Like most of the Newcomer buildings in Ruby Gulch, Darm's house doubled as her office, storeroom, and workshop—two rooms fabricated from recycled packing plastene and mounted on buttonwood pilings a meter and a half tall. Like most Newcomer buildings it stood just beyond the belt of terraformed land that followed the water seam, arable being too precious to waste, and its enormous transparisteel panels, double-glazed in an ineffective effort to keep the cold at bay, flooded the rooms with the harsh, broken, strangely colored sunlight reflected from below.

"What are they?" asked Luke, and Umolly shrugged, twisted her white hair up more firmly and reset its wooden combs.

"Exactly what they look like—ground lightning. They seem to start either in the mountains or from those crystal chimney formations—*tsils,* the Oldtimers call them—out on the wastelands. Couple of years ago one of 'em was strong enough to knock out Booldrum Caslo's computers, but they're usually not more than an inconvenience. I've been caught in them half a dozen times, out prospecting. It's like being knocked down and having your bones polished from the inside, and you're sick for a day and a half; Newcomers, anyway. The Oldtimers get over it faster. They don't even bother putting their houses on poles to avoid them, just pick themselves up afterward, dust off, and go about their business, though they do hang their kids' cradles from the ceilings to keep them clear. I used to hate 'em, but after that Force storm, if that's what it was, these don't look so bad."

The walls and furniture of Umolly Darm's little dwelling, like every other building Luke had been in since his arrival in Ruby Gulch last night, bore the marks of the maelstrom of poltergeist activity that had swept over them the very hour—Luke guessed the very minute—he had drawn on the power of the Force to confuse and distract the Theran raiders. Dishes, tools, furniture, even transparisteel had been broken; walls were gouged where small farm machinery or implements had been hurled against them as if by a giant, invisible hand. Sheds and fences lay smashed on the ground and cu-pas, blerds, and grazers had scattered at large through the Oldtimers' standing crops. In many cases the blerds had mixed in with the Oldtimers' alcopays, which had also escaped in the confusion and which carried parasites inimical to the more fragile blerds; and on his way across to Umolly's place that afternoon Luke had witnessed a dozen altercations between the two factions in the little town.

Aunt Gin informed him that morning that the two men injured when their smelter leapt off its base were still in critical condition in the Hweg Shul hospital. A woman who'd been in the care of Ruby Gulch's Oldtimer Healer—who by the sound of it used the Force to effect her cures—had died gasping as all the gentle psionics of the Healer's art had been stripped away.

He had done that. The thought made him sick with guilt.

"You said the Oldtimers talked about Force storms."

"Only to say their granddads and grandmas spoke of 'em being common, way back in the days." The delicate little prospector seated herself gingerly on the top step, keeping warily ready to leap up should the lightning below show signs of crawling up the pilings; Luke sat down beside her. "The last ones were two hundred and fifty, three hundred years ago, and even the Listeners don't have stories about how they started or what they really were. Except the Listeners say, there was a span of only about a hundred years when they took place. There weren't any before then, either."

Luke was silent, thinking about that. "Is there any chance. . . ? Do the Oldtimers ever talk about there being some kind of—of beings living on this world? Invisible, maybe? Or hidden, back in the mountains? Something that may be causing this?"

Umolly Darm chuckled. "Bless you, pilgrim, this

planet was surveyed six ways from next week by the Grissmaths before they ever dropped a soul here. You can bet they'd never have set up a prison colony where there'd be the least chance of getting local help. I've been darn near all over this rock myself and never saw nor heard a thing. Even the Listeners will tell you, there's nothing out there."

"Then what about the voices they claim to hear?"

"They say those are their old saints, Theras and the others. There's sure no invisible natives who're causing the Force storms, any more than they'd cause the ground lightning or those killer blows we get in wintertime. Me, I'm inclined to think it was sunspots."

Sunspots, thought Luke, later in the day as from the bench of Arvid's speeder he watched the white stucco buildings, the floating antigrav balls, and topato towers of Hweg Shul grow in distance. *Or maybe a Jedi who had come and settled on the planet, perhaps taught a pupil? Who had never realized what was causing the Force storms? Or who had tried, with no regard for the storms, to control the effect?*

A Jedi who had learned something previously unknown about the Force?

He was deeply aware of the Force as, later in the day, he sat in the window of the room he took above the Blue Blerd of Happiness Tavern, watching the green-clotted antigrav balls being slowly cranked down out of the hammering of the evening wind. Aware of its weight and its strength, disorienting, frightening; aware of the impenetrability of it. He couldn't push, couldn't search for Callista through it, and in any case he didn't know how much he could manipulate it without causing further harm.

But he had to find Callista. He had to.

The grief came back on him, like a cancer choking his lungs, his throat, his heart. There had not been a day when it hadn't come back to him like this, with knifing pain, that she was gone. And without her laughter, without the wry glint of amusement in her eyes—without the scent of her hair and the strength of her arms wrapped around him—there was only night without end.

There was an old song, one that Aunt Beru used to sing—a verse of it echoed in Luke's mind.

Through dying suns and midnights grim,
And treachery, and faith gone dim,
Whatever dark the world may send,
Still lovers meet at journey's end.

He had to find her there. He had to.

The eight months since the descent of the *Knight Hammer* in flames to Yavin 4 had been a darkness in which there were times when Luke wasn't certain he'd be able to go on. He knew academically that there was still some point to life: that his students needed him; that Leia, and Han, and the children needed him. But there were mornings when he could find no reason to get out of bed and nights spent counting the hours of darkness in the knowledge that nothing whatsoever awaited him with the dawn.

He closed his eyes, and pressed his forehead to his hands. Ben, and Yoda, and his studies with the Holocron, had taught him about the Force, about good and evil, about the dark side and the responsibilities that went with the bright. For eight months now he felt that he had walked utterly alone.

His mind relaxed into the silence of the room, seeking only rest. He listened to the noises of the taproom downstairs, the dim *gronching* of blerds stabled somewhere near; smelled the chemical stinks of the processing plants that were the town's heart, the musty curtains of the transparisteel behind him, and the not-terribly-clean blankets on the bed.

His mind settled and adjusted to the alien roaring of the Force.

And through it he felt the presence of a Jedi.

There was a Jedi in the town.

8

They had released the Death Seed.

Even through the haze of sweetblossom, the anger that filled her was a blind, sickened rage.

From the rail of her balcony terrace, Leia watched one of Ashgad's numerous synthdroids walk slowly, haltingly, out onto the greater terrace below. She knew these creatures weren't genuinely alive, only quasiliving synthflesh sculpted like a confectioner's buttercream over a robotic armature. But seeing the dark patches of necrosis on its face and neck, she felt a surge of rage and pity.

The voice of the pilot Liegeus—whom she had deduced was considerably more than a pilot—rose to her from below, soft and deep and patient. "Every day at noon you are to come out onto this terrace and stand for fifteen minutes in full sunlight. This is a standing order."

He walked out to where she could see him, clothed in a many-pocketed gray lab coat with his long dark hair pulled out of the way with ornamental sticks. He was a middle-size man, slight beside the synthdroid's powerful height and bulk. Ashgad must have been trying to impress someone—probably the local population—when he ordered these creatures, Leia thought. The muscular bulk was purely ornamental. Their hydraulic joints had the limitless, terrifying strength of droids, and would have had they been the size and shape of Ewoks.

Liegeus took the synthdroid's hand, stripped open the sleeve-placket, and examined its arm. Leia could smell the decaying flesh.

"You're quick to give orders," murmured the soft voice of Dzym, out of sight within the shadows of the house.

Liegeus turned his head sharply. Leia could see his face, though she was too far away to read any expression. Still, even hazy with the drug, she could feel his fear. It was in his voice, as he said, "These synthdroids are my workers and assistants. They don't die of the Death Seed but over a period of time their flesh dies. I won't have you . . ."

"You won't have me what?" Dzym spoke slowly, a deadly silence framing each word. "You would prefer that the plague went aboard those ships in your body rather than those of their fellows?"

Liegeus backed a pace, farther into the zone of the sunlight, and his hand moved almost unconsciously up to his chest, as if to massage away some cold, sinking pain.

"You would prefer that I took a little pleasure, a little sustenance, at your expense rather than theirs?" Dzym went on, and his voice sank still further. Leia could feel his presence, as though Death itself stood out of sight below her balcony, where the shadow lay thick. "I was promised, little key tapper. I was promised, and I have yet to receive the payment for those things that only I can do. You remember that there are many hours in a day, and only half of them are hours of light."

He must have gone then, because Liegeus relaxed. But

he stood for a long time in the sunlight, and even from the distance of the upper terrace, Leia could see that he trembled.

He was still shaky when he came up to her room, only a few minutes later. He must have come directly from the terrace, she thought, when she heard the door chime sound softly—Liegeus was the only one who ever used the door chime. Ashgad, and the synthdroids who brought her water and food, simply came in. She thought about going into the chamber to greet him, but somehow couldn't come up with the motivation. Cold as it was outside, and uncomfortable with the bitter dryness of the air, she found the sunlight soothing. So she remained curled up on the permacrete bench, wrapped in the quilt from her bed and the now-rather-scuffed red velvet robe, watching him as he looked around the room for her, checked the water pitcher, and then, turning, saw her.

He always checked the water pitcher. They all did. Leia was rather proud of herself for finding a place on the terrace rail where it could be poured out, to make it look as if she were drinking the stuff. In the hyperdry climate she had been flirting for days with dehydration and had a headache now most of the time, but it was the only way to keep her mind even a little clear. Since the first day she had been trying to figure out a way of tapping the pipes that supplied the internal mist fields that made the house livable or of distilling some of the moisture from the air, but the drug in her system made it difficult to actually *do* anything. She'd think of solutions and then discover with a slight feeling of surprise that she'd been sitting staring at nothing for two or three hours.

Liegeus came out onto the terrace. "Your Excellency," he greeted her gently. She hadn't meant to speak of what she had seen—hadn't meant to let him know she knew anything—but with the sweetblossom it was difficult to remember any kind of resolve.

He looked so pale, his dark eyes so haunted, that she said, "You're as much a prisoner here as I am."

He flinched a little, and looked aside. He reminded her of an animal that had been mistreated and would shy at the raising of any human hand. Compassion twisted her heart. "You seem to have the run of the place. Couldn't you leave?"

"It isn't that easy," he said. He came over to the bench where she sat, looked gravely down at her. The synthdroid, Leia could see, still stood on the lower terrace, the pallid sunlight turning its dead, doll-like hair to gold. "How much of that did you hear?"

"I . . . Nothing." Leia fumbled, and she cursed her own weakness for not being able to do without some of the drugged water every day. But she knew that most people were not aware of how their own voices carried. "I heard you and Dzym talking, that is, but I couldn't hear what you said. Only the way you shrank away, the way you fear him."

Liegeus sighed, and his shoulders slumped. A wan smile flickered over his lined face. "Well, as you can see for yourself, Your Excellency, even should I leave—and I'm being very well paid for my work here—there really isn't anywhere for me to go." He gestured around them, at the wild crystalline landscape, the dazzling gorges and razor-backed ridges of glass. Then he was silent a moment, looking down at her, helpless grief in his eyes.

"Do you spend much time out here on the terrace?" he asked abruptly.

Leia nodded. "I know it probably isn't a good idea. It makes my skin hurt . . ."

"I'll get you some glycerine," said Liegeus. "Did you hear what I said to the synthdroid? It's convenient to have them all operated from a central controller but it means you never can tell them apart."

"The only thing I heard was that it's supposed to spend fifteen minutes a day standing on the terrace."

"I'd like you to do that, too. More, if you can."

"All right." Leia nodded. It couldn't be sunlight that was a cure for the Death Seed, she thought. Billions had died of it, daytime or nighttime, on worlds across half the galaxy. "Liegeus . . ."

He was starting to leave; he turned back within the shadow of the house.

"If there's anything I can do to help . . ."

The minute the words were out of her mouth she felt like a fool. *The drug,* she thought, and cursed it again. Here she was a prisoner, her very life under their control—for it looked to her like Dzym was able to call the Death Seed into being and to take it away again—and *she* was offering to help *him.*

But something changed in Liegeus's eyes: Shame and gratitude for even that small kindness, replacing the fear. "Thank you," he said, "but there's nothing." He disappeared into the shadows of the house.

The house Luke sought lay deep in the heart of the Oldtimer quarter. In many respects it bore a rather surprising resemblance to Seti Ashgad's, which Arvid had pointed out to him that afternoon on the way into town. Like Ashgad's, this house was built at ground level—something that surprised Luke until he remembered that Ashgad's house had been built forty years ago by Ashgad's father—and like Ashgad's was now, this one had evidently once been surrounded by a luxuriant growth of plants, not just the standard vegetation common to low-light terraformed planets, but rarer growths and trees watered by a complex of droppers and pipes.

But while Ashgad's dwelling still supported this arrogant display of wasted water, this house bore only the detritus of former glory. Broken pipes crossed the dirty white stucco of the walls. A few dessicated stumps clung to niches, overgrown with snigvine like almost everything else in the grubby Oldtimer quarter. The milky-white stucco of the walls themselves had been smashed by winter windstorms, and beneath the gaps showed the grayish plastopress of which everything in the town was constructed. On the roof, most of the solar panels were broken as well, the cables rattling in the wind. Decay seemed to ooze from the boarded-up transparisteel like the foetor of a swamp: Decay and the enormous sense of something terribly wrong.

Not here, thought Luke.

It was something he had not considered: That in eight months, Callista would have ceased to be the woman he had known.

She had lasted thirty years inside the gunnery computer on the dreadnought *Eye of Palpatine.* Could she have deteriorated so quickly in less than one?

But whoever it was, whose strength in the Force he had felt, was here.

The door opened before he knocked on it. The woman standing on the low slab of crystal before its threshold wasn't Callista.

She smiled, and held out her hands to him, the smile transforming her to beauty. "Another one," she said softly. "Thank all goodness."

It was impossible to tell her age. Luke knew immediately she wasn't young, in spite of the porcelain perfection of her face. It was like a very good reproduction of youth that succeeded only in not looking old. She lacked the wrinkles and lines of human sorrow and delight around her mouth, the crow's-feet at the corners of the eyes that made Leia's so wise, lacked the print of even the smallest thought on her forehead. Her hair was raven black and hadn't been washed in weeks. Neither had her trim, high-breasted, long-legged body or the dingy green dress that wrapped it.

"Welcome." She drew him into the dense shadows within the first of the house's many rooms. Her hand was like that of a goddess who bit her nails. "Welcome. I am Taselda. Of the Knights." Her eyes met his, jewel blue under the flawless brows. "But then, you knew that."

Luke looked around the shabby darkness. Most of the transparisteel had been boarded shut and the room was illuminated only by a string of old-fashioned glow-bulbs tacked to the ceiling. His heart went out to her in compassion. Obi-Wan Kenobi had hidden himself for years in the obscure deserts of Tatooine, mocked at as a crazy old hermit, willingly surrendering the use of his Jedi powers that he might guard the last, chosen hope of the Knights. But he, thought Luke, had had the disciplines of the Force to help him bear it. This woman had been here for who knew how long, unable to use her powers for fear of harming the innocent in another Force storm. From the Newcomers she must have heard that Palpatine was dead, unable to harm her . . .

"I'm called Owen," he said, realizing that Skywalker was probably a name anathema to most of the old Jedi still alive after Vader's persecutions. "And I'm looking for someone."

"Ah." The blue eyes smiled again, wise and twinkling. She crossed to a cupboard and took out a pair of goblets, old Corellian glasswork, tulip shaped, and very valuable. She flicked a droch off the base of one. Past her shoulder, Luke had seen that the cupboard skittered with them.

She had a bottle of wine hanging out one of the few unboarded windows into a shady courtyard's chill, which she retrieved and poured. When she pushed aside the shutters and let a bit of pallid light into the room Luke saw that her white arms were boltered with droch bites. The smell of the insects was fusty-pungent above that of dirt and uncleanness. "Callista."

"You've seen her?" His whole body, his whole being, was a shout of triumph; he couldn't keep it out of his voice.

"How not?" smiled Taselda. "I am her teacher now in the ways of the Force."

The wine was from Durren and not very good. It had been cut with fermented algae sugar a number of times and had all variety of odd backtastes, but Luke sipped it, his eyes on the woman before him.

"Is she here? How is she?" he asked softly. "How does she look?"

Taselda brushed back a lock of hair from her forehead, and behind the gentle smile there was sadness in her eyes. "Like a woman who has endured much," she said. "Like a woman torn in her heart, trying to turn her back on her own deepest need."

It was a curious thing about Taselda's smile. It was wide, and flat, and at first sight little more than a stretching of the lips. But after a moment, looking at it across the rim of the wineglass, it came over Luke that it was very similar in some ways to old Ben's: quirky, gentle, amused with human nature. He wondered who this woman reminded him of. Aunt Beru, a little; Leia, a little; and someone else, a woman he had only the dimmest traces of in deep-buried memory. His mother?

The deep sense of warmth was the same, the giving kindness and the comfort of boundless, unselfish love.

"Where is she?" he asked, sensing that this woman

knew and understood all. "Can you take me to her?" The wine was sweet now on his tongue, subtle with resonances he had not comprehended before. He drank deep of it, and she refilled the glass. It soothed his weariness, as her smile did, and like her smile left him thirsty for more.

"Of course. I have been waiting for you, since she spoke your name." She reached out and took both of his hands in both of hers again. "There's a cave in the hills, not so very far from here. The Force is strong there. It's one of the places where the ground lightning emerges. I sent her there to meditate. I'll take you, for it's impossible to find without guidance."

She got to her feet and drew a deep breath, as if steadying herself, pulled her raggedy romex dress more closely around her, and looked vaguely in the corners for her shoes. Luke noticed, as if from a great distance away, that her feet were filthy and her toenails overgrown, like yellowed claws. His flash of disgust was followed immediately by his memory of Yoda—unprepossessing to say the least—and then by anger at himself.

How could he think so about Taselda?

And when he looked again her feet did not seem that dirty at all.

He stood, too, and set his goblet on the edge of the table. To his own surprise he almost missed the corner. It must be the dim lighting in the room, he thought, for the wine she'd given him had cleared his head rather than clouded it. Cleared it, it seemed to him, as if for the first time in his life.

"Have you a speeder?" she asked, and he nodded.

"I have to get it fixed, but I can do that in a day or so." It crossed his mind that he hadn't the money to do such a thing—he'd intended to sell the grounded vehicle for cash to get himself and Callista off the planet. But now that didn't seem to matter. His heart pounded faster even at that mental phrase: *Himself and Callista.*

"And weapons?"

He touched the blaster and the lightsaber at his belt.

Taselda's face fell. "It isn't enough," she said softly. "We will have to wait." Her brow creased in a frown.

"Wait?" Luke felt a twang of panic. The hills were dangerous. Callista would come to harm if he didn't get there soon. They might arrive and find her gone once more, or dead. It was unendurable, to be so close. "What's the problem?"

Taselda shook her head, with the air of one not wishing to burden a friend with her troubles, and averted her face a little. A droch crawled out of sight behind her collar. "It's nothing."

"Can I help?"

"I couldn't ask you to," she said. "It's my affair alone."

"Tell me." The world would be a bleak and terrible place if he didn't aid her. He might not find Callista. And somehow it had become important to him that she not seek the aid of another than he. "Please."

Her smile was shy, and a little self-deprecating. "It's been a long time since I had a champion. Your Callista is lucky, Owen." She raised those flower blue eyes to his again and touched his chest with confiding fingers.

"It's an old story, a long story, my friend. When first I came to this world—oh, many years ago—I had only intended to accomplish the minor mission the Masters of the Jedi had ordered for me and to depart. But seeing the way the people here lived, squabbling endlessly over pump rights, and tree rights, and who was entitled to grow which crops on which piece of land, I could not leave. There were Warlords, petty bullies with hired bravos, and though it is against the way of our order to take sides, I could not allow the deeds I saw to go uncorrected. I lent my skill, and such talents as I possessed, to the side of the people. With my lightsaber in hand I led them to a stronger and more peaceful way of life. My craft was destroyed one night while I was away leading the rescue of hostages from the enemy; and I knew that I must stay. After the fighting was over, these people made me their ruler. And I was happy."

Luke nodded, seeing in his mind this beautiful woman in her warrior youth. The house, indeed, was of the sort that a grateful people would build for a just ruler who had saved them from tyranny.

"But many years later another Jedi came to this world, an evil creature: selfish, lying, but very plausible. He came here because he had heard that the Force on this world is strong. It lies close to the surface of reality here, close enough to reach out and touch, though he was not capable of doing so. His own abilities to use the Force were not strong, and he sought to twist and gather them to fulfill his own emptiness. Beldorion he was called. Beldorion of the Ruby Eyes. Beldorion the Splendid."

She sighed and passed her hand across her forehead in a gesture of weariness and grief.

"As you know, Owen, there are always those who will follow such a one. He worked not only through violence and the threat of violence but through lies and calumny, turning the truth and people's memories of the truth, until everything I had done here was given a different meaning, a sinister significance that those whose power to work evil I had curtailed were delighted to believe.

"My friends turned against me. Beldorion was too feeble an adept to manufacture his own lightsaber, so he stole mine from me. I was driven into poverty. Feared by the weak and courted by the venal, Beldorion came to rule Hweg Shul like a king, and I was forgotten."

Her voice faltered, and she put up her hand quickly,

to cover whatever expression might have pulled at her mouth. In the quiet street behind them a blerd brayed its monotonous tenor screech; an Oldtimer woman drove past in a high-wheeled cart pulled by alcopays, flipping her long whip at their feet. Luke saw in his mind's eye this beautiful woman before him, hurrying along these densely twisted walled streets with her dirty dress fluttering in the endless wind and remembered Ben again and the way children in Tosche station used to run out in front of him giggling and making what they considered to be magic signs with their fingers. Even at this great distance of time—and he'd been only a small child himself—he remembered the genuine amusement that had tugged the corners of Ben's mouth.

Taselda went on, "Well, it was inevitable, as we true Knights know, that Beldorion should succumb to his own greeds and his own vices. He was usurped and ousted many years ago by a man named Seti Ashgad, a politician sent here by the old Emperor as punishment, even as the ancestors of these people had been sent here. Beldorion had become so sunk in debauchery that no power remained to him. His followers deserted him for Ashgad, and Ashgad took from him his very house, and all the treasure inside it. Treasure that he had stolen from me," she said somberly. "And most important, in that house somewhere is my lightsaber."

Luke said softly, "Ah."

"Because of injuries I suffered in my struggle against Beldorion it was not possible for me to make another. When I went to Ashgad, many years ago now, and tried to retrieve it, I was cast forth as brutally as Beldorion had cast me forth. Since then I have tried many times to recover it. See." With a movement of simple innocence, she slipped her dress from her right shoulder, and showed him, among the droch bites, a terrible bruise on her arm.

"We will be vulnerable, when we go to the cave to find your Callista," she said softly. "Ashgad's servants are merciless, the more so because they are no longer human, but only human-seeming droids. And because of that same injury, I no longer have the strength to enter Ashgad's house and get the lightsaber myself. Indeed, I'm no longer sure whether it is here or at the house he has in the wastelands, at the foot of the Mountains of Lightning. For Callista's sake, and for yours, I wish I could go with you, show you where she is, but I dare not."

She drew in a shaky breath and shoved back the dirty mane of hair from her face again with both hands. "I dare not."

Rage filled Luke at the sight of the bruises on her arm, self-righteous fury that anyone would have hurt this gentle, beautiful woman mingled with anxiety that they—whoever *they* were—would take out their anger at Taselda on Callista, should they come upon her alone. He said, "Where would your lightsaber be, in Ashgad's house?" Its high, glittering white walls came again to his mind, arrogant among the small cottages of the Oldtimers.

"There is a treasure room beneath the kitchens." Taselda's indigo eyes brimmed with grateful tears. "The entrance is through the kitchen courts, here." She turned away, and did something at a small table. Coming back, she handed him a sheet of coarse local paper, on which was inked a plan of the house.

Luke saluted her with it, feeling light and buoyant within himself, as if his bloodstream were filled with sparks of fire. He grinned at her like a boy. "I'll be back. We'll be out of town by nightfall."

"She told me that I could trust you, Owen," said

Taselda softly. "I saw the light in her eyes, when she spoke your name. I think you need have no fear of what you will find."

Callista. Luke's whole body seemed to be singing, as he strode away down the ill-paved back streets of the Old-timers town. *Whatever dark the world may send, still lovers meet . . .*

I've found her, I've found her, I've found her! 'I saw the light in her eyes . . .'

His steps slowed.

'. . . when she spoke your name.'

But Callista would not have known that he would be calling himself Owen Lars.

He stopped and realized he had missed his way among the near-identical white houses.

And he thought, quite calmly, *There was something in the wine.*

Luke had never been much of a drinker, and once he'd begun to study and understand the Force he had given it up altogether. It simply took too much edge off his concentration. Although, of course, Taselda's wine wasn't like other wine, still it surprised him that he'd imbibed the quantity of it that he had. Now as he turned his concentration inward on his own metabolism, to clear some of the alcohol from his system, he realized that there was something else there as well.

A synthetic mood-enhancer, he thought, leaning against a wall with one hand and closing his eyes. Pryodene or pryodase, or maybe Algarine torve weed—the kind of thing that made one accepting and friendly. Leia had told him there had been a time when consumption of pryodase had been *de rigueur* before dinner parties among the nobility of Coruscant, as a counter to the fad for dueling, and there were always accusations in labor disputes and divorce proceedings that one side or the other had slipped it into their opposite number's coffeine just before negotiations.

It was harmless and nonaddictive. It simply lowered one's guard.

Luke thought, *How wise of her, to use that method to overcome my prejudices so that I could see her as she truly is.*

He walked two steps, trying to reorient himself toward Seti Ashgad's house, and then thought, *What did I just think?*

A throb of pain seized him. Not physical pain, but the pain of loss, of abandonment, the deep-seated pain of a child who suspects from earliest awareness that his mother had given him away like a stray puppy, for reasons he could not understand. The pain of Callista's flight. The pain of losing the dream of the father he had invented in his lonely fantasies.

Cold flooded him, cold and anxiety. He couldn't lose Taselda . . .

Through the child's fear of loss, a voice came to him.

Search your feelings, it said, a black voice speaking out of blackness. *You know it to be true.*

His father's voice.

Vader's.

Taselda was using him.

The cold in him deepened, the panic of abandonment. If she was lying, using him only to get her lightsaber back (and what kind of injury would prevent her from making another lightsaber, if she'd had the skill to do it once?), it meant she wasn't Callista's teacher. She couldn't restore Callista to him. *No,* he thought, not wanting to believe it. Not wanting it to be true. *No . . .*

You know it to be true.

And as he had then, he knew.

He turned his steps back, toward Taselda's house.

As a Jedi, she would have been trained in the bending

of minds. Luke had seen Ben do it, had done it himself. The Emperor Palpatine had been a genius at evoking that kind of desperate loyalty, that need to serve him, calling forth the echoes of one's own fears like a skilled musician calling forth beauty from a flute.

And Taselda's ability in that direction was very subtle and very strong.

Wind slapped and howled stronger at him as he wound through the alleyways, as if forbidding him to return. Buried beneath the avalanche of wrenching desolation, the oceans of ambient fear that flooded his soul at the thought of a break from Taselda, Luke felt the cold knowledge he had felt, hanging on that projection above the Bespin abyss. He didn't want it to be true, but he knew it was.

He came to Taselda's house from the rear this time, and saw her through the back door across a grubby yard scattered with rusted speeders in various stages of disrepair. She was groping and picking in the shadowy corners of the room for something, behind furniture and under cushions. He saw her jam her arm under an armoire, then pull it out and stand, facing him across the yard, her blue eyes wide and furious, her black snaggly hair hanging in a mat of nastiness over her breasts. He felt her mind pull on his, angry and futile; felt the weak, diffused shoving of the Force, and though the wall sheltered them from the wind he saw around him in the yard the clapped-out water tanks, the bleached old rags, the scraps of wood and metal all flutter and twitch like live things.

Her eyes still on his, she was pulling things—drochs, they had to be—off her arm and eating them with her brown, broken teeth.

The anxiety in his mind had gone shrill, like a hectoring scream. There was desolation in his soul, fake as tinsel beads. Under it, a more genuine grief.

Luke turned away.

It was less the Force than his years with the Rebellion, his years fighting battles in vacuum in vessels moving at incredible speeds, that made him pick up almost instinctively first the sense of danger, and only in the next second the sound of running feet. He ducked as a spear buried itself in the dirt just beyond where he'd stood. Someone hurled a rock, and he sprang back as an old-fashioned yellow sodium blaster bolt ripped a charred line in the wall at his side. Ragged-looking men and women came running at him from all sides out of the alleyways—kids, too, wild-haired and barefooted, throwing rocks.

Luke could have scattered them with a blast of the Force, picked up any one of them and hurled him or her flying, but dared not. A girl of no more than sixteen ran at him with a club, and he swept it aside with his forearm as he sidestepped, dodged another blaster bolt from a weapon so run-down it probably couldn't have cooked a happy-patty, and fled. The little gaggle of Oldtimers ran after him, cursing and shaking their weapons.

"Murderer! Thief! Dirtball!" *(They should talk!)* They were fast, appearing around the corners of the houses and stabbing at him with spears and clubs. Two or three had blasters, but it took a good deal of practice to hit anything on the run, and Luke made sure to keep moving. Once two of the men grabbed him, tried to drag him back into the mazes of alleys—presumably back to Taselda's house, if as he guessed these people were remnants of those she'd "ruled" here, but Luke wasn't at all sure. He dropped his weight, swept one man's legs out from under him with a lashing kick, and used the falling body as a weapon against the other, then hurled them both into the angry pack. He dove over a wall, pelted across a thickly grown garden patch whose leaves slapped and smote him with the force of the gale winds, and heard the pursuers run around the long sides of the lot. If worse came to worst he supposed he could always use the Force to . . .

To what? Start a Force storm that would kill some other innocent old woman under the care of a Healer two hundred kilometers away?

He grabbed a rake from the tools along the fence, vaulted over the wall where he could hear the least of the shouting, and made a break for the wider streets and more open field of vision among the Newcomer houses. Dust and pebbles smote him and cut his face. Three Old-timers appeared in front of him across the width of the street, including the man with the blaster. Luke dove sideways, slipped past a spear that jabbed down on him from the roof of a shed, rolled to his feet, and set his back to the wall as more came running.

"Here, now, what's all this?" bellowed a voice.

The Oldtimers skidded to a halt, milled for a moment, then began to back away.

A weedy-looking eight-foot Ithorian and a fat, slovenly, dark-haired human male, both in the blue uniforms of the Hweg Shul municipal police, came walking down the alley.

"Shame on the lot of you," warbled the Hammerhead in its soft voice. "What do you think you are, piranha-beetles? Nafen?"

There was a muttering among the Oldtimers. One dropped a rock she'd had in hand to throw. Someone else said something about "the Evil One."

"Him?" The human jerked a thumb at Luke. His greasy black forelock flipped in the wind. No one replied. He turned to Luke. "You the Evil One, pilgrim?"

"Everyone is evil to someone." Luke dusted his sleeve, where a rock had nearly broken his arm.

The man chuckled. "Well, my ex-wife would agree with you there." He turned to the Hammerhead. "What about it, Snaplaunce? There anything in the City Statute about being evil?"

"Not to my knowledge, Grupp."

"You hear that?" Grupp the policeman turned back to the mob, only about a third of whom remained. "What's the guy done besides being evil?" He glanced sidelong at Luke, measuring him with a dark eye that was far from stupid.

"Evil is as evil does," yelled the girl who'd tried to brain Luke with a club.

"Yeah, well, mobbing a man who didn't even fire that blaster he's carrying sounds like *Evil Does* to me, sugar." Grupp gestured like a man shooing flies. "Get out of here, the bunch of you, before I run you all in for disturbing the peace. You okay?" He turned his back on the Oldtimers to speak to Luke, though Luke was pretty sure he was watching them still. They dispersed, muttering, in their eyes the anger at seeing Newcomers rescuing a Newcomer, not lawmen helping a man innocently attacked.

"I'm fine."

"Crazy Therans."

"Not Therans," warbled the Ithorian. "I know the Therans. These are the ones who have attacked Master Ashgad's house, four or five times since I have been here. I suspect they're the ones who killed the last of his human servants early this year, though I can prove nothing. I know it was they who kidnapped that young woman at about the same time."

"Young woman?" Luke felt as if he'd been kicked in the chest.

The Ithorian regarded him for a moment, speculation in its golden eyes.

"The tall woman who came in on one of the Durren planet-hoppers. She called herself Cray, but forgot on a number of occasions to answer when spoken to by that name. These ragged ones—the remains, I am told, of one of the old gangs that fought for control of this city between the crime-boss Beldorion and another, a woman, many years ago—surrounded and dragged her away one night, but before I could find where they took her I encountered her in the street. She said they were her friends." The sweet, low voice was dry—Ithorians have an astonishing range of emotional shadings to their words.

"When—when was this?" asked Luke, through dry lips. "Is she still in the city? Have you seen her?"

Grupp and the Ithorian exchanged a look. Not speculative, precisely, but a police look, asking each other whether he, Luke, constituted a threat of some kind to the order and well-being of their city. He saw Grupp take in the lightsaber at his belt and would have been willing to bet that whether or not the policeman knew what such a thing was, he remembered that Callista had worn one, too.

It was the Ithorian who spoke.

"She left Hweg Shul within a week of her arrival, of her own will insofar as we know. But whether she left in quest, or in flight, or at the behest of another, that we cannot tell."

They had reached the Newcomer area of town, the square white houses like truncated Imperial walkers on their stilts. The antigrav balls were all drawn down close to the ground, and the freezing wind roared like the vanished seas in their leaves and moaned around the permacrete rendering towers where brope and smoor were processed into edible form. Grupp and Snaplaunce looked Luke over one more time, bade him take care where he walked, and strode off to the shadows under a house where they'd left their speeder-bikes.

Luke stood for a long time, looking back toward the tangled walls and algae-covered rocks of the Oldtimer town.

Within a week of her arrival. Eight months ago.

Whether in quest, or in flight . . .

Luke shivered in disgust and abhorrence. He would have bet anything he possessed that, eight months ago, Taselda had tried to use Callista as her weapon, her striking arm, as Palpatine had used Vader and Vader had tried to use him, Luke. *One of the old gangs that fought for control of this city between the crime-boss Beldorion and another.* Was that what Taselda had sunk to, however and whyever she had come to the planet in the first place, the planet where the Force seemed to imbue the very stones like radiant light?

She had tried to enslave Callista with the promises of leading her to what she most wanted, with the illusion of belonging, of having found a home.

Callista had come seeking instruction in the Force and had found instead a terrible example of what could happen when you did not have it, when it decayed to almost nothing, leaving only cravings and anger and madness behind.

And Callista had fled.

Luke shivered and, leaning against the wind, turned his steps back toward his room above the Blue Blerd. His mind refused to release the horrible image of Taselda, once a Jedi, now a dirty old madwoman, picking drochs off her arms and eating them, staring at him out of the dark.

9

"Beldorion the Splendid sends his compliments, Your Excellency." In the doorway, the tall synthdroid bowed. "He would be honored by your presence at tea."

Oh, would he? Leia had to bite back the words. The adcube for synthdroids had mentioned nothing about their aural and visual receptors being wired as remote pickups so that their owners could see and hear what they did, but Leia knew in some circles it was routinely done. The sweetblossom sometimes made her careless, and she knew that with Dzym waiting, she had to be as careful as if she were walking the blade of a razor.

"Will Master Ashgad be present?" She exaggerated the sweet haziness of voice as she always did around the synthdroids or, in fact, around Liegeus—one of her schoolmates many years ago at the Select Academy had been stoned most of the time and the singsong quality was easy for Leia to fake. The mere fact that no one had come in to make her drink the drugged water had told her at least—belatedly—that the room wasn't wired; due to the effects of the drug the possibility hadn't even occurred to her until that morning.

"I do not know, Your Excellency."

"It's just that I need to know what to wear," she murmured dreamily, for the benefit of a possible listener.

"I do not know, Your Excellency."

Not, thought Leia, with the synthdroid's departure, that she had a whole lot of choice.

From her post on the terrace she'd counted at least five synthdroids, but some of them might be duplicates, so there could be more. At least two bore marks of necrosis, the slow dying of the flesh that covered their metal armatures that was apparently connected, in some way, with both the Death Seed and Dzym.

She wondered if it were indeed possible, as she was beginning to deduce, that Dzym could in some way control the Death Seed. It would explain the preciseness of the timing needed to take over the *Adamantine* and the *Borealis* and the fact that she had survived her bout with the disease. It explained why neither Ashgad nor Liegeus had contracted the plague, and at the same time explained Liegeus's fear. Or would she see some other explanation, some other detail, when her mind was clear again?

If she lived to look at the matter with a clear mind.

Leia shivered, and began to change into her red-and-bronze gown of state, and the heavy crimson mantle that covered it.

The synthdroid appeared a half hour later, as Leia was finishing putting up her hair. She took note as well as she could of the directions, the layout of the house: along a corridor, down a flight of steps. There were iron blast doors standing open near the bottom, and through them she glimpsed a vast compound like a docking bay, looking out over the open air of the plateau's edge. A blocky, medium-size freighter stood there, synthdroids moving around it carrying in what looked like the components of a computer core, which meant that construction was fairly far along. Liegeus came out, saying to one of the synthdroids beside him, ". . . all the green wires first, then all the red wires . . ." and across the open permacrete his eyes met hers.

He paused, startled: The synthdroid beside her said, "Please come this way now, Your Excellency," and she realized she'd been standing in the frame of the open blast doors; she hurried after. They turned a corner, proceeded down another flight of steps, and the smell of Hutt rose to meet her like a wave of heat.

"It is dreadfully slow here, dreadfully slow." Beldorion shifted his enormous, pythonlike bulk on the dais of air duvets and cushions on which he lay. Hutts tend to obesity as they grow older, but despite almost constant snacking, the Splendid One retained his air of physical power and enormous speed, completely unlike Durga the Hutt's thin and pitiful disciple Korrda, who back on Nal Hutta had been the butt of so many jokes. Unlike many of his species, he favored gold rings on his fingers, and in the folds of his head flesh, and a jeweled stud in his lower lip. On a baldric of gold and reptile leather he wore his lightsaber, the plain dark metal incongruous against the glittering harness. "It is good of you to join me, little princess. You must find the days weigh heavy in your room."

"They do, a little," admitted Leia, wondering what all this was leading up to. She recalled some of the more revolting aspects of her imprisonment by Jabba, but reasoned that even if Ashgad were ignorant of the invitation—which she was virtually certain he was—they were still beneath his roof. "Master Ashgad has been very assiduous about seeing to my wants."

"Oh, and to mine too, mine too," rumbled that gluey, bottom-of-the-well voice. "Not that I'm in anywhere near the same position as yourself, but well . . . I have my comforts, of course, and my chef, though quite frankly, little princess, this new fellow's not the cook Zubindi Ebsuk was. Zubindi . . . ah!" He sighed revoltingly, and groped around in his porcelain washtub of brandy for the spiky balls of marinated prabkros that floated therein. "Now, *there* was a chef! I was desolate when he died. Bereft. A Kubaz, like the new fellow—a genius at insects. 'Grant me the right hormones, the right enzymes to inject,' he used to say, 'and I will transform a sand flea into the center course of an Imperial feast.' And he could, you know." The deep crimson eyes fixed on her. "He could."

He rumbled deep in his belly, and she felt the touch of his mind on hers. Faint and weak, but there, subtly drawing at her will. She felt herself in danger of becoming hypnotized by those scarlet orbs and looked away. With that much sweetblossom in her system it was difficult not to submit her mind to his dominance.

"Ashgad, now . . . he's made himself the champion of these Newcomers, but what is that? When I ruled Hweg Shul, all the people came to me with their problems, that I could render judgment. And my judgments were just to all, you know." The red eyes caught hers again, held them. "I was the better ruler—the stronger as well."

It was an effort to look away. "I'm sure you were."

He chuckled again, and slithered one tiny yellow hand around among the satin cushions, almost absentmindedly plucking forth a droch nearly the size of the tip of Leia's finger, which he popped into his mouth and cracked absently with his tongue. "He couldn't have taken over from me if I hadn't been tired. That's all it was. All that fighting with that Taselda woman. It wore me out. Now taste this, little one."

He extended his hand, and across the room a beaten-silver plate stirred where it lay on the sideboard of black-wood and crystal, then lifted and floated across to them. It had almost reached them when it tipped in midair and fell. Even dazed with the effects of the blossom, Leia's reflexes were quick enough to let her dive from the pillows and catch it. It contained roulades of some sort surrounding a bed of what smelled like petroleum by-products, topped with a weird blue thing like an enormous berry. In a lifetime of diplomatic banquets—admittedly brief—Leia had never seen the like.

"Who was Taselda?" she asked, handing him the plate.

"A former colleague." He plucked the berry from the top of the dish. "She and I came to this world together—oh, many years ago. But she grew jealous of the reverence in which the local population held me and of my greater skills—she couldn't even manufacture the, ah, basic tools of our order. She did everything in her power to discredit me. Pinpricks, mostly, but annoying just the same. Henchmen trying to break into my palace, that sort of thing. Even after I came to live with Ashgad. Now, my dear, tell me if this is not the most exquisite taste in the galaxy."

Leia picked up the fruit knife and fork from the small table nearby, cut a section from the berry, and watched as Beldorion slurped down the rest with Rabelaisian enthusiasm before she ate her own fragment. She wished at once that she'd taken a larger hunk, because it was delicious, both sweet and meaty, juicy and subtly chambered.

"Zubindi used to grow them three times this size," Beldorion said with a sigh. "And of a flavor to make this seem a cast husk by comparison. Would you believe it, child? It's a common Rodian kelp gnat, raised on growth enzymes and kept alive and growing for a year instead of the day of its natural life span. Zubindi could keep them going for five years, turn them into a whole different life form! They'd sing and whistle and move around on little tentacles they developed toward the end of that last year of life. Heaven knows what they would have been, had he been able to prolong them further! And the way he could torture britteths! Britteth flesh, as you must know, improves with the enzymes secreted when they die in pain . . . ah! Sometimes I think I shall never get over his death."

He groped in his brandy bowl for another prabkro, and shed a sentimental tear. Leia tactfully took a tiny bite of one of the roulades. Kubaz chefs were famous through the galaxy for injecting insect life forms with growth enzymes and gene-splicing them in quest of newer and more perfect designer foodstuffs, so it was anyone's bet what these actually contained.

"What brought you here in the first place?" asked Leia.

He shook his great head, narrow eyes like cabochon jewels peeking out at her from beneath heavy lids. "I think you know," he said, and his great voice sank to a basso murmur, like the mutter that presages typhoon winds. His long, purplish tongue slopped around the edges of his mouth, questing for stray droplets of juice, then vanished within. "I think you've felt it—that light. That ocean of brightness that fills the universe; that fills each of our Order with light. Travelers' tales—old log books. They said it was here. But you know that."

His eyes held hers again, inescapable. "Now a young lady of your—particular—talents might find herself needing allies in a situation like this. Ashgad can't be trusted, you know, little one. And he was never that good a ruler." He held out one small gold-ringed hand, and Leia found herself unable to pull away.

From the doorway a deep, very quiet voice said, "At least he never sold one of his slaves to Dzym."

Beldorion swung around, hissing; Leia sprang back and pulled her gaze away. Liegeus stood in the doorway, graying hair hanging down in his eyes, broken out of his fear, thought Leia, by anger. For a moment he only stood there, looking at the two of them, then he stepped lightly down and crossed to the dais.

Softly, Beldorion said, "Have a care, philosopher." The whole terrible length of him twitched, the great seven-foot tail creeping back and forth like a separate, angry being as his red eyes narrowed. "Upon another occasion I told you I do not brook interference."

Liegeus hesitated for a moment, his dark eyes widening with some evil memory. Then he came forward again and took Leia by the hand. "What did he offer you, my dear?" His voice was steady, but she felt his fingertips cold, and shaking a little in hers. "Partnership in ruling this planet? Or just that he'd let you go free if you'd put him back in charge?"

He raised Leia to her feet and led her back to the door. Beldorion made no move to stop them, but as Liegeus reached to touch the opener plate Leia saw the Hutt gesture pettishly in his direction. Liegeus gasped as if struck, half-doubled over in agony, his free hand going to his temple. He was ashen with shock and pain as Leia slapped the opener plate with the backs of her fingers. The door sliced open, and she led him through, stumbling blind and clinging to the wall for support.

They were halfway down the corridor, opposite the blast doors that led into the docking bay, before Liegeus straightened up and drew a shaky breath. "Migraine," he managed to say through lips drained of color and blood. "He does that—sometimes—when I beat him at ho-logames, too. Sometimes—worse than that."

He shook his head, his hand stealing to his throat, cast a quick glance at the open blast doors, and putting a hand behind her elbow led her rather rapidly toward the stairs. "Did he try to influence your mind? Don't trust him, my dear."

"And I suppose I should trust Ashgad?"

Liegeus looked away.

They mounted the stairs in silence, passed down the corridor toward the doors of her room. He had punched in the code—carefully keeping his body between her and the pad—before he said, "He doesn't keep his promises. Even should he do so, he couldn't protect you from Dzym, and he could not defeat Ashgad. Even years ago, when Ashgad first reached this planet, Beldorion was no match for him."

Leia looked up, startled. "But the original Ashgad . . ." she began, and their eyes met. Liegeus looked away, and she could see by the flinch of his mouth that, still disoriented from the migraine, he'd said more than he meant. He ushered her gently into her room and, stepping quickly out, closed the door between them.

Leia groped blindly for the head of her bed, sat down, weak in the knees. She felt light-headed from thirst and a little ill from the struggle with Beldorion; glancing in the direction of the water pitcher, she got to her feet, carried it outside to the terrace, and dumped all the remaining water over the railing. Right now her thirst was too great, and she might forget later that she should not drink.

She needed her mind clear. *Is it because of the sweetblossom?* she wondered. *Did Liegeus mean something else, and I'm reading this into it because I'm drugged? Is there some other real explanation?*

But the only one she could think of for Liegeus's words—the only conclusion she could draw—was that the man who had proclaimed himself the son of Seti Ashgad, the Emperor Palpatine's old rival for Senatorial power, was in fact the man himself.

"Okay, what have we got?" Han Solo swung himself down the ladder from the observation port, crossed in two strides to Lando Calrissian's station at the long-range scanners. Bands of red and yellow light played upward across the conman's swarthy features; Lando flicked a calibration switch, altering the flow of the reflections to show the glitch in the spectrograph readings that had caused him to send a flag signal up to Han.

"Looks like a heat reading on the fifth planet of that system there. Damonite Yors B—nothing there, never has been. The graph's cooling fast . . ." He tapped the black bands in the colored spectrum, ". . . but those are reactor fuel lines."

Han reached past his shoulder to punch through a more accurate readout and swore.

"Good thing I brought my mittens." Lando reached to adjust another screen. "That's sure big enough for the *Adamantine*. By the heat streak in the atmosphere they've been down there for about ten hours."

Han was already at the main console, keying the course. "Hang on, Leia," he whispered. "Don't check out on me now."

Planetfall was a nightmare. The whole atmosphere a whirling wrack of storms, the *Falcon* was buffeted and thrown like a plastene plate in a riptide. Han and Chewbacca worked side by side over the console, fighting ion storms that struck them in sheets and fritzed out the sensors that were their only guide to the terrain below. Han allowed himself to think of nothing, to be aware of nothing except the elusive spot of heat on the readout—the spot that slowly dimmed from orange to brown in the hours it took them to struggle down through titanic gales.

She couldn't die, he thought. He had literally no

idea—none—of what he would do, what would become of him, if she should die.

He couldn't imagine life without her.

Through a millrace of flying atmospheric garbage, the sensors began to pick out the debris track on the ice below. Most of it was imbedded meters deep already in the long, hard melt slick where the primordial planetary ice had been liquified by the passage of the crashing ship, to refreeze within minutes; a rummage of hull fragments, broken-off stabilizers, deformed nodules unrecognizable already from atmospheric friction. The slick ran at a steeply acute angle toward a chasm in the ice, kilometers deep and nearly half a kilometer across. Han brought the *Falcon* in low over it, holding his breath as he followed the trail—*It didn't go over. Tell me it didn't go over.*

The ice slick ended in a shallow vee at the chasm's edge.

"There she is," said Lando.

For a minute Han thought his friend was speaking of Leia herself, rather than the wreckage of the ship.

There was a ledge that you could have put a small manufacturing plant on, forty or fifty meters below the edge of the chasm—the drop was unguessably deep beyond that, and the visibility appalling. The crashing ship's hull had ruptured when it had gone over the edge of the glacier plain above, and the whole business balanced near the dropoff to the deeper chasm like a billion-credit house with a seaside view. A dull rubicund glow showed where the dying engines lay, through the buckled panels and flying ice.

The serial numbers were visible.

"What ship is that?"

Chewie was already punching them in. The *Corbantis,* out of Durren orbital. Reported missing barely two hours before the *Falcon* had lifted out of Hesperidium.

Not the *Adamantine.* Not the *Borealis.* Han didn't know whether to feel relief or despair.

It was a fight to bring the *Millennium Falcon* around for another pass, to put her down on the lip of the first drop, a dozen meters from the V-shaped notch where the *Corbantis* had gone over. They dropped a towline first, using the notch as a site, so that the weighted end of sixty-five meters of megafilament cable hung down the face of that first cliff only a short distance from the wreck. Leaving Lando at the *Falcon*'s controls, Han and Chewie suited up and went out, following the line across the waste, hanging on for dear life against the butcher winds that obscured the face plates of their e-suits with flying ice, and let themselves down the ragged black mess of frozen cliff toward the dying glow of the wreck.

Even the powerful sodium glare of the e-suits' lights couldn't pierce the swirling murk to show much of the damage on the ship. Against the howl of static Han yelled into the helmet mike, "Small craft!" and pointed at the burn marks that scored the hull. Chewie roared assent. "You see any kind of Destroyer track on the sensors, Chewie? Anything that could have carried TIEs or fighters?" The Wookiee demurred. Farther on, the smashed silvery disk of a shield generator dangled from the ice- and blast-scarred metal in the wobbling white glow of the e-suits' light. "That's heavy guns for a planet-hopper, even if you could get one out this far."

Chewbacca's growl rumbled in Han's earpiece. The Wookiee pilot knew more about out-of-the-way smuggler bases in this part of the galaxy than the average miser knew about the contents of his or her creditbox, and Han believed him when he said there was no place in forty parsecs where a planet-hopper fleet could have put in.

Great, Han thought. *So there's a Destroyer—or a fleet of*

Destroyers—roving around out here someplace. Just what I needed to make my day complete.

The crew they found in the outer holds were dead. Under the white mounds of frost and ice it was difficult to tell, but Han thought these were men and women who'd died during the initial battle. In addition to the ruptured coolant lines and dangling wires indicative of major systems blowouts, the holes in the outer hull through which Han and the Wookiee climbed were too huge for the emergency sealant systems to cope with. The blast doors had shut at once, to save the atmosphere in the rest of the ship, and Chewbacca had to cut out the switch boxes to manually let himself and Han through.

Beyond, the bodies were simply white with frost. They glittered softly in the dark, hundreds of them, oriented along the corridors like iron filings in a magnetic field, crawling inward to the warmer heart of the ship as the cold seeped through the breached insulation and killed them as they crawled.

They lay facedown. Han was glad of it. He'd seen men and women who had died of cold, and mostly their faces were peaceful. Still, picking his way among the corpses like some clumsy intruder in his green plast e-suit, he would just as soon not see their faces.

Farther in, a few panels still glowed with power, candle-dim spots of amber or red. Radiation warning lights were on all over the ship, and a garbled female voice from the tannoy repeated over and over, with the pleasant persistence of a droid, that radiation levels were critically high, and all crewmembers were advised to implement antiradiation procedure D-4 in mitigation. After seven or eight times through the announcement Han wanted to find that droid and hammer it into tiny fragments, but it went on as a demented background to the escalating hell of the search as long as he and Chewie remained on the dying ship.

There was enough heat now to make their suits smoke—the gauges on his wrist showed Han that they were just a touch below the freezing point of alcohol— and the dead were not so thick on the floors. Into his helmet mike he said, "They're in the reactors."

Chewie nodded. Night caught on the snows of Hoth, Han had slit open the body of his dead tauntaun so that its lingering warmth might keep his friend Luke from dying of cold and shock. What remained of the *Corbantis* crew, by the same expedient, had made their way inward, to crouch by the fading heat of the reactors in a last despairing bid to outlast the cold until rescue could arrive. This was where Han and Chewie found them, radiation burned as if they'd been rolled in a supernova, seventeen of them still alive among twisted heaps of the dead. Two more died during the agonizing process of loading them onto antigrav tables from sick bay and struggling out across the windswept waste and up the cliffside to the *Falcon* with them: One by one, fifteen exhausting journeys that left Han and Chewbacca numb with fatigue as they rigged salvaged life-support equipment in holds originally stocked with the smuggled glitterstim and rock ivory that had been Han's stock-in-trade years ago. On the last of the journeys to get extra stasis fluids and antishock drugs, Han downloaded the vessel's logs.

"Where do we take 'em?" asked Lando, as he guided the bucking, heeling freighter up through the insanity of the atmosphere again. Han stood slumped for a moment in the doorway of the bridge, almost too tired to move. It was one of the few times he'd seen his friend shocked out of his cockiness, quiet in the face of catastrophe. Then he crossed to the auxiliary controls, stumbling with fatigue as he walked. "Hey, I can do this, man," added Lando, looking up quickly. "You go back there and lie down. Some of those guys in the holds look better than you do."

Han gave him a universal gesture and dropped into the chair, but beyond this he made no attempt to help in liftoff. It had taken nearly ten hours to transfer all the survivors, and he knew he was far too tired to be at the controls of anything more complicated than a self-conforming chair. Battered as he felt, it itched him to see anyone handling the *Falcon* but himself.

"Bagsho is probably our best bet." He shut his eyes, leaned his forehead on his fists in an attempt to block out the memory of the reactor core, the huddled shapes of the bodies pressed against one another in the small pockets of heat from the coils. Most of those who'd survived were the ones who'd had time to put on some kind of protective clothing, but there were over a dozen in radiation suits who'd died anyway, blind, burned husks of flesh. There'd been no chance, none whatsoever, that Leia had been anywhere on or near that vessel since she'd snipped the ceremonial ribbons at its maiden launch. His near-hysterical desire to double-check every corpse in the reactor chamber, every corpse in the ship, was, he knew, only that: hysteria.

But he couldn't stop seeing her there: flesh burned purple and slick, hair gone, eyes gone . . .

He pulled a deep breath and made himself continue, fairly casually, "The sector medical facility's there, and a small base. At least we can check in about enemy movements in this sector. I didn't see signs of really heavy artillery but it takes more than just a couple of planet-hoppers to put out a cruiser."

"Enemy?" Lando didn't turn his head—he was concentrating hard on keeping the *Falcon* from being flipped

into eternity by the tearing forces of the stratosphere—
but there was a world of gesture in his voice. "What
enemy? The partisans in Durren? That crazy wildcat pirate fleet or invasion or whatever it is that's supposed to
be hitting Ampliquen? The palace coup that's going on in
Kay-Gee? There isn't . . ."

Something hit the *Falcon* like the zap of a live wire.

Solo gave a yelp of protest and was diving for the
control panel even as the lurch of impact hurled him off
his feet. Behind him down the corridor he heard Chewie
roar. Lando yelled, "What the . . . ?" and Solo scrambled to hands and knees, almost made it to his feet when
another impact jolted him halfway across the bridge.

"Where are they coming from?"

"There's nothing out there!" screamed Lando, slamming the controls into a straight-up dive that took them
out of the final whirling shrouds of the atmosphere and
into the black of space. Another laser beam caught the
shields and overload lights went on like a red-and-amber
Winterfeast display over the main console. Han was already piling up the ladder to the gunnery turret, cursing
and wondering if this had anything to do with Leia's
disappearance, with the dying battlecruiser on the planet
below, or if this was just some little dividend from bored
galactic gods who thought Solo had had it too easy
lately.

There was nothing on the targeting screen.

Another laser bolt hit them and the readout showed a
thin patch the size of a sabacc table in the port underside
shield.

Solo cursed and hit the recalibrate switch. At the same
moment Lando's voice yelled in his earjack, "You see
'em?"

Solo saw.

They were like microscopic dust on the monitor—

Blast it, those things couldn't be more than a couple of meters long! Each was about the bulk of a laser cannon, barely large enough to accommodate a pilot. . . . *How the blazes did they get them out here? Where was their command base?*

Another jarring impact, and the stars veered wildly as Lando evaded. Against the black of space he saw only a quick gleam through the turret ports. Whatever they were, they were painted matte black and bore no lights at all.

Blast it, they were everywhere! Solo got off a scattering of shots but it was like trying to hit gnats with a smashball club. At the same time his hands jammed the controls before him, ratcheting down to the lowest calibration, trying hard to get a look at the things. "Where are they coming from?" he shouted again into the comm.

"There's nothing on the scan!" yelled Lando's voice back. "No base, no ship . . ."

"Well, they sure couldn't come through hyperspace at that size! Blast it!" Another hit, and the thin patch in the shield was registering as a hole now. Han tried to get off another couple shots, but Lando was flipping and swerving the ship to cover the open shield. Han hoped those guys in the holds were still strapped in tight. Not that any of them was conscious enough to care.

"Drones?"

"You can't send a drone through hyperspace! And that's no drone shooting!"

The methane storms of Damonite fell away behind them, a glowing acid yellow disk against the blackness that whirled past the glassine ports as Lando dropped and cut and dodged. Han wasted another couple of shots and had a quick look at something as the *Falcon* swept through a little gaggle of the attacking ships.

Were they ships at all? thought Han. Did they *have* live pilots? He wasn't sure. They were maybe two and a half meters long and less than a meter through, fulgin cylinders bristling with the knobs of what looked like miniaturized laser cannon. What did they have in there, little guys the size of his thumb?

"Get us outa here!" he yelled, though he knew for a fact that was exactly what Lando was trying to do.

The tiny ships surrounded them like a cloud of piranha-beetles, whipping and following every move and quite effectively impeding any chance of breaking into hyperspace. Another red light went on, meaning another shield had gone. There was a perceptible jar, and from the gun turret Han saw the white flicker of lightning spread across the whole surface of the *Falcon* below and around him as the shields tried to compensate. At the same moment Lando yelled in his earjack, "They're not going for the decoy transmissions, so they can't be drones!"

"I'm gonna clear us a path!" Han yelled back, as a blast of white at the corner of his eye told him the miniature ships had taken out some part of the *Falcon*'s upper structures. "Straight through seven by six bearing zero, punch it on three!"

"Han, old buddy, what . . . ?"

"Do it!" At the same moment he hit every fore cannon he had, straight columns of white destruction flowing out in an almost continuous burst at seven by six. Like a pittin chasing its shadow, the *Falcon* followed the path of the light, faster and faster, Han watching the slow-growing flare of destruction ahead of them and calculating by feel rather than by instrumentation when the last possible moment would be to jump without hurling themselves into their own fire. The little bronze toothpick ships came pouring back in the wake of the blast, firing at the now-steady target following the heels of the light.

He counted, "One . . . two . . ." *(This had better work . . .)* The last of the shields went in a flare of white, and red glare bathed Han's face from the sides, white from the front as the *Falcon* dove toward the laser ruin ahead . . .

"Three!"

Lando hit it—he had reflexes like a tingball set—and the stars stretched into lines of white.

10

"I never thanked you." Leia stepped through the tall arch that led from her small terrace into the shadowy chamber. Liegeus, who had come in with a synthdroid bearing food and another pitcher of water, paused in the act of setting them down, shook his head.

"Don't," he said, and the pain in his voice, the shame, told her a thousand things that he hadn't meant. Their eyes met for a time. Then he said to the synthdroid, "You may go."

The door swished shut behind it. Leia could see the dark patch of necrosis on the back of its neck, and smell the faint stink of rot in its wake. She didn't know how to ask what she wanted to know without raising suspicions, so she only said, "Why are you here? How did you come here? Beldorion called you a philosopher."

"And I am," sighed Liegeus. He made a move as if he would fuss with the water pitcher, the covered dish of aromatic and exquisitely cooked insect life, but let his hand fall to his side again. He faced her. "A wanderer. A blot on the familial escutcheon. They don't speak my name. Alas, it has also been my misfortune to be a competent designer of artificial intelligence systems for space-craft, and a very, very good holo faker."

"A holo faker?"

"Of course, my dear. It was my art, my hobby—the source of my joy and the material for a thousand silly pranks in my youth. The bane of my existence, now: Beldorion has drafted me into editing and retaping his formidable library of Huttese pornography. Even my stint on Gamorr, ghost-writing love poems for the boars to pass off as their own when they go courting in the win-tertime, wasn't so fearful."

Leia laughed, like sudden summer breaking the ice lock of her fears, and Liegeus laughed, too. For a mo-ment she thought he might have reached out and taken her hand, but he drew back at the last moment, saying instead, "Is there something you'd like me to make for you? I have digitalized holo scrap of every imaginable background, face, animal, and bit of furniture that's ever been recorded: motions, sounds, the slightest variations of movement. You would not know that you weren't there. I can give you the hatching of the glimmerfish by starlight, in the lake of Aldera below the palace where you were raised, or the Starboys in their heyday . . . or your husband," he added diffidently. "I have scrap of him, you know. And your children."

It gave Leia a queer pang to hear him say so, but she knew that Han was a public figure, the children were public figures and had been holo-taped tens of thousands of times. Liegeus's dark eyes were like those of a dog who fears to be kicked—he was afraid, she realized, that he'd offended her, and she reached out reassuringly and touched his hand. "No," she said. "Thank you, no. It would hurt too much, I think."

He opened his mouth to give her a reassuring lie, as he had before when he'd brought her water, but closed it instead, the lie unsaid. Their eyes met again, she in the light and he in shadow. He began to say something else and lost his nerve, and before he could find it again the door opened and the synthdroid returned.

"Master Vorn, Master Ashgad wishes to speak with you on the terrace."

Leia followed him inside the chamber, and to the door, and was careful, when he took his departure, not to let herself be seen as she crept back to the railing of the balcony, where she could hear every word said on the terrace below.

"I trust everything is proceeding on schedule?" came Ashgad's voice.

"It is, sir. I can begin bringing the core up the day after tomorrow; I'm feeding in escape trajectories to establish an exit program now."

"Try to set the work forward as much as you can, Liegeus," said Ashgad. "The longer we delay, the more possibilities exist for something going wrong. We're bringing in boxes tonight, both kinds. See they're properly stored."

Liegeus's voice was almost inaudible. "Yes, sir."

"It will be up to you for the next three days," Ashgad went on. "I'm leaving in the morning for Hweg Shul, to start things in motion there. I should be gone . . ."

"Leaving?" Liegeus sounded aghast.

"Oh, things will be all right." Ashgad spoke rather quickly, like a man who hopes things will be all right. In the five days Leia had been under his roof she had neither seen nor spoken to the man; he evidently did not like being brought face-to-face with the victims of his crimes. "Beldorion will be in charge, but you're not to permit him to come near Her Excellency. I heard about that little incident yesterday, and I've had words with him. He knows it's not to be repeated."

"But will he honor his word?" asked Liegeus, clearly alarmed. "If he tried yesterday to gain control over her, he may . . ."

"He'll do what he's told," snapped Ashgad. "As will Dzym."

"No," said Liegeus softly. "He won't. And Dzym won't."

"You worry too much," said Ashgad, too loudly and too swiftly. "I'll be back in three days."

"But—"

"I said, don't worry about it!"

Leia heard his footfalls retreat and felt through her knees on the terrace's tiles the heavy *whoosh* of a closing door. She sat back against the railing, feeling curiously sick with dread.

Ashgad was leaving. She would be alone in this house with Beldorion. And with Dzym.

"You find your friend?"

Luke raised his head quickly from the valves he was cleaning—in a dust-heavy atmosphere like Nam Chorios's, engines needed almost constant regrinding and refitting—as the doorway of Croig's Fix-It Barn darkened, and he grinned a greeting at Umolly Darm. The prospector had the grimy look of one just into town from the wastelands, her baggy trousers and thick, padded jacket pregnant with dust. Beyond her, in the street, Luke saw her heavy X-3 Skid piled high with a load of boxes, crystals glimmering like great heaps of broken blue-and-violet glass in the thin sun.

"Not yet," he said. He wasn't terribly surprised to see Darm. Arvid had told him when he'd recommended him for the job as mechanic at Croig's that it was the biggest repair shop in Hweg Shul, which meant on the planet.

And it was big, for Hweg Shul, meaning it housed about thirty repair bays that refitted anything from pumps to speeders to small household appliances for little more than the cost of a cheap lunch for his workers. Like every other Newcomer building it sat on stilts—the T-47 being worked on in the next bay had shorted all its coils from being too close to the ground during the recent storm. Croig was a Durosian, and Luke was positive he had connections to half the smugglers in the sector.

"What can I do for you?" He set aside the valves and crossed the dirty, oil-streaked floor. Unshaven and clad in the local mix of homespun and blerd-leather, after three days in Hweg Shul, Luke had so completely blended with the scenery that even Taselda's tame fanatics would not have noticed him in the street.

Darm handed him a banthine sonic drill. "Ruptured core sheath," she said. "I don't know whether you can do anything with it or not. And I wanted to ask your boss if I could bring in the skid after I unload it—again. We're sending a shipment up tonight, or trying to. Loronar's got a pick-up cruiser in high orbit."

"Loronar?" asked Luke, suddenly curious. "You sell the crystals to Loronar Corporation?" The way Arvid had spoken, he'd gotten the impression of a small-time operation—Darm digging around in the desert for crystals to make some kind of obscure optical or medical equipment, useful only to high-level boffins at the university research labs. Loronar was anything but small time.

"Sure." Darm dug in the pocket of her sand-scored red vest and fished forth a hunk of crystal the length and width of two of Luke's fingers, and perhaps twice the depth. "Smokies we call them, or Spooks. This one's a little small for what they want, and they look for better color than this—see how pale it is?—but they'll buy as many as we can ship. Watch this. Hold it up to the light?"

Luke nodded.

"See the shadows in it? Those gray lines? Now watch." She carried it across the bay floor to where the heavy coils of the recharger—smuggled in piecemeal and Croig's pride and joy—crouched like a greasy metal monster in the corner, the center of an organic-looking nest of cable and tube. Gingerly—the recharger had been set up in a corner of the room to protect it from sand, and because it was in the dark, it was always crawling with drochs—Darm pulled out a recharger block, set the terminals against the crystal, and thumbed the switch.

Luke flinched, appalled and disoriented, though Darm didn't appear to feel anything: The disturbance in the Force axed his brain like a scream. The woman regarded him in surprise as he fell back a step, trembling. "What is it?"

"You didn't feel that?" His mind was still ringing with it, though it had ended in a split second, even before she turned off the switch. Sweat stood out on his face and he felt vaguely sick.

She shook her head, clearly puzzled. "You okay, Owen? What happened?"

Luke hesitated. It was impossible to explain matters of the Force to those unaware of its existence and, given Taselda's attempt to control him—and Officer Snaplaunce's account of her attempt to kidnap Callista—in the town he was very careful to whom he spoke. "It's nothing."

He took the crystal from Darm's hand, and held it to the nearest window once more. The threadlike gray striations in the Spook's heart had changed their orientation, forming two starlike blotches where the terminals had touched.

"If that Spook had had the proper color," said the prospector with rueful amusement, "I'd just have done myself out of a hundred credits. They can program them, realign the structure to act as a receiver." She flipped the pale arrowhead of quartz in her hand, then tossed it to Luke.

His hand jerked back, and the crystal fell to the floor and shattered into glittering slivers. "Sorry," he said. "I'm sorry . . ."

She kicked the fragments casually out of sight under the recharger. "Not to worry. Like I said, it wasn't anything they'd take, but even the tiny ones can be re-oriented like that with an ion zap." She frowned at him again, studying his face, which still, Luke feared, showed too much of the sickened shakiness he felt inside. "You sure you're okay?" She probably meant, thought Luke, that it wasn't like him to drop things—and after years of a Jedi's hair-trigger physical training it certainly wasn't.

Whatever their other properties, the Spook crystals somehow seemed to be foci or triggers for the Force.

"Yeah," said Luke, and rubbed his temples, trying to gather his wits. "Yeah, I'm fine." No wonder the planet reverberated with the Force. Could they be used to . . . ?

"There's a meeting tonight," went on Darm, her voice breaking into the half-formed train of thought. "Seti Ashgad's back. Turns out he met with some bigwig in the Republic, how do you like that? We're all going to his place tonight—you know it? That big old joint that used to belong to some Hutt who ran things around here way long ago. Pretty fancy, but it must get fairly exciting during ground lightning. If you wanted to go I could get you in, introduce you around. People will be there from as far away as Outer Distance. If your friend's still in settled territory at all, someone will have seen her."

"Thanks," said Luke, his sense of confusion, of despair, returning at the mention of her presence on this world.

He'd walked past Taselda's house two or three times in the past twenty-four hours, carefully—had walked past Ashgad's, too. At least this would be a way in without rousing the suspicions of the too-intelligent Officer Grupp. "I'd like that."

Darm waved his thanks away, with the easy friendliness of communities where humans—or at least humans of a certain persuasion—feel that they have to stick together. "We'll find her for you," she said. "Sooner or later, somebody'll know. Tonight at twenty hours, then. I'll come by here at quarter of. Arvid and Gin'll probably be there as well."

Luke nodded. After Umolly Darm had left he knelt and touched the broken fragments of crystal with his fingertips, trying to recapture—trying to understand— what it was exactly that he'd felt. But they were only bits of silicon, like the rubbish heaped in all the corners beneath the repair shop's stilts.

So Taselda's enemy—whose house had been taken over by Seti Ashgad—had been a Hutt.

An evil Jedi? wondered Luke. Or was that just another of her lies? A "crime boss," Grupp had called him, but that could be only a layman's description of something he did not understand.

Could Hutts be born, imbued with the Force?

There was a time when someone would have asked that about the Khomm people as well, until Luke's pupil Dorsk 81 had made his appearance on Yavin Four.

Had Taselda tried to get Callista to break in and search for her lightsaber?

Ashgad's palace itself, though typical of Hutt dwellings in its burrowlike arrangement of rooms leading out of rooms, round doors, and feeding niches in every available wall, had been in human ownership long enough to have had windows put into it and been cleansed many times. As Luke, Arvid, and Aunt Gin struggled against the millrace of the evening wind, Luke fingered Taselda's sketch map in his pocket.

"You know anything about the meeting, Grupp?" asked Arvid, as the paunchy cop fell into step beside them. Grupp shook his head.

"Far as I can tell nobody did. I did sort of wonder where he's been these past few months." Howling out of the fast-falling darkness, the wind thrust them this way and that, making it almost impossible to speak. "Snaplaunce and I have been keeping an eye out here and most times there's been nobody."

Luke didn't think it likely that a prisoner—especially one who'd already attracted the man's notice—could be kept here undetected. Nevertheless, when they entered the house, he took the occasion to slip away from the others and make his way to the old kitchen courtyard.

Though sheltered by its high walls from the wind, the place gave him the willies for reasons he couldn't quite define. On one side, wide transparisteel showed him a long room embellished with what he vaguely recognized as state-of-the-art culinary esoterica: Four types of electronic stoves; freeze and slow dryers; dehydrators and rehydrators; bowls and measures and work surfaces of every conceivable size and material; bottles, boxes, and sacks on shelves that reached to the ceiling. A glutton's heaven, but little more.

Across the court the corresponding chamber was shuttered close. Opening its door, Luke had a dim vision of glass-enclosed vats of every size, tanks of oxygen and methane, feeder-tubes, shunts, and apparatus to which Luke could put no name. He couldn't imagine the pur-

pose of such a display, but the whole long room reso-
nated with ugliness and evil.

But there was no sign of Callista, no sign of any prisoner. The doorway to the treasure vaults that Taselda
had described stood shut behind an iron grille, grille and
door both covered with a thick blanket of podhoy of
clearly many years' growth. He reached out with his
mind, calling Callista's name, searching for some trace of
her in this place. But whether because of her loss of
ability to use the Force or because of the strange, thick
presence of the Force in the ether of the planet or simply
because she was not and had never been there, he felt
nothing.

A tall, androgynous individual whom Luke recognized
as one of Ashgad's synthdroids—either a member of the
party who'd escorted him aboard the *Borealis* or an identical creation—appeared behind him and inquired politely,
"May I help you?"

Luke meekly allowed himself to be herded back to the
others in what had clearly been the house's banqueting
chamber in earlier times, the biggest room in any Hutt's
dwelling. It was now filled with men and women, some
of whom Luke recognized from the abortive attack on
the gun station. Others he knew by sight from his brief
tenure at Croig's Fix-It Barn. Their clothing marked
them all as Newcomers, following standard cut and fashion in the Core worlds even if they could no longer
acquire the usual materials, and there was more diversity
in complexion than he'd seen in the limited Oldtimers
gene pool.

Croig was there, grayish, orange-eyed, and glum,
keeping close to his brother (or sister—the Durosian
word was the same) and the two or three other aliens of
Hweg Shul: the Arcona who operated one of the majie-
processing plants and a couple of Sullustans who owned

the biggest branswed towers in the district. Luke noticed that all were vaguely ostracized by most of the Newcomer humans. He'd encountered this a number of times at the shop, this unspoken prejudice against the nonhuman species of the Core worlds. Stupid, when you thought of their technologies. But then the prejudices of the Empire *had* been stupid and had, in fact, brought about its downfall.

More synthdroids guarded the door. He doubted that most of the people in the room realized that the guards weren't alive or human. They were realistic to the smallest degree, though the hair was a giveaway—perfect, human, but with the oddly dead look that replants frequently had—and the smell. Everyone in the room smelled: of sweat, of beer, of coffeine; of the salt of work and life. Synthflesh, until it grows into organic matter as a patch, requires no nourishment and excretes no byproducts. Luke recalled an article he'd read about Loronar Corporation's efforts to make synthdroids that would be acceptable to scent-cued species like the Chadra-Fans and Wookiees. There were even humans who reacted badly to the deeply buried anomaly of something that looked like a human and smelled like nothing.

The conclusion of the article, as he recalled, was that the project was low on the Loronar priorities list. Chadra-Fans and Wookiees had little purchasing power and were considered an insufficient market to take the trouble over, even at a hundred thousand credits a throw.

"Arvid." Gerney Caslo jostled over to them through the crowd as people began to settle themselves on the edges of the low daises that were scattered around the room and on the compressed chairs set between. The whole place had been carpeted in a kind of dense industrial weave, which lent it an odd hybrid look. What had been food niches were now filled with the sort of cheap knock-off artwork available to the wealthy on thinly settled worlds: bad holos of famous sculpture, sometimes edited to substitute the faces of the new owner and his or her family, or cheap little sixteen-color-lights displays that ran through their cycles in a minute and a half. Luke had seen some beautiful sand-glazed Oldtimer pottery, and wondered that neither Seti Ashgad nor his father, after all those years on the planet, had thought to include it in the house.

Had the elder Ashgad so much resented this world that he'd have none of its works? But surely the son, who had been born there, or at least raised there—he didn't look more than forty—wouldn't share the prejudice to the same degree? Or was Ashgad's other house, his dwelling in the Mountains of Lightning, more his than his father's?

"We're looking for a couple of boys for a job," Caslo went on, speaking from the corner of his mouth like a bad guy in a holovid. "There's a drop coming in tomorrow night."

"Where?"

"Ten Cousins."

Luke had heard Croig speak of the place. The Cousins in question were *tsils,* the crystal chimneys standing in a ring instead of a line, markers of some unknown geological process. A smuggler's dream, a formation easily identified on a scan but small enough to search in a night.

"Can you use Owen here, too?" Arvid nodded to Luke. "He's working for Croig. He could use the cash."

Booldrum Caslo, a thickset, smooth-faced little man with heavy sight-amplification equipment bolted into his head, grinned, "Anyone who works for Croig could use cash."

Caslo studied Luke for a moment, then nodded. "We

can use as many as we can. I hear it's a good-size cargo. You got that speeder of yours running yet?"

Luke nodded, though *running* was a matter of interpretation.

"You'll work pickup, then," said Caslo. Arvid sniffed as the older man walked away.

"Doesn't trust you as a perimeter guard."

"Hunh?"

"To keep the Therans away," explained Gin, coming over and perching on the edge of the dais where they sat. "Oh, the Listeners sometimes get word of drops and try to stop them, but mostly I think it's just keeping tabs on whatever's going on. Mostly they seem to concentrate on . . ."

The lights dimmed, save for a single one on the main dais, set unobtrusively in what had been an olympian feeding niche. A curtain at the back of the room parted, and Seti Ashgad stepped through.

Do not trust him, Callista had said. *Do not meet with him, or accede to any demand he makes.*

Why?

It was the first time Luke had seen the man face-to-face, though on the *Borealis* he'd glimpsed him and his escort in passing. He had not been born when Ashgad's father had been exiled by the Emperor Palpatine, but his teenage interest in the Rebellion had made him familiar with the older politician's easygoing charm and chameleon promises from holos. The old man must be in his eighties now, thought Luke, watching the son mount the dais and exchange jokes and pleasantries with those in the audience who knew him best.

He hadn't heard Croig or anyone at the Blue Blerd of Happiness speak of the older man at all. Yet he'd defeated the (possibly Jedi) Hutt, taken over his power and his house. So he must have been a remarkable man. Was he dead, or just retired to the house in the Mountains of Lightning?

"Now, now, we can't have any of that," Ashgad was saying, to a raucous suggestion that Republic troops would soon be on hand to "settle for" the Therans. Good-natured sarcasm dripped from his deep voice. "They're the *majority*, after all, you know. It's *their* planet."

"It's our planet, too!" yelled Gerney Caslo, springing to his feet. "We bust our backs putting plants on this motherless rock. Don't that count?"

"Does it?" Ashgad swept the crowd with a green eye suddenly cold and angry. "I thought so. I was optimistic enough to assure you I could do something about that. It appears that I was wrong."

Silence fell, but Luke felt anger pass like ground lightning through the crowd.

"As you know," said the politician, now suddenly the focus of the entire quiet room, "I had high hopes. Through connections I was able to obtain a meeting, not with some politician, not with some bureaucrat, not with some committee member, but with Leia Organa Solo herself—not," he added bitterly, "that she was at all enthusiastic about coming, as she made clear to me from the outset."

They'd called the senior Ashgad the Golden Tempter. Luke knew, listening to his son, what he must have sounded like. Ashgad used his voice like a master artist used a light organ, evoking nuance, shade, twilight, and brilliance with the slightest shifts of tone and volume.

"I apologize," went on Ashgad, "for my enthusiasm and for my folly. I owe you all that apology, for raising hopes not destined to be fulfilled." He gestured, and another man—at this distance Luke couldn't tell whether it was a synthdroid or not, though there was something suspiciously smooth about the way he moved—slipped through the curtain and set up a holo player in the niche.

"Perhaps I should let Her Excellency tell you in her own words."

The light in the chamber dimmed still further. The holo of Leia was of crystal-clear quality, appearing almost solid in the near darkness, as if she were bathed in radiance from an unseen source. The scale was perfect—lifesize, so that she truly seemed to be in the room, hands folded on her knees, the heavy folds of her robe of state spread around her. The Noghri bodyguards squatted on their hunkers, nearly a dozen strong, like shadows behind her. Her chin was up, and she spoke with a cold precision Luke had only heard her use when she was truly angry.

"I'm afraid that any help from the Republic is out of the question, Master Ashgad," she said. "The Republic cannot afford to be seen to support a minority—*any* minority—by prospective planetary councils still undecided about joining. Too much trade depends on our maintenance of the status quo and too many people see the efforts of the Rationalists on your planet as disruptive, unruly, and criminal."

A buzz stirred the crowd. Beside Luke, Gerney Caslo mutttered, "Criminal—I'll show you criminal, honey!"

"Criminal to make an honest living pumping water . . ."

"What's disruptive about wanting medicine for my son . . . ?"

Leia's image went on, "I understand your problems, Master Ashgad. But the Republic must look at the larger picture. And, quite frankly, the discontent of a handful of settlers on a world that isn't even a member of the Republic is not worth the two billion credits it would cost—not to mention the damage done to the Republic's image—should we intervene in your quarrel."

Her last words were drowned in a rising roar. Someone yelled, "Festering hag witch, what in blazes does she know?" and Luke was on his feet, his whole body aflame with rage, not at the man who had shouted insults at his sister but at the man who stood on the dais, just visible beside the glimmering holo, his head bowed in pious resignation and regret.

Luke yelled, *"Liar!"* but his voice was drowned in other outcries, and before he could draw breath for another shout he realized that to protest that the holo was faked would only reveal his own identity and make it impossible for him to locate Callista. The holo was as much a fake as the cheap sculptures in the niches, holographically altered to resemble family members. For one thing, even before Leia had eliminated the bodyguards, she had *never* appeared in public with the Noghri. When "Leia" rose from her chair Luke was sure of it: the chair itself was nothing like those in the *Borealis*'s conference room or indeed anywhere on the executive flagship at all. The crimson robe was one she'd worn on a dozen state occasions over the past few years, easily copied. Luke had never seen it done this effectively, but presumably a really good slicer could get a holo of Leia's face and alter the movement of the lips to mesh with any voder-modified script.

But all this, he realized, was something he'd learned over the course of years with the Rebellion, years of dealing with the sophisticated technologies and scientific neepery available on Coruscant and its inner worlds. As a kid on Tatooine—and had he grown to adulthood there, as Uncle Owen and Uncle Owen's friends had—he'd had no more suspicion that truth could be skillfully edited than he'd had the ability to fly.

They believed what they saw.

They believed Seti Ashgad.

And they were furious.

Ashgad was up on the dais artfully giving the impression that he was mollifying the crowd without in any way lessening their outrage. Luke slipped past the synthdroids by the door, crossed through the smaller chamber beyond, his boots making no sound in the carpet, too angry to remain. He was aware of the synthdroids watching him—their Central Control Unit, wherever it was, was undoubtedly programmed with the faces of every Rationalist on the planet. But no one stopped him. He stepped through a pair of long windows to the outside, breathing hard with fury, and made his way through the thickets of blueleaf and aromatic shrubs to the street. The wind had died to a dull hammering with the coming of full darkness. The voices in the dining hall still echoed in his ears, yelling vituperation at his sister.

Beyond the edges of the settlements, the *tsils* glistened like spikes of ice in the cold-eyed starlight of the wastes. The ground was lustrous with frost, and the cold was like iron. He felt the Force all around him, breathing—waiting.

There were people out there in the waste, not far away. Though they bore no lights he sensed them dimly: eddies, stirrings in the Force. Therans?

Probably. Watching Seti Ashgad's house.

Release your anger, his father had said. Release your anger.

He had meant it then as a lure, a come-on—use your anger in combat—a fool's trick.

But now Luke truly released his anger, let go of it: let it rise like steam, to be absorbed and defused by the stars.

There was entirely too much anger afoot that night anyway, deliberately being stirred up, raised like a magician raising power back in that house. Rid of it, Luke was able to think clearly again, to ask questions. And the chief question was: What does Seti Ashgad stand to gain?

11

Under pouring rain, the port of Bagsho on Nim Drovis
crawled with troops.

Han had alerted the Med Center from orbit that he
had fifteen critical cases of radiation sickness on board.
Ism Oolos, the Ho'Din physician he'd talked to over subspace, awaited him in the docking bay with an emergency
team, surrounded by a squad of uniformed Drovians who
seized Han's arms the minute he came down the *Falcon*'s
ramp, shoved him up against the nearest wall, and
searched him none too gently.

"Is this really necessary?" demanded Dr. Oolos indignantly; Han also expressed himself to the head of the
Drovian squad along the same lines but with considerably
greater emphasis.

"Doc, if you'd seen some of the armaments coming in
for the Gopso'o tribes, you wouldn't be asking that." The
Drovian sergeant pulled out its esophageal plug to make
the remark, and shoved it back in with a *squish*. Since the
onset of high-tech civilization in the wake of Old Republic military bases, most Drovians—who had been a pas-
toral network of tribes when contacted—had acquired

the habit of sucking zwil—a cake-flavoring agent common to Algarine cuisine—through the mucous membranes of their breathing tubes via fist-size spongy plugs saturated with the stuff. Four-fifths of the soldiers wore plugs of various sizes and the air was thick with the dreamy, cinnamon-vanilla scent, where it wasn't heavy with the odors of wet vegetation, mildews inadvertently imported from every corner of the galaxy, and the oily smoke of burning.

"You must excuse us." Dr. Oolos ducked his bright-tentacled head as he accompanied Han, the sergeant, two troopers, and the med team back up the ramp. "The Gopso'o have been restless for months—ancestral enemies of the Drovians . . ." He lowered his soft voice and his twenty-five-meter height to speak without the sergeant hearing. "Not a particle of difference between them, you understand, except that they have been at blood feud for, literally, centuries. I have heard the original issue was whether the root word for *truth* is in the singular case or the plural, but so many atrocities were committed on both sides that, of course, it barely matters now. The Drovians were the ones who made interstellar contact first, so, of course, they're the dominant tribe, but . . ."

"They're killing each other over a festering grammatical construction?"

Han couldn't keep his voice down. Dr. Oolos winced and gestured him quiet, but it was too late. The Drovian sergeant grabbed Han's arm in a viselike pincer: "I'm killin' those moldspawns because they killed my family, see? Because they disemboweled Garnu Hral Eschen, because they tore the flesh off the bones of the children of Ethras, because they . . ."

"All right," said Han hastily, as the sergeant was dragging him closer and closer to the muzzle of its gun.

"Uh—Chewie . . ." He turned just in time to make it appear to the Wookiee, emerging from the door of the bridge, that he was in no actual danger and manufactured a cheerful grin. "Chewie, this is Sergeant . . ."

"Sergeant Knezex Hral Piksoar." The sergeant shoved its plug back into its breathing apparatus again; a little thread of greenish mucus squirted out around the side to join the glistening crust that caked the lower part of its face.

"It's necessary that they be permitted to search the ship," the Ho'Din informed them gently. "It's purely a formality. With local unrest as violent as it has been, and with forty deaths from the plague so far on the Republic base . . ."

"Forty?" Han stared up at the willowy form towering over him, aghast.

"I fear so. It's why I questioned you so closely before I was permitted to give you medical clearance to make planetfall. Authorities here have put the whole base under quarantine."

Hral Piksoar followed them into the first of the several storage holds Han had converted to emergency sick bays. It held its weapons trained in four directions while Dr. Oolos and his team passed swiftly from victim to victim, injecting antishock and stabilizers, transferring the suppurating, hairless, muttering forms to stasis boxes on antigrav tables. The other two troopers disappeared down the hallways to continue their search for illegal weaponry. Han felt the back of his neck prickle at this violation, but knew that a Donnybrook at this point would result in not only himself, Lando, and Chewie spending the night in the local chokey, but these fifteen survivors in all probability continuing for hours longer in their nightmare pain.

For himself, he'd have taken a poke at Hral Piksoar in

a heartbeat, the minute the goon laid a pincer on him. But he'd been through two parsecs of hyperspace hearing the feeble whispers of agony from the men and women hooked up to makeshift life support every time he walked down these corridors.

Maybe he was learning something from Leia, he thought, willing the flush of anger from his face.

"What's the story?" he asked softly, as the treelike physician ducked through into the next hold. "You tell me there's forty guys down with the plague on the base here; we get attacked by something I've never seen anywhere out there—a partisan revolt on Durren—somebody sure shot down these poor bastards . . ."

"Galactic Med Central is trying to contain the plague," said Dr. Oolos worriedly. "Trying hard." His head tendrils flexed uneasily, a hundred shades of crimson and scarlet ribbed and straked with violet; his dark eyes were filled with concern. "They bring them to us dying of no perceptible ailment—no virus, no bacteria, no poison, no allergy. Bacta-tank therapy only seems to accelerate the progress of the slow bleeding away of life."

He shook his head, and glanced across at Sergeant Hral Piksoar, who was peering paranoically around the corner and into the hall. "With Gopso'o raids on the suburbs— bombings of public buildings—they've seized one minor spaceport already—the atmosphere here has been terrible, unbelievable." He touched a gas mask hanging from his belt, and followed his team back into the corridor with the last of the victims, Han striding in his wake. "Take one of these with you if you plan to leave the vessel for any reason. The Gopso'o are rumored to be using bilal and rush gas in their attacks, though we haven't had any documented cases yet at the center."

"Think again if you think we're gonna leave this vessel." Lando Calrissian stepped through the door of the bridge as they passed it, dark face taut with anger but fear in his eyes. "My advice to you, old buddy, is to seal and lift."

"Not without finding out something about what's out there." Leaving Lando and Dr. Oolos in the corridor, Han ducked back onto the bridge and scooped up the five wafers onto which he'd downloaded the unfortunate *Corbantis*'s log. "Can you get me an unscrambler for this, Doc? I need to know what and who axed that ship and anything else they might have seen out there before it happened."

"I'll certainly try." Dr. Oolos held out his hand for the wafers—Han glanced at Sergeant Hral Piksoar, coming down the corridor toward them, and simply pocketed the information himself. Through the *Falcon*'s open boarding ramp the sound of shots could be clearly heard, the heavy, percussive cough of ion cannons almost drowning the harsher zap of blasters.

To Lando he whispered, "Don't take the engines all the way down and keep an eye on the lift-off window. I'll be back in two hours."

Lando followed them to the doorway. The med team made a little caravan across the rain-pocked permacrete of the bay, water sluicing off the mist-filled coffins of the stasis boxes. Drovian guards surrounded them, weapons at the ready, as if they expected the burned, pain-racked husks inside to leap out with guns blazing in the cause of the Gopso'o tribe. "And what if you're not?"

Han ducked his head against the rain, which was as warm as bathwater as he stepped out into it. "If I haven't linked with you by then," he said, feeling for the com-link in his pocket, "take off. Tell Chewie whatever you have to, to keep him from coming to look for me." By the sound of it the shots were closer, and a confusion of voices. The wet air was rank with smoke. "But find Leia. Whatever it costs."

Human beings were most odd.

Given the capabilities of a high-quality protocol unit to reproduce any given language, complete with its inflections and tonalities, See-Threepio could, of course, duplicate nearly any of the thirty thousand songs popular in the Core Worlds over the past seventy-five standard years verbatim, note by note and tone for tone. It was not a function he filled particularly often, for there were automatons and semianimates with larger speaker units and better bass range who could do the job more efficiently, but he could do it. Postulating that on a relatively backward world such as Nim Drovis those in quest of entertainment would pay a certain amount per song (with the appropriate royalty percentage figured for members of the Galactic Society of Recording Artists), he had calculated that even in such a moderate establishment as the Wookiee's Codpiece he and Artoo-Detoo should be able to earn enough in an evening to defray the costs of third-class passage to Cybloc XII.

But, as the assistant manager of that pink plush-lined cavern had phrased it, "You sound like a festerin' jizzbox. I *got* a festerin' jizz-box right over there in that corner."

And Threepio, even had his programming permitted him to argue with a human, would have been hard put to find grounds for disagreement. Before seeking another resort of public entertainment, therefore, he gave the matter some thought.

It was, as usual for Nim Drovis, pouring rain, and those citizens for whom consumption of liquid befuddlement took precedence over defending their homes and families, if any, from the street fighting in sporadic progress all over the city were scarcely a promising lot. The denizens of the Chug 'n' Chuck seemed to consist mostly of Drovian soldiers on three-hour furlough, professional mold-and-fungus removers—a hard-bitten lot with their flame and acid throwers slung over their backs, Drovian molds and fungi being what they were—a scattering of the small-time providers of goods and services prohibited at the more polite levels of society; and the joy-boys and lolly-girls associated with every species represented on the planet, together with their forbidding-looking business managers. Given their wholesale absorption of alcohol, sundry chemicals, and spice, Threepio did not hold high hopes for his and Artoo's success in this venue, either, but he was surprised.

Entertainment, he had long ago deduced, seemed (as far as he could judge) to be based on random mixtures of incongruous elements. Therefore, taking into account the words of the assistant manager of the Wookiee's Codpiece, he had acquired a concertinium, a set of violion twitch bells capable of activation through one of his chest jacks, and a drum for Artoo. Randomly digitalizing patterns of notes for every one of those thirty thousand songs popular in the Core Worlds over the past seventy-five years for reproduction on these three instruments and recalibrating his voice circuits to reproduce the tones of such luminaries as Framjan Spathen and Razzledy Croom, he was able to produce quite passable music, although Artoo, as a result of the switch boxes and *Pure Sabacc*'s computer circuits still taped and jacked and wired into him, was a little eccentric as far as the rhythm line was concerned. Threepio was quite proud of the result; and had his audience been sober, he was sure they would have appreciated just how good the entertainment was.

And indeed, the one individual in the Chug 'n' Chuck

not engaged either in boozing himself into insensibility or behaving toward the opposite sex in a manner usually reserved for one's honeymoon did applaud Threepio's rendition of Gayman Neeloid's "The Sound of Her Wings" and tossed a credit piece into the basket perched, hatlike, on Artoo's domed cap.

"Can you play Mondegrene's *Fuge in K*?" he asked, naming a classical piece of great antiquity and grandeur, which Threepio had only heard performed by full orchestra with thunder cannons and a dual-spectrum light organ.

It was one of Threepio's favorites, the mathematical complexity of it a source of endless delight to his logic circuits. He leaned a little over Artoo's bass percussion. "In its entirety?" he inquired hopefully.

His audience, a sturdy little Chadra-Fan whose silky golden fur could have been much improved by a session in one of the spaceport's grooming parlors had any been open, nodded enthusiastically. He signaled the bartender for a refill on his megavegiton ale. "Do you have it all in your programming?"

"Hey," grunted the bartender. "You ain't playin' none of that sithfesterin' classical chunder in here."

The Chadra-Fan turned indignantly on his seat, and waved an expansive little paw at the other five patrons of the bar. "You think they're going to care? All of you!" He raised his voice to a sharp tenor shout. Fifteen assorted eyes focused briefly on him, with a certain degree of effort. "I propose to buy from you all rights to the time and talents of these good musicians for the price of a drink apiece. Done?" He whipped a handful of credits from the sporran at his silken belt, slapped them down on the bar.

"Festerin' classical chunder," groused the barkeep, lumbering back to her ale taps but pocketing the credits.

The Chadra-Fan signaled Threepio with a peremptory wave of his paw and settled back in his chair, eyes shut, all his silk-fringed nostrils quivering. "Maestro, over-whelm me."

The swelling strains of Mondegrene's *Fuge* had the effect of emptying the bar of all customers still clearheaded enough to walk, but Threepio didn't care. Even on the concertinium and twitch bells—with Artoo's enthusiastic if inaccurate assistance on the drum—the *Fuge in K* was an intellectual masterpiece, like a closely reasoned philosophical argument, and the transposition to the unfamiliar instruments added, in an odd way, to Threepio's understanding and appreciation of the complex structure of the piece. The barkeep, with no customers to claim her attention, leaned back against the corner of the bar sucking plug after plug of zwil, listening to the wide-ranging variety with skepticism that, Threepio felt, was slowly turning into something else. Respect, perhaps. Appreciation of his capabilities. Maybe even a dawning enthusiasm for classical music.

Or maybe not. At the conclusion of the piece she crossed the room to them, hands tucked through the heavy leather of her belt, blue eyes sharp and calculating under their (to Threepio's mind) excessive maquillage of blue-and-gold paint and all the diamond rings through her snout twinkling in the bar's intestinal light. She looked down into the basket on Artoo's cap and said, "Ten creds. You boys ain't half bad."

"Why, thank you, Madame." Threepio removed the violion jack from his chest so the bells wouldn't jingle an accompaniment to his speech.

"Your boss going to be by here later? Maybe he and I could work out a deal of some kind."

"Oh, we don't have a boss, Madame. Our master is . . ."

"Now, don't confuse the poor lady, Threesie."

Threepio turned in complete astonishment as the Chadra-Fan—who had at the conclusion of the *Fuge in K* gone to the doorway to listen to such street noises as were audible above the steady patter of the rain and to sniff at the dark moving air of the coming night—came padding back.

"Igpek Droon—he's a buddy of mine on the Antemeridian route—he *hates* to have even his droids call him 'boss,' " the Chadra-Fan went on, looking up at the barkeep with his sharp little black-coal eyes. "Spent a pile reprogramming every droid on his ship to call him 'friend' and 'comrade.' He was raised by Agro-Militants— would you believe it?—and he says it's just sand in his gills to have anything subordinate to him. Has a terrible time whenever he gets a Gamorrean or a Griddek in his crew, spends the whole time arguing with them over what they're going to call him. I'll be heading back with these boys . . ." He slapped Threepio with one hand, Artoo with the other, with a familiarity the protocol droid found more than a little offensive, ". . . to Pekkie's ship, just to make sure they get there okay and don't get picked up."

"I beg your pardon," protested Threepio. "But do I . . . ?"

"Sure you remember the way," cut in the Chadra-Fan, and the next moment snapped at him in the meeping, flurrying speech of Chad's indigenous inhabitants, "Go along with me, you silly pile of tin! You want to end up playing sparkle-bop at this meat market for the next thirty-five years? She's trying to steal you!"

Threepio squeaked, "What?" in the tongue in which he had been addressed. "Steal us?"

The Chadra-Fan rolled his eyes, turned back to the barkeep, and said with a laugh, "Damn technical sticklers, these See-Three units. They'll give you an argument over which side of the street they're programmed to walk down. Let's go, uh——" He glanced quickly and unobtrusively at Artoo's serial numbers, "Let's go, Artie. Pekkie said you had to be back before full dark, and it's close to that now."

He put a furry little paw behind Threepio's golden elbow and tugged, and so disoriented was he that Threepio followed, trying hard to frame his objections to the deception. Artoo rolled obediently in their wake, leaving the barkeep squinting suspiciously after them, fingering her snout rings and twitching her ears.

"I'm terribly sorry," said Threepio, once they were in the rain-slick street. "I have reviewed all my files and I can find neither your name nor your likeness in any of my records."

"Yarbolk Yemm. Reporter for the *TriNebulon News*. Not that it'd be in any of your circuits, Threesie—where *is* your boss?"

"My counterpart and I are the property of . . . Artoo, what are you doing?" The little astromech swung sharply around in a ninety-degree turn, banging his golden counterpart with the drum that was still attached, like a mammoth mechanical pregnancy, to his leading surface. Artoo followed up the assault with a trilling obbligato of beeps, tweeps, and wibbles, to the effect that it would not be a particularly good idea to inform a reporter for *TriNebulon* of their mission, goals, or concerns.

And there was much, Threepio had to admit, in what he said.

"Our master is waiting for us on Cybloc XII," explained Threepio, after considerable thought that fortunately took place so quickly as to make the remark have the promptness of truth. "Through a shipping error my counterpart and I were dispatched to Nim Drovis instead, and we have been unable to get in touch with our master to arrange for our transport. It is vitally important that we rejoin our master with the utmost speed. Hence the regrettable exigency of acquiring sufficient funds by these means." He gestured to the concertinium, folded into a neat red lacquer box and hanging by its straps from his chest, and to Artoo's drum. They stood on one of the myriad little bridges that led from the Old Town to the New, the lightening rain flecking the brown water beneath them and trickling down the two droids' casings and the Chadra-Fan's black-wet silk tunic. Across the canal, rising commotion and the sound of shots grew louder, voices shouted orders, feet splashed through the puddles.

Yarbolk turned his head sharply, long ears twitching; then he looked back at the droids with speculation in his black little shoe-button eyes. "Cybloc XII, eh? There's been no word out of there in thirty hours, from everything I've heard. They sent out two cruisers to deal with the wildcat pirate fleet out of Budpock—the *Ithor Lady* and the *Empyrean.* Nobody's heard word of them, either. Now the talk all around the bars here is that somebody's supplying the Gopso'o with weapons, and promising them the guard stations on the roads are going to be down—and aren't they just, tonight? You boys be careful," he said, pulling up the wet silk hood over his head. "There are laws governing ownership of droids, but I've yet to see them enforced, anywhere, and anyway they're only as good as the last memory flush. There's any number of people in this town who'd welcome a windfall like a free See-Three unit and an astromech with nobody's name on them."

He fished in his sporran again, and brought out a red-burnished twenty-credit cylinder, which he dropped into the half-full basket of credits on top of Artoo's cap. "Buy your tickets in a human name—Igpek Droon really is a small-time trader, if you want to use his—and get yourselves out of here. Good luck. Thanks for the music."

There was another crescendo of mayhem, closer this time, and with it the bass roar of ion cannons. Yarbolk Yemm shifted to the front of his belt the small recording devices he wore, and scampered off across the bridge in the direction of the noise, a bright, wet little form of pink-and-blue silk and matted fur. A moment later combatants came pouring out of the narrow street visible some twenty meters farther down the canal, a knot of uniformed Drovians, a couple of humans, and a Ho'Din all defending themselves against a much larger contingent of differently uniformed Drovians, whose shaved crania bore long topknots in which random shapes of colored plastic and rubber had been braided—animal totems, Threepio's programming informed him, and a lively trade item from the larger interplanetary corporations seeking to purchase the bulk protein from the Gopso'o slug ranches.

"Good gracious!" exclaimed the protocol droid. "Artoo, that's Captain Solo!"

Heavily armed and aided by strategic betrayals of the outlying guard stations, the Gopso'o clansmen poured into the town. In the enclaves within Bagsho itself where the Gopso'o lived in low-paid, ill-educated obscurity, they emerged from their foul-water tenements with new weapons in their hands, shouting the names of their murdered ancestors and of the Twenty-Five Personifications of Virtue and firing on their oppressors and anyone they associated with their oppressors.

"Stinkin' scumtoes," growled Sergeant Hral Piksoar, voice nasal and bubbly around the zwil plug because its pincers were fully occupied with the ion cannon it was trying to site. "Well, you better be proud of your handi-work, Solo . . ."

"Me proud?" yelped Solo, and flattened behind the corner of an alley wall to return fire. "I never even *heard* of Nim Drovis until last week!" Down in this district the canals hadn't been disinfected for weeks. At the sound of voices and the trample of feet, the scummy, rain-pocked waters bulged and surged, and Han could see the molds beginning to emerge, glistening vilely in the dim reflection of streetlamps blocks away.

"Republic'll send us troops, they said. No need to have big standing armies. The festerin' Republic will help out if there's need. Well, we sent for troops, pal . . ."

"Captain Solo had nothing to do with the dispatch of emergency forces," put in Dr. Oolos severely. He leaned a long viridian arm around the corner and popped off four or five shots at almost complete random—Han guessed the physician had never had a weapon in his hands in his life—and ducked back under a storm of return fire. "There is a plague in the military bases of this sector . . ."

"All I know is your festerin' Republic said they'd be here, and they festerin' ain't." Hral Piksoar cursed as laser fire clipped the back of its rearmost tentacle. "And where have your patrols been that that kind of armament's gettin' through, hunh? Those maggot suckers got canister guns, fer the love a' Truth and Beauty!" It spit a yellowish stream of zwil.

"Lando!" Han thumbed the toggle on the comlink, keeping a worried eye on the molds creeping toward them in a slobbering orange line. "We're on our way back. The Gopso'o are overrunning this whole sector. Alert the port guards if they don't know already and tell 'em we're coming through. Have the *Falcon* ready for liftoff the minute we're on board."

"What the blue blazes is goin' on?" yelled Lando's distracted voice back. "We already know about the Gopso'o, old buddy, we just got done drivin' 'em off the docking pads. You better get here in the next ten minutes or there ain't gonna *be* liftoff."

Solo cursed, and fired a blast of hot plasma at the oncoming molds, which melted in an unbelievably foul-smelling sizzle under the blast itself and kept right on coming. At the head of the alley, Hral Piksoar and its fellow troopers were holding their own, though two were down, Dr. Oolos plastering in synthflesh and cauterizing arteries with grim speed. It would be fairly simple, thought Han, for himself or the long-legged Ho'Din to dash, jump, and spring through the mottled field of advancing molds—they moved in clumps, and an agile human could get through between them if he or she kept moving—leaving the bottom-heavy Drovians behind. By the same token, once they were through the molds and across the canal—there was a ramshackle plank bridge about ten meters farther down—the oncoming Gopso'o would be too slow and heavyset to pursue through the molds.

His eyes went immediately to the high walls that hemmed them in.

Since from time immemorial there had never been a day on Nim Drovis without torrential rain, the architecture of Bagsho was of a solid order, heavy stone walls broken by lines of the thick timbers that supported additional floors. Even in these shoddy tenement districts by the Thousand Stinking Ditches, this type of building prevailed, the residents using the round, projecting ends of the floor timbers as fastening points for balconies, plank gardens, and bird traps. Han tore the length of emergency cable from his belt, primed the stubby firing tube, and shot the cable hook upward, to lodge in a timber some five meters down the alley and nearly that distance above the mold-crawling pavement.

"Can you swing?" he yelled to Hral Piksoar, pointing to the low balcony above the canal bank beyond the advancing molds and close to the plank bridge.

The sergeant regarded the thin cable with extreme doubt—Drovians averaged twice the weight of moderately sized adult humans—but Han said, "It's tested at a thousand."

"What about my pals?" Hral Piksoar nodded back to the two downed troopers.

"Are you kidding, Sarge?" said the larger of the two, struggling to sit up. "Between the slime-festering Gopso'o and them molds, believe me, I'll try it. I got one good tentacle still."

At their weight, Drovians are not good acrobats, but by scrambling up a makeshift heap of boards, broken doors, and furniture looted from the ground floor of one of the buildings opening into the alleyway, they could get enough height to make the swing to a low balcony, and thence clamber down and across the plank bridge. There was no problem of them throwing back the weighted end of the cable to the next swinger—Drovian tentacles are like mechanical pistons and with that many different sensory devices on their bodies, their aim is exceptional. Han and Dr. Oolos went last, maintaining cover fire against the Gopso'o who maneuvered, crouching, everywhere on the street outside and on the balconies of the various tenements above street level. It would only be a matter of time, Han knew, before they made their way through the mazes of alleys and tenements to surround the retreating party; only a matter of time, he reflected dourly, before the masses of advancing molds grew too thick and too insistent to be driven back. Since their first run-in with the Gopso'o, every summons Hral

Piksoar had sent out for reinforcements had been met with, "We'll be there when we can." A polite euphemism, Han knew, for "You're on your own, pal."

Laser fire skinned the wall above him, tearing his face with burning chips of rock. He aimed for the muzzle flash but didn't know whether he scored. No body fell from the balcony where it had originated, but no return fire came, either. Behind him, Dr. Oolos yelled, "Solo!"

The last Drovian had swung to safety. The molds were thick over the street now, churning sluggishly, the whole enclosed seam of the alley rank with oozing digestive acids and with the smoke of charring where the Drovians were forcing them to keep their distance. "Can you make it?" yelled Solo. After the physician had volunteered to escort him back to the docking bay—Solo suspected out of a very real fear that the Drovian troops would abandon him in the event of an attack—he'd hate to see the Ho'Din miss his grip and have the flesh burned off his bones by carnivorous fungi.

Dr. Oolos fired off a last shot at the molds that were now only fractions of a meter from his and Solo's boots. He caught the end of the cable the waiting Drovians had flung to him, clambered up the pile of broken furnishings. "I can but try."

"This way!" insisted Threepio, pausing in the mouth of one of the warren of noisome, unpaved alleyways between the end of the bridge where they had parted from Yarbolk, and the spot where they had last seen Solo and his party duck around a corner. "I can hear the shooting!"

Artoo made no reply. He could have remarked that there was shooting all over the district now—the shrill, zapping whine of hand blasters, the unmistakable crunch of Caspel cannister shot, the vibrant roar of ion cannons and blaster rifles—but did not. He only set off determinedly across a small, muddy square.

"Artoo, don't be foolish!" cried the protocol droid, deeply distressed. "Oh, dear, I'm afraid those circuits we couldn't get out of you on the *Pure Sabacc* have disrupted your directional system! That alley won't take you anywhere *near* where we last saw Captain Solo!"

Nevertheless, he toddled in pursuit of the determined astromech, well aware that on his own he did not possess the information necessary to facilitate Her Excellency's rescue. It was his responsibility to deliver Artoo safe and sound to Captain Solo whether Artoo cooperated or not.

And to his great surprise, the next corner they rounded showed them Solo, the tall Ho'Din, and the Drovian troops, just pelting across a plank bridge while a much larger force of Gopso'o fired at them futilely from the other side of an alleyway choked with slobbering, aggressive orange and yellow fungi, like a knee-deep river of mucus between the confining alley walls.

Unfortunately, Artoo had led them out of the maze several meters too far up the alley, so that the Gopso'o, the molds, and the width of the canal lay between the two droids and the fleeing Drovians. Amid a welter of blaster fire Threepio called out, "Captain Solo! Captain Solo!" but such were the vocal volume modulations necessary for a protocol droid, his words did not carry over the razor-wire shriek of the blasters. Even as Threepio was trying to ascertain how to get through the Gopso'o and the molds—which though they could not digest the two droids they would certainly gum up their means of locomotion—Solo, who was in the rear, made it across the plank bridge and turned the cutting ray of his blaster on the jerry-built catwalk, exploding it in a dazzle of flame and dropping it into the canal.

Solo, the Ho'Din, and the Drovians disappeared at a run down the narrow street beyond.

What ensued reminded Threepio of nothing so much as an obstacle course of the sort invented by military computers to test the reflexes of humans and droids—such droids as were specially fitted for military usage, he reflected bitterly. Artoo, who seemed to know where he was going or to think he did, led the way around corners, across tiny squares where recent shell holes from grenades or cannister shot were rapidly filling with muddy rainwater, down narrow walkways above canals oozing with purulent, creeping life. And everywhere there was shooting, small bands of topknotted or nontopknotted natives of Nim Drovis firing at one another from doorways and balconies, groups of them looting burning stores and houses with the oily smoke thick in the air. Bodies lay in the street, soaked with rain and half-covered, some of them, with slowly feeding molds. In places the narrow streets were so torn up by blaster shot and grenades that the underlying dirt, soaked with the pouring gray rain, made an impassable soup of muck. In others, barricades had been erected of furniture, broken paving stones, and timbers, sometimes occupied by combatants of one side or the other locked in deadly blaster duels, sometimes festooned only with the dead.

"We have to find Captain Solo," nattered Threepio, catching his balance on the wall of a narrow through-passage where the flooded goo came up to his precisely articulated knees. "He will be here in search of Her Excellency, of course. The Council must know by this time that something has befallen her. Even without free communication, he'll be searching the sector."

Artoo, brown as if painted with a slurry of mud, tweeted in response.

"The docking bays!" cried Threepio. "Artoo! You're a genius! Of course that's where they'll be going!"

They reached the docking bays only moments after the advancing Gopso'o closed in around the spaceport facilities. Blaster fire splattered hot and vicious among the wide, sheltered permacrete pads. In places the Drovian troops had set up ion cannons, driving the Gopso'o back or holding them to the few pads they'd managed to take over. Artoo stolidly led the way along walls scorched by waves of smoking plasma, through baggage tunnels, and under temporary plastic shelters burning in clouds of stinking smoke.

Threepio cried, "There!" as they emerged into the sheltered cargo porch fronting the wide permacrete space of a bay, where the familiar shape of the *Millennium Falcon* crouched, entry ramp down, like a great gray-and-rust heap of junk in the streaming rain.

A spattering of blaster fire tore up the pavement before them. Two troops of natives—one the uniformed Drovian troopers, the other a band of Gopso'o—held the two entrances to the bay. Those under the same porch as Artoo and Threepio were, unfortunately, the Gopso'o, a ragged assemblage of ill-clad guerrilla fighters armed to the teeth with the finest of weaponry. The Drovians under the other porch, which lay at ninety degrees, were fewer in number, but Threepio could distinguish the red-and-violet headstalks of the Ho'Din who'd been with Solo, and, crouched behind a barricade, Captain Han Solo himself.

"Captain Solo!" cried Threepio. "It's us! Don't leave us!"

More laser fire drowned his well-modulated voice. Solo broke cover, dashed across the open pavement in a lightstorm of covering fire. The Gopso'o in the porch fell back—Threepio could not but observe that most of them were far inferior shots when compared with the Drovians—he said to Artoo, "Now!" and called out to the sergeant of the Drovians, "Let us through! We're friends!"

He called out—for better understanding—in Drovian, a language used chiefly by Gopso'o; the ruling Drovians tended to speak Basic, even to one another.

A storm of shot drove them back.

Han Solo made a long rolling dive and plunged up the boarding ramp. Someone within the ship was surely watching, for the ramp started to lift the moment the captain's body touched its end. It almost literally gulped him up, like a steel monster slurping up a treat. Threepio made a despairing try at stepping out into the bay and retreated hastily with a scorch mark across his stained and muddy chest perilously close to his power-supply jacks.

"Don't leave us!"

White fire poured from the *Millennium Falcon*'s vents.

Artoo let out a despairing wail.

The souped-up freighter tore a hole in the rain-black clouds and was gone.

12

Luke was still sufficiently furious the following evening to consider telling Gerney Caslo to pick up his own smuggler drop and take it to perdition in his pocket, but something Arvid said to him changed his mind. It was only a chance remark, when Luke met the young farmer the following day, to the effect that Caslo was Ashgad's business agent in Hweg Shul, but it caused Luke to think. Ashgad had clearly been doing everything he could to rouse the local Rationalists to fury. It didn't take many data to figure out that it was to Ashgad's benefit to have a private army ready to drive the Therans out of the gun stations and open the planet to trade. As the wealthiest man Luke had so far encountered, heir to the crime boss Beldorion, Ashgad would be in a position to act as middleman for the community once trade started coming in.

Only for a few years, true, thought Luke. Did he think he could control the place longer than that, once the gun stations weren't there to limit imports? Or did Ashgad just want to seize the gun stations for himself and keep the status quo for his own profit?

The planet itself was dirt poor. Its only export seemed

to be the rather friable Spooks, and having lived for several days on topatoes, smoor, and blerd exudum, Luke couldn't imagine anyone paying the shipping costs to acquire any of those delicacies. But having been raised there, Ashgad might very well desire only the power that he knew.

Was that logical? he wondered that evening, as he waited in the darkness of the Blue Blerd's yard. Ashgad had been raised on the planet, true, but he had been raised by a father who had dreamed of taking over control of the Senate himself. Had Palpatine not become Emperor, Seti Ashgad might very well have done so. Hardly the man to raise a son who sought only to rule what was almost literally a barren ball of rock.

Only minutes after the easing of the evening's torrential winds, he saw the line of speeders make the corner between the buildings in ghostly silence. Six of them, shadows only, running without lights above the machinery-cracked permacrete of the roadbed into the hangar yard. He recognized Arvid's lopsided Aratech with the crude balance-leg beneath it, and Umolly Darm's skip. Gerney Caslo was riding up beside the prospector, a small, black, vicious-looking blaster rifle cocked up against his thigh. A couple of volunteer guards rode cu-pas behind them, blaster rifles slung in the ready position, faces blacked and eyes glittering in the watery flicker of the stars.

"Fourth in line," whispered Gerney, and tossed Luke a small, flat can of the dark camouflage paint that hunters used to take the glint off their weapons. "Rendezvous at Ashgad's if we get split up. Overload the charges on anything you pick up, if it looks like the Therans are going to be able to take it away from you." Luke blacked his face, and touched up the crude pair of infrared goggles he'd been lent by Aunt Gin with the camo paint. A dozen or more riders met them among the topato towers, the rounded, chubby bipeds moving with surprising quiet. Luke noted that these guards, too, were extremely well armed.

Ashgad was putting out a lot of money to get himself in the position of leader of the ruling faction of the planet, he thought as they left the towers and slowly rising antigrav balls of newer cultivation, glided between the scrubby fields of brope and the algal meadows where blerds grazed like wrinkled lapis mountains. The smell of growing plants faded in his nostrils as the sterile prickle of the wastelands crept over his skin.

There was something he didn't know. Some piece of information he didn't have that would make sense of this.

The wastelands stretched out around them like a blanket of salt. The terrible velvet weight of the Force grew heavier on his mind.

Few on the planet seemed to be aware of the Force's presence here, thought Luke. No one at all seemed to realize that there was some kind of invisible life, some unseen civilization here, silent among the dazzling, wind-scoured canyons. Was Ashgad? Was that what he sought to control here?

Or like Taselda's enemy, did he seek to control the Force itself?

Ahead of them Luke saw the red-orange spark of laser cannon illuminate the spine of the hills. As if in answer another glinted, sixty degrees around the horizon. Before them, the loose ring of the crystalline Cousins pointed mutely at the stars.

Tiny, tiny in the hard black vault overhead a pinlight exploded, faded. Someone in one of the other speeders cursed the Therans, called them fools and fogeys, and worse things yet for their refusal to welcome outside influences to their world. Raised as he had been, Luke understood. Nobody he'd known as a boy and a teenager had ever considered the rights of the Jawa or the Sand people to the territory occupied by the human colonists of Tatooine, and every one of his adult acquaintances in those days would have been outraged had either indigenous species asserted its undoubted majority rights to determine policy for the planet as a whole.

Stop the import of farming equipment, metal, chips, just because nine-tenths of the population of the planet thought it was wrong for trade to come down out of the skies? Ridiculous! Why don't you just forbid us to use tools at all and be done with it?

He scratched at a droch bite, slowed his newly repaired speeder as a flicker far up in the sky signaled a red-hot meteorite in entry, a minute capsule of smuggled goods. The mounted guards scattered, minuscule yellow lights from their sensors and heat detectors briefly outlining their camouflaged faces, cu-pas silent, muzzled and booted in the dark. Caslo marked where the capsule came down, every driver triangulating on the ten icy pinnacles, and they raced for them over the vast flat, glittering dish of the plain.

Equipped with primitive retros, the capsule hadn't even buried itself in the twinkling gravel. A percussion rifle crackled somewhere far off, and Luke sensed the distant presence of more riders. He wondered, as Caslo scrambled down the side of the smoking impact crater a hundred meters from the nearest *tsil,* how Ashgad managed to pay for weapons for his followers. Had Palpatine left revenues in the hands of his rival? *When rocks dance.* But the weapons Ashgad was buying were all new or near new, the most modern, the most expensive that bore the Loronar double-moon logo. "All the finest—all the first." The man had money from somewhere.

Had Callista entered his house? Learned from Taselda, perhaps, where the money came from and where it was being sent? Was that why she'd fled Hweg Shul?

Men were handing crates up out of the pit, passing them to the drivers. A flurry of shots in the flat distance told Luke of approaching Therans, held off by the ragged perimeter of guards. Someone gave Luke a bale of blaster rifles, which he stowed in the back of his Theran speeder; a crudely tied together bunch of spare energy cores.

So they were getting at least some secondhand, thought Luke, turning the sleek black-and-red cylinders over in his hand before stashing them in a corner. Even at smuggler's prices, those would be cheaper than new, and Ashgad was clearly out to arm every man and woman of the Rationalist Party. They were passing rifles up singly now. He caught one thrown to him, held it briefly in the dim glow of the speeder's console lights to see the make. His mind went back to the gun station, to the embattled, dirty Therans ducking through the shadows of the crazy superstructure, the gawky, dancerlike figure in red swinging down on the cable to throw the grenade.

The gun was a white-and-silver BlasTech, this year's model, small, solid, and familiar in Luke's hands. He knew it well. They were the type of guns with which the entire Honor Guard of the New Republic had been newly outfitted only last month. He'd practiced with them, to while away time, on board the *Borealis.*

Luke turned it over, and his blood went cold in his veins.

On the butt was the silver coding plate of the Honor Guards, marking the weapon as the property of the New Republic, assigned to the flagship itself.

The gun had come off the *Borealis.*

"Yo, Lars!" somebody called from the ground. "Asleep at the switch?"

Luke stashed the weapon quickly, caught another handed up to him. He didn't need to hold this one to the console lights, his fingers found the coding plate by themselves. When he carried the next several guns to the back of his speeder he flicked on the glowrod to check the others.

There were a couple from the *Adamantine,* but most of these had come off Leia's flagship.

There was one—a Flash-4 with a custom grip and a lanyard ring—that he recognized as the one Han had given Leia herself.

I have to escape.

From the corner of her balcony that overlooked the dawn-colored crystal flatlands far below, Leia watched the luxurious black landspeeder that bore Seti Ashgad and his two bodyguards dwindle and perish with the distance. He had avoided her since the kidnapping—probably, she thought, because he knew himself unable to sustain the masquerade of being his own son before someone who had studied holos of him as she had—but she had always been conscious of his presence and protection. His plan, whatever it was, was clear in his mind, and at least for the moment he had to keep her alive.

But Dzym and Beldorion had plans of their own.

Three days. If she lasted that long.

For the first time in days, she had awakened with her mind clear. The water Liegeus had brought her last night had been clean. Whether that had been an oversight or some kind of gift to her, she knew she had to take advantage of it without delay.

On the threshold of her room she paused, blanket

wrapped around her over the thin white nightshirt she wore, long chestnut hair hanging in a braid down her back. Around her—around the high cinder-gray walls of Ashgad's fortress, the spiky, crystalline rocks of the plateau—the greater mountains towered, huge chunks and teeth and masses of crystal, like enormous jewels flashing in the eternal twilight, reminding her of just how steep a drop it was, to the glittering plain below.

Her heart twisted inside her with a sick terror, an awful almost-wish that they'd kept her under the soporific peace of the blossom.

Closing her eyes, she reached out with her mind and heart, formed the image of Luke. He'd come for her once before, when she was trapped in the Termination Block of the Death Star; when she was weak and sick after torture, numb with a grief that it was years before she'd actually feel. *I'm here to rescue you,* he'd said.

She would have smiled at the memory, had the fear in her not been so great.

In her mind she cried his name: *Luke!!!* sending it echoing, blazing out across the emptiness of air and crystal and early light. *Luke!!!*

He had to hear. He had to.

But in the still cold, the deep, heavy movement of the Force seemed to surround her, filling her with the alien sense of its presence. It was like the sound of the sea, drowning all other voices in its great voice.

Luke wouldn't hear. She was trapped there alone.

She shook the fear away almost at once, and with it the horrible recollection of the man Dzym's hands on her face, the dreadful, sinking coldness of death.

Luke wouldn't hear. He wouldn't come. She had to figure out what to do and what was going on.

They had released the Death Seed.

She returned to the shadowy bedchamber, sat on the

end of the bed where the sunlight fell on it, and drew her feet up under the blanket. She felt a droch bite her and scratched furiously, the insect dropping from the bedding into the dazzling carpet of mottled light. It curled itself into a tight brown-black pellet no bigger than a pinhead and died.

Blossom made you accept almost anything, she thought, revolted. Even lying down in bedding that you knew was alive with parasites. She was bitten all over from sitting in the dim chamber at tea with Beldorion the Splendid, too.

They had released the Death Seed. If they could control it, or thought they could control it, through Dzym, it was an easy guess what their negotiations with Moff Getelles and Admiral Larm were. *Curse them,* she thought. *Curse them!*

Dzym was somehow a key. He could lay it on them somehow—transmitted by the synthdroids?—and call it off, as he had called it off of her. She remembered the ecstasy on his face, and at other times, his air of paying attention to something else, listening to something else, like a man counting down time.

And yet, what was the point?

But did Moff Getelles really think that he was strong enough to take over the Meridian sector, once quarantine and containment procedures got under way? To hold it in the face of a concerted Republic effort to drive him out?

And for what purpose? Pedducis Chorios, that nest of smugglers and Warlords, would be impossible to control effectively. Durren's planetary coalition was solidly behind the Republic. Budpock had been one of the Rebellion's most loyal supporters. Nam Chorios was a waterless, lifeless, poverty-stricken rock.

To complete the Reliant, Ashgad had said.

But she'd seen the *Reliant*. It was not a planet-killing Dreadnought, but a midsize freighter. *Boxes . . . of both kinds.* What kind of payload could a midsize ship carry that would make this all worthwhile, even were the gun stations to be eliminated?

Leia shivered, and rubbed her wrists, where the memory of Dzym's cold hands remained.

The door chime sounded politely. Leia swung around, startled, drawing the comforter close around her and sliding her hand toward the lightsaber concealed among the pillows.

But it was only Liegeus, bowing shyly in the doorway, a porcelain pitcher of water in his hands. "I'm pleased you're feeling better, my dear." His eyes went—as Leia's had, automatically—to the empty pitcher beside the bed. She had drunk all the water the minute she'd realized it wasn't drugged.

By his gentle smile she saw that he knew.

"I couldn't bear to see you killing yourself like that, in this climate." He held out to her the glass goblet. "Ash-gad's never noticed any difference. I've brought you some holovids, too; imprisonment without them is only bearable if one is drugged."

Leia studied the man's face warily across the rim. "And what now?" she asked softly. "What happens to me while he's gone? Or was that why he left, so that it wouldn't be his fault?"

"No," said Liegeus quickly, "no, of course not. He isn't a bad man, my dear."

"He is the worst kind of man." Leia turned her face aside. The words, *Death Seed,* lay close to the tip of her tongue and she knew she must not say them, must not let even Liegeus know how much she knew. He might stand up to Beldorion for her sake, but she knew—she had seen—that he was unable to stand up to Dzym. And who could blame him for that?

He was like Greglik, she thought. She was fond of him, she pitied him, but she knew she could not trust him.

"No," insisted the holo faker. "Ashgad . . ." He hesitated. "I understand what's making him . . . do all of this. And it . . . I can't explain."

Her long dark braid whipped as she turned back to him, to meet the utter wretchedness of his gaze.

"I can't," he said. "But please, trust me." Sitting beside her on the divan, he fumbled in the pocket of his lab smock, brought out a black cylinder half again the length of his palm and perhaps twice the thickness of his thumb. "This is for you," he said. "I'll have to have it back just before he returns, you understand."

Leia turned it over in her hands. A comlink. Dedicated circuitry, at a guess—there wasn't a keypad. Probably made of standard components, though. And old, like everything else on this planet. The new ones were half that size and you needed micron tools to work on them.

"I've changed the combination on the door pad," Liegeus went on. He didn't quite glance back over his shoulder, but almost. "He shouldn't be able to get in here." He didn't say of whom they spoke—he didn't need to. "He has no computer skills, he can't . . . do that kind of thinking. Whatever he tells you, don't let him in. If he tries to come in, or if he does manage to, somehow, use the comlink. I'll only be moments away, in the . . ." He stopped himself—at a guess, from saying something that would reveal to her that there was a ship under construction on the premises. Why the secrecy about that? What part did it play in their plan? "In the other part of the house."

He made a move to turn away, and Leia caught his sleeve. "Who is he?" she asked. "What is he?"

The dark eyes looked quickly away, and she saw the too-sensitive mouth flinch. "He is . . . what he is. He's a native of this world . . ."

"There are no natives of this world." Leia felt his hand cold under the grip of her fingers. "Before the Grissmaths started shipping political prisoners here there was nothing but stones. What is it he wants to do with me? What is it he tried to do, that night? You said Beldorion sold him someone he had enslaved. For what purpose? And what became of him?"

"Nothing," said Liegeus quickly. She looked down and saw his hands were trembling. "I can't explain. It's . . . it's something few people would understand."

The fear in his eyes was terrible to see, and her heart went out to him in pity. She put her hand over the cold, slender fingers. "Try me," she urged.

Liegeus got quickly to his feet, and backed to the door. "I . . . ." Then he shook his head. "Beldorion may invite you to tea or to supper again," he said. "Don't go, or make sure that I go with you. Just remember to spend as much time as you can on the balcony, in the sunlight, and you'll be all right."

The door opened, and he stepped through. In the instant before it closed Leia met his eyes again, and saw in them longing, and grief, and a terror that had swallowed nearly everything within the man's soul. She said quietly, "Thank you," and the metal panel *swished* between them. A moment later the outer locks clicked.

After he had gone, Leia sat for a moment, gathering her breath and her courage. Then she got up, crossed to the dresser where she kept her gown, the pins and jewels that had been in her hair, the folded-up mass of the red velvet robe. Two of the flat-backed cabochon jewels from the robe's chest piece, picked loose, gave her enough purchase to bend the end of one of the hairpins into a makeshift manual screwdriver. It took her five minutes to open up the comlink, and recalibrate the beam.

Picking a simple keypad lock by means of a micron beam was an excruciatingly tedious process, but she had all day, and nothing else to do. Judging by the number of holovids he'd brought, Liegeus didn't expect to be free of his duties on the *Reliant* until evening.

Lock picking was one of those skills she'd acquired in her years with the Rebellion, one of the minor guerrilla survival skills pilots had taught one another, just in case, like making explosives out of certain brands of game tokens, or tinkering water filters from sand and flightsuit liners. Something simple that might just save your life. Winter—who'd taught her this particular trick, which she in turn had learned from an outlaw slicer on Coruscant—had said, "Be sure to write down every combination as you try it. Sure as little hawk-bat eggs, the minute you get bored and quit writing them down, you'll score, and then you won't remember what the combination was."

Leia wrote them down, laboriously, with another hairpin scratching in the soft buttonwood back of one of the drawers pulled from the chest. An hour and a half after noon, as far as she could judge from the angle of the sunlight, the lock opened.

With the sensation of having been unexpectedly knocked breathless she stepped back, closed the doors, let the lock click over again. She had to be sure it would open at need—that it hadn't been a fluke. If they caught her outside and she couldn't get back in, she would be incarcerated indeed.

It opened a second time. Leia slipped the converted comlink into her pocket, not without a qualm. But the likelihood of encountering Dzym was marginally less than the likelihood that she'd have to get back into this room on less notice than the ten minutes it would take to switch the beam over from comm to micron. She reached back to feel the comforting hardness of the lightsaber tied around her body beneath her shirt and stepped out into the hall.

13

Luke had said to her, over and over on those occasions on which she'd put aside the pressing demands of state to train with her brother's pupils, *The eyes are the most dangerous of the senses, because you'll believe them first.* Pausing at the foot of the stair, Leia shut her eyes, slowed her breath, and listened deeply to the house around her. Reached out with her mind, as Luke had taught her. Felt for the flow and movement of the Force.

It was everywhere, a singing vast as light. The ocean of light, Beldorion had said, utterly unlike anything she had experienced on Yavin, on Coruscant . . . anywhere that she had ever tried this. Strong and frightening, as if something huge stood just behind her shoulder, watching her with sad wisdom.

Is there a reason to fear this? she thought, holding her fear in check. A minute passed, two. Beneath that deep, humming strength, she was able to sort out true sound in the rooms around her.

Beldorion's thick voice came from his quarters close-by: "Beautiful, beautiful! All that, from just those unprepossessing little glet-mites!"

And the harsh, nasally whine of a Kubaz's inflection: "It's all in finding the correct solution, you see, Master." That would be the chef, she thought. The unworthy heir of the great and lamented Zubindi Ebsuk. "Under ordinary circumstances, of course, glet-mites would never have contact with a solution of *hall d'main* excretions—their worlds aren't even in the same Sector! But it so happens that the hormones contained within *halles d'main* are the exact physiological complement of the glet-mite teleological systems . . ."

And under it a *cheeping*, tiny voices protesting. Leia shivered.

Of Dzym she could hear nothing. Did he make sound, when he moved? Pressed to the harsh plaster of the wall, she ignored the sudden jab of a droch bite on her ankle, probed deeper with her mind. There was a kind of heavy vibration somewhere in the house, the steady whine, as of machinery. The house generator, of course. Liegeus had said Dzym wasn't capable of "that kind of thinking," to cut into the household computer and make it tell what the security keypad numbers were.

Leia wondered how good their security was.

Whether it was the smell of Hutt or revulsion over the drochs or just overwrought nerves, she was feeling light-headed by the time she found her way out of the dim, curtained quarters of the Hutt to a door into what was clearly Seti Ashgad's portion of the house, the long, sun-flooded chamber that looked out onto the terrace below her own balcony. Here the ceilings were higher, the heavy, heat-trapping curtains drawn back from the line of transparisteel panels that gave onto the terrace. There was an airy functionality about the place, with its immobile wood-and-leather chairs, its desk put together from planks of buttonwood, its simple sideboard. The monitor screen in the niche above the desk was new, Leia

saw, a high-definition Sorosuub X-80—they'd had to cut
the niche bigger for it, and so recently that the chipped-
out plaster hadn't yet had time to discolor. Leia paused
in the doorway to listen again—*If Dzym's mind doesn't work
in terms of computers, how did he get a job as secretary?*—then
crossed to the desk and brought out the board, keying in
quickly a request for systems shell. Once she knew the
type of system she pulled up data on the house itself.

Wiring diagrams showed her the shaft that led down
through the heart of the mesa, to the garage from which
she'd seen Ashgad's henchmen take that elegant—and
nearly new—black speeder at dawn. After a little puz-
zling she identified where she was and where the head of
the shaft lay on the other side of the house near the
docking bay and its compound of workshops and labs.

She ran a print, then called up another instruction
and asked for further data. The docking compound beyond those blast doors she'd seen was enormous. For a
world where equipment of any sort was scarce, there
seemed to be no shortage of it there.

A complete complement of the extremely expensive
equipment that charged the antigrav coils of speeder
buoyancy tanks. A major computer system hooked to an
independent generator and dedicated to hyperspace engineering. Liegeus's holo faking works: Good grief! Millions
of separate data clips, far beyond hobby or art. That, too,
had to have been part of their plan, and might explain
why in five days there'd been no attempt at rescue.

Another system centered in this very room—probably, thought Leia, behind the slatted cupboard doors to
her right. She got up, still reading down at the backup
systems screen: high-security locks with backup wiring
on various doors, including, she saw with a certain annoyance, that of the lift from this level down to the
garage.

She ran a zoom check on the schematic. No such backup existed on the lift shaft's repair stairway. Her calf muscles would ache, but she could do it. She keyed a further command to open the combinations on file. Yes, she'd gotten that of her chamber door correct—silly, but it gratified her to have her skill officially confirmed. It was listed as having been changed shortly after dawn that morning, probably the moment Seti Ashgad disappeared into the morning glow. She ran a print, folded the sheets of plast together, stuffed them into the pocket of her trousers, and went to investigate what was behind the slatted doors that rated a separate power backup.

It was a CCIR board. The central control unit for synthdroids—How many of the things did he *have*? Leia counted wiring for two dozen. *Two dozen?*

She tried to remember what she'd learned about synthdroids from her one tour of the Loronar Corporation facility on Carosi's larger moon. That had been during the Daysong uproar about the relative rights of synthflesh. Synthflesh, Leia recalled, was supposed to retain automatic immunities to virus and antibodies, but obviously they'd gotten around that one. She did remember the officials of Loronar telling her that CCIR technology operated on near-instantaneous transmission between a special variety of programmable-matrix crystals. Was that an intrinsic part of the plan, she wondered, or just a convenience?

Leia returned to the computer. Every second she remained in this room increased the likelihood of encountering Dzym, or Liegeus, or Beldorion, but this might be the only chance she had. It was hard to know what else she might need. She ran a compressed print of a Corewide scan on the names she had overheard: Dymurra. Getelles. *Reliant.* When it was over she copied the information to a wafer, shoved both the wafer and the formidable sheaf of flimsiplast into the thigh pockets of her trousers, and replaced the plast in the printer with fresh so that it would not be obvious that some two hundred sheets had been printed out. Heart beating hard enough to sicken her, she closed her eyes again, probing at the stillness of the house.

She heard nothing, but she wasn't sure if she was doing this right or not. If she'd had more training—if she'd concentrated more on it—could she have reached through this strange, heavy miasma of the Force to summon Luke?

That way lay despair, and she shook the thought away.

She studied her first printout of the wiring schematic again, identifying the lift shaft, the stairway that wound down its side. By overlaying the schematic of the backup systems, she could easily identify the room that contained both the CCIR terminal, and the main computer station: The room where she now stood.

Through that door. Down another flight of steps to a round reception area that contained nothing more important than an enormous light sculpture and a couple of artificial waterfalls. The lift doors opened there, as did the access hatch for the maintenance stairs.

She glanced over her shoulder at the wide transparisteel panels leading onto the terrace, aware of how secure the light made her feel, how safe. As she headed toward the reception area, the doors to the lift and the access stairs, she found herself hoping that the room would have transparisteel.

It didn't. It was dark, save for the flamboyant rainbows of the light sculpture, whose colored patterns twinkled and flashed in the murmuring waterfalls, half-seen in the gloom. It stank of drochs and Hutt, and Leia dared not touch what she thought were the glow panels, for fear of activating something that would reveal to others where she was. Picking her way between the pale mushroom shapes of cushioned furniture years unused, by the dim reflections of the light sculpture, she thought, *The stairs will be unlit.*

She pulled her shirt out of the waistband of her trousers, fumbled underneath to untie the lightsaber from around her body. The cold laser blade didn't give much light, but at least, she thought, it was better than groping downward in utter dark.

"True Jedi can see in the dark, *barúm,*" Beldorion had rumbled to her once a day or two ago, when he'd asked her to join him for lunch and a bask on the terrace—she no longer even remembered how the subject of Jedi powers had arisen. "They see not with their eyes—they see with their noses, with their ears, with the hairs of their head, and with their skins. You have neglected your training, little princess." He'd shaken a tiny bejeweled finger at her. "They used to have us run races in the Caves of Masposhani, miles below the ground. Used to drop us on the dark sun worlds of Af'El and Y'nybeth, where there is no spectrum of visible light. But the great Jedi, the Masters—Yoda and Thon and Nomi Sunrider— they could summon light, could make metal glow so that their puny little friends wouldn't stumble either. They'd hold a pin—so . . ." He'd reached one slimy hand to pluck a hairpin from her head, Leia flinching but too dazed with the drug to pull back.

The Hutt had held the pin between thumb and forefinger, vast ruby eyes looking past it into hers. And she saw, like a dream she'd dreamed and forgotten, a fragment of his memory, a man's thin face, bone-thin and horribly scarred within a great gray tousle of hair, holding a hairpin as the Hutt was holding hers, the metal curve of its upper end incandescent and shedding light enough to see the pillars and frescoes of the room in which he stood.

Leia had shivered, as the memory vision died: Shivered to think of all that ancient learning, all the techniques and knowledge that Luke had been so painstakingly trying to jigsaw together for years, sunk in the mucky well of the Hutt's indolent mind. All that unlimited power, put, not to evil use, as Vader and Palpatine had put it, but to the service of utter pettiness, even as he could think of enslaving her for no better purpose than to regain his rule over defenseless farmers or to beat an old rival who had no more actual power than he.

The lightsaber weighed heavy in her hand. *You must learn to use your powers,* Luke had said. *We need champions of the Force. There aren't so many of us that we can afford to choose.*

But every time she thumbed the toggle, every time the cold, clear sky-hued blade hummed to life, Leia saw only shadows: the shadow of Vader. The shadow of Palpatine. The shadows of her own anger, her own impatience, and the righteous certainties she had come to distrust. And now, the moldy shadows of Beldorion and the pettiness of greed.

The shadows of the future she feared, when Anakin, Jacen, Jaina—those three incalculable fragments of her body and her life—came to the age when they would choose either the light or the dark.

Still, at the moment she had no other option. She activated the blade, and pushed open the discreet access hatch that led into the service stairs.

Something she couldn't see clearly whipped out of sight down the first curve of the flight. The smell of drochs was choking. The dim glow of the lightsaber's blade showed her only the faintest of outlines a meter around her, the steep little wedge-shaped stairs—cut into the rock of the mesa itself—the descending curve of the ceiling close over her head. Right hand clutching the weapon's haft, left hand touching the centerpost of the stairs, she moved downward, the scald of adrenaline cold fever in her veins. She didn't know what she'd do if she reached the garage to find one of the synthdroid servants on guard there or if there were no landspeeders to steal. From the high balcony outside her room she had looked west and north as far as she could and had seen nothing but the wastelands of crystal mountains and endless, glittering plains.

There might, of course, be a resort casino and greenputt playing fields a hundred meters south of this place. She could almost hear her friend Callista's wry, soft comment, and her heart ached with the hope that Luke would somehow find her, here on this world. *But I wouldn't bet the rent on it.* Just the memory of the kind of thing Callista would say made her smile, the ironic image giving her courage in the darkness.

She stopped.

There was something sitting on the step ahead of her, just beyond the range of the cold blade's light.

It was about the size of a pittin, sitting upright twenty or thirty centimeters high—glistening, crablike, cocking its long eyestalks at her with malign awareness. Sitting upright. Waiting for her.

Leia took another step, and extended the blade.

The thing swayed back. In the dense shadows it was extremely difficult to make out what it looked like, but glancing up, Leia saw that there were other things, things like long-legged spiders splayed out on the ceiling and walls, things like short-legged slugs that scooted along the walls, catching and eating the huge drochs that rustled in the shadows. As she watched, the upright thing on the step bent and turned, extruding what looked like a single spiky limb from itself to pounce on a particularly gross droch, catching it in a pincer that seemed to alter in shape and transform into a gulping mouth. For a moment she heard it purr, a soft little thrum of deep pleasure. Then it swung back, eyestalks swiveling to face her again. Sickened, overwhelmed with the sensation that this was an evil that could not be fought, Leia extended the lightsaber so that the glowing tip advanced on the crab thing.

Movement flickered in the corner of her eye and she swung around as something dropped from the ceiling, landing on her shoulder with a wet plop. Pain stabbed through her, like a droch bite but far worse. The soft-bodied thing that had fallen on her morphed out grabbing legs, hooks that sank into her flesh as she cried out and tried to pull it loose.

Weakness. Pain in her chest. Cold and dreamy sleep.

Something else fastened on her leg. The crab thing on the steps purred louder, a sound of dreamy pleasure. She felt as if she were dropping down in a lift bound for the center of the world.

She whipped the lightsaber around in her hand, shrinking in terror from the glowing blade that she knew could take her own arm off as she touched it to the parasite on her shoulder. It frizzled horribly and the pain it felt went through her like a knife, and in her dreamy, sickened weakness she felt it die. It was like a part of her own flesh dying. She turned the blade, fried the thing on her leg, taking the pain, taking the sense of black slipping death, and moved another step down.

The crab thing scuttered ahead of her, vanishing into the dark, save for the orange sparks of its eyes. Around

the curve of the stair she could see the walls moving
with them, all shapes, shifting one into the other, feeding
on one another but all turning as one toward her with
the awareness of the light. Leia backed up, catching her
heel on the stair in her weakness and almost falling.
Another one, whatever they were, dropped from the ceiling onto her neck, smaller, so that both the sinking
weakness of dying, and the pain of its death, were less;
but they were coming after her.

Two more bites. She felt like she would faint from lack
of air. The crab thing's soft throb of delight made her
long to find it, cut it to shreds, wherever it was. Her hand
fumbled with the lightsaber's hilt, pain of a different sort
lancing through her arm as the tiniest edge of the blade
brushed her flesh in killing another parasite. If she fell,
she thought, if she lost consciousness, she would die.

Clinging to the walls, sobbing, trying to breathe, fighting not to sink into that cool welcoming sleep, she stumbled upward, fifteen steps, twenty. The crab thing was
following in the darkness behind, as if relishing, reveling
in her exhaustion and pain. *They'll find me,* she thought. *I
won't be able to make it back to my room and they'll find me.*

Seti Ashgad was away, Seti Ashgad who had warned,
Skywalker will know if she dies. She had tried, again and
again, to call out to Luke, to send him signals with her
mind, but wasn't sure that he had heard. The humming,
singing power of the Force in this world might have
drowned out everything else. Only Dzym was there, silent in this silent house. *If he finds me I shall die.*

She fell through the door, lay panting, cold, unable to
breathe or think, while the wan particolored glow of the
light-sculpture flickered over her, and the lightsaber, its
blade vanished with the relaxation of her grip, glinted an
inch or so from her fingers. *I have to pick it up. I have to stand
up. To get out of here. To get back to my room.*

Dying would be easier, she thought. She wondered if Luke really would know.

At least if I died, they could appoint a successor.

As an idea it had its merits. But in the slow-sinking dimness of cold that surrounded her, she heard movement, the heavy, thick, sluglike panting of Beldorion. Somewhere near, she thought. Heading this way.

Don't let him find me, she prayed, trying to stand. She couldn't, but on her hands and knees she crawled, across the darkened chamber, up the endless stairs. He would take her prisoner for his own purposes, Liegeus had warned—but in time he would trade her to Dzym, as he had some other poor slave.

She thought there were parasites still on her, the pain of them chewing her arms and thighs and back, the weakness draining her, sapping her strength away. But when she crawled into the long, narrow office where the computer was, and lay in the ghastly tinted grayish purple bands of the setting sunlight, she felt better, and feeling herself after a time, found no sign of them.

I can't let them find me, she thought. *I can't.*

It took everything she had left to climb the stairs again, holding to the walls, exhausted and sick with the pain of the lightsaber burn. She collapsed again on the floor after letting herself in the room, and lay there for a long time, curled in a fetal position in the fading bars of sunlight, wanting only to sleep until the universe was made new.

In time she got up and hid the lightsaber, the wafer she had copied, and all the printouts under the duvet and pillows of her bed. She called out again, reaching out with her mind, but it was little more than a despairing whisper: *Luke* . . . then she did pass out, into dreams like the colorless wells of death.

     ·   ·   ·

"Igpek Droon," boomed the deep voice of the masked and hooded passenger, and what looked like a bad prosthetic hand in a cheap black glove—so bad it might almost have been a droid's jointed metal fingers under there—held out fifty-seven credits worth of various bars and tokens to the captain of the freighter *Zicreex.* "I'm in the employ of the Antemeridian Freight Lines. It's necessary that my droid and I reach Cybloc XII as soon as possible."

The captain counted the money, looked at the glowing yellow lenses that were visible through the full-face breathing mask that covered most of her prospective passenger's head. Long, pale hair flowed out around it, giving it the eerie look of a decorated skull.

With the driving back of the Gopso'o rioters by government troops, every docking bay still operable in the port was jammed: with business people, stranded travelers, aliens of all sorts and descriptions fleeing the fire-ravaged city. Most were paying lots more than fifty-seven credits, but then, most were trying to get on to better vessels than the *Zicreex,* which would have been termed unprepossessing even by the charitable.

Captain Ugmush didn't care. She had a human for an engineer who kept the thing running, and her several husbands, when they weren't fighting one another, made a fair team for trading goods to the rougher worlds of the sector, which was about as good as Gamorreans could do in competition with more sophisticated species. Ugmush herself, her long hair dyed pink and her heavily muscled arms and breasts sporting fifteen parasitic morrts to demonstrate her strength and endurance, was aware that few aliens could stand to travel on Gamorrean ships. She knew it wasn't likely she'd be besieged with offers as long as there was one other vessel in port.

"You got a deal."

The black-robed alien who called himself Igpek Droon, clanking just faintly as he walked, made his way up the ramp and into the ship, trailed by his little R2 unit droid. Ugmush wondered if this person Droon might be talked into selling his droid when they got to Cybloc XII.

14

It was all there, in black on the pale green plast.

Seti Ashgad's communication with Moff Getelles of Antemeridian, making arrangements to destroy the gun stations in return for weaponry and first cut of the profits when Loronar Corporation moved in on Nam Chorios to strip-mine it for its crystals.

Memos from Dymurra—who turned out to be CEO of Loronar for the Core systems—detailing which minorities, disaffected factions, and splinter groups would rise in revolt, suitably armed at Loronar Corporation's expense, in order to split the Republic peace-keeping fleet and allow Getelles's Admiral Larm to move in.

A comparison chart by Seti Ashgad, showing the trade-offs in cost between the expenses of weaponry, bribes, agitators, and planted atrocity stories against the first year's profits on programmable CCIR crystals.

Details of the meeting, including a payoff to Councillor Q-Varg, coordinating Leia's disappearance with the poisoning—not to death, the memo assured Getelles, so that no successor could be appointed without hopeless legal wrangling among the Council—of Minister of State Rieekan.

At no point in his letter did Ashgad mention the Death Seed plague of centuries ago. "The plague vectors do not appear on any sensor, since within the body they mimic exactly human electrochemical fields and tissue composition," he said—which explained why they needed the quasi-living flesh of the synthdroids. "Once the illness has taken hold, even regenerative therapy has no effect. However, be assured that it is in my power to completely control the outbreak and spread of this malady, and I offer you my personal guarantees that it will not affect anyone other than those on the Republic ships and bases."

And bases! thought Leia, breathless as if she had run for miles and hot with anger to the core of her being. *Idiot! Idiot! "It is in my power to completely control the outbreak," my grandmother's left hind leg! Don't you have any idea, any concept, of what will happen if there's an accident? A miscalculation? Something you hadn't thought of, Master Know-All Ashgad?*

She was almost trembling with rage. Accounts were scanty of the original Death Seed, but huge segments of the population of dozens of spacegoing civilizations had perished before it had burned itself out. In places it had been combated, but she wasn't sure how, or how effective those remedies had been. As far as she had experienced, Dzym, and Dzym alone, seemed to have any control over it.

She thought about Ezrakh, and Marcopius, and her eyes grew hot with tears. *I will kill them.* Rage made her tremble, made her wonder how quickly she could master the Force, how quickly she could build strength to wreak wholesale vengeance for the innocent. *I will gather the Force together in my hands and I will bring it down on their heads like a thunderstorm.*

Vader had done that.

And Anakin, in her dream.

She wrapped her arms around herself, fighting not to weep. It was better, she thought, not to know that you had the potential for that kind of power. Better not to know that you really could do that, if you wanted to turn your heart and your life over to your rage.

Han would be looking for her. Han would be with the fleet. *It will not affect any but those on the Republic ships.*

The Republic was in chaos. They'd dared poison poor Rieekan, for no better purpose than to cause trouble . . .

And for what?

Hands shaking, she shuffled through the flimsiplast pages.

There it was. Loronar Corporation's plan to build a new facility on Antemeridias, for the manufacture of both synthdroids and something called Needles: controlled by the same CCIR crystals, programmable, long-distance miniweapons with infinite range and hyperspace rendezvous capability.

And the source of the crystals was Nam Chorios.

CCIR technology. Deep-space Needles, carving up the fleet like the Quamilla of the Kidron system carving up sodbeasts. And with Nam Chorios firmly in their sphere of influence, they'd have as many of those programmable crystals as they cared to use.

The *Reliant.* Paperwork was complete on that, too. A modified I-7 Howlrunner hull, with extra capacity. Loronar Corporation had been making drops of components and materials for months. Ashgad's requests and specs were very precise—Leia recalled her father saying that the man had been a ship designer himself—and his communications indicated where and when his Rationalist friends had picked them up. There were occasional indents for second and third drops where the gun stations had blown the incoming cargoes out of the sky. Liegeus Sarpaetius Vorn was mentioned as the vessel's A.I. designer and programmer, but his chief value lay in expert holo faking. There were requests for specific digitalized scrap of her and of her flagship and escort, to be mocked up into transmissions describing the safe conclusion of the conference between Ashgad and herself, and the two vessels' departure from the rendezvous point and entry into hyperspace.

Her stomach twisted with sick betrayal. He couldn't not know what was going on. He couldn't not know the dangers of the plague. Then bitter anger swept her, that she had liked the man.

Grand Moff Tarkin was probably good to his wife and children, too, if he'd had any, she thought, disgusted with her own naïveté. *The man who pulled the lever on the Death Star that destroyed Alderaan would undoubtedly have been kind to someone he cared for.* Her hand closed tight on itself for a moment, her breath shaky with rage.

Then, face cold and still, she began looking through the plast sheets again, searching for something . . .

There. Invoices for the building of the *Reliant*. A charging mechanism for antigrav lifters and speeder buoyancy tanks, to make prospecting for crystals easier once the gun stations had been destroyed and the big trader vessel was free to take off. She studied the schematics for the vessel. A curious amount of shielding, she thought. Double and triple hulls with internal baffles—What kind of radiation did they think they were going to encounter?

Leia sat back, staring out the windows at the gaudy sunset sky.

She felt she'd slept longer, though by the light she'd only been out for a few hours. There was fresh water in the pitcher and signs that someone—probably Liegeus—

had been in the room. She'd waked with a blanket over her, and was gladder than ever that she'd forced herself to conceal the flimsiplast and the lightsaber before finally passing out. When she had lain down she felt like she was dying.

In fact, the sensations had been curiously similar to her brush with the Death Seed.

But Dzym hadn't been around. If Dzym had known where she was, and what she was doing, she certainly wouldn't have waked up here.

She pushed up her sleeve. Her flesh was reddened in a few places and she had picked up a couple more droch bites, but there was no sign of violence. No sign of the broken capillaries, the bruising that the secretary's fingers had left.

The purplish twilight of day was dimming into deeper night, windless and still with sunset. Leia thought about waiting until dawn, then shook the thought away. It wasn't as if any natural predators walked Nam Chorios's nights. Delay would only bring Ashgad's return eight hours closer. If she acted now, there was a good chance they wouldn't miss her until morning.

Leia got to her feet, unsteady at the knees. The water pitcher was of the vacuum type. A turn of the cap sealed it shut. It was heavy, hung over her shoulder by a make-shift strap of torn bedsheet. She rolled together two blankets and put on the two spare shirts Liegeus had given her. At the touch of them, her anger at him faded. He could not have known what he was getting into, and once in, it would have been too late.

The doorpad combination had been changed while she slept, and she activated her lightsaber and drove it into the innards of the lock. It was now or never. She could afford no delay.

Ashgad's study first. There were two more things she needed to find out.

The study faced north, like her room. Its inner wall was curtained in shadow, but the faded sunset reflected from the cliffs and faceted towers of crystal of the mountains beyond the plateau, and the ghostly crazy quilt of light lay across the white tiled floor with a strange radiance that was somehow comforting. Leia called up the main files, ran a scan-and-print on everything concerning the Death Seed. It was fifty or sixty sheets, double sided, closely spaced, and she shoved those into her bedroll with the rest of the printouts she'd gotten earlier.

Then she paged through the directories until she found what she needed: maps of the area, elevations, travel guides. There was a village twenty kilometers away, on the other side of the mountain spur on which the fortress stood. Ashgad would look there, she thought. Odds were good they wouldn't have equipment strong enough to send a signal offplanet, anyway. Sixteen kilometers in the other direction was one of the gun stations, on a shoulder of the mountains called Bleak Point. She thought she could reach it, keeping to the hem of the foothills for cover. Deserted it might be, its automatic systems guarding this world as they had guarded it for nearly a thousand years, but there would be equipment of some kind there that she might be able to use.

She checked the household plan again. Through that door, right up the hall where she had turned left before; a flight of stairs and a locked door whose combination, according to the computer, was 339-054-001-6. The antigrav tanks were stored behind the second door. The light in the sunset sky was dimming, and she felt an obscure pang of fear. Though she knew Dzym was active in daylight as well as at night, by day she felt safer from him. Whoever and whatever he was, she wanted to be out of the house before full dark.

A thought crossed her mind. Turning back, she opened the slatted doors into the small chamber where the CCIR Central Control Unit stood, amber power lights glowing like eyes in the dark.

This would have to be fast, she thought. Liegeus would be working with the synthdroids in the docking compound. Beldorion would certainly have one or two about his quarters and maybe one in the kitchen with his grubby little Kubaz cook. The synthdroids' wholesale collapse would get them on her trail, but the only ones on her trail would be Liegeus and Dzym, not twenty-something centrally controlled and extremely mobile synthetic humans.

Her hand was on the toggle of her lightsaber when the *swish* of the outer doors froze her where she stood. The next second voices sounded in the room, and she barely had time to pull shut the slatted doors that concealed the Control Unit in its vestibule.

Three days! she wanted to scream. *He said he'd be gone three days!*

The voice was the voice of Seti Ashgad.

"I told you not to go near her!" he was saying, and Leia was shocked to hear how broken and shrill was his voice. An old man's voice. "Skywalker's her brother, and a Jedi Knight. He'll know if she dies, and it's too soon to have them know they can choose a successor! Our whole plan will come adrift if . . ."

"You've told me that before." Dzym's voice hissed in the twilight. "Don't treat me like an imbecile, Ashgad. Are you telling me that you believe this puling little wreck over me? Are you?"

Leia turned one of the slats of the door, put her eye to it. No light had come up in the long study, and the fading daylight outside did not reach to its inner wall. She could make out faces, and the sharp white V of Ashgad's shirtfront . . . she thought he was wearing a gray or white cap of some sort, blurring into the blur of his face. Of Dzym she could distinguish almost nothing, save a slumped dark suggestion of evil, a gleam of eyes that reminded her unpleasantly of something else. Other eyes, recently seen . . .

Liegeus stammered when he spoke. "I—I merely said—I thought when I found her yesterday afternoon . . . she hasn't wakened, my lord. She's lying up there cold and barely breathing. I've checked on her all through today . . ."

"And you thought," whispered Dzym, and the shadow of him shifted with the slow ophidian turning of his head, "you jumped to the conclusion that I had disobeyed my lord's request—that I would only wait until his back was turned . . ."

Leia thought he reached out one hand toward Liegeus's face. Though it was difficult to make out what was happening she thought the holo faker fell back a pace, his back to the wall. Thought she heard him whisper, "Please . . ." with utter terror in his voice.

"Did you check the room?" asked Ashgad, rather quickly. "Could it have happened another way? Could another . . . ?"

"Of course not!" Dzym swung around on him, Liegeus stepping quickly out of his reach. "What other besides me has the strength? What other besides me is old enough, developed enough? I have told you. Told you that *and* not to treat me as if I haven't a brain! Let us go to her and see if this whiner is even telling the truth."

Liegeus turned hastily, and Leia heard the *swoosh* of the door in the darkness; Ashgad said hoarsely, "Wait."

It was hard to see, and the murmuring voices were

barely audible, but Leia thought Liegeus had gone ahead, leaving Ashgad and Dzym alone in the darkening room. Ashgad spoke almost too low to hear, but she thought he said, "It was a long journey. I should have taken you."

Dzym made no reply, or if he did speak, it was too low to hear.

"I'd have taken care of that woman in Hweg Shul somehow. Kept her from you. Kept her from talking. Next time . . ."

"There is no necessity," whispered Dzym, "for 'next time.' "

"When Larm's troops land I'll have her taken care of. I promise. You won't need to worry about her betraying you. No one believes her anyway. But I . . . look at me." The shrill, old-man voice cracked, and Leia, without quite knowing how, realized that he wasn't wearing a cap, as she had thought. His black hair had grayed almost to whiteness. "I had to get out of there late last night, after the meeting. I had to . . . to come back."

"To come back," whispered Dzym mockingly. "To someone you don't trust. To someone you think will disobey . . ."

"I never thought you disobeyed."

"You believed the whiner."

"I—I didn't. I was just—taken off-guard. We need him, Dzym, until this is over. He was the best we could get, one of the best holo fakers in the business. After Larm's troops land, after the *Reliant*'s launch tracks are in, you can do with him what you will. But please. Please don't be angry. Please . . ." She didn't hear clearly what he said; she thought it was "help me" or maybe "give me."

Dzym stepped sideways a little. Leia saw the sleek black topknot silhouetted against the glint of the computer's power lights, and the spidery motion of his

gloved hands as he unfastened the breast of his robe. In
the reflected gleam of the lights in which he now stood,
she saw clearly that below his neck his skin changed. It
was hard, chitinous, catching green and amber glints—
broken and blotched, too, all over Dzym's bare chest and
shoulders, with tubes and orifices and groping little
mouthed nodules that had no business on any human
form. All those little mouths and openings gaped and
stretched, dark matter running down, glistening. Dzym's
human mouth opened as well, the long tongue groping
like a serpent.

With a noise that was not quite a whimper, not quite a
sob, Ashgad bent his head down. He pressed his mouth
to the dark, chitinous chest, and with a horrible movement impossible for a human neck, Dzym moved his
head around, tongue probing at Ashgad's nape. The
thready radiance sheened on a trickle of blood. Ashgad
made noises for a while—thin ones, small and desperate—then was silent. The silence lasted nearly a minute,
though it seemed to Leia, trapped in the dark of the
shuttered vestibule, to go on longer than that.

At last, barely audible, Ashgad whispered, "Thank
you." The crackle of age was gone from his voice. The
room was fully dark now, and only the faintest stain of
orange remained in the sky outside, but Leia thought his
hair had darkened perceptibly, and when the two left the
room, Ashgad moved like a young man. Leia thought,
but couldn't be sure, that he wiped something from his
mouth and chin.

She timed their footfalls ascending the stair, knowing
she had only minutes now. The sky-colored blade of the
lightsaber flashed to life in her hand, and she drove it
deep into the center of the control unit in a vicious hiss
of sparks and smoke. Then she caught up bedroll and
pitcher and fled across the tiled floor, stabbing the combi-

nation of the locked door that led to the rest of the house, right down the hall, up the steps. Another combination, another door—a synthdroid standing in the laboratory beyond, blue eyes glazed and staring, androgynous mouth open as it staggered, numbly, from wall to wall. Leia brushed past it and it fell. Guilt touched her as she stepped past the body. In driving her lightsaber into the Central Controller, she had mass-deactivated them, destroyed them . . .

They're not living, she told herself. *No more living than a droid that might have been deactivated or its memory flushed.* But the guilt remained, as if she'd wiped Artoo's programming or Threepio's.

They'll search, she thought. *Ashgad and Dzym and Liegeus. They'll get Beldorion to use his Jedi perceptions, to touch the Force.* To feel for the vibrations of her mind, if the sluglike mass of indolence still had the capability of doing so—if the weird, overwhelming vibration of the Force that filled this world would permit it.

The storeroom containing the antigrav units was exactly where the schematic said it was.

But only one unit was active. The rest—nearly a dozen—lay in boxes of styrene and goatgrass along the wall, dead, useless as so many rocks would have been.

Leia felt as if she'd had a bucket of cold water hurled in her face.

Her hands shook uncontrollably as she pulled the single unit whose lights were green from its shelf. It was a 100-GU unit—a speeder usually took four—and about half charged. She clicked it to neutral buoyancy and pulled it after her like a balloon on a string to the lab outside, where a synthdroid lay on the floor, eyes staring, near the half-assembled parts of a new buoyancy charger. The old one, on a table nearby, was an outmoded model held together by Y-bands and silver space tape. A scattering of antiquated, blown-out, and depleted tanks lay around it.

Next time they vote to have trade come in, I'm all for it, thought Leia grimly, as she dug through drawers. There was a belt reel of cable and a hook there, standard in mountainous terrain; also a small glowrod, and two rolls of silver space tape, which she threaded onto the makeshift bedroll strap. *This business of never having the right equipment is ridiculous!* She pocketed a couple of emergency mini-heaters, crossed the room at a run to the big double doors that the schematic had told her would lead to the docking bay.

As the schematic promised, the great permacrete pad that formed the southeastern quarter of Ashgad's compound overlooked open space on two sides. The *Reliant* sat on five short legs close by the workroom door through which she emerged. In smaller hangars to the side she made out the needlelike nosecone of an elderly Headhunter, and the blunt silhouette of a gutted Skipray Blastboat.

Synthdroids, fallen with equipment or tanks of Puffo-Shield in hand, lay about the *Reliant* in starlight like wet black heaps of laundry. There was no light, for the Central Control Unit knew where every step and cable and piece of machinery lay, no matter which droid set it down, but it seemed to Leia that the great gulfs of air beyond the permacrete apron were filled with the softest echo of brightness, the glow of the merciless stars amplified by the wasteland of faceted ridge and scree.

Leia looked down from the edge of the apron and her heart froze. *I can't.*

It was easily three hundred meters to the base of that first, sheer drop. From there the slope tapered steeply, a shamble of diamonds, bled of color in the etiolated light. An antigrav unit's lifting capability was directly proportional to the distance from the surface of the ground. The first drop might be so fast that when the lift finally kicked in, it might not do so soon enough or hard enough.

The cable wasn't even a quarter long enough, and with no way of detaching the hook, she might as well set off flares to announce in which direction she'd gone.

Behind her, in the dark bulk of the house, she saw a light go up, then another.

The image returned to her mind, of Ashgad bending his head down to the mouths and tentacles and groping, wormy nodules of Dzym's chitinous chest; of Dzym's ungloved, unseen hands on her face, her wrists. Of the cold sickness that pulled her down toward death.

Here in this high place, unshielded by any walls, she had the curious sensation of the Force being all around her, as if she stood not on a boat in the sea, but on the living ocean bed itself. Strong, strange, it called to her, she thought. Spoke in words she could not understand.

She checked the antigrav unit in her hands.

It wasn't enough.

It is. The thought was warm wind breathing in her mind. *It is.*

You've got to be kidding!

Leia looked over the edge again. Darkness and starlight and scintillant wastes dropped away like a vast subconscious thought. She knew that the slight difference in weight wasn't going to have any effect on the immutable law of twenty-six point six meters per second per second, but nevertheless she dropped her bedroll first. The sealed pitcher would shatter and couldn't be risked.

What am I thinking about? she reflected cynically, as she ripped a double strip of space tape and fashioned a make-shift handle. *I'm the one who's going to smash to a million pieces.*

The night around her, the subtly flashing darkness, whispered, *You won't. We're here. Trust.*

More lights sprang up like startled glowbugs on a summer evening, and she heard Ashgad's oratorial baritone call, "Liegeus! Here, at once!"

They'd found the synthdroids.

Leia slipped her arm through the handle, clicked over the antigrav unit to its highest output, and stepped off the edge of the platform.

Leia was calling him.

Luke jolted out of sleep, shocked breathless in the chilly dawn.

Encircled by the towering crystal shapes of mountains like molten glass, the image of her was etched on his mind, alone in a world of glass and sky. She was on a stone terrace, wrapped in a white blanket, cinnamon hair lying in a long disheveled braid down her shoulder. There was something about the image that told him that this had happened some time ago, that it had been caught up in the distortions of the Force, but he knew it was real. She looked thin and fragile and badly scared.

Ashgad.

He hadn't just destroyed her ship, looted it for its weapons. He'd taken her off. Ransom? Negotiation?

An illusion, the result of last night's discovery on the smuggler drop?

No. As surely as he knew the bones of his body, he knew she was there or had been there. Alive.

The foot of the Mountains of Lightning, Taselda had said. Arvid or Aunt Gin would know the spot. For a moment he considered taking Taselda, only to reject the thought in the next heartbeat.

He rose from his bed, walked to the rear transparisteel, looked down on the peacefully prosaic yard of dust and belcrabbian, water pumps and broken speeder parts, the dark-leaved antigrav balls beyond the walls floating still as cutouts in the clear, early light. It was difficult to remember that this was all manufactured, laboriously carved from a world that admitted no life.

From here, the great, lawless presence of the Force could only be felt a little, dim and far away.

Luke reached out with his mind. *Leia. Don't despair. I'm on my way.*

He didn't know if his thought even reached her, tangled in the distorting effects of the Force on this world. Didn't know if she could hear, even when it did.

But Callista had told him once that hope, too, can sometimes affect the Force.

"What's that?"

Muffled in the folds of the black hooded robe and cumbersome breath mask and wig, See-Threepio considered Captain Ugmush's question to be purely rhetorical. Even one unused to the noises of war, riot, and rebellion should have been able to accurately identify the sound of heavy artillery shelling, the crash of crumbling walls, and the harsh clashing of human voices and blasters.

The Gamorrean captain's three husbands, however, seemed to take their lady's exclamation as a straightforward request for information, and went barreling to the round portal that led onto the boarding ramp to see. All three reached the entryway at the same moment and immediately undertook a slugging match for precedence. Captain Ugmush, who had taken on another commission to transport cargo offplanet and was waiting impatiently for delivery, heaved herself from the bridge workstation, where she'd been checking through projections of launch windows and hyperspace jump points, and proceeded to break up the fight with slaps, squeals, and head bashing, following which the entire family group piled out the door and down the ramp. Engineer Jos, chained to his console, didn't even raise his eyes.

A further explosion that made the ship rock on its landing gear brought Threepio nervously to his feet. "Captain Ugmush . . ." He realized his vocal modulators had gone into default register and quickly reset them to the deeper tone that, though it took up far more memory in mimicry of organic resonators, exhibited less of the characteristic droid "metallic" quality. "Captain Ugmush, do you really think you should leave the ship at this moment?" He toddled toward the door as another flurry of shots and outcry came echoing from somewhere uncomfortably close by. "In the event of an emergency takeoff . . . Oh, dear, Artoo . . ." His voice dropped back to default again. "Do you have any idea how to get this model of vessel lifted off?"

The astromech, trundling toward the doorway in his wake, denied any expertise in the piloting of the lumpy Gamorrean cubeship. Threepio muttered, "Oh dear, oh dear," as he followed Artoo out the door and down the ramp, hoping against hope that the situation outside wasn't going to get any worse.

The moment he emerged at the foot of the ramp it became evident that it was unlikely that it would—or *could*—get worse. The next bay over was in flames, black oil smoke and thirty-foot columns of fire pouring skyward and Gopso'o troops and Drovian government forces searing one another with blaster fire and cannister grenades across the wreckage.

For a moment the docking bay in which the *Zicreex* lay was quiet. None of the Gamorreans was to be seen. Then under the arcade a door opened and a muddy, shabby

little figure darted through. The fugitive slammed the
keypad to close the door behind him, pulled a crowbar
from the nearest heap of scrap under the arcade, and
smashed the lock. The effort was to little avail. It was
clear that whoever was on the other side of the door also
had crowbars, battering rams, and grenades. The fugitive
dashed madly across the open permacrete, and Threepio
said in surprise, "Why, it's Master Yarbolk from the Chug
'n' Chuck! Master Yarbolk! Over here, Master Yarbolk!"

The Chadra-Fan needed no further encouragement.
He bolted past them and up the entry ramp, instants
before the doors gave way and an exceedingly mixed con-
gregation of Drovians—some wearing the Gopso'o scal-
plock and others, though presumably sympathizers, not
so decorated, accompanied by a couple of Durosian and
Devaronian lay-about spaceport types—came smashing
through. Someone yelled something about a stinking
traitor sellout swine, and Threepio, correctly interpreting
the remark to reflect on the fugitive Master Yarbolk,
pointed toward the doorway that led to the unburning
bays beyond.

"That way!" he boomed in his alternate alien voice.
"Unclean hairy undersize journalist!" He hoped the in-
vective was as acceptable to them as it was informative.

Hollering imprecations, the mob smashed its way
through the farther doors at the same moment a twenty-
centimeter shell struck the arcade between the burning
bay and the one currently occupied by the Zicreex.
Threepio let out a squeak of panic and retreated up the
ramp as the Drovian government forces scattered, re-
grouped, and fired on the Gopso'o who were attempting
to advance over the wreckage. At the same moment
Ugmush and her husbands appeared at a run. They must
have passed the mob just within the other doorway, and
they added their mite to the battle, firing on the Gopso'o

as they lumbered across the permacrete and up the boarding ramp, an assortment of parcels and packing boxes hung over their shoulders and backs.

Dirty pink curls flying and morrts clinging to her for their very lives, Ugmush burst onto the bridge, screaming, "Get yourselves strapped in, you stupid garbage eaters! What in sithfestering blazes do you think this is, a luxury liner?" She flung herself down behind the console, jabbing keys and flipping levers with far more speed than seemed possible in hands so huge. "Close that festering boarding ramp, you muck-sodden flapdragon, do I have to do everything on this maw-sapping ship? Jos, get us out of here! Fruck, open fire on those festering Gopso'o—hang on, the lot of you! Bunch of crab-sucking morrtless soap-using cheesebrains!"

She rammed the activation levers over, the engineer cut in the power overrides, and in a roar of ground fire, ion cannons, and retro lasers, the *Zicreex* was airborne and heading out of the ragged billows of smoke, flak and wreckage like a spinning overweight glet-fruit shot from a catapult at the sky.

Threepio, who hadn't had time to buckle himself down or even take a seat, picked himself gingerly up and readjusted his breath mask, hoping that either his robe hadn't come disarranged enough to exhibit his undeniably droidlike legs, or that Ugmush had been too occupied with her velocity computations to notice. Yarbolk, who like him had been hurled to the far corner of the bridge, limped over to assist him in righting Artoo-Detoo, who had rolled a considerable distance and whose distress lights were blinking in several systems, including one of the bolted-on components they hadn't been able to get rid of after disconnecting him from the *Pure Sabacc*. Most of the distress lights went out. Artoo tweeped a wan thanks, and without a word, Jos removed the elastic tie from his long hair and offered it to Yarbolk to tie up some of Artoo's stray cables.

"Thank you—er—Igpek," said the Chadra-Fan. "I owe you one."

Ugmush turned in her seat, and glared at the furry little journalist out of orange pinhead eyes. "And what the festering muck is that troublemaker doing on my ship?" she demanded. "Don't you sapheads know there's a reward out for him on seven systems?"

15

They were there.

Luke froze, lying under the pitted steel belly of the speeder. Listening.

No sound.

But they were there, watching him. He knew it. Even through the silent trumpets of the Force in the deep stillness of the wastelands, he could sense their presence. He'd sensed awareness of him again and again since leaving Hweg Shul.

The invisible watchers.

The planet's unseen original inhabitants.

Effortlessly following his speeder, keeping him in sight.

Where he lay under the speeder he could see nothing. When the starboard antigrav unit had started to go he'd prudently set the vehicle down with one edge on a sort of bench of basalt, the other side on a lump of frost-green quartz the size of a hassock, so his only view from underneath, as he rejiggered the generator wiring to recharge the defective a-g coil, was straight ahead or straight behind, identical vistas of harsh reflective gravel broken by bigger fragments and hunks of crystal, and, farther off, crystal chimneys piercing the sky.

He sensed that should he emerge from beneath the speeder and look around him, he would still see no one.

He lowered his eyelids, trying to call the shape of them within the Force. But such was the interference of the Force on this world, the sheer magnitude of its presence in alien guise, that he could get no clear picture of those invisible ones. Maybe, he thought, that was the point of the interference to begin with.

Nor could he tell exactly when they had begun to dog him, or feel whether their interest was beneficent, malicious, or merely inquiring.

They were only there.

"Who are you?" he called out, aware of his vulnerability, lying on his back under the speeder. "I mean you no harm. You don't need to be afraid to show yourself to me. *Can* you show yourselves to me?"

Their presence drew closer—or *something* drew closer, a distinct awareness of their awareness of him. He wondered how he knew it was *they* and not *he, she,* or *it.*

Carefully, he crawled from beneath the speeder, and stood up.

Pale shadows lay about him; pale daytime stars pierced the dark blue of the sky. Pale sunlight fragmented from the glittering gravel that stretched in all directions, empty to the farthest shore of the long-forgotten sea.

"It's the Loronar Corporation." The Chadra-Fan journalist Yarbolk lowered his husky alto voice, brought out from the pocket of his singed and stained silk vest a handful of green datacubes, held them out as if their mere presence on his hairless, pink palm were proof of what he said. "On every one of these planets, every place in the Meridian sector where there's been an armed revolt or religious rioting or uprisings from minority tribes or groups or whatever it's been . . . the dissident forces are always armed with Loronar weapons. Not bottom-cut sellouts, mind you, like the gunrunners are always peddling to aborigines if they think they can get away with it. Top-of-the-line blasters and grenades and ion cannons. Look at these."

He rattled the datacubes like dice in his hand. Artoo-Detoo, taking him at his word, promptly extruded a gripper arm, picked up a cube, and withdrew the arm into his own vitals. "Hey, give that back!" protested Yarbolk, loudly enough that two of Ugmush's husbands, an armed guard, two very nervous Aqualish smugglers, and the dozen or so others who shared the waiting chamber of the Quarantine Enforcement Cruiser *Lycoming* turned to glare at them, as if blaming them for their present situation.

The *Zicreex* had not even made it to the hyperspace jump point when it ran into trouble. Just outside the outlying asteroid fields of the Drovian system they had encountered the Republic cruiser *Empyrean,* firing furiously with all guns in all directions without any target immediately apparent—not until the flash of one of the cruiser's shield generators blowing up had illuminated what at first appeared to be a cloud of space debris surrounding the vessel like flies. Within moments, however, it was obvious that the tiny slips of matte black metal were vessels of some kind, pouring concentrated fire on the huge ship and slipping and scattering from return fire like a cloud of butterbats.

Since the battle lay between the *Zicreex* and the outer reaches of the system, where it would be safe to jump to hyperspace, the small trader was trapped where it was. Ugmush, the droids, and Yarbolk clustered by the viewport and watched as the *Empyrean* tried first to battle, then to flee the swarming attackers.

"Fascinating," Threepio said, looking over Ugmush's shoulder as the captain tried to scan up a reading on the nearby area in the hopes of not running afoul of whatever larger vessel was controlling the swarm. "They seem to be nothing more than ambulant weapons. Don't be silly," he added, to Artoo, who had surreptitiously hooked into the console behind Ugmush's broad back. "There has to be a principal ship. Whatever it is, it must have amazing range."

Yarbolk, crowding at Ugmush's elbow and peering back and forth between Artoo's readouts and those on the console, whispered, "No principal ship. Just weapons. It's got to be CCIR of some kind."

Light flared over their faces as a bolt from one of the tiny ships achieved target. The fire cloud from the exploding cruiser enveloped the daggerlike little weapons; a hundred white stars flared in the dissipating ball of heat and gases as they, too, were destroyed. The score or so which survived simply pivoted, like a school of glimmerfish in the darkness, and moved away. Black painted as they were, they were swiftly lost to sight.

Yarbolk whispered, "By the Big Green Fish . . ." And then, "What are you doing?" as Ugmush moved the levers, and the *Zicreex* swung around.

"Salvage," the Gamorrean said. She jerked one meaty hand at the viewport, where the two or three huge chunks of what was left of the cruiser hung glowing in blackness, surrounded by whirling fields of half-melted shielding, metal shards, spears of glass, and vacuum-bloated corpses. "Lots of stuff."

Ugmush and her husbands, resplendent in deep-space environmental gear customized to their species for use by mercenaries, were looting the wreck when the Quarantine Enforcement Cruiser *Lycoming* made its appearance. Its captain, a much-harried Gotal female in charge of a small troop of fighters and a squad of medics from the Coruscant Institute, had picked up the *Empyrean*'s distress call, and was not amused by the presence of the Gamorrean free traders at the wreck site.

Threepio supposed it was a credit to his disguise that he'd been put under arrest with the others. Artoo-Detoo had simply been impounded.

Now the little blue access hatch in Artoo's side slid open again and his gripper arm deposited the cube on the table in front of Yarbolk. Yarbolk snatched it up possessively and bestowed it in his breast pocket. "*TriNebulon*'ll pay me a fortune for that," said the Chadra-Fan. "More so than ever, now." He hadn't been groomed in days—most of the grooming parlors in Bagsho had been boarded tight—and his silky golden fur was a mass of dirt and knots. "Did you get a look at that wreckage? The hulls of the attacking vessels, the weapon vessels?"

"I didn't examine them closely, no." Threepio turned his head to look at the pieces of wreckage that Ugmush had taken on board the *Zicreex* before the QEC had put in its appearance. They were stacked in a corner of the enormous waiting room, labeled and under a very tired-and crabby-looking Sullustan guard.

Yarbolk lowered his voice still further. "They're modified Seifax shielded transport shells," he whispered. "Thousands of them were shipped to Seifax's new plant on Antemeridias a few months ago—and Seifax is a dummy corporation for Loronar."

"You can't really be serious." Threepio modulated his voice down, shocked. Though he was not physically uncomfortable in the all-enfolding black robe and leather mask with its breathing tubes and filters, Threepio found the disguise massively inconvenient because the fabric bunched in his joints, interfered with the delicate operation of his hydraulic retractors, and—since like many droids his balance was less acute than humans'—threatened to trip him at every other step.

"Loronar Corporation is a subscriber to the Republic Registry of Corporations. Their board of directors is made up of individuals of the highest probity and credentials. They were responsible for a good deal of the armament that made the Rebellion possible!"

"And they turned a five hundred percent profit in the ten years of active Rebellion that preceded the fall of the New Order. Now the Rebellion had its own financial sources, but not that kind of money. Loronar was selling to both sides, probably through dummy corporations like Seifax. And the Seifax plant on Antemeridias has been buying miniaturized hyperspace drives from the Bith. I have a connection in the processing office. Hey," he added, snatching back another of the datacubes from Artoo, who, apparently still under the impression that *look at these* was an order, had been systematically picking up the cubes on the table with his gripper and taking them into his data-retrieval port. "You give those back."

The droid promptly spat them out in a line onto the table. Yarbolk snatched them up, counted them, and glanced quickly over his shoulder again at the other occupants of the quarantine hold. They were a motley bunch: a scrofulous-looking gray Wookiee and a couple of Aqualish who held together and kept looking from the guards to the doors, the crew of a Squib prospector vessel who protested vehemently and often that they hadn't heard about any plague, and a rather extravagantly hued Ergesh who occupied three seats and smelled like the garbage pressers of a candy factory.

"There have been three attempts on my life, since I started on this story," whispered the Chadra-Fan, and his four wide nostrils quivered in the velvet of his snout. "Loronar Corporation can't afford for this to be made public. Half their contracts come from the Republic."

"Surely Loronar Corporation wouldn't frank an assassin!"

Yarbolk sniffed and jabbed one short finger at the protocol droid for emphasis. "Loronar might not do it themselves, but they'd get Getelles to do it. Who do you think put those Gopso'o on me, back on Drovis? My sources at Getelles's court tell me Loronar is pretty much backing Getelles's whole household. The local CEO, Dymurra, lives there like a king: sex droids, vibrobaths, plug-ins, glitterstim, four different chefs, self-conforming slippers, independently controlled environments in every room of his mansion, you name it. Some stuff that isn't legal *anywhere*. He couldn't get it without Getelles's okay. That all adds up to . . ."

"Igpek Droon?" called a voice from the inner doorway.

"That's you!" hissed Yarbolk, when Threepio didn't respond.

"Oh—oh, yes." Threepio rose quickly, stepping on the hem of his robe as he did so; Yarbolk inconspicuously caught him by the elbow to keep him from going over. The *Lycoming*'s Captain and Chief Medical Officer both stood in the doorway: female Gotals, their flat gray faces already turning toward him with suspicion as he hastened in their direction, their hornlike sensory organs picking up the synergistic energy fields that betrayed him as a droid.

"Thank goodness we've finally contacted someone in authority!" cried Threepio gratefully, unhooking the straps of his mask and pulling free the blond wig. "You have no idea . . ."

He found himself looking down the barrels of two blasters and a disruptor.

"Don't come any closer, droid," snapped the captain. "Tuuve, get a restraining bolt for this one."

"But you don't understand!" protested Threepio. "You must communicate with the New Republic Council immediately! Her Excellency, Chief of State Leia Organa Solo, has been kidnapped! You must . . ."

"Not another one," muttered the Chief Medical Officer to her captain. "What was the last one? A wrecked shipload of Carosi pups with two hours' oxygen left? And how much tenho-root extract did that one have stashed in its casing?"

"I beg your pardon!" Threepio drew himself up to his full height, though he had been carefully engineered to be nonthreatening to a wide spectrum of sentient species, Gotals among them. "I am a certified protocol droid belonging to Her Excellency herself! The very idea that I would be programmed to smuggle illicit drugs . . ."

"Whoever programmed this one picked a doozy of a cover story," remarked the captain. She nodded to the Sullustan engineer who had come up behind Threepio with a couple of restraining bolts. "Get His Excellency down to the impound hold and go over him good. And take down the serial numbers."

She rubbed her eyes. Her thin, fleshless lips were gray with fatigue and the soft tissue around her eyes was swollen. When he considered it, Threepio supposed that operating a quarantine enforcement vessel along the perimeter of a sector involved in half a dozen separate revolts—without any centralized authority to back up her decisions—must be an extremely wearing task.

"We'll put Enforcement on whoever he really belongs to after this is all over, but for now, tag anything you find hidden in the casings and send the microprocessors down to the lab. We need them bad. They need wiring in Maintenance, too."

"I protest!" cried Threepio, as the Sullustan troopers laid hold of his arms. "Her Excellency has been kidnapped and . . ."

"Her Excellency, for your information, my friend," said the Gotal, with a weary, gritting edge to her voice, "just transmitted authorization for our mission in this sector, under her personal seal. I've just spoken to her."

"She left authorized holograms of herself for contingency purposes before she left on the secret mission!" cried Threepio. "That's standard procedure. Of course they would need her authorization to establish a quarantine zone, but she isn't really there! My counterpart and I are the only ones who know her true whereabouts!"

The two Gotals—members of a species notoriously distrustful of droids, an understandable prejudice given the sensitivity of their sensory organs—exchanged an eloquent glance.

"But I tell you I was there! Two battle cruisers disappeared! The *Borealis* and the *Adamantine* . . ."

The surgeon frowned. "Your cousin's on the *Adamantine*, isn't he, Captain?"

The captain nodded. "And the *Adamantine* left for Celanon at the beginning of the week."

"That was only a cover story!" wailed Threepio, as the guards pulled him in the direction of the doors. "Her mission in this sector was top secret! The *Adamantine* was destroyed . . ."

The captain's eyes hardened to steel. "Get him out of here," she said softly to the guards. "Get that R2 as well, would you? You tell them in Impound to flush those microprocessors good."

The guard saluted, and asked, "What about the Chadra-Fan they came on board with?"

The Gotal captain fished in her pocket for a slip of pink flimsiplast. Threepio thought it was a message slip of some kind, but there was no official heading, only a private scramble code across the top. Her eyes narrowed furtively as she looked over at Yarbolk, who was still sitting next to Artoo and trying to look inconspicuous. Then she turned to Threepio. "What's your friend's name?"

Unless programmed to give alternate information, droids are devastatingly truthful, even those whose business is protocol and diplomacy. "Yarbolk Yemm," provided Threepio unhesitatingly. "I understand that he's a journalist for *TriNebulon.*"

There was momentary silence. Then the captain said, "That's him," and signaled to another guard as she started across the room toward the Chadra-Fan.

Yarbolk saw them coming and sprang to his feet. Everyone in the waiting hall had been relieved of whatever weaponry he or she'd possessed, and in any case the guards were heavily armed. He bolted toward the doors, but they did not open. Turning at bay, he raised his hands in protest or surrender as the Gotal captain pulled her blaster from her side and fired a stun beam into his chest from a distance of less than a meter. The shock of it threw the little journalist back against the door, where he slumped slowly to the floor in a tangle of golden fur and pink-and-blue silk.

The Gotal captain glanced around her. Under the watchful eyes of the guards, none of the others in the room had moved. Perhaps, deduced Threepio, they had their own reasons for wishing to remain inconspicuous. The captain spoke to the guards nearest her, in a voice so low that only a droid's acute audio receptors could pick up what she said.

She said, "Airlock three."

•   •   •

Stretched in the crevice of a glittering cliff face, Leia shaded her eyes against the rising sun glare. Wind made her face feel as if it had been chemically processed. From her high ledge she could see back along the maze of canyons, harsh edged and broken as old tectonic upheavals had left them, every surface a mirror magnifying the heatless light.

If they were looking for her, she couldn't tell it.

Certainly she saw nothing. Ashgad could easily program simple tracker droids to her physical parameters: movement, mass, and body temperature. For this reason she had sacrificed the antigrav unit and one of the heaters, sending it drifting away down the canyon as a decoy. Beldorion's decayed powers might sense the difference, but Leia was willing to bet that even had the Force not lain like a crackling magnetic field over the entire planet, the effort was beyond the one-time Knight.

She closed her eyes for a moment, weary to exhaustion. She still didn't know why she hadn't been dashed to jelly at the foot of the mesa—there must have been more juice in the coil than she'd thought. She felt like she'd dodged, and run, and scrambled a hundred kilometers since then.

Opening her eyes again, she unfolded the map. Years on the run with the Rebel forces had taught her to read elevation maps. She identified the canyon she'd climbed up, and the two peaks between which she had to clamber to come down on the deserted gun station at Bleak Point. There was no water marked anywhere on the map, so she didn't know whether there would be a pump of any kind at her destination. Only about a quarter of the water in the pitcher remained, and she didn't know how long it would take her to get a message out . . .

. . . If the gun station still contained working equipment capable of subspace range.

Stiffly, achingly, she bent to examine the wreckage of her gold-stamped ceremonial boots, and with bleeding fingers ripped another length of silver space tape to add to the existing crisscross of repairs.

If Ashgad didn't have some means of picking up and tracking such a signal.

If there were anyone alive to hear.

She tried not to think about the Death Seed and about how much her feet hurt.

The Death Seed.

The echo of it returned again and again to her mind.

Idiot, idiot, idiot. She slung the sealed pitcher over her back once more and started the long, cautious, terrible process of following the ledge back along the cliff toward the high-up cluster of amethyst peaks that were her next landmark.

She'd seen records of other governments, other armies, other men who had attempted to use plague as a weapon. Hathrox III came to mind. It had been twelve centuries, according to the records unearthed there, and the place was still on the Registry as a Standing Hazard. The team that had retrieved the records had all died, as had the crew of their rescue ship and the entire staff of the quarantine facility to which they'd been taken. According to the records—tapped into by remote at a distance—the terrorist organization that had developed that particular quasivirus had had a "fool-proof" antivirus.

Are you familiar with the term mutate, *boys and girls?* Leia's mouth twisted in cynical despair. *Have you ever heard the words* human error? *Minor equipment failure? How about that little phrase 'Oh, we didn't think of THAT'?*

Death Seed.

Don't you dare. Don't you DARE.

But they already had dared. If Ashgad's memos were correct, the Death Seed was already spreading through the fleet, crippling it as revolt after revolt broke out across the sector and Admiral Larm's ships moved in. Apparently Dzym could control the timing of its starts if he were in the area or cared about doing so—otherwise it spread on its own.

Would Beldorion hear her, if she tried to call out to Luke again?

Her hand touched the lightsaber at her belt. She should have listened to Luke, she thought. Spent more time in training. Luke wouldn't have this trouble.

Neither would Vader, of course.

Panting, hands bleeding, knees torn from the bitter mangling of uneroded stone, Leia gained the crest of the ridge between the two peaks and looked down on the gun station below.

It looked tiny, hundreds of meters below. A blunt black cylinder, doorless and without so much as a centimeter of transparisteel, set close beside the heavy shoulder of rock that gave the place its name. The original black stone had been added to with rude defensive works, reminiscent of a woman in a formal senatorial robe wearing a shade-drinks-and-stereo picnic hat. She could get in, thought Leia, through those bristling wood-and-metal upper works, were she willing to sacrifice her blanket by cutting it into strips to lengthen the cable.

She managed, but only just. Throwing the hook from a precarious balance point at the top of the rock spur, with the help of the pouring wind she was able to lodge it among the bristling beams. Releasing the cable to hang free along the wall, she climbed to the ground again, and stumbled to the place where the cable, added to by blanket strips, reached to within a meter of the gravel.

It had been years since Leia had shinnied up a wall. Once, twenty meters up, pummeled by the wind, arms burning and breath short and hard in her lungs, she felt a wave of dizziness rise over her and thought, *I'm going to faint.*

She wrapped the cable around her arms, pressed her forehead to the black stone, wind crushing her like a torrent of ice, willed the giddiness to pass. Her body trembled with hunger and fatigue. *I'll never make it.*

But she did. She pulled the cable up after her when she reached the top, and crept like an exhausted old woman to the cluster of shielded coils, reflectors, and modulators that rose through the pavement among the jury-rigged defensive works: The great laser cannons pointed at the sky.

Night brought the dim white daytime stars to unwinking brilliance among the tangle of beams and razor wire and lessened the pounding brutality of the wind. Leia cut through the locks on the doors that led down to the station below, afterward barricading the doors as well as she could behind her. The gun station, being without transparisteel, might well be haunted with the same groping, mutating vermin that had attacked her in the stairway of Ashgad's house. If that were the case, she would be forced to sleep on the roof, and would probably freeze.

She saw none of those things, but there were hundreds of fingernail-size drochs in the stairway. Some turned toward her in the muted beam of her downward-pointing glowrod, and began to crawl purposefully in her direction up the steps. Leia activated her lightsaber and flicked them with its tip. Those she touched sizzled and curled into balls of charred death. The others crawled after her, as she descended the stair.

The equipment in the station was old, but serviceable.

Most of the gun coils themselves were sealed, but the controls were open, a simple switching mechanism transferring targeting from the sealed computers to manual. *They have to have teaching of some kind.* She flicked the test switches experimentally, studied the readouts. The targeting equipment was elementary, but nobody who hadn't been trained could have used it. *Something the Listeners pass along with the doctrines they hear from the voices in the wastelands?*

Why would they want to destroy ships coming in and ships going out? Just because they want to keep the world primitive?

Or was there something else?

Sharp pain stabbed the calf of her leg. Looking down, she saw three or four huge drochs burrowing through the strips of space tape wrapped around her legs. Exhaustion and a slight breathlessness dragged at her, as it had after the attack by the creatures in the stairwell. *They must be related to drochs,* she thought, backing away from the targeting consoles and shining the glowrod all around her. The floor was dotted with the round, flat shapes of the insects. *Keep moving,* she thought. *Don't let your feet stay too long in any one place.*

The gun chamber was enormous, round, obviously occupying all of one level of the squat tower. Nothing in it even suggested communication equipment to her. Lamp fixtures hung dead from the smoke-black vaults.

A steel ladder in the center of the floor communicated with the lower level, and there was equipment there, too, sealed behind soot-stained and filthy black metal. Wornout blankets, heaps of arrows and spears, boxes of metal bullets, explosive ceramic pellets, and paper-wrapped gravel shot strewed the floor. Leia leaned against the ladder, fighting a wave of dizziness, her body trembling and suddenly cold. *Drochs,* she thought. *Sunlight will make me feel better.* But she realized it could just as easily have been exhaustion, hunger, and the fatigue of unaccustomed hardship.

Far above her, she heard the sudden slither and crash of falling beams and furniture.

The barricade! Her heart froze. Boots clumped with muffled tread on the floor above, and the hard white beam of a sodium light veered and flickered down the opening in the floor. Voices murmured. A quick glance around showed her there was no further ladder down—the rest of the tower must be taken up with the power supply of the guns themselves. Though she knew the dark spaces between the equipment were crawling with drochs, Leia wedged herself between two anonymous black boxes, bruised hand gripping the lightsaber. The light from above grew stronger, moving with the movement of being carried, turned, scanned along the floor. Someone said, "Look," and was shushed.

The dead drochs, thought Leia. And then, *I must have left tracks in the dust of the floor as well.*

Her whole body ached with the thought of having to fight. *Luke,* she thought, *if I get out of this alive I'm going to start training with you, at least to get into condition.*

Her cold hands slid over the switch on the lightsaber.

Light poured from above, and a shadow came down two steps of the ladder, then dropped lightly to the floor and stepped at once into shadows, a trained warrior seeking cover. Other shadows clustered above, blocking most of the light, but a stray beam of it caught a sand-scoured red coat, a whirlwind of smoke-colored veils, the metal plates and buckles of heavy boots. There was movement, and with a faint hum the sun-yellow blade of a lightsaber stabbed into existence.

A woman's voice said, "Come out."

Leia lowered her weapon, suddenly dizzy. "Callista?" she said.

The blade lowered, and the red figure before her put up a black-gloved hand to push away the veils that wrapped her face. "Leia?"

16

"We are the weapons of the Force." Callista's strong fingers pulled the roll of silver space tape taut, while she fished one-handed in the pocket of her crimson coat for a knife. Above her, the iron beams of the gun station's defensive works lost themselves in the darkness, like a deadly sieve of razor wire set to trap the cold diamond stars. "We always have been, since the beginning of the Order; since people first began to understand the existence of the Force."

Leia said softly, "That's what scares me."

"I know."

She sliced off the tape, finished attaching a cutout sole of cu-pa leather to the broken ruin of Leia's boot, and handed it back, folding up and pocketing the knife, one-handed again, with the quick economy of a longtime jury-rigger. The face that had been Cray Mingla's had changed. Look as she might for the features of the young scientist she had known, the woman who had given up her body to Callista that she herself might seek her lover on the Other Side, Leia could see only the lost Jedi, the woman her brother so deeply loved. In colorless starlight, no trace of Cray's blond remained in the thick masses of Callista's hair. Dark with the darkness, in daylight it would be the soft, medium-brown that it had been turning when last she'd seen this woman with Luke. Her gray eyes were mostly hidden in the shadows of level dark brows.

"I don't think Luke understands that, really." Callista moved her head a little at some sound on the other side of the great black gun muzzle, pointing skyward in the center of the station's open roof. It was only one of the other Therans setting up a small but powerful electroheater to make supper, calling out to a couple of the young women of the troop. The evening wind had stilled. Bé, the troop Listener, a twig of a man who might have been thirty or fifty, passed like a shadow among the riders who spread blankets, cleaned weapons, spoke softly among themselves all around.

The Force was a dark sea, sounding in the night. Leia wondered if Callista could feel it as she could.

"People have tried to use him," Callista went on, "from the moment he put out his hand and summoned his lightsaber to come to him. Vader wanted to turn him. Palpatine wanted his services. Palpatine's clone managed to enslave him for a time. But Luke is strong, stronger than he knows. And Luke has a single purpose. I suppose you could say that he has a pure heart."

She folded her arms, more relaxed than Leia had seen her toward the end there, in Luke's presence. Her breath made a smoke of diamonds as she spoke. "Luke doesn't hunger after power. In some ways I don't think he understands those who do."

"No." Leia had never thought of it in those terms, but she recognized that Callista was right. Luke had never sought to be a commander of anything except a wing squadron. He wasn't the tactician Han was. At the Jedi

Academy, all he sought was to teach, to learn, to further the ways of the Force for all. He wanted a Jedi Order so that he could be part of it, not for the sake of having pupils at his beck and call.

"But you understand."

"Yes."

"Then you understand why I had to leave."

Leia sighed, a whisper of regret. "Yes." In a way, she had always understood.

There was silence for a time, the crystals of the high peaks catching the fragmented glare of the bitter stars. "I'm like Luke," Callista went on, speaking softly, almost to herself. "I never wanted power. Only to learn. Only to be with other people who understand. But people use those who have our power, Leia. Vader wanted to use you. If he hadn't spoken of his intention to do so, I don't think Luke would have been angry enough to go after him, to fight him to the death. You told me how Thrawn and Pellaeon tried to kidnap your children, how C'baoth wanted them as weapons of his own ambition. I've seen how hard you try to teach Jacen and Jaina to listen to their own hearts, to have a sense of fairness, of justice. So they won't be pawns. So they won't be twisted. But for a long time they'll be weak, because they're children, and it's easy to influence children by love and hate and lies."

"Yes," said Leia again. She pulled on her boot, drew more closely about her the thick coat of rough-woven raw majie that someone had lent her, and walked over to the parapet beside which Callista sat. She had told the younger woman of her dream and of the fear that had followed her since.

"I want them to be happy," she said, and leaned her cheek on the wind-scoured metal of the beam. "I want them to be children, to have the birthright of their inno- cence. But at the same time, I know they can't just follow any path they want. With their powers in the Force, I have to teach them to distinguish lies from truth, to seek justice the way my father . . . the way Bail Organa sought justice. I have to . . . to protect the next generation from them. The way I have to protect the present generation from myself."

Looking down at the woman still seated against the parapet, she saw in the lost Jedi's starlit eyes the understanding of what she meant. Of the darker fear that lay wrapped in the images of the dream.

"To protect this generation from yourself," said Callista gently, "you have to embrace the way of the Jedi, Leia. Not flee it. Luke is right."

She stood, unfolding herself to her lanky height, her crimson clothing almost black in the star glimmer and the pallid glow reflected from the shining stones. Nights on Nam Chorios, without benefit of warming oceans, were unbelievably cold, even in this summer season. Leia huddled her gloved hands in her armpits and wondered how the Therans managed, night after night, under the open stars.

"There's a woman in Hweg Shul named Taselda, a small-time Jedi adept who came to this planet centuries ago, seeking power. The way I came."

"Beldorion spoke of her," said Leia. "Was he her partner?"

"They came here together. After this long, telling lies to themselves, to each other, to everyone, I'm not sure exactly what took place. They were both adepts, but neither had much power. Only one of them had sufficient training to make a lightsaber, but I don't know which. I don't think either of them has the capacity for it now. Like me, they came here seeking an easy answer."

"I didn't think Hutts *could* be born strong in the Force."

"Don't underestimate the Force, Leia," said Callista. "Anyone—anything—can be born in its light. There's a tree on the planet Dagobah that's strong in it. Sea slugs in the oceans of Calamari use it to draw plankton into their mouths until they grow to be bigger than starfighters. But they haven't the sentient mind to learn to use it beyond that. And that is for the best."

She sighed.

Suddenly sure of it, Leia said, "You were the slave Liegeus spoke of, weren't you? The one Beldorion sold or traded to Dzym."

Callista stood so silent for so long that Leia feared she'd angered her, but in time she nodded. "Having been Taselda's slave before," she said. "I let myself be enslaved, because I was so hungry, so desperate. She used me, as Beldorion would have used me, had I been any good to him. As he'd have used you."

Leia nodded again. The pain in Callista's face was frightening to see, and she felt anger stir in her again, this time not anger at Ashgad specifically, but at them all: Beldorion, the Rationalists, Moff Getelles, all those who grabbed for petty goals and broke and ruined lives in the process, not seeing anything beyond their own wants. But it was sour anger, like brittle ice above a still well of endless grief.

"As long as I can be manipulated like that," Callista went on, "as long as I can be used—as long as I lack my own power in the Force—I am a prime candidate for the dark side. I'm standing in its shadow now. If there is a way for me at all, I have to follow it alone. I will love Luke until the day I die and beyond, but I will not pull him into that shadow with me. Please, Leia. Make him understand."

•   •   •

"What do we have?" Han Solo strode into the bridge still stripping off the helmet and gloves of his e-suit, registered immediately the blinking red lights over the comm board, the worried note in Chewbacca's growl that had summoned him and Lando back onto the ship in double-time. Outside, terrible stillness lay over the pitch-black lava plains of Exodo II, the eternal dust that lay around the bore holes of the ghaswars that were the planet's most plentiful life form stirring uneasily in the glare of the *Millennium Falcon*'s lights. The wrecked scout cruiser they'd traced there had been in much the same shape as the *Corbantis* had been, save that the engines had been long cold, the crew dead of radiation poisoning, asphyxiation, cold, and ghaswar bores.

Chewbacca rumbled a reply and put up the readout. Han stared at it, aghast. "That's gotta be wrong."

Lando came striding down the corridor. He'd taken off his e-suit and was combing his crisply curling black hair. He'd been badly shaken by the bodies on the destroyed cruiser and more so by the evidence that it, too, had been destroyed by the tiny, knifelike missiles that had cut up the *Corbantis* and almost demolished the *Falcon*. "I've had a look at those barometric readings, old partner, and if we want to get off this planet before the next atmostide we'd better . . ."

His voice trailed off. He stood staring at the screenful of data the Wookiee had transferred to the main viewer.

"What the hell is *that*?"

"What's it look like?" demanded Han, shaken. "It's an invading fleet, coming out of hyperspace and heading right this way."

"Artoo-Detoo, what in heaven's name do you think you're doing?" Threepio toddled after his counterpart as the astromech wheeled into life again the moment the doors of the impound bay were shut, heading over to the access panel by the door. "Honestly, ever since poor Captain Bortrek installed those extra interface circuits you have been behaving in a most extraordinary fashion! You know as well as I do that with these restraining bolts we're not going to be able to leave the room!"

Artoo merely tweeped a request.

"Why?"

Artoo explained.

"I don't see that," protested Threepio. "I don't see at all how removing that panel, even if I could do it, would save poor Master Yarbolk from being put out the airlock. If we're discovered, as we surely will be, we could get into terrible trouble!"

Artoo pointed out that as troubles went, being dissected for one's microprocessors and later paid for at a ninety-five percent discount to one's owners was as terrible as it got.

"I'm really not programmed for this kind of thing at all! Oh, why will not anyone believe me!" Threepio pressed one forefinger against the center of the access plate above the door panel and thrust, with all the strength of his hydraulic arm joint. Never, in any circumstances, would he have exerted his strength against living flesh of any variety, but metal was metal, and not being up to military standard, this metal buckled along the edge sufficiently for him to get his fingers under the plate and pull it free. Artoo proceeded to deliver a string of instructions.

"Honestly, I think those additional circuits disrupted your logic modifiers! Green wires connected to coaxial links—you don't *possess* coaxial links! Oh." Threepio flipped open one of the silvery gray add-ons screwed to his counterpart's side. "Well, I'm sure that they aren't good for you."

Nevertheless, he hooked the links into the green wires, and listened to the flow of bleeps, twitters, and chirps that Artoo-Detoo poured into the quarantine ship's internal relay system.

"Artoo-Detoo, that is a patent untruth!" declared Threepio indignantly. "First you disable the opening mechanism on the doors of airlock three, then you cause the system to believe that those doors *have* been opened . . . and even should you help Master Yarbolk escape from that airlock, that doesn't do *us* any good, you know. We're still unable to leave this hold while we have the restraining bolts on, and *he* is still unable to get off this vessel."

The golden protocol droid turned away, arms folded in the human-form expression of indignation and uninvolvement. "I won't have anything further to do with this."

Artoo made a sad little noise, but no request to be unhooked from the access hatch. Indeed, he produced small blips and whirrs every now and then, which indicated to Threepio that the astromech was still monitoring something in the QEC's main computer. It became clear what it was when he rocked a little on his wheels and tweeted excitedly. The next moment the doors of the impound hold opened, and Yarbolk hustled inside.

"I owe you," he whispered excitedly, fishing in his pocket and producing a magnetic bolt extractor and a pair of wire snips. "Brothers, I owe you plenty. This whole ship stinks! The Big Green Fish only knows who paid that captain how much to put me out the airlock. Maybe she thought the order was on the up-and-up."

"It could be," surmised Threepio, as the Chadra-Fan popped the restraining bolt from his golden chest.

"Artoo here claims there is a traitor, or at least a major information leak, on the Galactic Council."

"And the Rebels have taken Coruscant," muttered Yarbolk, going to work on Artoo. "Tell me something I don't know. You went and blabbed that Ashgad had kidnapped Lady O-S. Is that true?"

Threepio hesitated, belated visions of galaxywide coverage cascading into his deductive logic circuits.

"Because if it is, you better keep damn quiet about it, my tinny friend, if you don't want her getting what I nearly got. And as for a traitor on the Council—Fish, I figured that one out weeks ago! Loronar buys and sells Senators and governors in the Republic and out of it. All it takes is a few strategic contributions to good causes. Hold that door, would you, Threesie? It's gonna close again once I get Artie unhooked . . . ah. Thanks."

He looped up the wires and coax cables into the interface box on Artoo's side and replaced the strip of silver space tape that had held its hatch closed. "All those Senators have blind spots. Pet causes. Like 'order in the galaxy' or 'the rights of all sentient species' or 'the rights of one obviously superior sentient species to put all other sentient species straight whether they want to be put straight or not.' And it's Loronar's business to know what those blind spots are."

He was hurrying down the corridor as he spoke, furry feet making no sound, wide nostrils snuffing softly. Once he halted, pushing the two droids back into the niche of a bay door. Two Sullustan guards walked by, weapons slung casually over their shoulders, bodies slumped with fatigue. "Thank your lucky nuts and bolts the whole ship's understaffed and occupied with those Aqualish smugglers up in the holding area. Which one of these bays is their ship in, Artie?"

Artoo cornered determinedly and made his way down

a short passage to a landing bay whose doors, surprisingly, stood open. They passed inside, Yarbolk pausing to crank the doors shut manually from within. The bay was tiny and almost completely filled by the lumpy ovoid of the Aqualish smugglers' vessel. Beyond the dark, silvery green egg of the ship, the magnetic field glimmered faintly around the oval shape of the entry port. Yarbolk hooked Artoo's coax links into the access hatch beside the bay door: "Figure five minutes should do us?"

Artoo tweeped.

"You can get that baby started in that short a time?"

Artoo tweeped again, indignantly.

"Okay, okay. Once you get it to turn over those things are candy to fly. I doubt she's got the juice in her to make it to Cybloc, but I know a fellow on Budpok who'll buy her, no questions asked, cargo and all. The proceeds should get me back to the Core, and you to Cybloc no problem."

"Not again," groaned Threepio, as he, Artoo, and Yarbolk hastened across the decking to the Aqualish ship. "I do hope we can arrive at a more convincing disguise this time. I must say that I am quite frankly becoming very tired of being treated as the potential personal property of every sentient being we meet."

"Not to worry." Yarbolk pulled the hatch shut behind them and twirled the locking rings—for a space-going civilization, the Aqualish had some surprisingly primitive features on their ships. He toddled ahead of the two droids to the bridge, where he hooked Artoo into the computer core again and perched on the stool before the console, his furry little feet dangling.

"I have a plan—one that *doesn't* depend on you two pretending to be anything you're not."

Threepio said nothing, but in the portion of his central processing unit that formed opinions as protocol paradigms for communications facilitation, he reflected that he was heartily sick of plans.

They were undoubtedly doomed.

From the dense shadow at the base of the plateau, Luke looked up the striated cliff-face at the matte black jumble of Seti Ashgad's compound, and wondered how many of those glowing rectangles of yellow and white denoted occupation. Was one of them Leia's prison? Or were they holding her somewhere in the heart of the house, within the rock of the plateau itself?

Shivering in the dense cold, he reached out with his mind, seeking to touch hers—*Leia . . .*—but did not know if she could hear. In the darkness, the whisper of the Force around him was very strong, pressing on his mind, tugging at all his thoughts, so that he was hard put to keep it at bay. Even as there were ways of using the Force to keep from being seen, so it was possible to keep from making an image on certain types of sensors. Luke hoped that such minor use wasn't sufficient to trigger a reaction elsewhere on the planet.

What was happening elsewhere in the galaxy as a result of Leia's kidnapping—what other events that kidnapping would have been coordinated with—he didn't like to think.

He'd brought a toolkit from Croig's shop—leaving most of his slender finances to pay for it—and it didn't take long to rewire the alarm and spring the doorcatches. His small glowrod showed him a permacrete parking bay containing a sleek black Mobquet Chariot, and by the stains on the floor there were two other speeders usually in residence, one of them with a faulty rear coil. Turbolift doors gleamed dully in the light. Luke ran the beam along the wall, seeking a stairway door, and drochs the size of his thumb waddled and skittered out of his way.

The stairway, he thought, was going to be bad.

The Force was life, Yoda had said. Connecting all living things. What he felt, standing in the doorway to the stair and reaching up with whatever senses he could muster, Luke had never felt before and never wanted to feel again.

Life, thick and cloying. Life huge and all-encompassing—there couldn't *possibly* be that many creatures in the stairwell! Billions, billions. . . . The sense of life there was overwhelming, and yet there was something hideously wrong with it. Something ugly, evil, rotted. A dirty miasma, a sense of fermentation, swollen like cancerous tissue, rotted and foul. Luke had no idea how to interpret this, no concept of what this meant, or even if his perception were accurate. He couldn't even tell if it was billions of lives he felt, or only one, huge and vile and waiting.

But Leia had to be up there.

The lightsaber hummed to life in his hand. He maneuvered the little clip-on glowrod from the toolkit onto the front flap-pocket of his coverall, flicked it on.

Permacrete steps ascended to a landing, then turned out of his view. Darkness, and something moving along the walls. With the choking inner sense of evil it was impossible to determine anything else about what might be up there, shape or size or sound or smell.

Cautiously, Luke began to climb.

He passed one landing, two, then three. Each break in the stair was twenty steps up. The plateau looked well over three hundred meters high, but there was no telling how deep the foundations of the house extended. As far as Luke could tell, there were no holocams or viewers in the stairwell: only a close-crowding monotony of permacrete walls, grimy with the brown tracks of drochs. The join of the walls and floor was almost sepia with the noisome exudations of their bodies.

Pain stabbed him in the calf and he looked down to see half a dozen huge drochs—the length of his thumb—wriggling and climbing up his boots. Several had bitten through his pants leg and into the flesh already. Disgusted, he pulled a hypo-driver from his belt and used the shaft of it to dislodge those that hadn't bitten yet, but more were crawling purposefully toward him across the floor.

As he bent down, the light of his little glowrod fell on them, and to his surprise he saw that several of the biggest had definite limbs, pincer-clawed or tentacular, sometimes both on the same organism. He stepped quicker, reminding himself that Arvid said they simply died and dissolved in the flesh. . . .

But the pain in his calf was followed by weariness, a cold lassitude, an ache in his chest, and the sudden, overwhelming desire for sleep.

He stepped around a corner, and onto another landing, and there they were.

The floor was brown with them. Among the glistening mass there were half a dozen nearly the size of Luke's hand, spider-shaped or arthropod, some with the batrachian, springing legs of a Cabuloid pad-hopper. . . .

Luke fell back, appalled, and something struck him from behind, fastening to his back between the shoulder blades, and pain like the slice of a chisel jabbed the back of his neck.

He flung himself back against the wall, crushing whatever it was against the permacrete, but as if that had been a signal the drochs on the floor hopped and skittered and flowed toward him. The pain on his neck still reechoed, though a sticky fluid trickling down his back told him that whatever had attacked him was dead. He turned to flee down the stairs and saw that the drochs had gathered in behind him, big and small, some of them huge, legged, toothed, and fast as lizards. Weakness flowed over him with the agony of a hundred bites, as if all his veins had been opened—not blood loss, he knew at once, but life-loss, the draining of the electrochemical field of his nervous system, of the life essence of his flesh and heart.

He fell against the wall, clinging to the permacrete to stay upright, knowing that if he went down among them he was a dead man indeed. They evaded the slashes of his lightsaber, a weapon too big to touch them, too slow for all its speed. On the steps ahead of him Luke saw the biggest droch of all, nearly twice the size of his two fists bunched together, carcinomorphic, staring at him with two bright eyes on short stalks, and he thought, *It's sentient. Or nearly so.*

And he knew somehow that it was this thing that had orchestrated the attack on him, letting him come so far up the steps that there was no chance of descent.

He cut at it, staggering with weakness. The thing sprang aside. Luke's knees gave out and he fell, gasping, dizzy, pain stabbing him as if he were rolled in needles. . . .

And he summoned the Force.

Like a shining wind he called it, and like a shining wind it came, tearing the drochs from his body as Vader had once torn cabinets and spools and railings from the infrastructure of the carbon-freeze chamber on Bespin to hurl at him. But the drochs he hurled away, crushing them against the walls, staggering to rise as more flowed toward him, from up the stairs and from below.

He thought, *I can't do this. The balance of the Force is broken. This will destroy some other place.* . . .

But when they fastened on him again, stabbing with

greedy mouths through the ripped cloth of his suit, panic and horror seized him, and he knew that he must use the Force or die.

Like a whirlwind the psychokinetic energy ripped and chopped at them, plucked them up and flung them against the walls, down the steps, and Luke had glimpses, in the jarring swirl of splintered light, of the bigger drochs seizing and fastening their mouths upon the smaller, then hurling themselves at him. The choking sensation of rotted, fermented life blotted his brain, more and more life, as if each droch were bloated on the lives of those it drank.

In for two creds, so let's rob the bank, thought Luke. *No sense in being inconspicuous now.* He directed the Force before him, and staggered up the stairs, climbing on his hands and knees, while above him he had the sense of the big arthropod droch retreating, claws clicking on the floor, eye-stalks watching him like evil stars out of the darkness.

17

"What's that?" Leia whirled at something that was less a
sound than a stabbing in her mind, a tightening in her
chest, flicking her consciousness like a whip. From deep
below them in the locked and sealed tower came a crashing sound, something falling. The Listener Bé caught up
a white lamp and sprang up the steps to the downward-
leading door, pressed himself to it like a spider. At the
same moment one of the other Therans camped on
the roof cried out, pointing. With a shiver Leia saw one of
the clapped-out grenade launchers rise from where it lay
and begin to smite itself against the black shielding of the
central gun.

Eerie in the uncertain starlight, it crashed against the
metal wall, over and over, bending the metal of its own
barrel in its violence, untouched by any hands. Leia
pressed back against the parapet, wondering if she were
the only one to hear a sound like dim shouting, the
clamor of voices within her own mind, crying something
she did not understand.

Then the voices dimmed. The grenade launcher fell to
the pavement again, its barrel bent nearly ninety degrees.

In the silence the yammer of the cu-pas on the ridge behind the gun station sounded suddenly clear.

"The Force," whispered Callista. "Someone is using the Force."

Leia shuddered. All desire that Callista's words had roused in her to learn to use the Force for good trickled away like ice melting in the summer sun. *Not if that's what it is. Not if that's what I could become, mindless power hammering in rage.*

"Beldorion?"

"Maybe," said Callista. "He still has that power within him, though he can't use it, or control it, as once he could. That's why he wanted you under his control."

Leia shook her head. "I don't understand." The very air seemed to whisper with a lambent horror, violence waiting just beyond the finger touch. "The . . . the Force here. Could it have done something to him?"

"Not the Force," said Callista. "Dzym. And the drochs. They're lifedrinkers, Leia. *They* are the Death Seed plague. The Grissmaths knew. They seeded the planet with drochs, hoping those political foes they exiled here would die. But the light of the sun fragmenting through the crystals here generates a radiation that weakens the electrochemical bonds of their tissues. It prevents the larger drochs from damping the electrochemistry of organic life until they're absorbed harmlessly by their hosts. The smaller ones it kills outright.

"I don't know how the prophet Theras knew this," she went on. "So little is known of him. Certainly he never knew that it was the drochs who caused the plague, only that no ship large enough to carry heavy shielding should be permitted to leave the planet. He may have been a spy, or a politician opposed to the Grissmaths. But at least he understood that the planet must be kept in quarantine. Over the years that must have extended to forbidding larger ships to land. Somehow he must have known there was a connection."

"And Ashgad took them out in the flesh of the synthdroids," said Leia softly. "How could he do that? How could he get them past the quarantine screens? How can Dzym control them the way he does?"

"I can't prove this," said Callista softly. "But I think the drochs are sentient, after a fashion. Even the littlest ones. They mimic shapes, chemistry, electromagnetic currents, anything, down to the cellular level. That's why they can't be detected. I think in some ways they mimic intelligence as well. They become of the same substance as their hosts, even as they're drawing the life out of them and into themselves. And the big ones, the captain drochs, can draw life out of the victims *through* the smaller ones, without themselves attaching to their hosts. That's when they get dangerous," she went on, shaking her head. "The more life they drink—their victims' or each other's—the more intelligent they become. Bigger, and more capable of mutability. Those things you described in the stairwell of Ashgad's house weren't related to drochs, they *were* drochs. Drochs grown big from eating one another, from absorbing one another's energy. People used to eat them, to absorb life and energy into themselves."

"Does it work?" The memory of Beldorion digging around in his cushions and popping drochs into that huge, slime-dribbling slit of mouth came revoltingly back to her.

"In its way," said Callista. "In its way."

The stab of pain, of terror, struck Leia again, the voices clamoring in her brain, and a hundred meters off the black mouth of a canyon suddenly spewed forth a whirl of dust, like sparkling smoke in the starlight. Not a breath of wind stirred, but she saw boulders, slabs of crystal and granite and basalt, leap like fish in the maelstrom, and heard the hammer and crash of them striking the canyon's walls. Panic closed her throat. Callista sprang to the top of the parapet, barely touching the maze of beams and wire for balance, staring out across the salt-white wasteland at the sudden whirl and rise of dust from that direction that collected slabs and boulders as it came. Beneath them in the gun station, other things were falling, or hammering frenziedly against the walls.

Then the horror sank again, the voices in her mind stilled. Leia wondered why she thought they had been saying her name.

Callista stepped down, her gray-black veils stilled, though they had whipped around her as if wind-blown while she listened. "That's too big for it to be simply Beldorion looking for you." Her eyes were grave. "Something else is going on. This is only my opinion, you understand, but I think that the drochs become part of the brain of those who eat them. And the bigger ones, if they're eaten, exert influence even after they're consumed. I know the bigger drochs—the truly big ones, the size of a pittin—can control the little ones. Dzym. . . ."

"Callista!" Bé cried out a warning. At the same moment sudden wind erupted from below the parapet, pouring out of the canyons all around the gun station. Grit ripped Leia's face, chunks of gravel and flying arrowheads of broken crystal gouged her cheeks and forehead. Above them and on all sides the beams and timbers of the defensive works began to shake, wire and rivets groaning and writhing like live things. Scarred face cut by shrapnel, arms covered with drochs digging into his flesh, the Listener emerged from the doorway of the tower and ran to where Callista stood, even as the grenade launchers, the stacks of pellet guns and spears, were sent sprawling by the kick of some giant, invisible foot.

One of the flamethrowers began to spout fire. Bé caught it up, hurled it over the parapet—Leia saw it flare like a torch on its way down before it exploded, halfway down the face of the tower. While other Therans grabbed metal cable that fell from the beams, snaking and snatching at them, Callista knocked ammunition loads and power-cores out of every weapon she could lay hands on, hurled them after the flamethrower into space. One exploded seconds after it left her hands, and by the reflected glare Leia saw the other woman's face, calm and weirdly peaceful in the whirlwind of her long dark hair.

Leia stooped, caught up a blaster rifle whose whole chamber glowed violent red, flung it over the parapet. Visibility was down to almost nothing with the dust, and the violence of the storm was fast tearing the swaying beams free. A coil of razor wire sprang loose and lashed across Leia's back like a whip, blood soaking into her clothing as Callista dragged her to the cable the Therans had used to climb the tower.

Climbing down a cable after having scrambled up only hours ago was the last thing Leia wanted to do. But she felt the force of the horror building, not diminishing. Through the voices crying in her mind she thought she heard Luke's voice, sensed Luke's terror and desperation. She knew to the marrow of her bones that to remain in this place, with the forces being unleashed, might well mean death.

She swung over the parapet, wrapped her hands around the cable, icy wind ripping at her long hair and raking her back with sand through the rent in her shirt. It seemed to her she descended forever, alone in howling darkness, with flying boulders shattering against the tower walls and beams and wire raining down past her. How Bé and Callista guided the band to the cu-pas and speeders clustered on the canyon ridge, she didn't know.

Unlike ordinary winds, these terrible upheavals in the Force were not averted or thwarted by the canyon walls. They ripped and tore at the Therans as they worked their way upward along the canyons, away from the center of the storm. Leia clung to the neck of her borrowed cu-pa, glimpsing only now and then Callista riding beside her, dragging the beast along by the rein.

All the time she could hear Luke's voice, feel his consciousness in the storm.

"Leia!" The cry echoed down the stairwell, a man's voice wrung with agony and despair.

Luke stumbled, and let the Force around him fade and ease. *She's there. Or someone up there knows where she is.* Clinging to the wall, knees jellied with weakness, he readied his lightsaber again, made himself find the strength to climb.

The psychic stench of the drochs was overwhelming. It washed over Luke as he neared the door, and saw what lay in the room beyond.

It was far too deep in the plateau to be the foundation of the house. Probably a guard chamber or security watchroom of some kind, long abandoned. Walls, ceiling, and floor, it swarmed with drochs, a vast hideousness drunk and re-drunk from droch to droch until the whole air was black with it. Luke saw, scuttling along the wall, the carcinoform droch that seemed able to command the others, weirdly like a general reviewing troops, but that awareness was only for an instant.

A man lay in the midst of the room. He had ceased trying to get up, though Luke saw him pluck weakly at the brown, squirming things as they covered his face. The stalk-eyed commander-droch scuttled in now and then to pluck smaller drochs from the dying man's body, drinking them dry and casting them aside to be picked and finished by the tinier fry that skirmished around the edges. Luke was raising his hand, ready to summon the Force again, when movement flickered in the doorway on the opposite wall, the doorway that led to a further-ascending flight of stairs, and a soft voice whispered,

"Now, now, what have we here? Shoo-shoo."

The drochs scuttered from their victim, and Luke slapped the glowrod on his chest into darkness, and stood back out of the room's single dim orange ceiling-lamp. They retreated, but remained close around the man, who lay now in the midst of the floor, smallish and slim and graying and vaguely familiar. His clothing was torn in a thousand places to reveal flesh all dotted with the red marks of their bites, and his chest rose and fell with the desperate effort to breathe. The man walking toward him from the doorway Luke definitely recognized as Seti Ashgad's secretary, Dzym, said to be an inhabitant of this planet. . . .

But his mind still open, still conditioned to the reactions of this place, Luke felt the miasma of him, the vast, dark, stinking aura of rotted power, an aura so huge, so dense, that it nearly made him sick.

Dzym whispered, "Shoo-shoo," again, and the circle of drochs expanded infinitesimally. The big stalk-eyed one started to scamper for the doorway, where Luke stood, and Dzym strode forward and caught it in two steps, lifting it up between his gloved hands. The thing clawed frantically at him with its pinchers, and Dzym laughed, a horrible sound, like a computer recording of laughter, or a bird that has been taught to mimic the sound. Dzym released one hand, and with small, sharp brown teeth pulled off the violet leather glove, and Luke saw that his hand bore only the most superficial resemblance to a human limb at all. It was, in fact, a sort of mouth, orifices gaping on the palm and at the ends of the fingers, tinier mouths all red and probing, like the heads of maggots, which Dzym then fastened around the crab-thing's body.

Dzym closed his eyes, and drew deep his breath. The droch in his hand squirmed horribly, weaker and weaker, and Dzym smiled in his reverie. "Ah, I've been hunting you for a long time, my little friend. Sweet . . ." He drew another rapt breath, like a man savoring wine. "Sweet."

At his feet the prone man rolled over, and started, feebly, to try to rise.

Dzym put his foot down hard on the victim's chest. "I thought we had an understanding about this, Liegeus," he said in his soft voice. "I thought you knew what the boundaries of Seti Ashgad's house were to be. Tell me that you knew."

The man Liegeus whispered, "I knew," while Dzym closed his eyes again, and lifted the still-wriggling super-droch to his face, where he bit and chewed at it with his mouth for a time, murmuring in his throat and sighing while brown matter ran down his chin and neck. In time he dropped the thing, and smiled, his blotted mouth like nothing human.

"They're so good, when they get that big," he murmured. "So sweet. Such a deep rush of life, such a concentration—though that little fellow was getting a wee bit big for his boots." He went to his knees at Liegeus's side, and the man tried to roll away from him, bringing his arm up over his face for protection.

Dzym reached out with his bare, dripping mouth-hand, and drew him back over. "As I suspect you are, my friend."

Liegeus made a weak noise of protest, whispered, "Please . . . Ashgad . . . I haven't finished installing the launch vectors . . ." but Dzym was clearly not paying any attention. He pulled off his other glove and began to stroke and caress the man's face and arms, leaving trails of bites and gashes along the major arteries and along what Luke recognized as the energy tracks of certain healing systems, the paths of electromagnetic synapse from heart and liver and brain. Dzym's eyes were shut in ecstasy, his head bowed forward, and Luke thought he could see restless, thrusting movements among the man's clothing, as if there were other limbs twitching on his back and chest, other mouths gaping and closing. Liegeus wept a little, and then lay still; he whispered, "Leia . . ." and that decided Luke.

Lightsaber flaring to life in his hand, Luke reached out with the Force and pulled Dzym from Liegeus, as he had pulled the drochs from himself, and hurled him against the wall. But Dzym was nimble and swift. He scrambled around, twisted as he struck the wall and fell to the floor, gummed mouth parting in a hiss of rage, and for a moment Luke felt the Force used to strike at him in return.

Not an expert's blow, not trained, but present, like poltergeist anger or the aimless psychokinesis of certain animals. Weakened as he was by the drochs, it was strong enough to knock him back against the wall. He caught his balance, sprang forward, and Dzym backed from him, pale eyes glaring, the front of his robe falling open to reveal the squirming mess of tubes and tentacles and secondary mouths beneath. The Force smote Luke again, weak and secondhand and stinking in his mind. Secondhand, absorbed from someone else, he thought. . . .

Then Dzym was gone. The door to the stair leading up slammed—Luke could hear the locking-rings clang over. He was readying his lightsaber to cut through the wood when a tiny breath behind him whispered, "Run. He'll use the drochs who've bitten you. . . ."

Luke turned. The man Liegeus tried to reach out toward him, to move his bloodied hand.

"They're his to command. They'll be in the stair."

Luke reached him in two strides, went to one knee at his side. "Lady Solo . . ."

"Gone. Fled. Looking for her—Beldorion and Ashgad. I thought I could . . . make good . . . get out . . . synthdroids down . . . thought I could find her."

In the open doorway to the downward-leading stair there was a dark glitter along the floor, a skittering movement that turned to a slow, sluggish flow. The dense, fetid sense of a million rotted lifetimes rolled out, like the smell of clotted blood. Luke slipped his arm under Liegeus's shoulders, pulled him to his feet. "Do you know where she might have gone?"

The lolling head rolled; the older man breathed, "Bleak Point gun station. Or a canyon in the hills. I don't . . ."

"Never mind," said Luke, breathing deep, gathering to him the strength of the Force. "We'll find her."

It was use the Force or die, he thought, and he wondered what they would say about it: Obi-Wan, and Callista, and Yoda. That he should die, rather than cause what he had caused last time—Tinnin Droo the smelter in agony from his burns, his assistant unable to walk? How was he to know that Leia's absence, Leia's death, wouldn't cause greater grief, greater destruction in the Republic?

And in his mind he could almost hear Obi-Wan's voice whispering, *Trust your feelings.*

And his instinct—he hoped completely detached from a desire not to be sucked of life by the filthy swarm flowing toward him across the dirty permacrete floor—was clear.

He smote them with the Force, clearing the way like a

maniac broom. Half-dragging, half-carrying Liegeus, Luke descended the stair, shaky himself and sickened with weakness, feeling the drochs still buried in his legs and arms drawing strength from him, feeding the strength into the monstrous creature, human only in form, that went by the name of Dzym.

The hangar doors were locked. Luke dumped the unconscious body he carried into the sleek black Star Destroyer—like Mobquet, ran the green laser blade of his lightsaber through the lock, and shoved and hauled the door open far enough to admit passage of the speeder. Mobquet Chariots started up with a coded ignition, but Luke hadn't tinkered with speeders for twenty-five years to no purpose—Han joked that Luke could hot-wire an Imperial torpedo-platform with one of Leia's hairpins.

Then they were running through the night, under the stars.

The Theran riders took refuge in a grotto deep in the hills, an enormous geode of amethyst away from the storm's heart. Two or three Therans illuminated glowrods or torches, and the glare of them twinkled on the rough jewels around them, the shadows moving strangely through the fugitive brightness. There must, thought Leia, be something in what Callista said about the crystals generating a radiance that killed the drochs. There were none in the cave.

After a long time of silence, hearing the boulders crashing like pebbles in the surf against the canyon walls outside, Leia asked softly, "Who is Dzym? What is he? He's keeping Ashgad alive, isn't he?"

Callista nodded. "As he's kept Beldorion alive—and Splendid—all these years. I think he had dealings with Taselda, too. The original split between them may have been on his account." Torchlight splintered over the faceted pocket of jewels in which they sat, made strange brightness over her thin face, in her colorless eyes.

"He's the key to Ashgad's deal with Loronar, the key to your kidnapping along with poor old Liegeus's ability to cut a perfect holofake: the one who could set the drochs to drink the life out of the ships' crews at a certain moment and no sooner. He controls them—drinks life through them."

"And he enjoys it," said Leia softly, remembering Dzym's face. "That's what he wanted me for, wasn't it? Because I'm a Jedi. So he could touch the Force."

"I don't think that was conscious in him," she said. "He couldn't use it, really, or not use it to any degree of skill. He just wants that life, that addition to his own life. He thinks he can control them all, no matter how far they spread. I don't know, but I think he's wrong. I believe it's only a matter of time—and not very much time—before they get far enough from him to slip from his control, before they breed in such numbers that they'll be controlling one another, not obeying him. But he doesn't believe that. And at heart he doesn't really care. All he wants is to get off this planet, into more fertile worlds."

"That doesn't tell me who he is," said Leia. "Or how he can do this."

"He can do this," said Callista, "because Dzym is a hormonally altered, mutated, and vastly overgrown two-hundred-and-fifty-year-old droch."

"Hills," whispered Liegeus. "Up the canyon. Death Seed—takes less than half an hour . . ."

The cold within Luke was unmistakable, terrifying. He couldn't even touch it with the Force, because its molecular structure was so precisely his own. He was surprised that his voice sounded so calm. "Can we outrun it? Get clear of his range?"

"Have to . . . cross the galaxy . . . to do that. No." Dzym's victim struggled to sit up, long hair flowing back with the wind. "Another way."

Luke's breath was beginning to drag hard by the time he halted the speeder, as far up a jagged crevice of crystalline scree as he could manage to ascend. His companion had fallen silent, and for a heartstopping time Luke feared that the man had died and in so doing condemned him to death as well. But Liegeus raised his head when Luke shook him, regarded him with dark eyes drunk with fatigue.

"Ah. Knew I couldn't . . . get out of it . . . this easily. Ground lightning kills them. Rig a jump-circuit field through the crystals . . . lots of them here . . ."

Luke was already dismantling the speeder's engine with fumbling hands.

Even a Mobquet Chariot could not generate one-thousandth of the power of the ground-lightning storms, but once a crude circuit had been wired to push electricity through the huge fragments of crystal that littered the talus-slope underfoot, the dim tingling of low-level current was palpable to someone sitting between the points of exchange. "It won't kill them," whispered Liegeus, as Luke handed him one of the thermal blankets from the Chariot's emergency kit, and sat down beside him. His hands and body itched with a discomfort that never reached the level of pain. "But it weakens them to the point that they can't kill us, can't draw off our energy and transmit it to Dzym. When the sun rises we'll be well."

Luke shivered and glanced skyward at the huge, cold, unwavering stars, wondering how much was left of the night. The electricity passing between the crystals and over the two men was too weak to throw light: Only now and then, a quick spark or a glow, like luminous swamp gas, seemed to wicker in the air. Of greater brightness were the stars themselves, whose pallid bluish gleam seemed to be picked up by the slabs and clusters and formations of shining stone that clustered the canyon walls.

He pulled his own too-thin blanket close around him. His words smoked in the wan electrical glare.

"Is she all right?" he asked. "Leia?"

The older man nodded. "Ashgad forbade Dzym to go near her. He's almost completely enslaved to Dzym, but at least until the *Reliant* was ready to take Dzym off-planet, away from all danger of the daytime radiance of the crystals, they couldn't let anyone be sure of her fate. Dzym couldn't argue with that—and this whole treaty with Getelles to get the mining rights for Loronar Corporation was Dzym's idea, to get himself off the planet—but he doesn't think like human beings. I kept him away from her as well as I could."

He let his head fall back again, on the jacket Luke had wadded up underneath it. "I say that as if I think it mitigates what I've done. It doesn't. It's just that I . . . that Dzym . . . I could not go against him. But when she escaped, I couldn't let her go alone. Unarmed, with nothing. She's . . . It's been a long time since I cared for anything or anyone except remaining alive another day. But Leia—Lady Solo, I should say . . . she was kind. And very brave. Certainly braver than I, though that could be said of the average lizard."

Luke's head was swimming. With part of his consciousness he was acutely aware of Dzym's malice, of his attempt to draw away the energy that kept Luke's flesh warm and his heart beating. But through his dizziness he heard the voices again, whispering, very close to him now. They were saying something. Saying something to him. About Leia, he thought, or at least about the image of her. He saw a slim dark-haired woman doing something with what looked like an antigrav unit. Programming it?

The vision slid away.

Who are they? he wanted to ask. Those invisible beings, the watchers in the hills? Where were their cities, or where had their cities been before the dying of the seas?

Instead he asked, "Who are you?"

In the dark at the bottom of the canyon, Liegeus was only a sense of living, an echo of the Force, but he heard the man's chuckle. "A failure," he replied softly. "The blackest sheep the House Vorn ever produced. A philosopher, I've styled myself. But my art has always been imitative, mocking up holos, striving for perfection and the belief of others. I was a harmless prankster as a child, and I loved the precision of it. I think that usually reads as 'holo forger' to law enforcement agencies, though men of my talents can make fortunes in the entertainment industry. But for my sins I was that rare treasure for such as Ashgad: a man whose family would not miss him. To them, for years, I have been as one dead."

He sighed, and for a time there was no sound but the faint hissing of the speeder's electrical system, and the occasional pops of the free-flowing circuits jumping.

"Don't be too hard on Ashgad," he whispered. "He's more a slave to Dzym than I am.

"Ironic, isn't it? That Dzym, who started out his life as an appetizer, should . . ."

"As a what?" asked Luke, startled.

"An appetizer." Liegeus blinked up at him. "I'm sorry. I'm getting ahead of myself. Forgotten . . ." He shook his head, trying to clear it, but the lassitude did not leave his eyes. "It was Beldorion's greed—or I suppose one could say his gourmandism—that was his downfall. That Kubazi chef of his, Zubindi, was always experimenting with enzymatically enhancing and gene-splicing new types of insects so they'd be tastier, juicier, more fun for Beldorion to eat. Hutts like to eat sentient things, you know. They like the game of chasing them around the plate for a bit. Vile things."

He shook his head again, and this time Luke glimpsed the echoes of ugly scenes long ago witnessed in his eyes.

"Well, Zubindi finally got the idea of enzymatically enhancing, feeding, raising a droch, mutating it in the dark, far longer than its normal lifespan. Before anyone realized what was going on, the droch had grown, and achieved intelligence, to the point where it enslaved Zubindi. It drained energy from him, but at the same time gave him back strength and energy—which goodness knows he needed, in dealing with Beldorion—in a sort of double vampirism. And in the end, of course, the droch Dzym enslaved Beldorion as well."

He managed a faint laugh, gazing up at the stars. "It's certainly a lesson to us all, though I'm not sure about what. And, of course, once Dzym began draining his strength, Beldorion was finished as a power in Hweg Shul. It was easy for Ashgad to take over, when he arrived on this planet. He stepped into Beldorion's power, into his household and all his servants. . . . And, of course, into Dzym, too."

Luke wondered if that was the reason the old Senator had built the house in the desert: to protect his growing son from the influence of the creature that he himself could not be rid of. And of course it hadn't done any good.

"In fact, I'm not sure how much of Seti Ashgad is left, in that body and that brain." Liegeus's voice had sunk to a murmur—for a moment Luke could not tell whether he was speaking of the elder Ashgad or the younger. "Certainly not enough to go against Dzym's will. And as the resident expert on local conditions here, it was his job to assure Getelles and the CEOs of Loronar that the drochs were in no way connected with the ancient Death Seed plague. It's not that difficult. They truly don't want to know. As I didn't want to know, and managed not to know, up until seven or eight months ago."

His breath went out in another sigh. By a flicker of the moving current, Luke saw his hand grope feebly at the glittering pebbles beneath his fingers, stir at them aimlessly. "Eventually of course the matter was pushed under my nose in unmistakable terms. I told myself I had to do 'something' about it, get word out 'somehow.' But the problem with 'somehow' is that it really means 'later.' And there was always Dzym, waiting there for me. Hungering for true life, true energy, not that pitiful low-level field that synthflesh generates, though he absorbs that if he can get nothing else. It wasn't until Leia—Lady Solo—came, and fought so hard, worked so hard, risked everything, that I understood how completely contemptible I had become. I did not . . ." He hesitated. "I did not wish to appear so in her eyes. Does that seem contemptible to you?"

Luke remembered his days of puppy love for her, and the way he and Han had vied with each other as pilots to impress her. Not only they, but every unattached pilot in the Rebel fleet, it seemed, had been in love with her. "It's the destination that matters," he said softly. "Not the road."

"I fear I've left it rather late." The philosopher's voice sank to a whisper again. "I was lying to Dzym. The program that will take the *Reliant* out past the gun stations is finished. It just needs to be input. And the first load of Spook crystals is ready to be shipped."

Luke winced, as sudden pain stabbed through his head. At least, he thought, growing up on this world, Ashgad wouldn't have the education that would permit him to input something as complex as a launch-vector.

"And crystals," went on Liegeus, not noticing, "are not the only thing it will carry. It will bear Dzym to some headquarters, where he will not be affected by the sunlight and radiance of this world. Dzym and as many drochs as he cares to take with him, to draw lives from others that he may then drink those lives from them in his turn. And so it will go on, until half the worlds of the galaxy are planets of the dead."

Deep in the dark of the Transit Galactic Shipping Warehouse on Cybloc XII, a flare of white light sparked. There was a hiss, as of an electric welding arm, and the sudden, choking stink of sizzling plastene.

"Artoo-Detoo," complained a voice, close by but somewhat muffled, "would you *please* take a few more precautions to ascertain that it is safe before you undertake activities of this nature?"

No reply. Plastene fizzled with heat; then the tenor snarl of popaway fasteners breaking loose. From outside came the dim, swift squeaking of wheels, the fleeing patter of feet.

"Really, if I had known that Master Yarbolk's 'plan' to get us to Cybloc XII consisted of mailing us parcel post . . ."

The light vanished. Silence returned, a dreadful silence far too deep for the hub of trade between the Meridian sector and the Republic whose gateway this lifeless moon was. Then another creak and pop, and the white plastene side of a particularly large crate fell with a clatter.

Artoo-Detoo set forward his balance wheel and trundled slowly out, raining styrene packing in all directions. The white glow of his visual receptor moved across the contents of the warehouse: crates and boxes stamped with shipping labels and addresses from every corner of the Meridian sector, bales of raw materials, machinery and computer equipment still muffled in goatgrass casings. Apart from the cluster of containers stamped with the name and shipping number of the freighter *Impardiac,* out of Budpock, every crate, every bale, every casing had been opened and rifled. Machinery lay strewn across the rough gray crete of the floor. Gobbets of packing material surrounded broken boxes like wads of gristle after a butchering. Near the door, two men in the uniforms of the shipping company lay dead, with the blue faces and bloated bellies of those who have ceased to worry about the cares of this world quite some time ago.

The huge chamber stank of death.

Artoo's wheels squeaked softly as he moved around the pile of crates, seeking a particular one. The voice that had spoken before said impatiently, "Over here! Really, this may be the safest way for droids to travel, but it certainly has its drawbacks."

The label on the crate said:

CALRISSIAN, CYBLOC XII
HOLD FOR PICKUP

The return addressee was one Yarbolk Yemm, of Dimmit station, on Budpock. A sharp sound in a corner of the warehouse made Artoo swivel his cap, the light following the source of the noise. It was only a small, fanged, insentient scavenger, sniffing for what it could get.

Artoo began to pry open the pop fasteners on Threepio's crate. The silence was dreadful.

"Well, of course, it's quiet," said Threepio, when Artoo remarked on that silence. He carefully unfolded his much-mangled joints, stepping out of the crate and picking goatgrass and styrene beads out of his joints. "It's quite late at night. I suppose even major ports have to sleep sometime. Oh, all right," he added, "the main port on Coruscant is never quiet. Nor on Carosi. Oh, I suppose the one on Bespin is active even at the bottom of the graveyard watch. But that's no reason to say that it's 'too quiet.' What is 'too quiet'?"

The door of the warehouse hissed open. Artoo rolled immediately behind a gutted bale of dwimmery and, when Threepio showed no sign of following, reached out with his gripper arm and dragged the taller droid into concealment with him.

The creatures that entered the warehouse were unrecognizable in e-suits. They could have been anything from Sullustans to Ishi Tib, though one of them, by the nasal inflection of his voice, Threepio identified as a Rodian. What he said in that nasally voice was, "This must have come off that last ship."

"Good," rasped another voice, tinny through the e-suit's voder circuit. "They haven't been touched . . . no, fester it, looks like some of 'em have. Let's see what we got."

They entered, the tallest hauling an antigrav sledge behind him. The sodium light on the Rodian's helmet made jarring white slices of glare, huge black rhomboids of shadow. Vermin scampered behind the crates. One of the invaders kicked aside the bodies of the dead, and while he and one comrade began systematically prying open every crate and parcel in the untouched corner, the third knelt by the bodies and checked their pockets.

"What you got there?"

" 'Puter system. X-70."

"Piece of garbage." They loaded it onto the sledge nevertheless. "That silk there?"

"Yeah. What's in the crate?"

"Looks like wafers. Company payroll records."

"Take 'em. We'll sell 'em wiped. What . . ."

The speaker turned quickly, as the door of the warehouse slid open again. Two low, blocky forms stood framed in the almost-total darkness outside—and whatever hour of the night it might be, Threepio knew that a working spaceport was never *that* dark. Gold rounds of light from their visual receptors identified the newcomers as droids. Both opened fire without hesitation or parlay on the looters, who fell in their tracks. The internal weapons had been reset—these droids had not fired to stun.

Threepio was so indignant he would have spoken out in protest, had not Artoo sent a quick subsonic prod with his welding arm into Threepio's exposed wiring.

The two new droids wavered and hissed a report over their remote transmitters, then, receiving an answer, proceeded to take up where the human looters had left off, loading up the sledge with everything of value that had been in the *Impardiac*'s delivery, then stripping the e-suits off the looters before they left, silent as they had come.

"What in the name of the maker," asked Threepio, "is going on?"

The streets of Cybloc XII's main transit base were lightless, save for the occasional flicker of dying emergency circuits. Most of the docking bays were empty and dark, the buildings of its transport facilities a furtive whisper of scavengers, vermin, and occasional looters, the helmets of their e-suits glistening in the dark. The offices of the Port Authority contained horrors, bodies long dead and rotting in the alien bacteria that even the carefully controlled atmosphere of the domed facility could not completely exclude.

The Port Authority, the Republic Consular Offices, the fleet headquarters—all had been looted of their communications equipment. In the main infirmary of the base, bodies occupied every bed, every centimeter of spare floor space, every office and closet: bodies unmarked, rotting, curiously peaceful in aspect, as if they had all slipped into sleep and from there to dissolution. Those bodies, that is, that had not been turned over, tossed about, pockets and clothing checked for what they might contain. The medical equipment in every laboratory was gone or partially dismantled for its microprocessors and transistors. A couple of decapitated Two-Onebees remained in what had been the bacta-tank room—the tank drained of its fluid and bereft of its control panel—silent, their chest cavities open and dangling wires, like corpses themselves in the horrible gloom.

With a slight hiss, the emergency lighting of the medical center browned out and gave up its final, feeble ghost. With darkness came a skittering, brown insects with which Threepio was not familiar scrambling along the walls.

"What are we going to do?"

Artoo maneuvered his way into one of the offices, where an Ithorian in the white coat of a physician lay dead over her console, and plugged into the computer jack in the wall. He tweeped worriedly, light from the street outside falling across him in pale orange bars.

"At the same time as the *Adamantine*?" said Threepio. "That's absurd. Plague vectors don't operate that swiftly and the odds against a simultaneous mutation are seven thousand four hundred twenty-one against."

A couple of tweets and a wibble.

"When were the last reports from anywhere in the facility?"

Artoo reported. Though the street below the med station had been deserted for some time, a small band of e-suited figures hurried along, dragging sheets heaped with what looked like random gleanings—monitors, circuit boards, jewelry, shoes. One of those figures staggered, caught itself against the corner of a wall. The others conferred hastily among themselves, not going anywhere near their afflicted comrade, and ran. The man they had left tried to stagger after them, then sank down, helmeted head resting on his knees. In ten minutes or so, during which Artoo gave Threepio a précis of the progress of the plague in all reported quarters of the Meridian sector, the green light on the looter's e-suit went to amber, then to red, visible as a tiny dot of brightness across the street.

Through the smoky transparisteel of the facility's environmental dome, the orange streak of a departing ship could be seen.

A few moments later, the streetlamps went out.

The nights on Cybloc XII are long. The small moon on which it is built has a rotation period almost synchronous with its orbit. The great, glowing mass of the planet Cybloc is only occasionally visible from the port facility there, as a huge gold-and-green disk low in the sky. It did not show that night. Until the harsh light of the primary, Erg Es 992, flooded through the port's dome, Artoo worked alone, sending Threepio out on scavenging expeditions to various laboratories for what he needed and improvising what the protocol droid could not find. By that time it was safe, the streets were deserted save for the dead.

In time Artoo was ready.

"But it's useless," Threepio protested, looking down at the little stack of circuit boards and wiring that the astromech had hooked into the medical center computer. "There isn't enough amplification in that modulator to get a signal out of the system. Don't get smart with me," he added, to Artoo's tweeted reply. "I found the only thing on your list that was available. You should be glad I was able to retrieve that. There's absolutely nothing usable left in the Port Authority, or in any one of the shipping companies."

Artoo hooked another circuit into the loop.

"And I don't see what good that's going to do. If there's known to be plague here, no one's going to come near enough even to hear a distress signal except more looters."

Threepio did not even add, *We're doomed*. There was, perhaps, enough true doom, enough complete hopelessness, in the silent streets he had spent the night traversing to have stilled that particular observation. Threepio had seen dead humans, but the scale of this devastation awed him. The implications of looters innocent of quarantine regulations scattering even now to every corner of the Republic in all available transport horrified him still more.

So when Artoo gave him his instructions, Threepio obeyed. Thin as a thread, on a beam that wouldn't get much past the world that had been their goal for so long, the signal went out, in Basic and every one of six million galactic languages, just to be on the safe side:

"Help."

18

"Whaddaya mean, you can't get a response from Cybloc Twelve?" Han Solo slapped the comm button on the office viewscreen of the Durren Base Comptroller, much to the annoyance of the Comptroller herself. "There should be a half-dozen cruisers in port there . . ."

The Comptroller shouldered her way past him to be in full view of the screen. "Is there no signal at all, or is there interference?"

"No signal at all, ma'am." The extremely young midshipman in charge of the communications room saluted nervously. "The *Courane* and the *Fireater,* both out of Cybloc, both reported in as of three hours ago . . ."

"Where are they?" demanded Solo.

It had been a nightmarish flight to the Durren orbital base. By the time the *Millennium Falcon* had cleared the dense and stormy atmosphere of Exodo II, the advancing fleet had been close enough to pick them up on sensors. TIE fighters, of the old-fashioned LN type but perfectly serviceable, had been dispatched. While Lando, a good pilot but a less-than-reliable shot, had dodged and veered through the gas clouds of Odos and the nearby fringes of the Spangled Veil Nebula, Chewie and Han had manned the gun turrets, accounting for two of their pursuers before the thickness of the glowing dust clouds and the danger of floating chunks of ice the size of small moons, which swam up with horrifying unexpectedness from the shimmering soup of visual and electrical interference, discouraged pursuit. Han had geared and tinkered with the engine to reduce impulse power below the range of detection; and at greatly reduced speed, the *Falcon* had all but drifted out of the fighters' range.

"Either they're too shorthanded to risk a scout in this mess," Solo had remarked, watching the engine vibration of the remaining two TIEs retreat into the distance—the only dependable means of detection on board—"or they're in a hell of a hurry and don't think we're worth stopping for."

"Or they think they got us with that last shot." Lando was nervously calculating the probable locations of the huge ice chunks that were out there, somewhere, in the soaked screens of glittering whiteness that drifted everywhere in both visual and sensor pickup.

Chewbacca had growled and snarled a retort that they *had* gotten them with that last shot: That black chunk rapidly disappearing into the dust clouds was their rear starboard stabilizer.

Because of the extreme lightness of the floating ice mountains within the nebula compared to the density of the *Falcon,* seven or eight of these enormous blocks began to drift toward the smuggler vessel and followed it, like banthas in love with a speeder, for some distance, until out of range of the fleet's sensors Lando was able to lay on a little more speed.

But it was not a pleasant journey. By the time they fetched up in the Comptroller of Durren's office, Han was in no mood to be told that no vessels or crews could be released to him from the slender reserves still at the station.

"Captain Solo, *if* you please . . ." The Comptroller thrust her way around him, to face her communications officer again. "Have you attempted to contact Budpock base and inquire, Midshipman Brandis?"

"Budpock doesn't know anything, ma'am. They say communications with Cybloc went dead about forty-eight hours ago, no reason given. There's been a lot of static interference; nothing's getting through. They sent a drone visual but it hasn't come back yet."

"Thank you, midshipman."

Solo was reaching for the comm button and taking in breath to demand the whereabouts of the two ships out of Cybloc. For an elderly, diminutive, and rather stout woman, the Comptroller had very quick reflexes and cut the transmission before a word could be spoken.

"As you know, Captain Solo," said the Comptroller, with quiet precision, "the Republic's treaty with Durren specifies protection, not only of the existing majority planetary regime but also, as a backup, of the system itself. We have barely gotten the plague isolated on this base. The planetary government has only just regained a foothold in the capital and over the transportation and communication systems, and the insurgent faction is equipped with suborbital and supraorbital vessels that have already wreaked great havoc on this station. This is not the time to strip our forces . . ."

"The sector is being invaded." Han spoke slowly, trying to hold down his temper, knowing that this was an officer who would meet shouting with an icy stone wall.

"Then why have I not been contacted by either the Chief of State or the Senate Inner Council?" When she said "Chief of State" she fixed him with a beady dark eye—she knew perfectly well who he was married to.

Because the Council is deadlocked over the appointment of a successor, and nobody's going to risk starting a war they may have to repudiate when Leia shows up again, if Leia shows up.

Han drew a deep breath and let it out. "You're right," he said. Leia always started negotiations by saying, *You're right.* He'd frequently told her that such untruth would eventually cause her tongue to turn black and fall out of her mouth. "Maybe I'd better see if I can contact the Chief of State on the private channel—it sometimes works better than the military ones."

Lando and Chewbacca were crowded together with the single clerk in the outer office—because of the outbreak of the Death Seed plague in its lower quarters the entire orbital base was short staffed—every screen around them covered with readouts.

"This's bad, old buddy." Lando turned in his chair. "We got two more scouts missing. There's a whole corridor right down the center of the sector blacked out. I'll bet you any money it's those little whatever-they-are missiles, coming out of hyperspace shooting . . ."

"Come on." Han grabbed him by the arm and hauled him out of his chair and out of the room, Chewbacca striding like a giant, fungus-covered tree at their heels.

"What the . . . ?"

The corridor was deserted. Quarantine signs and barriers were everywhere, at every gateway to the lower levels. Han's skin prickled at the thought of being in the same installation with the Death Seed. He wondered how soon anyone would know of infection. How was it transmitted? How long an incubation period did it have? Months? Minutes?

"Does Wing Tip Theel still operate out of Algar?"

"Wing Tip?" Calrissian looked confused at the sudden introduction of one of their less-reputable computer-slicer colleagues into a military operation. "I think so. He did last time I talked to him."

"How soon can you get there? And can he still slice into the Algar Pleasure Dome's central computer core?"

"Hell, Wing Tip could slice into Fleet Central and forge the personnel records of any corporation in the galaxy back to the Old Republic without anybody being the wiser. But what . . . ?"

Han shoved his friend against the wall and frisked him for his pocket recorder. "Get the first ship you can out of here and get there. Take the emergency cash from behind the *Falcon*'s starboard bulkhead . . ."

"But what about fixing the stabilizer? What about . . . ?"

"Just do it, okay? Tell Wing Tip I need the best holo fake of Leia he can make, absolutely top class, narrowest bands, latest recordings, background perfect, the whole nine meters. Give him the emergency cash as a down and tell him I'll give him thirty thousand in two weeks— swear anything, sign anything."

"*Thirty thousand?* And you're planning to rob which bank to pay for this?"

"Let me worry about that." He checked the pocket recorder, glanced around to make sure they were unheard, though the corridor outside the Comptroller's office was deserted. The whole quadrant of the base was deserted, the crew and guards of the two cruisers still on base confined to their ships in the hope of avoiding infection, those few not in sick bay—or the morgue—keeping to their rooms.

"Best and latest scrap of Leia, understand?" he said softly. "Tell him to futz it up with a little interference so the join lines don't show. I want him to gimmick up the broadcast so it looks like it's being relayed in on the main line from Coruscant. And this is what I want her to be saying."

"You're the brother, aren't you?" After long silence, in which he seemed to have sunk into sleep or death, Liegeus stirred. His voice was barely a thread, and Luke, shivering uncontrollably in the night's bitter cold, wondered if either of them would survive till morning. "Skywalker. The Last Jedi."

"The first of the new batch, I hope." He thought about those he had trained: Kyp, so intense and so frighteningly powerful. Tionne and her music. Clighal with her talents for healing. Some had already departed Yavin Four, to seek their own paths, their own work. Some, like his faithful Dorsk 81, were already on the Other Side. There was a new recruit, a Bith, of all things. . . . And more, over the years. With the help of the Force, many more.

If he died tonight, they'd be able to go on, somehow.

The memory of Callista on Yavin Four was piercing, pain more intense than any he had experienced in his flesh. He remembered her teaching Tionne the finer points of the lightsaber or sitting on the terraces of the old temples in the apricot sunset light, speaking of her own master Djinn Altis and his floating stronghold in the gas clouds of Bespin. The morning Luke had brought the image tank that Han and Leia had found in the crypts of Belsavis, Callista had showed them all how to call shapes in it, how she had learned to use such a thing as a tool to strengthen her command over the Force. While the students shrieked with laughter and congratulations at one another's successes, Callista had left in silence. Coming out a half hour later Luke had found her stand-

ing on the terrace, staring out across the jungles at nothing, willing herself not to feel.

"I should have realized it earlier," went on Liegeus.
"The planet . . . draws Jedi. At least Beldorion always
claimed to be a Jedi, and he got that lightsaber of his
from somewhere, though that horrible woman Taselda
claims that it was originally hers. She sent that poor girl
of hers to steal it back . . ."

"Girl?" Luke's heart stood still in his chest. He tried to
keep the flare of fear, of hope, from his voice, but must
not have succeeded, for in the starlight the older man's
eyes seemed to change, understanding.

"A young woman named Callista."

Luke felt for a moment unable to breathe. He remembered his own willingness to do whatever Taselda asked,
not only in the hopes that she would lead him to Callista
but out of the urgent desire to please her that seemed to
be one of the uses of the *control mind* of the dark side of the
Force.

Of course Callista would have lied to Officers Grupp
and Snaplaunce about leaving Hweg Shul of her own free
will. She had left to do Taselda's bidding.

If she came to harm, he thought, *I will . . .*

Will what? Kill Taselda? And Beldorion? And who else?
None of it would bring Callista back.

Release your anger. Truly release it, and let it evaporate
like the drochs in the sunlight.

Liegeus was still watching his face. "Beldorion took
her prisoner, of course," he said, his voice gentle, as if
speaking to a man who had been hurt in some accident,
or who had fallen hard and far. "She was no match for
him, and Ashgad's synthdroids. She seemed to think
Taselda could make her a Jedi, and Beldorion wanted her
taken alive because he thought she had some kind of
. . . of Jedi power, though that wasn't the case. Beldo-

rion had some thoughts of enslaving her himself, but he ended up giving her to Dzym. One . . . one does."

"And you did nothing?" Luke's hand balled tight. The urge swept him to strike this helpless man where he lay, and Liegeus knew it. He flinched, but made no effort to ward off a blow.

At the whisper of his indrawn breath Luke remembered him dying among the drochs, remembered Dzym with blood and brown slime running down his monstrous mouth and pity for him swept away his rage. "No," he said softly. "What could you have done?"

The Force, he thought. *The dirty echo of the Force I felt in Dzym's power . . .*

As if through a mouthful of dust, he asked, "What happened to her?"

"She escaped. I overheard Beldorion and Dzym; I told her what they had agreed. She escaped that night. I don't know what became of her after that. She was . . . very bitter."

Luke found that he was breathing hard. "I have to find her," he said softly. "I have to tell her . . ."

His voice trailed off. In the lifeless silence of the canyons, ground lightning flickered somewhere far off, as if in echo of the tiny, artificial field in which they sat.

"Tell her what, my friend?" Liegeus's voice was gentle. "That you love her? She knows that. It is the one thing that she has never doubted."

"You spoke to her?"

He moved his head a little, *Yes,* thin hands folded on his chest.

"Then you know that I have to see her."

"Do you think she thinks so little of you, that she believes you'd turn against her for her lack of power?" From the darkness his voice came, tired and disembodied. "Many years ago I loved a woman—a girl, really. She was very young. It was . . . like nothing I have known, be- fore or since. At times it felt almost as if we were brother and sister, two halves of the same whole, and at others it seemed as if our passion for one another colored the world like firelight. I can't explain it, if you haven't felt the same."

Luke whispered, "I have felt it."

"Like me she was a wanderer, wanting to know what lay beyond the stars. Like me she was adept with ma- chines and tools. A bit of a cynic, like me, but with a passionate heart.

"But she had her own road," he said. "I don't think she ever loved me less, but it was a road that I could not follow. I did try. But sometimes . . . you have to let them go."

"Not this."

Not Callista.

Not the one thing in his life that he'd wanted . . . That he'd ever wanted this badly. The words came hard. "I can't."

"Well, every case is different." Liegeus's deep voice was so thin that Luke risked illuminating the glowrod on his torn and ragged flightsuit, so that he could check the philosopher's fingertips and eyelids. His pulse was weak but steady, his breathing shallow and slow.

"I went after her." Under the discolored lids his eyes moved, as if he could still see her face. The brows pinched. "Like a fool I thought I was the only person who could ever teach her what I thought it was she had to learn in this life, that I was the only person who could give her what she needed for all that long and winding road of the human span. And all I managed to do, in clinging to her as I did, was hurt her terribly."

Luke said nothing. Callista's face came back to him in the morning light of Yavin Four's temple tower, and the voices of the adepts playing with the image tank that she herself had instructed them in.

"In the end," said Liegeus, "I understood that the most truly loving thing that I could do would be to let her go, to seek her own road. I suppose it was vain of me to believe myself the only guide she would ever have or need. Or to believe that she was the only one I would ever love."

Luke was silent for a time, his whole soul crying out against the darkness of the past eight months. At last he whispered, "Was she?"

Liegeus smiled, and touched his wrist. "I think the human capacity for loving is too great for a single loss, however enormous, to blight. At least I hope that's the case. You do not believe me now, but I have walked this road, Luke. I can tell you, if you keep walking, you do come out of the dark at last. The love I have for your sister is no less for the love I felt for both my wives, bless their long-suffering hearts. There is always love."

Not like this, thought Luke. *Not like this.*

He had meant to stay awake, to fight the drag of weariness that seemed to be pulling him to the edge of a bottomless dark well. In any case it seemed impossible to sleep with the itching crawl of electricity tingling in his flesh, cleansing the vile energies of the drochs, and with the night's unplumbed cold. But he found himself nodding, dragged himself awake with all his strength only to nod again. As darkness gathered him in the voices that had, it seemed, all this time been whispering in his mind stepped to the fore again, like men and women stepping out of shadows, and as he drifted from the mooring anchors of his consciousness he could hear what they said.

They spoke of time and of still, tideless waters imbued with life and heat. They spoke of the heartbeat of the moonless world, and of the stars. This was a deep-colored background on which the bright flashes of closer consciousness moved like ephemeral dayflies: amusement and concern at the flurrying little creatures come to live in their minute enclaves of soil and water and vegetative fluff. Worry about danger, some terrible danger.

And then anger. Deep, burning, violent anger, the anger of those who have seen their friends and family members raped and murdered and enslaved before their eyes, the memory of voices outcrying in pain as their minds were stripped from them, helpless fury and pain.

Don't let them. Don't let them. Why did he think they were standing all around him, looming shadows in the canyons' rocks, looking down at him while he slept. *We can still hear their voices. Still they cry to us. Still they are part of us.*

Luke shook his head. *I don't understand.*

He was on Tatooine. He was standing in the courtyard of his old home, restored, no longer just a subsidence half-filled with sand, as the stormtroopers had left it so many years ago. There were stormtroopers in the courtyard, and out of the kitchen doorway that led into the court they were dragging Jawas—shrieking, pleading, kicking, jabbering. Aunt Beru, of course, would never have permitted a Jawa into her clean kitchen, but dimly Luke realized that this wasn't the point. Someone standing just beside and behind him, someone he couldn't see, was making these images, someone very old and very patient and very angry, trying to make him understand.

Two stormtroopers seized a Jawa by the arms. A third one raised up a huge hand drill of the kind used for taking water rock samples, and drove the spinning bit down into the Jawa's head. Horribly, the Jawa continued to kick, continued to struggle, as the drillmaster set aside his drill and withdrew from a tub at his side a brain, naked and gray and dripping clear fluid, and packed the stuff into the opening in the Jawa's head like a sapper packing explosive into a hole. Then the Jawa ceased to struggle and remained standing passively while the two stormtroopers released it, picked up white stormtrooper armor from a giant pile in front of the workshop door, and stuffed the Jawa inside it, closing up the armor like a trooper-shaped box and locking it along one side. Though the suit was rigid while it was being manipulated, once the hapless Jawa was inside it, it became articulated, like regular armor. Though it was impossible that anything as small as a Jawa would be able to fill it out, it seemed, within, to have grown to size.

It saluted the others and walked smoothly up the steps and out of sight, just as if there were a man inside.

Hunh?

A second Jawa was brought out of the kitchen *(Aunt Beru must be having a fit!)*, had its head drilled and packed with brains, and was in its turn packed into armor—given a weapon, he now saw, an Atgar-4X blaster rifle, and sent on its way.

I don't understand. He turned, to try to get an explanation out of the one who had invented the vision, but found himself back in the canyon with Liegeus. He was standing over his own body and that of the engineer, and though he could have sworn that the one who had shown him the images, the one who was trying to communicate with him, had returned to this reality with him, he saw nothing behind him by the dull-gleaming facets of the rock wall.

Callista's voice said to him, "It's their world, Luke. It's their world." He saw her walking away from him, her long brown hair hanging in a tail down the back of her jacket of leather and nerf wool that, though it was black in the starlight, he knew was red.

Walking away down her own road in the starlight, toward a destination that he could not see.

Around her, Leia was conscious that the glittering walls of crystal had changed. When she had entered the cave, a crevice far up the canyons above the Theran camp, she had been dazzled by the lights thrown from the thick encrustation of gems. But as she extinguished her lamp, as she had been instructed, and walked farther into the dimly radiant chamber, she was aware that somehow the deep-buried geode had been transformed, morphed into something familiar, a room she knew . . .

Dark pillars ascended to the striated green-and-gold glass of the vaults. Shadows chased one another across the dull gold intricacy of the floor.

Palpatine's audience hall. Why did she dimly hear the funky jizz-wailing of that horrible band Jabba the Hutt had kept to play in his palace? Why did she smell, behind the perfumes and incense and subtle hurlothrumbic gas with which the Emperor had flooded his court hall, the rank stink of Hutt, the greasy odor of mercs and soldiers of fortune?

She walked farther. The fear that came over her she attributed to the gas. Her father had warned her about it, the first time she'd had an audience with the Emperor, when she was a youngster. "Don't be afraid," Bail Organa had murmured as he opened the door for her. "It's just a trick he's playing on you, to make you think he's more dangerous than he is."

She had been afraid, but had known it wasn't real. That memory remained with her, that knowledge, whenever afterward she felt fear.

There was someone on Palpatine's throne.

Leia stepped clear of the pillars. A robed figure,

stooped forward, face in the shadow of a hood. She saw the gleam of eyes. At the foot of the throne huddled a woman, nearly naked in scraps of gold and silk, long chestnut hair braided down her back and a chain collar around her neck.

Herself, eight years ago. Eyes downcast, beaten, submissive as she had never been, not even in Jabba's awful palace. Hopeless, knowing that this time there would be no rescue.

Her hand went to the lightsaber at her belt, but she remembered what Callista had said, that it was better not to use a weapon until she knew against whom to use it. Leia stood still, but her heart hammered in her chest.

"Draw it," drawled a deep voice, a woman's voice, like smoke and honey, and she recognized the voice as her own. The robed figure on the throne put back her hood. Leia saw herself, matured and beautiful, beautiful beyond description: nearly six feet tall, with the attenuated, slender grace she had always envied Mon Mothma and Callista. Though there was maturity and wisdom in her face the crow's-feet around the eyes were erased, the mouth was fuller and stronger and redder, the hair a cinnamon cloud. Every beauty idealized and raised to terrifying perfection.

"Draw it. You must give it to one of us."

She stood up from her throne, shrugged aside Palpatine's robe so that it folded down her back in dark curtains. Leia saw that she, too, wore the gold slave harness, jeweled and flashing, but she wore it like an Imperial gown. The Empress Leia leaned back her head and laughed and stretched forth her hands to the shadows of the ceiling. Force lightning rained from her fingers, crawled up the pillars, illuminated the perfect cheekbones, and cold auburn eyes. Behind her, as in Jabba's palace, Leia could see on the wall a man frozen in carbonite, but the contorted face was Luke's, not Han's.

She didn't know where Han was. Dead, she thought. Dead of the Death Seed, somewhere in Meridian sector. And she, the Empress, was free of him at last.

"Which of us will you give it to, Leia?" The Empress jerked the golden chain, pulling the slave Leia sprawling. The wretched girl buried her face in her arm and wept, as Leia had sometimes longed to do at that time, in that place, in her life. "Draw your lightsaber, and give it to one of us. This is what you must do."

Leia unhooked the weapon from her belt. She hefted it in her hands, slender and silvery, the weapon she had made under Luke's tutelage and later feared to use. The hands of the slave Leia, clutched into fists of frustration and hopelessness, were nerveless and weak. Those of the Empress before her throne were large, strong as a man's, long-fingered, and white as Leia had always wished her hands could be. Behind the throne she could see Jacen and Jaina, smiling, lightsabers in their hands, and just visible was the corner of her father's white robe, the one he had been wearing in her other dream, when Anakin had cut him dead.

There was no sound but the slave girl's sobbing.

The Empress walked toward her, Palpatine's robe billowing around her like wings of smoke containing the flame of her golden harness. "Give it to one of us," she commanded. "Give it to me."

Leia backed away, frightened of the woman's power. *Even as bad as I am with this, I could kill her here. She deserves it, for what she did to my father.* She wasn't sure why she thought this or of whom she actually spoke. If she gave it to the slave, the Empress would only take it from her. Besides, the slave was a crawling weakling, sobbing miserably, not raising her face. Leia felt a stab of shame and embarrassment, knowing that, too, was her.

I could kill her. I could kill them both.

She backed farther, holding the lightsaber in both hands, her breath coming fast. The auburn eyes—her own eyes, raised to the glory of suns—stared into hers, compelling her, as Palpatine could compel. On the dais, the slave girl groveled and wept. Leia clutched the weapon's hilt, not willing to surrender it, yet feeling she must. She was almost panting with fear, and the thin choke of gas in her throat was what brought her to her senses.

It isn't real. Her father—her true father, the father of her heart—had said. *It's just something he wants you to feel.*

She stepped sideways, out of the Empress's path.

"I don't have to give it to anyone," she said. "It's mine, to do with as I choose."

And turning her back on them, she walked out of the palace, out of the cave.

19

"Luke was able to confront Vader," said Callista. "To be defeated by him—to cut off his hand, as his own had been cut off—to accept that this was his father. To surrender that fact, and go on from there. You never had that chance."

"It's not an experience I'd stand in line for," remarked Leia drily. "I knew Vader. I saw him tagging after Palpatine every time I went to Court. Believe me, I'll never accept that he was my father."

"Then you'll always be the slave to his shadow."

Anger sprang to Leia's eyes. For a long moment they met the other woman's gray gaze in the campfire's wavering glow, the chilly flare of sodium lamps set here and there around the Theran camp. Most of the cultists had lain down around the mouth of the largest of the glittering caves, when the aftermath of the Force storm had blown itself out. Save for a few mounting guard farther up the canyon, they had given themselves up to sleep. Bé had disappeared, to commune with the night, someone said. Apparently this was what Listeners commonly did, because everyone just nodded.

Leia and Callista, apart from the others, were virtually alone.

It was Leia who looked aside first. Her nightmares came back to her, the shape and face of her fears. She recalled the rage that came over her, the need to prove herself other than Anakin Skywalker's daughter. She had taken and used his weapon, the Noghri, for her safety and that of her children and to repair the damage that he had done them; but she flinched from the thought of standing up and saying, *I am Lord Vader's daughter.*

"I don't know what it would mean," she said slowly, groping for words, "if I accepted it. If I made him a part of me, the way Luke has."

"You mean for others?" Callista wrapped her long arms about her knees, sitting perched on a smooth hunk of crystal like fused glass, her dark hair frayed by straying winds across the crimson leather of her jacket. "Those who would ask what his daughter was doing ruling the Council?"

"Maybe," said Leia. "Mostly for myself. And for the children. It will take time." The thought of it revolted her, furious anger succeeded by the heat of tears in her throat.

"No one is asking you to do it tomorrow. But if you know what parts of him are inside you, you can know what to build a wall around and what to take into yourself. Because you cannot afford not to be strong, Leia," she said. "You cannot afford to let this kind of thing happen to you, ever again."

"No," she said softly. "I know that."

Callista stood and unhooked the lightsaber from her belt. The sun-yellow blade slid forth like a lance of summer into winter's dark. "Then let's begin."

Sparring with Callista was in some ways easier than

sparring with Luke, though the lost Jedi was of a height with her brother and no less exacting a teacher. Still, Callista understood the differences in technique required of Leia's lesser height and lighter weight, knew the finer points with the instincts of one who has been rigorously coached for many years, and was far more conscious of distance and timing than any man Leia had ever worked with. As when she worked with Luke, Leia had no sense of danger whatever, no fear of the softly humming laser blades that could slide through flesh like a hot silver wire through cheese; only a strange exhilaration, a sense of freedom that she mistrusted instinctively because it felt so utterly right.

"Footwork," said Callista dispassionately, searing a tiny curl of smoke from the rock a centimeter from Leia's much-taped golden boot. "Footwork. Don't be afraid of your spirit. Don't always be watching yourself."

Leia stepped back, the blade whispering, shedding pale azure light over her sweating face, the long tendrils of her cinnamon hair hanging down in her eyes. "If I don't watch myself I'm afraid I'll do something wrong."

"I know," said Callista. "You've watched yourself like that all your life. What are you afraid you'll do?"

"Hurt someone," said Leia, and knew it for the truth from the bottom of her soul. They weren't talking about combat now. They both knew that.

"You'll know when the time is to strike," said Callista. "And when to step away. The only way to learn it is to do more of this, not less."

"I don't want to be another . . ." The words froze in her throat.

"Another Palpatine?" asked Callista. "Another Vader? You aren't. You're not even another Bail Organa. You're Leia."

Leia was silent, regarding the soft-shining blue light of the blade, the paler glow of Callista's just beyond. Those two heatless beacons illuminated the darkness around them, isolated the two women in the heart of an ember fire, statesman and warrior, thinker and feeling heart.

"Haven't you seen that yet?" asked Callista, her voice more quiet still. "Luke has."

Leia's panting breath steadied. The weapon felt more stable in her hands, more a part of herself. For the first time ever when she had held the lightsaber, she smiled. And smiling, signed to the younger woman and stepped into the fray again.

It was Callista who gestured to stop. Leia lowered her weapon. Callista turned her head, listening, her dark, level brows drawn together. A moment later Bé came into the circle of torchlight, his scarred, thin face intent in the braided frame of his long hair.

"They're moving on the gun station," he said. "From Ruby Gulch, dozens of them. On other gun stations as well."

"How did he know that?" Leia asked, as she and Callista followed the others to the caves where the cu-pas and speeders were hidden. She climbed onto the back of a repulsor-lift sled with three other cultists; Callista swung into the saddle of a pale golden cu-pa, wrapped the gray veiling close around her face, and settled her rifle and grenades over her shoulder.

"Voices tell them, they say. Voices that speak in their minds if they sleep in certain places, far back in the hills, or drink preparations of certain herbs—as far as I can tell, that suppress left-brain linear activity. Bé is a Healer, strong in the Force. Many of the other Listeners are, too."

She tossed Leia a rifle and a bow. There were arrows in the back of the sled, being passed among those who clustered there, men and women alike, as the vehicles and animals began their swift trek through the icy darkness of predawn, flowing like water down the silent canyons.

"The Force is so strong here," she said softly, her gloved hand steady, easy on the cu-pa's rein. "I'd heard the rumor of it from Djinn, my Master. There was a story about two young Jedi who came here centuries ago seeking gifts and strength in the Force that they themselves lacked. Nothing further was known of them, but one of them supposedly was a Hutt. I know Hutts live a long time."

She shook her head, wonderingly, as if regarding that desperate young woman of nearly a year ago, fleeing the ruin of Admiral Daala's demolished fleet and seeking a place to go, a clue to lead her through the labyrinth of her quest for her own lost gifts.

"What I found, you know. Pettiness, old feuds, slavery to the base . . . And I thought, never again. Never again am I going to be anyone's pawn, because of the powers I was born with, the powers I don't even possess anymore. But while I was a prisoner I saw the *Reliant*. I had seen Dzym and guessed what he was planning. I take it you didn't get my message?"

"I got it." Leia grimly shifted the rifle on her shoulder, clung to the struts of one of the sled's makeshift gun turrets. "It's just that by that time things had progressed too far to be called off. It reached me the day I left."

"You should have said you were sick."

"It took Q-Varx and the Rationalists months to set up the meeting. They were operating in good faith—pawns, not spies. I read their correspondence. I wasn't willing to risk the political repercussions of refusal."

Callista shook her head, and Leia said, "You have to make these decisions." She hesitated, and then, because she herself despised surprises, added, "Luke came, too. He was on Hesperidium to see me off. He took a fighter to the planet's surface, to look for you."

Callista's head turned sharply.

"I don't know where he is."

She looked away. What could be seen of her face was still as ivory, but above the edge of the veil, the wide gray eyes filled with tears.

They rode for a time in silence, winding down the trails that were barely familiar, scattered with broken rock and shards of crystal, with dunes of gravel hurled up wholesale from the flats below. Dawn winds had started as the wan sun warmed the endless dead sea bottom. Squinting against it in the silky gray light, Leia could make out the taller masses of the cliffs around the gun station, the fretwork of the shattered upper works, black against the pearlescent air.

"I found nothing here that would help me," said Callista quietly. "The Force is here, but not in a form that I can touch or understand. Whatever is alive here—if anything—is invisible, intangible. Believe me, I've tried to reach it, to touch it. The Listeners say it's the ghosts of the old holy men and women that speak to them, but I think they're wrong. The voices only use the shapes that the Listeners have already in their minds."

She shook her head, her eyes narrowing against the shadowless twilight of distances and wind. "There's a woman in Hweg Shul who has interests in shipping. When this is over I'm going to contact her, see if I can get myself off-planet in one of the little cargo lifters and work my passage elsewhere. Are you going to tell Luke you've seen me?"

"Whatever you wish," said Leia. "I'd like to, yes, but I won't if you'd rather I didn't."

Callista started to say something, then thought about it and asked, "What do you think would be best?"

"I think it would be best if I did."

"Then do so," said Callista. "Make him understand, if you can. Tell him that I will love him to the ending of my life, but that mine is a life of which he cannot be a part."

Across the crystal ridges, sudden snakes of white lightning flickered, cold and pale in the dawning light. Leia grabbed the railing of the speeder as it rocked and swayed, jolted by what felt like a groundquake, though the ground beneath the antigrav lifters was steady. An obsidian boulder several tons in mass wrenched and twisted in the rock side of the mountain before them, and the glittering talus of crystals at the foot of the cliffs around them leapt upward into funnels, like toothed whirlwinds.

The Therans in the speeders cried out, looking around them with weapons at the ready, and Callista and Bé fought their cu-pas to a standstill moments before the beasts could bolt in panic.

"Another," said Callista softly. "Worse than before, I think."

"There's one with them who moves this storm." Bé's lizard-black eyes were shut, listening deeply. "He brings this storm at his will, summons and directs it."

"That will be Beldorion."

"What do we do?" asked a man on Leia's repulsor sled, looking nervously around at the cold cliffs sparkling in the new light, the world paused, it seemed, on the brink of chaos.

Bé shook back his tangled braids. "We can do no other than we are instructed," said the Listener. "We meet them, and die."

• • •

If the horrors of watching the dying corpses of Cybloc XII being looted had been bad—the squabbles between looters, the remote-operated droids patrolling like whirring insects, the sight of those few expiring survivors being relieved of jewelry and credit cylinders by thieves—the darkness that followed was infinitely worse. The dome lights were gone. The dim auxiliary circuits were going. In the medical offices where, with a droid's infinite patience, See-Threepio was broadcasting his distress call in alternating bands of Basic and various of his six million language repertoire, the light had gone utterly, and only a few buildings were lit in the next square, leaking stray glims to show him the street below the windows, where nothing at all now moved. The body of the dead looter lay where it had been left, naked of its e-suit, which others had taken along with the computer equipment that he'd been dragging. It was little more than a black shape to Threepio's visual receptors, though it registered on his infrared for some time. The smells of alien bacteria and decay organisms choked the air.

"It isn't any use," he said in time. Artoo-Detoo, sitting inert as a heating unit in the corner, illuminated a single red light, inquiring.

"The entire base computer core has been gutted. Even should someone attempt a landing, we wouldn't know it."

Artoo wibbled a reply.

"Oh, very well. But it will do us no good. I expect we'll sit here until our power cells run down, and chaos and destruction will encompass the Republic." At another time Threepio would have spoken out of a personal conviction of impending doom. Now he realized he was saying no more than the truth.

"We did our best."

The astromech bleeped and settled back to his resting

position. It was inconceivable that either of them would do other than his best.

Threepio returned to the jury-rigged microphone. "Distress on Cybloc XII. Distress on Cybloc XII. Please send an evacuation team. Please send an evacuation team.

"Ee-tsuü Cybloc XII. Ee-tsuü Cybloc XII. N'geeswâ el-tipic'uü ava'acuationma-teemâ negpo, insky.

"Dzgor groom Cybloc XII. Dzgor groom Cybloc XII. Hch'ca shmim'ch vrörkshkipfuth gna gna kabro n'grabiaschkth moah." He dug down into the bottommost registers of his voder circuits. The Yeb language had few technical terms, and it was necessary to patch together a linguistic equivalent from: "Several conglomerates are urged strongly but respectfully to coordinate activities to prevent the drowning of another conglomerate that is not a threat to any of them, nor will be in the immediate or distant future to them or to their children." He did the best he could.

Bith was easier. "Six-five. Twelve-seven-eight. Two-nine-seven." In many ways, Threepio was very fond of the Bith.

"Distress on Cybloc XII. Dis—Artoo, look! It's an incoming vessel!" He pointed to the dark transparisteel, through which the transpariflex panels of the dome could be seen. Against the livid gloom of the sky the red track of descending retros had appeared. "Can you get *any* sort of reading on the computer?"

Artoo, who had tried already a dozen times, simply twitted a negative. Threepio was already toddling toward the turbolift. "They'll be coming into the port bays. By the time we reach there they should be just about landed. Oh, thank goodness."

Artoo simply lowered himself down onto his third wheel, and rolled after his golden counterpart, without comment. If he had reservations about the nature of the rescuers, as deduced from the make and serial numbers of their vessels, he kept them to himself.

It wasn't that Threepio hadn't considered the possibility of smugglers, looters, or space pirates. But the events that had transpired since the two droids and the unfortunate Yeoman Marcopius's escape from the doomed *Borealis* had given the protocol droid a little more confidence in his ability to negotiate possible transport. In any case his power core was dangerously close to reserve, and even another *pas de deux* with space pirates seemed preferable to going cold on the dead world, leaving Her Excellency to her own devices with no one who knew where she was. All the way through the dark, utterly silent streets of the plague-stricken dome, he composed scenarios and arguments to talk his way into passage to Coruscant without informing potentially hostile—or simply verbally incontinent—hosts what his message and mission might be.

And they all fell silent within him as he and Artoo stepped through the doorway of the largest of the docking bays, and he saw before him in the actinic glare of its landing lights the black ship that stood there, an Imperial Fleet Seinar IPV System Patrol Craft, like a sleek-shelled crab, lowering its boarding ramp.

Threepio said, "Oh, dear."

On the face of it, there seemed very little chance that any amount of money would persuade the inhabitants to drop him and Artoo off at Coruscant.

It was too late to turn tail, however. Figures in dark e-suits were coming down the ramp—both men and women, judging from the way they walked, which was unusual for the Imperial Service—followed by two black, spider-armed floating remotes that scanned the base with hard beams of white light while the troopers crossed the stained floor of the bay to where the two droids stood.

One of them, a dusky Twi'lek woman with an enormously extended helmet, touched the comm button in her suit and said, "Two of them," and again Threepio wondered. The Imperial Service would ordinarily no more employ nonhumans than it would employ nonmales. On closer study he identified the e-suits of Imperial design—CoMar 980s—but without emblems, though the sleeves and chest bore marks where emblems had been removed.

"No other signs of life on the base?" inquired a very small, very tinny voice from the comm.

"No, Admiral. Looks well and truly looted to me."

"There was, in fact, extensive looting during the final throes of the epidemic," provided Threepio helpfully. "My counterpart and I counted five separate parties of looters, and the Computer Core of the base system was so extensively dilapidated that we could not even use it to signal out."

"Put them through cleansing procedures," said the tinny voice. "Bring them to me. I want to find out once and for all what's taking place in this sector."

"You know, Artoo," surmised Threepio, when after a very thorough passage through two radiation chambers and a chemical bath the two droids were conducted, still by the Twi'lek Sergeant, to a small lift marked "Private," "I think this isn't an Imperial mission at all. The ship, though of Imperial design and manufacture, does not bear the markings of any of the various satrapies of the former Empire. Neither do the uniforms of such crew members as we have seen. We might be dealing with a case of extensive theft of Imperial matériel by a completely neutral third party."

The doors of the lift closed soundlessly. There was a shivering vibration as it ascended. Artoo tweeped.

"Clandestine operation? What kind of clandestine op-

eration would be undertaken by any of the remaining
Imperial governors? I'm sure it can't be that."

The doors slid open. Imperial Captains and Admirals
always tended to favor a black sleekness in their offices,
in part in the interests of spare unclutteredness, in part,
quite frankly, in the interests of intimidation. The chamber into which the two droids stepped now was no excep-
tion. Threepio was quite well aware that computer
screens and consoles lurked behind those obsidian-
mirrored panels, that a touch on an access hatch would
summon chairs, if necessary; more lamps; dictation
equipment, if required; implements of torture; articles of
restraint; a mirror and shaving equipment; or wine, coffeine, and beignets for that matter . . .

But all of that was secondary to the digitalized tallying
of recognitive factors concerning the woman who sat in
the room's single chair: tall, tough, and athletic in her
stripped-down version of the Imperial officer's uniform,
red hair hanging like a comet's tail down her back and
eyes cold as ball bearings in a pale, expressionless face.
Threepio had never seen her in person, but as a specialist
in protocol he was programmed with all sorts of files
about people who were or had been in positions of authority, and he identified her at once.

"Good heavens, Artoo," he exclaimed, "I seem to have
been given inaccurate data. According to my most recent
information, Imperial Admiral Daala should be dead."

Daala said softly, "I am."

Han Solo wondered whether there was any insanity in
his family.

He folded his arms, considering the vista afforded him
by the hard transparisteel of the viewport: two CEC gun-
ships, the *Courane* and the *Fireater,* half a dozen smaller

cruisers, and maybe twice that many escorts, X-wings and E-wings. They hung pale silvery against the darkness of realspace, sleek white fish among the stars. The newest Republic equipment, true—unlike the clunky, crotchety horrors of the Rebel fleet—but all of them, he knew, understaffed with men and women pushed to the brink of exhaustion. None of them a match for what he knew lay ahead.

But not a bad turnout for a faked video and a lot of bluster and fast talk.

He turned from the *Falcon*'s viewport to the main screen, where Lando, who'd hitched a ride back from Algar with the fleet, and his Sullustan co-pilot Nien Nunb, were handling the jump extrapolations while Chewbacca studied the sensor readouts beamed in from the few remote stations on the other side of the Spangled Veil Nebula.

"Pick 'em up?" Solo asked, and the Wookiee yowled assent.

"Where they headed?"

"Well, judging by the point at which they came out of hyperspace," said Lando, tapping in a few more numbers, "it could be either Meridias itself, which would be stupid on the face of it considering that planet's been dead for centuries, or any of the Chorios systems."

Lando looked a little tired from his fast trip to summon reinforcements, but was shaven, bathed, and sleek as usual. Han, who felt and looked like many kilometers of bad road, didn't know how he managed.

"For my money it's Pedducis Chorios. They'll have their work cut out for them getting rid of all the pirate Warlords who have alliances with local chiefs, but there's a lot of profit there. Nam Chorios is just a rock."

"Yeah," agreed Han softly. "But by an amazing coincidence, it's the rock Seti Ashgad comes from, with all his swearing up and down he saw Leia off safe and sound. And now all of a sudden while everyone's all in a tizzy because Leia's disappeared, by gosh, somebody comes along and tries to invade Nam Chorios."

"But that's crazy!" protested Lando, every entrepreneurial bone in his body offended to the marrow. "Who'd want anything on Nam Chorios?"

"I don't know," said Han. "But I think we're gonna find that out." He leaned over the comm, opened the main link.

"Captain Solo here. We're taking hyperspace jump bearing seven-seven-five; coming out bearing nine-three-nine-three-two . . ."

Lando's eyes flared wide at the nearness of that jump point. "Han, old buddy . . ."

Han put his hand over the mike, "We want to get there before them, don't we? I know what I'm doing."

"What you're doing is smashing us into Nam Chorios if somebody gets one hair off."

"So don't get a hair off," said Han bluntly, and turned back to the comm. "Course for Nam Chorios. Possible interception on return to realspace, so keep your heads up."

He turned back to the readouts. Three Star Destroyers. Half a dozen carracks. Two interdictors.

And the swarms that didn't even register on the readout, the silent, deadly clouds of CCIR space needles, waiting to cut them to pieces the minute they came out of hyperspace.

He had to be crazy.

"Punch it, Chewie," he said.

20

Luke felt the violence of the Force storm that surrounded the Bleak Point gun station kilometers away, as a throbbing in his head and a clutch of terror and rage in his chest. As the Mobquet flew down the canyons like a great black glide lizard, crystal boulders and whirlwinds of gravel would spontaneously leap and swirl in the air, spattering against the speeder's sleek body and scratching the tough transplex of the passenger hoods. Liegeus whispered, "Beldorion. He can still wield the Force after a fashion. But I've never seen it like this, never." Luke gritted his teeth, knowing that this random torrent of energy was being duplicated elsewhere on the planet, wrecking machinery on which people's lives and livelihoods depended, overturning other forges to cripple other men.

So that Seti Ashgad could disable a gun station, he thought, and create a corridor through which a ship could fly.

He'd only need to disable one.

As they came out of the hanging canyon above the gun station Luke said softly, "They're in."

Most of the wood and metal palisade that had crowned the ancient tower had been torn away by the violence of the uncontrolled Force. Beams and shards and huge mats of razor wire strewed the gravel at the base of the walls; and with the sheer poltergeist wildness of the Force, these would rise up and hurl themselves like rabid things against the walls, the remains of the defenses, the surrounding rocks. As Luke watched, a rusted beam flew like a javelin from the ground, dragging after it a whole tangle of wire, and fell among the struggling forms that ran and dodged and fired on one another on the top of the tower. The beam thrashed and whipped until it fell, dragging two of the Rationalist fighters down with it in a snarl of debris.

On the flat top of the tower they were still fighting before the door that led down into the building itself. From the mouth of the hanging canyon Luke couldn't tell, but he thought that there was another, smaller scrimmage going on around the coils and shielding of the barrel of the laser cannon itself. Rationalists were struggling to get up on top of it, raggedly dressed Therans fighting them hand to hand to keep them from damaging the gun. The flare of blasters and ion cannon burst like pale lightning in the morning air, but such was the nature of the Force storm that not many of the shots were getting in, and the Therans had quite clearly stopped even trying to throw spears or shoot arrows. Even pellets and bullets from projectile weapons were whirled away like chaff.

"Beldorion's there," said Liegeus. He shoved back the long ash-colored hair hanging in his eyes. "Back out of the front lines somewhere, I should think—there!" He pointed down to the silvery shape of a round floater, some distance from the base of the walls. Luke could see the coiled shape of the giant Hutt on it, muscular and serpentine, not at all like Jabba's slothful bulk.

The sense of decayed Force, of rotted abilities and spent purpose, rose to Luke like a stench, as it had from Taselda.

In many ways it was worse than Vader, worse than Palpatine. At least their dream had been grand.

"What do we do?" said Liegeus.

Luke began to back the assault speeder up the canyon again, the way they had come. A speeder wasn't an antigrav platform and generally couldn't be used as one without restructuring of the buoyancy tanks, but Chariots had motors on them that would do credit to many of the combat vessels Luke had flown. "We hold on tight."

Liegeus gasped, "What are you going to do?"—*A silly question,* thought Luke, as he slammed the speeder into full-bore acceleration and readied his hand on the turbothrust lever. It should have been patently obvious what the only possible course of action was. The walls of the canyon blurred into a shining curtain, wind and flying gravel scorched back over hood and metal, the gap of the canyon walls rushed toward them and beyond that, the wide break in the tower's defensive crown beckoned like a ridiculously enormous bull's-eye.

Liegeus wailed, "Luke!" and hid his eyes.

The speeder cleared the twenty-five-meter gap between the last ridge of the mountain's shoulder and the top of the tower like a nek battle dog, like a trained Tikkiar rising for a kill. Luke cut the turbos and hit the brake, skidding in among the combatants who scattered before him. He recognized Gerney Caslo in the fighting around the door and, springing out of the speeder, plunged across the stained and battered paving blocks of the tower's open top and up the steps to where he stood.

"You've got to stop this!" he yelled. Everyone was so

startled for a moment by the appearance of the Mobquet among them that they did halt.

"You're being duped!" shouted Luke, turning to the men and women who crouched behind makeshift barricades, guns in hand, to those who had for the moment fallen back from fighting on the laser gun itself. "You're being used! Seti Ashgad has only one reason for wanting to open this planet—so that he can sell the whole place to Loronar Corporation to strip-mine! He doesn't care about your farms! He doesn't care about medical supplies, or water pumps, or machinery for you!"

He looked around him, at the dusty, cut, bloody faces, the battered forms stepping cautiously forth from their places of cover, at the angry eyes, not wanting to believe. Arvid was among them, and Aunt Gin, and the brother-in-law of the owner of the Blue Blerd.

His arms dropped to his sides. "He isn't doing this for you."

Someone said, "Shoot the whiner," and Luke reached forth with the Force and pulled the man's blaster away before he could get the shot off. The white bolt of energy scattered chips from the wall of the stairway housing behind him.

"A lot you know about it!" yelled someone else.

"I know," said Luke quietly. "I've been into Ashgad's house. He isn't doing this for any of you."

"He's right."

Behind Luke, the door opened, very quickly, and closed again—Luke could hear the locks slamming open even as Gerney Caslo and the two men with him made a jump to catch it as it opened.

Leia had stepped through.

Leia grimy, in tatters, her hair hanging down in strings in her eyes and her palms and knuckles bandaged. Leia with strips of space tape and leather binding what remained of her ornamental golden boots, empty-handed but with a blaster on one hip and her lightsaber on the other.

But definitely Leia Organa Solo, known on a thousand news holos to many and certainly, from Seti Ashgad's faked video, to every man and woman there. There was goggling silence.

"He's telling the truth," she said. She reached into one of the thigh pockets of a pair of far-too-big trousers she wore and produced a wad of computer printouts. "Here's a copy of Ashgad's correspondence—with the CEO of Loronar, with Moff Getelles of Antemeridian, with pawns and cat's paws in the Republic Council. Is anyone here a neep?"

Booldrum Caslo stepped forward. "I am, ma'am."

"Then you'll recognize the system codes as coming from Ashgad's computer."

The chubby man changed the lens ratio of his visiamps and flipped quickly through the hardcopy, then glanced back at Gerney, apologetic. "She's right. This is Ashgad's. I installed the components myself."

Caslo blustered angrily, "Which doesn't mean *you* didn't compose this yourself, girl." But others were pulling the papers from his cousin's hands, reading the memoranda, the deals, the concessions.

"An installation in Thornwind Valley? Six-month forcible recruitment? A man can't live a week up there!"

"Mandatory labor pool?"

"Transfer of matériel—isn't the real word for that *theft*?"

"Price freeze standardization on Spooks?"

"At *sixty-seven creds*?!?"

"Occupation fleet . . . who said anything about an occupation fleet?"

"The occupation fleet is in orbit now," said Luke. He

pointed upward. Several of the Rationalists had electrobinoculars and focused them skyward, where far overhead pinlights of brightness flared in the star-prickled twilight sky.

Under the spate of exclamations and curses, Leia threw her arms around Luke in a fierce hug. "What about Dzym? Ashgad's . . ."

"I know about Dzym," said Luke.

"If there's really a battle going on up there—if the Council really did manage to get ships to stop Getelles's fleet—he'll still try to lift off in the *Reliant* with all the drochs he can take."

"The lift programs aren't installed."

"Any competent engineer can do that." She looked up quickly as Liegeus emerged from the Chariot, dodged through the milling men and women, the angrily stirring cables and beams, the lawless Force winds. "Liegeus . . . !"

She flung her arms around him, and he held her tight, graying head pressed to hers. "My dear child, I'm so glad to see you safe! I never, never in my life thought you'd try to escape . . ."

"Then you didn't know me very well." She grinned at him and a moment later he grinned back.

"Well—I suppose I did know you'd try it." He shook his head.

"Listen, Liegeus, how much does Ashgad know about the software on that vessel?" demanded Luke. "How much of an education has he had? Can he install it? Can he get the thing off the ground?"

"Of course he can," said Leia impatiently. "Seti Ashgad was one of the top hyperdrive engineers of the Old Republic. The original Z-95s were his design!"

"*His* design?" Luke stared at her blankly. "They were making Z-95s fifty years ago!"

"Seti Ashgad is the original Seti Ashgad!" said Leia. "Dzym's been keeping him alive all these years."

There was a rising clamor, men and women jostling and shoving aside Gerney Caslo's heated protests of Ashgad's good intent. Sheets and streamers of hardcopy were flourished in dust-covered, blood-covered hands, though Luke noticed that Umolly Darm and Aunt Gin were collecting the documents and tucking them into the safety of their pockets.

The Theran cultists had come down from their defensive positions on the gun shielding to join in the fray. With a yell of fury, Caslo broke from the mob and, with a nimbleness Luke wouldn't have given him credit for, seized a belt of grenades and sprang to the top of a broken girder, scrambled up another one toward the muzzle of the cannon.

Leia yelled, "Stop him!" but it was too late. Someone fired a blaster rifle just as Gerney hurled the grenades. A dozen lines of cold light stitched the man like deadly needles, but no one had thought to fire at the grenades he threw. They went over the stained black rim of the shielding. A moment later a deep, shuddering concussion shook the building, jarring everyone from their feet. White smoke belched from the cannon mouth. Gerney's body was trampled as people scrambled up the sides of the shielding to look.

Around them, there was sudden stillness as the Force storm relaxed its grip.

Leia swore. Luke's hand stole to the red, swollen marks the drochs had left on his flesh, and he shivered.

"Can you fix it?" he asked Liegeus softly.

"I don't know. I don't have tools."

"Umolly and Aunt Gin'll have some . . ."

"It won't be in time," said Leia. "There's an armored Headhunter in the same hangar and an old Blastboat.

You can mount the main turret guns in the Headhunter; that'll give you enough firepower to bring him down."

"The place'll be guarded . . ."

"The synthdroids are gone. Dead. I put them out of commission before I escaped and I don't think Ashgad's had time to get them back online. Come on."

Luke bolted back to the Chariot. Aunt Gin and Arvid were already tearing loose the antigravs from the two lifter platforms that had gotten the Rationalists to the top of the tower, affixing them to the black assault speeder's sides.

Only when the Mobquet had disappeared over the parapet did the battered metal doors of the stairway into the tower itself open, and Callista step forth.

"Liegeus?" She held out her hand to the philosopher. The earpiece of the ancient intercom system still hung around her neck. "We've got tools down here."

"And they'll be about as much good as those silly arrows," stated Aunt Gin fiercely, bustling over with her toolkit. She shoved the enormous, rusty box into Liegeus's hands. "Take this, son. I for one haven't spent ten years on this crummy rock to see it get taken over by those cheats at Loronar."

She led the way into the tower. Liegeus paused on the top step, studying Callista's face. Comparing the thin, tired features with those of the woman who had been Taselda's slave, the woman Beldorion had taken prisoner. "I'm pleased to see you well, after all that—er—unpleasantness," he said gently. "I owe you a kind of thanks, for opening my eyes to what Ashgad was doing, though I never thought I should be so mad as to say so. You were right."

Callista shook her head. "You were afraid for your life," she said. "All the knowledge could have done was hurt you, which it looks like it did. I'm only glad you were able to take care of Leia."

"After having not taken care of you?" There was a self-deprecating twinkle behind the genuine shame in his eyes, and Callista smiled.

"I can take care of myself. Most ladies can."

"How well I know. You know your young man is looking for you."

Callista said softly, "I know."

"Quite honestly, Madame Admiral, that's all I'm able to tell you." Threepio made one of his best human gestures, spreading his arms, palms out, at precisely the correct angle and positioning to indicate a friendly helplessness, a complete willingness to divulge whatever lay in his power.

And his digitalized recognition of human body language indicated to him that Daala was not buying it one credit's worth.

But she said, her harsh voice slow, "My title is 'Admiral,' droid, not 'Madame Admiral.' I am—I was—an officer of the Imperial fleet on exact parity with others of my rank, and you will employ that usage whenever you address me."

Her eyes were like ash—burned out, exhausted, defeated. Threepio did not think he had ever seen such ruin, such bitterness, on a human face.

"Once, Tarkin and I together could have ruled the Empire," she continued slowly. "Looking back on it, I can't even remember why. All I seek, now, is a place to live out the rest of my life where I will not be disturbed. I thought I had found such a place on Pedducis Chorios, a world in a neutral sector, with amenable local authorities, beyond the interference of those ham-fisted, brainless, contentious madmen who are engaged in the final throes of tearing to pieces what was once the finest system of government this galaxy has known. I want no more of it, or of them."

Her hands lay smooth over the arms of her chair, her knees together, the square bones of the joints and the hard bulge of muscle clearly defined where the drab trousers tailored to the flesh. Threepio's copious databanks contained a great deal of very alarming information about this woman: one of the most brilliant commanders in the Imperial fleet, but a mad bantha, a loose gun firing at random in battle. A woman of formidable competence and terrifying anger.

"And now I come to take up the advisory position I and my partners have been offered by the Pedducian Warlords," she continued in that quiet voice, whose hoarse timbre spoke of burning gases inhaled in the last battle on board the *Knight Hammer*, the battle in which Callista had destroyed her flagship and in which she and Callista had both been thought to perish. "And what do I find?"

Threepio had never been good at distinguishing rhetorical from actual questions.

"Invasion, the Death Seed plague, wholesale rebellion, looting . . ."

"Be silent."

He logged the interchange in his Later Study file under the heading of "Determinative Cues to Separate Rhetorical from Actual Questions." It was his duty as a protocol unit to achieve perfection in that area, and he was aware that it would probably prolong his period of usefulness as well.

"I find droids who have clearly been at large for some time in this sector, droids whose function is to accurately record all data taking place around them, whose answers to my questions are so comprehensively riddled with holes and omissions that they lead me to suspect that there is something going on."

She rose to her feet, and touched a wall hatch. With silent efficiency the panel revolved, exhibiting a complete and up-to-date electronic analysis kit. She activated the data screens with three taps of those long, square-tipped fingers, and unhooked a coaxial cable.

"Fortunately, many, many years ago I had a friend who taught me how to communicate with droids."

Threepio said, with genuine interest, "How very kind of him," but Artoo, quicker on the uptake, made a nervous attempt to back away, thwarted by the restraining bolt that Daala's Sergeant-at-Arms had taken the precaution of installing on both droids before bringing them into her presence. Daala checked over the various interfaces and cables added by poor Captain Bortrek and finally hooked her own coax into one of the ports he had space-taped to Artoo's side.

She flipped a switch on the analysis kit; Artoo quivered and gave a faint, protesting wail.

"Now," said Daala, her green eyes narrowing. "Tell me what's happening in the Meridian sector."

"What the blazes *are* those things?" Lando flipped through half a dozen data sectors, then cut back immediately to another screen of scan field to check on the next pass of the vicious, needlelike attackers. "And how much damage did that one do?"

Chewbacca yowled something through the comm from the rapidly freezing rear quarter, where he was floating near the ceiling to fix burned-out wiring through hissing masses of emergency foam. "Those things are the things that're gonna appear on our head-stones, pal," said Han.

"The most I can figure is they're some kind of CCIR technology, like synthdroids," said Lando, brown hands flicking and scrambling over the shield controls while Han whipped and pivoted the *Millennium Falcon* through the desperate series of zigzags and loop the loops that was the only possible defensive strategy against the things. "The Antemeridian fleet isn't anywhere near us, they can't possibly be guiding them in the usual sense of the word."

Around them, the *Courane* and the *Fire-eater*—and the light explorer *Sundance,* in which Kyp Durron had shown up to assist—were doing the same, snaking and weaving in a desperate attempt to remain in position near Nam Chorios until the actual invading fleet showed up to fight. Only the fact that they'd made orbit before the arrival of the gnatlike attackers, with barely forty minutes to spare, let them hold any kind of position at all.

"Are you kidding?" said Han. "You know what a synthdroid costs? That's crazy!"

"I know synthdroid technology is based on a kind of programmable crystal, and that's what kicks up the price . . . Blast!" he added, as there was a jarring flash and more red lights went up on the board. "Chewie, we've got another hit, starboard shield—yeah, I *know* about the hole in the port shield!"

Stars whirled and flashed past the viewport as Han put the vessel through another series of evasions. He wondered as he scratched past another line of laser light, perilously close to the main shields on the ship's spine, how long he could keep up this pitch of alertness and activity, not to mention how much more of this kind of activity the power supplies could take. Though everything was a spangled flash of stars and blackness, he had seen, in a rare moment of pause, the *Fire-eater* drifting helpless and being cut to pieces by the Needles at their leisure. He could only pray that the crew was already dead or at least unconscious from anoxia.

Lando, who could never leave an explanation unfinished, added, "If somebody's synthesized those crystals, or found a way to get them cheap, there's no problem."

"There's a problem for us!" yelled Han. *How did you fight things like that?* After long concentration and plenty of practice he'd managed to hit two of them, but with so many wasted shots it wasn't worth it. They could only evade, until the toll of the speed and hyperquick reactions wore them down.

The Needles, as far as he could tell, were tireless.

"One thing's for sure," yelled Lando, "they sure want that rock. You got any ideas how we're gonna deal with the main fleet when they show up?"

"I'll think of something."

There was a jarring concussion from somewhere in the ship, and more red lights went on.

"Moff Getelles."

Daala sat back from the primary readout screen, letting it go black. The lesser screens still held the record of Artoo's long, persistent battle to retain the secret files concerning Leia's disappearance, her doubts concerning the integrity of the Council, and all the information for which Yarbolk Yemm had been chased and shot at across half the sector. The little droid rested tipped back on his two main limbs, a posture curiously evocative of defeat. Cables and wires trailed from the various ports and interface hatches, short-circuiting through his defenses to every portion of his memory.

Threepio felt sorry for him and considerably apprehensive for his own safety as well.

It did not take an interrogation unit to deduce that this tall, red-haired woman sitting so motionless in her black chair was very, very angry indeed.

"The quibbling, incompetent, boot-licking, corset-laced little sand maggot," she said, in a perfectly soft conversational tone. "Still has his sycophant Larm on a leash, I see—with whom he shared the test results at the Academy, when he was promoted to captain over my head. Selling out to Loronar Corporation, a gang of legalistic thieves who'd peddle their sisters to either side so long as they got paid . . . Slime molds. All of them. Ranats and Hutts have more honor."

Threepio made a quick examination of his Determinative Cues subfile, but could not accurately ascertain whether a response was being solicited from him or not.

Daala slid from her chair to her knees, and began uncoupling the various cables from Artoo's innards.

As she worked she spoke, still softly, almost to herself. "I pity her, your Chief of State," she said—speaking to Artoo, Threepio thought, slightly indignant. "She was Prince Bail Organa's daughter. A man of honor, by his own rights, who raised her to be honorable. We had honor in those days. Honor and courage."

She stood and shook back her hair, which flashed like fire in the dim lighting of the office. Still her eyes were dead, but filled with the stony anger of the dead. "It was honor that drew me to the fleet. Power, yes, but honor and courage as well. And now they have come to this. Maggots feeding off the corpse of the Empire. Ghouls selling it to procurers and money grubbers. Tarkin would have died of shame."

She was looking in his direction, so Threepio ventured, "I have no conclusive data as to whether Loronar Corporation is in the business of procuration . . ."

"I was a fool." She touched the side of the electronic extraction kit, and it retreated soundlessly into the wall. "I was a fool to think that leaving them behind would be so simple as cursing them, and walking through the door. Maybe I've always been a fool."

She returned to her chair, and touched an almost invisible toggle in its arm. "Yelnor? Get me a conference with the captains of all the ships."

"Ships?" inquired Threepio, startled.

Daala raised her head, her poisoned eyes seeming to take in again that she was not alone in the room. "Ships," she said. "I am the President of the Independent Company of Settlers, over three thousand of us, counting spouses and children. We who were loyal to the old ways, loyal to the order and efficiency that was the heart of the New Order. Most were officers of the fleet, who sickened, like me, at this constant petty struggle for power, this stupid diplomatic bandying of words with upstarts and scum. Some others—the heads of business and their families, civil servants. We ask only to be let alone, and to that end we entered a contract with Warlord K'iin of the Silver Unifir for one and a half billion acres—the smallest of the three southern continents—on Pedducis Chorios, to colonize and to live as we see fit.

"And I have no intention," she concluded, reaching out and tapping Artoo on his domed cap, "of seeing my investment—*our* investment—come to nothing because a boot-kissing, talentless, jumped-up catamite like Moff Getelles wants to be supported in comfort by Loronar Corporation for the rest of his sycophantic life. Even if pushing him out of the sector means saving your Chief of State—and her spineless alien trash of a Senatorial

Council—from the embarrassment they so richly deserve."

She flicked over another comm button. Viewscreens revolved into existence all along the wall before her, viewscreens bearing the faces of eight men—three of whom wore, like her, drab variations of emblemless Imperial uniforms—and two women. Stern, disciplined faces, with those same bitter, burned-out eyes.

"My friends," said Daala, "it seems that there is one battle yet to fight."

21

"He's behind us." Leia reared up to her knees, wind and dust tearing at her long hair, and adjusted Aunt Gin's electrobinoculars. Whipping and veering through the fathomless, glittering gashes of the canyons, scaling hog-backs of diamond scree or dropping down precipices ten and twelve meters deep to catch again on the Mobquet's antigravs, it was impossible to see behind them for more than thirty meters at the most, sometimes only half that. But Leia knew.

"Beldorion?"

She dropped back down into the sheltered cockpit, began checking loads on the flamethrowers and blaster rifles that Arvid and Umolly Darm had thrust in after them on their departure. She smiled a little grimly at the truly excellent quality of the weapons, all sleek, all new, all black and silver, and all bearing the discreet double-moon logo:

LORONAR WEAPONS DIVISION

"All the finest—All the first."

As a rule Leia discreetly avoided riding in any vehicle

that Luke was driving; but for one of the first times in her life, she was grateful that her brother had developed the skill that had made him one of the best pilots of the Rebellion. And indeed, the Chariot was equipped with internal grav control as well, so she was able to prime and check everything without having her bones jounced out of her body every time the antigravs kicked in as they went over small cliffs—or big cliffs: She was being very careful not to look. She might have been sitting on her own bed at home.

"How'd they import this thing, anyway?" she asked, looking around her at the comfortable black leather of the seats, the small, enclosed bar and the bank of electronic toys and communications equipment. "It's nearly as big as a B-wing itself."

"According to Arvid, Loronar must have made seven or eight drops before they got past the gun stations." Luke flung the Chariot over a chasm that was considerably deeper than he'd supposed, whipped in a long, banking curve over the near-vertical face of a crystalline canyon to take some of the stress, and headed up a ridge like a mating sun dragon taking to the sky. "At least Aunt Gin found pieces of wrecked ones two or three different times. She's made a fortune charging Ashgad for repairs. She's bought parts from the Therans, too, so they've found some as well. All in the past year, she says."

"While Q-Varx was putting together the meeting with the 'head of the Rationalists' on this world." Leia shook her head. "I won't say I'd have trusted Q-Varx with my life, but he seemed sincere. Never in a million years would I have thought he'd be part of something like this."

"Maybe he was sincere," said Luke softly. "Maybe he sincerely thought that embroiling the whole sector in warfare and risking the spread of some plague he'd been *told* they could control were worth the rights of those who seek progress over stagnation. And he can't have known it was the Death Seed they'd be spreading."

"He didn't," said Leia. "But my point is that he should have. A man in that position can't afford to be that stupid."

And all the while Luke was flicking the controls, stretching out his mind and the Force to feel the ground beyond the next ridge, to slip past obstacles before they came into view, he was thinking, *There's something else. There's something I'm missing.*

There was life on the planet. Invisible, intangible, but intelligent, and lambent with the Force.

Don't let them. Don't let them.

Don't let who?

Why did he remember his vision last night, of storm-troopers and Jawas? Why did he feel that whoever it was, who had stood near the broken-down speeder in the canyon, watching him at his repairs, awaited him just beyond the next rise, around the next elbow of the rocky way?

But there was never anything there.

"And it's a sure thing," he added, almost to himself, "that Q-Varx didn't know about Dzym."

The hangar doors were locked. So were the doors that led from the hangar to the stairway, up to Ashgad's house. Luke was of the opinion that half-power on the ion blaster should be sufficient for the second pair of doors, for the first had nearly disintegrated when Leia had fired at them full-force. But the first blast only dented the inner ones, so Leia turned up the blaster to full and let them have it again. The noise in the enclosed space of the hangar was quite astonishing, and brother and sister waded to the resultant, gaping hole through a calf-deep rubble field and a choking cloud of dust.

"I told you three-quarters would do it."

"We can't waste time."

Leia might have learned diplomacy and patience with ambassadors, reflected her twin wryly, slinging one of the two flamethrowers into place over his shoulder, but it was quite clear that she still dearly loved the destructive force of small artillery fire.

"What did you do to the synthdroids?" Luke still couldn't get over the fact that there were virtually no human guards.

"Gutted the central controller." Leia swept the whole steps before them, floor, walls, and ceiling, as far as the landing, with a blast of fire. They both wore goggles picked up in the hangar, but Luke still had to blink hard to get his bearings back. The curled little black crusts that had been drochs crunched under their boots as they ascended to the landing. Leia fired again.

"We'll have to remember that if Loronar gets the Needles going. But any commander worth his ammo allowance is going to have the central controller locked up in the heart of the biggest battlemoon in the galaxy."

"Yeah, well, you were locked up in the heart of the biggest battlemoon in the galaxy, too." Luke grinned across at her as they dashed up another installment of stairs.

"And unless we've got somebody on the inside willing to let us go again with a homing device stuck on our tails," retorted Leia, pushing her goggles onto her forehead, "we'd better not count on that kind of luck again." The jewels on her gold-headed hairpins glittered incongruously through the soot and filth. "There has to be a weakness to them. One that doesn't involve access to the central controller."

The two halted in the doorway of the chamber, where Luke had met Dzym and had rescued Liegeus from the life drinker. The floor was a creeping sea of drochs. Brother and sister opened fire with the flamethrowers, swept the whole room in a licking, roaring sheet of yellow heat. It was like sprinting through an oven afterward, sweat rolling down their dust-streaked faces, the burned matter left after searing the soles of their boots.

The gateway that led through to the construction compound was locked, and Luke laid a hand on Leia's shoulder as she brought up the ion blaster again. "It's shielded." The green column of his lightsaber hummed into existence at the touch of a switch.

Leia glanced back over her shoulder, toward the blown-out door of the stairway. Luke knew what it was, who it was, that she felt behind them.

He was there, Luke thought. He could almost see him, ascending each step with a heavy, coiling loop of his great wormlike body, eyes malevolent rubies in the dark. The dark hurricane of the Force swirled around him, uncontrolled, while in his mind the voice of Dzym whispered, telling him that these humans, these pale little maggots, these defiant little play-Jedi, needed to be stopped at all costs.

Luke ran the lightsaber into the lock's works, tested the door switch. It vibrated, but held. "There's another lock," he said. "A hidden one, behind a wall-hatch . . ."

"Here." She had her own blade out. Luke wondered how she had managed to keep that with her, when Seti Ashgad had taken her from the ship.

There was no time to ask, for the floor shivered suddenly with the force of liftoff, the amber lights all across the lintel of the door turning red. Luke gritted, "They're

off!" and far above, over the top of the wall, they could
see the square, gray shape of the *Reliant* spring skyward,
lifters blazing, heading up the single corridor opened in
the planet's defenses by the destruction of the Bleak
Point gun station. At the same moment, Leia thrust her
lightsaber into the second lock, and the door slid open,
the hot winds of takeoff fountaining forth over the
threshold in a torrent of dust.

A couple of Spook crystals lay on the permacrete, a
trail from the cleared space where the boxes had been.
There were drochs, too, tiny ones, dying in the glare of
the pallid sunlight, where they had fallen out of whatever shielded container Dzym had carried them in.

And, on the other side of the open bay, stood the
Headhunter, its engine hatch open, a gutted tangle of
wires hanging down.

Luke swore, and raced across to it. Leia was already
running toward the Blastboat, which was likewise gutted
but otherwise unharmed. "Can you fix it?" she yelled,
scrambling up to the canopy. "They didn't have time to
cripple the guns."

"I think so. The readouts on the central core look
okay. They were in too much of a hurry. . . . Get me
the toolkit from the bench."

Leia sprang down, dashed to the repair bench, swung
the red metal energy cart around, and dragged it over as
Luke stripped off the remains of his shirt and began making a fast diagnostic. "Get the guns," he yelled, from
halfway within the hatch. "They just pull out once you
undo the locks, but you'll have to reattach the
cores . . ."

She snatched up an extractor and core couplers and
raced across the permacrete to the Blastboat as if they
were the children of the Rebellion again, with the Imper-

ials coming in and code scramble blazing from every makeshift klaxon on the base.

Listening. Listening. Knowing what was coming, power and anger and the decayed dark sludge of what had once been genuine, trained ability to use the Force.

She had one gun pulled and dragged over to the Headhunter and was starting on a second when she knew she could afford to wait no longer. Luke was buried in the hatches of the Z-95—the *Reliant* ascending like an ash-colored plague angel to the rendezvous with the Loronar fleet . . .

And she heard his breath. Stertorous, rasping, like the beat of gluey tides. The wave of ammoniac reek rolled across the permacrete, and the nigrous shock wave of decayed Force. Leia dropped from the Blastboat and ran lightly toward the door, stripping off and dropping her jacket, unhooking and throwing aside her blaster, knowing what the Force could do to blasters.

Beldorion the Splendid moved fast. He crossed the outer court in a series of great bounds and slithers, huge muscle rolling beneath his squamous hide. Fluid leaked from his mouth and his eyes were twin balefires, glittering with a single, evil obsession that he did not even recognize as being not his own.

In the curtains of sun-glittering dust that filled the open gateway of the launch bay a woman stood, slender and tiny in the moving aura of misty light.

Taselda? His old rival, his old enemy, flashed to mind . . .

No.

The little Jedi woman, the woman Ashgad had brought, the woman Dzym had wanted, a small shining figure in the shadows, with the pale glory of a lightsaber shining like tamed starfire in her hand.

"Don't test me, little Princess." His own blade

stretched forth with a deadly *thrumming*, a pallid and sickly violet. "It has been years. I may be a lazy old slug now, but I am Beldorion still."

Heart beating fast, Leia studied him, remembering how Jabba had moved, sidelong and looping, using the center of the body as a balance point. She recalled the one time Jabba had become displeased with someone at his court—the fat housekeeper who danced or was it his long-suffering cook?—and had gone after her or him with a stick. Recalled the deadly speed of even that obese and sluggish bulk.

Yet she felt no fear.

She didn't reply and could feel that it displeased him. He was the kind, she realized, who liked to expound before he killed.

Good.

"You were a sweet little girl. Don't make me—"

Leia struck. Step, step, thrust, as Callista had shown her, a hard clean slash like diminutive lightning, and Beldorion, still expounding, barely got out of the way. But his counterstrike was unbelievably fast, the strength of it nearly breaking her wrists as she intercepted it on the blade, the doubled vibration roaring in her head and in her bones. The blades twined, snarled, Leia twisting out from under another descending blow and barely dodging when the descending swerved to lateral—an old trick, Callista had said, but it took practice and left you open. Leia dodged back, shaken by the Hutt's sheer, animal strength.

She stepped back in, pressing him, her attention narrowed to nothing but the monstrous thing before her and the shining blades. Nothing else existed in her mind. He had enormous striking range, flinging forward like a serpent, so that she threw herself sidelong, rolled—*Thank you for the practice, Callista, Luke*—under the paralyzing wallop of his tail and was on her feet again and going in, the blade seeming to stream fire from her hand.

Not a second, not a moment, to lose—the plague rising up from this dim-shining world—the monster coming toward her again, rutilant eyes staring. He struck with his tail again, hundreds of kilos flashing with the speed of a whip. She barely dodged, wishing she had Luke's acrobatic training, his ability to Force-lift. The blades tangled, parted, Leia panting as she leapt sideways again, sparring for distance, watching the tail, fighting to remain close enough to strike. *In and out,* Callista had said—*It's the only way for a woman to fight.* Like a huge serpent he struck, and she raised her blade to defend, her mind open with the Force, feeling before he did so that he was going to switch to lateral again.

He did, and she was in under the blow and slashing a long, streaming, sidelong cut that went through the soft green body like burning wire. She flung herself past him, away from him, fast, for the huge bulk of him burst open, severed clean through, mammoth gouts of fluid and flesh and organs exploding suddenly forth.

She heard him bellow with rage, once—saw the hot smoke-colored blade of his lightsaber go whirling, end over end.

Then he was collapsing like a punctured balloon, like an empty sack, and Leia stood panting, covered in slime, her own blade burning in her hand, as Luke flung himself out from under the Headhunter and into its cockpit.

Dripping with filth, she saluted him with the blade, and Luke saluted back, their eyes meeting for an instant before he slammed the cockpit shut. Luke knew what it was that he saw.

Her first victory. The victory over the shadow of Vader. The victory of acceptance of herself.

And, he knew who had taught her that long characteristic side cut.

He hit the lifters, and the Headhunter slammed into life and rocketed like a falcon into the sky.

It rose faster than the *Reliant*, faster than most interceptors, for it had been designed to outmaneuver the gun stations, and had done so before. Course controls were adapted to the positions of each gun station, Liegeus's calculations, beautifully precise. He punched in the program, to hold the segment of sky guarded only by Bleak Point, knowing that had to be the way the *Reliant* was going as well. The flashes of light returned to his mind. Fighting, he thought. Fighting high above the surface of the planet, orbital battle. Someone must have come in to stop them.

Would they know to open fire on a ship rising from the planet's surface?

Blue sky darkened around him. The pale stars brightened to burning jewels.

He saw the gray ship, rising far ahead, making for the flurry of explosions and lights. There was a Republic corsair, hanging in space, far away to his left, being torn to pieces by tiny, darting CCIR Needles of black and bronze. The things the Empire wanted. The things Loronar was going to give them.

Beyond, at the farthest range of his vision, he saw the fleet.

Imperials. Two, three Republic vessels— Was that the *Falcon*? Dodging, twisting, like durkii maddened by parasitic kleex, trying to fire at the Imperial ships that were surrounding them. A thousand tiny flashes of fire as the Needles tore and swirled around them. He was out of signal range still, but coming into firing range on the square, awkward gray ship that contained Dzym and Ashgad, the monstrous life drinker and his pitiful pawn and the dark boxes of death that would consume the lives of all the galaxy, and relay that life back to him.

Only for that. Destruction, death, ruin stretching over planet after planet, only so that Dzym could drink of the lives of everything he touched, without fear.

Luke's thumb hit the firing button. White light lanced forth.

The next second a terrible concussion ripped his ship, tossed it spinning. He glimpsed the *Reliant* still going its way untouched, glimpsed something small and fast and black pass over him. . . . Another shot, and his whole console went red. He scratched and twisted at the joystick, trying to drag the Headhunter to stability, but he was spinning out of control, falling into Nam Chorios's gravitational pull. As the Z-95 rolled, he pulled her straight and got off a wing laser shot at the *Reliant,* saw yellow fire explode from her aft engines.

But she didn't go up. Only drifted, swinging off course, and his long-range pickups brought in the faint crackle of Seti Ashgad's voice, calling for an intercept.

As the Headhunter began its long fall, Luke saw a small carrack detach from the Imperial fleet, begin to make its way toward the drifting craft.

And before the Imperials knew what they had loosed, the Death Seed would grow across the stars.

Then he was falling.

Cabin grav was out. Against the sickening sensation of freefall, Luke worked to reroute switches, to shuttle power from the now-unneeded shields, trying to summon enough pickup to at least take him in alive. The heat in the cockpit was unbearable, suffocating, the ground a vast lake of molten reflection, rushing to smash him to powder. Hot spiky mountains, black shadow. The crystalline needles of the *tsils.* He felt the jolt and pull as one of the engines caught, dragged on the joystick, trying to even out into a long, sweeping curve. The retros fired, cutting his speed. He seemed to be descending in a column of fire, falling he knew not where. A laser bolt hissed near him and he thought, *Oh, thanks* . . . Presumably he had passed into the range of some other gun station.

Or they'd got Bleak Point fixed.

Flatten the curve. Hold the retros. Cut in the antigravs.

Callista . . . he thought, wanting more than he had ever wanted anything that he had been able to speak to her again. *Callista* . . .

He was above a plain. An enormous sea bed, blinding with the fire of diamonds to the horizon. Snaking lines of *tsils,* marching away into the distance. The Ten Cousins. Other circles, other lines, pointing toward the great glittering outcrops of Spooks in the hills.

There was a pattern to them, visible only when coming in from above like this. A pattern that tugged at his consciousness, reminded him of half-forgotten dreams.

He pulled back on the joystick as hard as he could, threw his mind open to the Force—because the ground was flashing by so fast he couldn't see anything of the terrain below—and brought her in.

Afterward he didn't remember getting out of the Headhunter before it exploded. He knew he'd probably used the Force to damp the physical reactions involved until he'd crawled to more-or-less safety. He had no idea where he was or how close might be his chances of rescue, and somehow that didn't matter.

If the Imperial Fleet picked up Dzym—Dzym with his enslaved front man Seti Ashgad, with his little dark boxes of crawling life, with his promises of controllable, invisible plague and limitless access to the crystals they needed for those tiny death dealers—there was going to be nothing left of the Republic, of the fragments of the Empire, of any space-going civilization whatever.

Only Dzym, fat and sated and looking around for more.

Luke lay on the spines of the crystal, eyes shut, the smoke of the burning Headhunter in his nostrils, knowing he should get up and knowing that he could not.

Feeling them standing around him again.

Silent, unseen.

If you're going to attack me, attack me, he thought, his mind slipping into a darkness and dreams of stormtroopers and Jawas again. *If you're going to have me, go ahead.*

And then, on the borderlands of consciousness, he remembered the pattern of the *tsils,* coming in from high above: remembered his dreams when they'd loomed in the background. remembered the voices that spoke to him in those dreams, like the Listeners said the rocks spoke to them.

You're alive, he said, enormously surprised—more surprised than he'd been about anything in his life.

Assent flowed out over him, colors in his mind, as blue as the crystalline core of the *tsils,* the green of the Spook clusters high on the rocks. *Alive alive alive alive . . .* like an echo.

And his dream of the Jawas came back.

They'd only used, after all, the images they could find in his mind: the indigenous inhabitant, brain gutted and forced to work for the stormtroopers.

You've been alive all this time.

All this time, they agreed, a gentle vibration like music, rising from the crystals beneath him, from the *tsils,* from the mountains; rising up into his bones. *From all time. For all time. Thinking and dreaming and speaking and singing. The sea formed us, and the sea went away. The planet fed us, from the fires of her heart. Little people here and there but not important. Not until they took us. Took our* . . . and the word was impossible to translate in his mind, *"brother/self"* he thought—a part of their minds.

The deep tide of their anger flowed over him, anger for their kidnapped kin.

Taken and enslaved, zapped with the horrible electronic realignment, as the Jawas had been zapped in his dream, so that they became slaves. Through the minds of the *tsils* Luke saw those enslaved ones, imprisoned both in the Needles and in the synthdroids; slaves but still kindred, still *tsils* in their hearts. He sensed the incomprehension of those slow timeless beings about what it was that they saw, but he himself understood.

The cabin of the *Reliant.* Two synthdroids lying dazed, eyes staring, on the floor, their flesh a rotting mass but their minds receiving impressions, still and calm, without pain. Seti Ashgad sat at the controls, his face a welted, bleeding mass, gasping, fighting for breath. His hair, his clothing, his body crawled with drochs, freed of their fear of the crystal-imbued light of Nam Chorios; while Luke, through the eyes of the synthdroids, watched, he saw a thumb-size brown insect crawl into Ashgad's mouth.

And Dzym stood behind him. Dzym with his robe open to the waist, every pulsing orifice and squirming pendule moving, while Dzym himself stared at the Imperial carrack's approach in the main screen with hungry delight in his eyes.

"*Reliant?*" crackled a voice over the comm system. "*Reliant,* this is Grand Admiral Larm of the Antemeridian sector."

Luke was so startled, so dazzled by the vision, that he could barely gather his thoughts. *Can you still talk to them?*

Confusion, murmuring—a dim comprehension of the horror, the pain, of those enslaved and taken away. But no focus. No direction or guide. They could see this, but could not understand, as Luke had not understood the dream that the *tsils*—the planet's Guardian inhabitants—had sent to him.

A second vision flashed in his mind, of the *Reliant* rising against the great glowing purple-white gem of the planet, seen from space. Of the carrack drawing closer to it, and, weirdly, of the voices transmitted between them, picked up over the electronic consciousness of the Needles themselves and relayed back to their kindred *tsils*.

"This is Grand Admiral Larm, of the Antemeridian sector Imperial Fleet. In the name of Moff Getelles, I am empowered to greet you personally."

With doubled vision he saw the square gray ship, the silvery carrack, and in the same consciousness saw the *Reliant*'s bridge again. Seti Ashgad raised his head like a drunken man, barely conscious of what was being said.

Dzym threw back his head and laughed, his eyes sparking in the darkness with two flames of unholy triumph.

Luke took a deep breath, and closed his eyes. It crossed his mind, very briefly, to wonder what this was going to do to his own mind, his own brain, but through the *tsils*, through the great white crystals in the ground, the green crystals in the high cliffs, he was aware of the pain of those that had been taken away, and he knew he could not let them remain in that agony. *Through me,* he said. *Focus through me.*

He felt their awareness converge on his. The Force in them, the Force that had been growing slowly, strangely, from their utterly alien life, twining with the Force within his bones and flesh and mind.

Tell them to destroy Ashgad's ship, he said, reaching out his mind to those hovering, darting consciousnesses out in the black gulfs of space. Understanding what they were now, and how to reach them. *Do this for me and I swear to you, wherever they are, whoever has bought them throughout the galaxy, I swear to you they will be brought back here.*

He felt the consultation of them, like an endless green wave spreading out across the plain, through the mountains, over the planet. A deep vibration, like the ripple on a still pond. And then it came back, Force and more Force—shining oceanic currents of it, streaming through his body, unbearably bright. Tearing him apart. He cried out in pain, kneeling upright in the diamond wastes, focusing his mind; calling the Force to his flesh. Reaching out toward the darkness of space, where the Imperial carrack was docking against the *Reliant.*

He saw Seti Ashgad trying to get to his feet from the main console, stumbling and falling among the dead synthdroids that littered the floor. Saw Dzym draw in a breath of ecstasy, of anticipation, of world-devouring delight.

Luke's eyes were closed, so he didn't see, far, far above in the hard blue unchanging sky, the tiny brightness of an explosion.

Then he fainted, and lay unconscious, alone beside the slow rising pillar of oily smoke in the midst of the wasteland of light.

22

Given the circumstances under which they had last parted, the eventual journey down to the surface of Nam Chorios could not be other than awkward for both Han Solo and Admiral Daala, once in charge of the security of the Imperial Weapons Installation in the Maw cluster.

See-Threepio, who accompanied them with Chewbacca, Artoo-Detoo, and a considerable number of Daala's co-émigrés, did his best to ease the tension by filling Solo in on the events leading up to Leia's kidnapping, on the state of the Meridian sector as observed by himself and Artoo-Detoo on their travels, and on Yarbolk Yemm's well-documented contention that the whole thing was a ploy originated by Gnifmak Dymurra, CEO of Loronar Corporation, as a means of obtaining hypercomplex polarized crystals from their only known source on Nam Chorios, for the manufacture of both synthdroids and CCIR Needles.

He was at a loss to account for the fact that those supposedly programmable Needles had unexpectedly left off attacking the small Republic fleet and had descended on the square gray ship rising from the planet's surface, blasting it and the Imperial carrack that had gone out to tow it to the safety of the Imperial fleet into sparkling fragments of eternity. A *prima facie* observation of the attack, even without the wildly furious and speculative jabber intercepted from Admiral Larm aboard the carrack, made clear beyond a doubt that this was *not* what Admiral Larm had had in mind.

Even as the debris cloud of the *Reliant* and its escort was dispersing, the entire squadron of Needles had turned with the precision of a dance troupe and had swirled down into the atmosphere, heading for the surface of the planet.

It was a moot point whether Admiral Larm's successor would have continued his attack—his forces still outnumbered the Republic ships almost three to one, and Solo's little fleet had been badly mauled—had not Admiral Daala's ships come out of hyperspace at that point, and descended on the Imperial vessels like black, avenging night.

"From the time I was sixteen, the fleet has been my life." Arms folded, booted feet apart, Daala glanced over her shoulder at Han, the growing glare of the planet below already so bright as to cast cold, queer shadows on her face. The forward lounge of a Seinar Sentinel landing shuttle included a curving sweep of viewport, as well as small amenities like a cold-cabinet containing wine and beer. Trails of condensation whipped and swirled up the transparisteel viewport, so that the Admiral seemed wreathed in misty light.

"Service. Order. The triumph over the forces of chaos . . ." She cocked her head, as the soft throb of the engines altered with the transfer to repulsorlifts. A hard fold appeared at the corner of her mouth, the track of some bitter thought. "All of my life, and all that I could have had, I laid on the altar of the fleet, and I was satisfied. And now . . . this."

"Well," said Han softly, "I can understand. You're not the only one who's ever been betrayed."

She started to jeer something back at him, then stopped herself and averted her face. Beyond the shifting vapor trails and their reflected brilliance, the starry darkness was yielding to a deep cobalt noon. "No," she said, her voice unwontedly quiet. "Perhaps not."

"Oh, look," exclaimed Threepio, from the other side of the lounge. "The CCIRs all appear to have crashlanded. There, see?" A thread of smoke curled into the still air. "How remarkable that they would have maintained so tight a formation in the face of what was quite clearly a controller malfunction."

"Yeah, well, maybe we better pick up a couple of them and see what we can learn about getting them to malfunction again."

As if Threepio had not spoken, Daala said, "You know her policies, Solo." Once she would never have acknowledged him as her equal, or spoken to him without scorn in her voice. "Will your Chief of State keep her hands off the Chorios systems, once their value is known to her?"

"I don't know what the Council's gonna say," said Han truthfully. "But I do know Lei—Her Excellency— just went through one laserblast raking over because she refused to interfere in a planet that couldn't get a majority for interference. So as long as you folks keep the majority on Pedducis I'd say you're pretty safe."

He rose, and walked over to stand beside her and look at the world that to him had, up until this time, been only a name.

"What a rock! There're people living down there?"

Chewbacca yowled an observation.

"Oh, right. One crummy little block there and about

four houses way over in the distance. I can see we're at a major population center of the sector."

Daala remarked drily, "At the moment, Captain Solo, I can think of few views more pleasant than that of an entire planet utterly devoid of human life."

The homing beacon from the surface brought them, not to the fortress of Seti Ashgad, but to the Bleak Point gun station sixteen kilometers away, where the plain of glass-bright crystal made a landing area for the shuttle. A light freighter already occupied the site—"As long as that station's out of commission," said a brisk little woman with long white hair, as the doors of the shuttle opened, "I'd be a fool not to take a cargo of majie off-planet and see what I can bring back. I'll get the cream of the market. Well, what do we got here?" she demanded, turning, as Han, Chewie, and the two droids descended the boarding ramp and looked around them at the glaring landscape.

Wreckage from the Force storm scattered the gravel for half a kilometer around the walls of the tower, snarls of wire, broken beams, weapons burst by the violence of Beldorion's uncontrolled will. Rationalists and Therans alike were gathering around the walls, and the plain was a parking lot of speeders, speeder bikes, and cu-pas warbling and wheezing and scratching themselves. A caravan of very dusty, very primitively dressed Therans clustered together, gazing in wonderment at the speeders; at Umolly Darm's freighter; and at the sleek, deadly shape of Daala's shuttle. From their midst two figures broke away, crossing to Han and Chewie at a run.

Battered, dusty, blotched with grime and smoke and blood, Han realized it was Luke and Leia. Leia cried, "Han!" and threw herself into his arms, crushed against him, face pressed to his shirt and leaving an enormous smutch of slime-dried dust there. Looking down into her face, he realized that he himself was unshaven and smutted with soot from that last burn-through of the defensive shielding that had almost accounted for the *Falcon* in the last moments before Daala and her fleet had made their appearance.

"Leia!" They were hugging like schoolkids, rocking in each other's arms—Han felt an idiotic urge to whirl her in his arms and dance.

"Admiral Larm . . ." she began.

"Is space dust," finished Han. "His fleet went back to Antemeridian to give him a nice memorial service. I don't think they're gonna be back."

"You know what happened?"

"Pretty much. The plague's over three-quarters of the sector, there doesn't seem to be any way of stopping it. The boys at Med Central say it's like the Death Seed . . ."

"It *is* the Death Seed." Luke came over to them, limping heavily with a stick, wearing the same sort of padded jacket and loose, ragged robe that the Therans had on. "And the—the Guardian *tsils* have agreed to send some of their number offplanet, to the sector medical facility, to be installed in apparatus that will destroy the drochs. Once we've got the sentient Spook crystals to channel light through, it shouldn't be hard to destroy the drochs wherever they are. All they ask in exchange is that we return every Spook crystal that has ever been taken off and programmed."

"And you're gonna explain that to Loronar how?"

"I'm going to explain," said Leia sweetly, "that without their cooperation, the entire story of their support of the epidemic will be released for general consumption, accompanied by sanctions that will put them out of business in a week."

Han nodded judiciously. "You got me sold."

"Once the Guardians are able to get offplanet," said Luke quietly, "I don't think Loronar's going to have much of a market for Needles anymore. The CCIRs worked because the central controllers mimicked the vibrations of the Guardians themselves. But even reprogrammed, the enslaved Spooks will know and obey the voices of the Guardians, their—their family, their alterselves. The living crystals that have inhabited this planet since first it was formed.

"They knew about the drochs," he went on, speaking to Leia. "They were aware, when the Grissmath Dynasty seeded the planet with them to kill its political émigrés. They did their best, for seven and a half centuries, to keep the drochs from getting offplanet. They invaded the dreams of the prophet Theras and his followers, taking whatever forms they found there, whatever they would believe, and instructing them to keep anything larger than about the size of a B-wing from taking off. Anything bigger would have sufficient shielding to protect the drochs from the radiation. But there's nothing, really, to keep large cargoes from coming in. And there are seams of mineral wealth, platinum and rock ivory, deep in the mountains that can be exported in small enough quantities to be ray screened and still support those who take them off."

"Which is just fine with me," put in Umolly Darm, hurrying past with Arvid and his aunt. "I never liked that Spook crystal business. Too fragile, the ones with good color were too far back in the hills, and even a box or two of the things gave me the willies. That Theran Listener Bé is already putting together an expedition for rock ivory with me and Arvid here."

She hurried on her way, Arvid waving back at Luke, to the stock freighter that stood some distance from the gun station's walls.

Leia glanced in the direction of the shuttle and then back inquiringly at Han. "An old friend," said Han, rather drily. "She showed up at the last minute to help us out. She wants to have a diplomatic discussion and some assurances from you."

Leia nodded, "All right."

She turned back, "Luke?"

He and Liegeus were among the Therans, shaking hands with those who had found Luke in the wastelands, sent by the voices in their Listeners' minds; bidding goodbye to the Rationalists, to Booldrum Caslo and his landlord and Aunt Gin. Luke paused for a moment, looking around, and Liegeus said, "We'd best be going, Luke. I've gotten the gun station back online again. It will be forbidding egress from this world in very short order now."

And, when Luke still hesitated, the older man added gently, "I think that there is nothing further that you can do here."

So close, thought Luke desperately. *So close. If I could just tell her . . .*

Whatever dark the world may send . . .

He remembered her eyes, in the sunset light of Yavin Four's towers. Remembered the pain in her voice, in that final message.

I have my own odyssey . . .

Tell her what, that would not give her still greater pain?

"No," said Luke softly. "You're right."

He turned, and followed his sister and Han, the droids and Chewbacca and Liegeus, to the shuttle. At least he'd have a reason to get up in the morning, he thought wryly—now, and for quite some time to come. He would be back to this world, he knew: to bring back the Guardians, when those who went offworld to form the droch-killing apparatus returned. To bring back the remains of the synthdroids and Needles, for the Guardians to try to rehabilitate and realign after their enslavement.

To learn what he could of the Force, as the *tsils* understood it and of this strange civilization of timeless minds.

But he would always wonder.

He stopped at the bottom of the ramp, for one last look at the cool-glaring sun, the twilight stars, the wind-scoured sea bottoms, and wastelands of colored glass, the towering crystal *tsils.*

She has her own road, Liegeus had said. And he was right. Where she had to go now, Luke thought, he could not follow.

The only way in or out of the gun station tower was over the walls. A Theran was rappelling easily down on a line, dark crimson coat and gray veils striking a familiar chord: the fighter who had thrown the grenades, thought Luke, during that first battle he had seen. When the gawky, graceful figure reached the ground and walked toward Umolly Darm's freighter, he saw the lightsaber swinging at the heavy leather belt, the long tail of malt-brown hair as she pulled loose her veils, and his heart leapt against his ribs.

She turned, at the other side of the landing ground, at the base of the freighter's ramp. She had always known if he was looking at her, even as he had known when her eyes were on him.

For a long moment they stood in stillness. She at the threshold of her long road, he thought, and he at the beginning of his.

He raised his hand to her, *Farewell.*

Her shoulders relaxed, and he could feel the tension leave her, the fear that he would cross that open ground to tear anew all those too-fresh wounds by taking her in his arms.

The time was past, for that.

In her stillness he read her thought: *Please understand.*
I understand.

She raised her hand to him, and he could feel her
smile.

The antigravs on the shuttle were so smooth that
there was no need to strap in for liftoff, though once the
vessel got moving Luke knew he'd be better to be sitting
down. He hurried his steps, to catch up with Liegeus as
they made their way to the forward lounge. The philosopher was right, he knew. *Trust your instinct,* Obi-Wan had
said, and curiously enough, once Liegeus had spoken of
loving and freedom, he could no longer deny what his
instinct had been telling him.

There was a time to embrace, and there was a time to
release.

Time was long.

He was at Liegeus's heels when they stepped into the
forward lounge, and the woman seated near the mist and
glory of the viewport rose from her chair. "Your Excellency," said the red-haired woman to Leia, who had preceded them in.

But she said no more. She only stood transfixed, color
draining from her face and with it draining the harshness
of its lines, the terrible stern bitterness that seemed as
much a part of her as the skull beneath the skin.

It seemed to Luke that there was another face looking
out from those bitter emerald eyes. A girl's face, almost
unrecognizable. A fierce dreamer's face, scarred by the
ecstatic knives of her dreams.

In a whisper, unbelieving, Daala said, "Liegeus?"

He was staring, as if at a ghost, only no ghost could
have brought that leap of amazed joy to any man's face.
"Daala?"

They crossed to each other, stopped inches apart, as if, after a lifetime of diverging roads, at the crossroad they feared to touch once more. It was Daala who reached out first and took his hand.

"Have you . . ." His voice hesitated. "Have you had a good road, all these years?"

"A long one," she said, the girl's voice, the proud dreamer's, audible still beneath the damage of battle and years. And it seemed to Luke that he saw death leave her eyes, and long-forgotten life stir there again. "Cruel, in places. You?"

"A long one."

She put up her hand, touched his unshaven face.

"I've missed you, Liegeus," she said softly. "I've missed. . . . This will sound foolish, but I've missed having someone to talk to."

Liegeus's fingers brushed her cheek, wonderingly exploring the footprints of the years, then gathered up the copper weight of her hair.

She had always been the stronger of the two, Luke thought, watching them together. And knowing this, he had released her into her strength.

Their lips met, tasting first, both afraid, then drinking deep, as if they could never again have enough. Her arms went around him, incongruous in the military severity of her uniform; he crushed her to him, medals, blaster, and all.

Nobody in the lounge existed anymore. It was as if Leia, and Han, and Chewie, and the droids, and Luke had all been wiped from existence, and with them the past twenty years.

No one in the lounge was the slightest bit surprised when Daala and Liegeus made their exit, without a word to anyone, handfast, into some other part of the shuttle. "I guess you'll have that conference some other time," remarked Han, drawing Leia down beside him on the black leather of the couch.

Leia sighed and laid her head against his shoulder, weary beyond words. "I guess we will." His arms were around her, strong and rock hard under the rough linen of his shirt. He smelled of salt sweat and burned insulation; his chin was sandpaper against her temple and his breath living warmth on her skin. She wanted more than anything simply to remain there, and drift into sleep.

From the viewport, Luke watched the thin yellow track of Umolly Darm's freighter as it lifted from the planet, streaked through the atmosphere and away.

She's all right, he thought. It was like watching a hunt bird when after its years of servitude, its owner frees it to return to the woods. *She is well, and strong. She'll find her way one day to the Force, to the light.* He felt weightless, at peace, and strangely free.

The blue air thinned to darkness and stars. The shapes of the fleet became visible, silvery pendants in the blackness—the world that he had sought since the age of eighteen, when he had looked into the Tatooine skies.

She had released him, he thought, to travel *his* road, wherever that road was going, to whatever end that journey would have.

He heard a soft step behind him, knew it was Leia before her hands touched his shoulders. Her voice was worried. "Are you all right?"

"Yes," said Luke softly. "I'm all right."

ABOUT THE AUTHOR

BARBARA HAMBLY'S first *Star Wars* novel was the *New York Times* bestselling *Children of the Jedi*. Her other novels range from high fantasies to historical mysteries to vampire tales. She holds both a master's degree in medieval history and a black belt in Shotokan karate. A multiple Nebula Award nominee, she has also been president of the Science Fiction and Fantasy Writers of America. She lives in Los Angeles.

The World of
STAR WARS Novels

In May 1991, *Star Wars* caused a sensation in the publishing industry with the Bantam Spectra release of Timothy Zahn's novel *Heir to the Empire*. For the first time, Lucasfilm Ltd. had authorized new novels that *continued* the famous story told in George Lucas's three blockbuster motion pictures: *Star Wars*, *The Empire Strikes Back*, and *Return of the Jedi*. Reader reaction was immediate and tumultuous: *Heir* reached #1 on the *New York Times* bestseller list and demonstrated that *Star Wars* lovers were eager for exciting new stories set in this universe, written by leading science fiction authors who shared their passion. Since then, each Bantam *Star Wars* novel has been an instant national bestseller.

Lucasfilm and Bantam decided that future novels in the series would be interconnected: that is, events in one novel would have consequences in the others. You might say that each Bantam *Star Wars* novel, enjoyable on its own, is also part of a much larger tale.

Here is a special look at Bantam's *Star Wars* books, along with excerpts from the more recent novels. Each one is available now wherever Bantam Books are sold.

The Han Solo Trilogy:
THE PARADISE SNARE
THE HUTT GAMBIT
REBEL DAWN
by A. C. Crispin
Setting: Before *Star Wars: A New Hope*

What was Han Solo like before *we met him in the first STAR WARS movie? This trilogy answers that tantalizing question, filling in lots of historical lore about our favorite swashbuckling hero and thrilling us with adventures of the brash young pilot that we never knew he'd experienced. As the trilogy begins, the young Han makes a life-changing decision: to escape from the clutches of Garris Shrike, head of the trading "clan" who has brutalized Han while taking advantage of his piloting abilities. Here's a tense early scene from* The Paradise Snare *featuring Han, Shrike, and*

Dewlanna, a Wookiee who is Han's only friend in this horrible situation:

"I've had it with you, Solo. I've been lenient with you so far, because you're a blasted good swoop pilot and all that prize money came in handy, but my patience is ended." Shrike ceremoniously pushed up the sleeves of his bedizened uniform, then balled his hands into fists. The galley's artificial lighting made the blood-jewel ring glitter dull silver. "Let's see what a few days of fighting off Devaronian blood-poisoning does for your attitude—along with maybe a few broken bones. I'm doing this for your own good, boy. Someday you'll thank me."

Han gulped with terror as Shrike started toward him. He'd lashed out at the trader captain once before, two years ago, when he'd been feeling cocky after winning the gladiatorial Free-For-All on Jubilar—and had been instantly sorry. The speed and strength of Garris's returning blow had snapped his head back and split both lips so thoroughly that Dewlanna had had to feed him mush for a week until they healed.

With a snarl, Dewlanna stepped forward. Shrike's hand dropped to his blaster. "You stay out of this, old Wookiee," he snapped in a voice nearly as harsh as Dewlanna's. "Your cooking isn't *that* good."

Han had already grabbed his friend's furry arm and was forcibly holding her back. "Dewlanna, no!"

She shook off his hold as easily as she would have waved off an annoying insect and roared at Shrike. The captain drew his blaster, and chaos erupted.

"Noooo!" Han screamed, and leaped forward, his foot lashing out in an old street-fighting technique. His instep impacted solidly with Shrike's breastbone. The captain's breath went out in a great *houf!* and he went over backward. Han hit the deck and rolled. A tingler bolt sizzled past his ear.

"Larrad!" wheezed the captain as Dewlanna started toward him.

Shrike's brother drew his blaster and pointed it at the Wookiee. "Stop, Dewlanna!"

His words had no more effect than Han's. Dewlanna's blood was up—she was in full Wookiee battle rage. With a roar that deafened the combatants, she grabbed Larrad's wrist and yanked, spinning him around and snapping him in a terrible parody of a child's "snap the whip" game. Han heard a *crunch,* mixed with several *pops* as tendons and ligaments gave way. Larrad Shrike shrieked, a high, shrill noise that carried such pain that the Corellian youth's arm ached in sympathy.

Grabbing the blaster from his belt, Han snapped off a shot at the Elomin who was leaping forward, tingler ready and aimed at Dewlanna's midsection. Brafid howled, dropping his weapon. Han was amazed that he'd managed to hit him, but he didn't have long to wonder about the accuracy of his aim.

Shrike was staggering to his feet, blaster in hand, aimed squarely at Han's head. "Larrad?" he yelled at the writhing heap of agony that was his brother. Larrad did not reply.

Shrike cocked the blaster and stepped even closer to Han. "Stop it, Dewlanna!" the captain snarled at the Wookiee. "Or your buddy Solo dies!"

Han dropped his blaster and put his hands up in a gesture of surrender.

Dewlanna stopped in her tracks, growling softly.

Shrike leveled the blaster, and his finger tightened on the trigger. Pure malevolent hatred was etched upon his features, and then he smiled, pale blue eyes glittering with ruthless joy. "For insubordination and striking your captain," he announced, "I sentence you to death, Solo. May you rot in all the hells there ever were."

SHADOWS OF THE EMPIRE
by Steve Perry
Setting: Between *The Empire Strikes Back* and *Return of the Jedi*

Here is a very special STAR WARS story dealing with Black Sun, a galaxy-spanning criminal organization that is masterminded by one of the most interesting villains in the STAR WARS universe: Xizor, dark prince of the Falleen. Xizor's chief rival for the favor of Emperor Palpatine is none other than Darth Vader himself— alive and well, and a major character in this story, since it is set during the events of the STAR WARS film trilogy.

In the opening prologue, we revisit a familiar scene from The Empire Strikes Back, *and are introduced to our marvelous new bad guy:*

He looks like a walking corpse, Xizor thought. *Like a mummified body dead a thousand years. Amazing he is still alive, much less the most powerful man in the galaxy. He isn't even that old; it is more as if something is slowly eating him.*

Xizor stood four meters away from the Emperor, watching as

the man who had long ago been Senator Palpatine moved to stand in the holocam field. He imagined he could smell the decay in the Emperor's worn body. Likely that was just some trick of the recycled air, run through dozens of filters to ensure that there was no chance of any poison gas being introduced into it. Filtered the life out of it, perhaps, giving it that dead smell.

The viewer on the other end of the holo-link would see a close-up of the Emperor's head and shoulders, of an age-ravaged face shrouded in the cowl of his dark zeyd-cloth robe. The man on the other end of the transmission, light-years away, would not see Xizor, though Xizor would be able to see him. It was a measure of the Emperor's trust that Xizor was allowed to be here while the conversation took place.

The man on the other end of the transmission—if he could still be called that—

The air swirled inside the Imperial chamber in front of the Emperor, coalesced, and blossomed into the image of a figure down on one knee. A caped humanoid biped dressed in jet black, face hidden under a full helmet and breathing mask:

Darth Vader.

Vader spoke: "What is thy bidding, my master?"

If Xizor could have hurled a power bolt through time and space to strike Vader dead, he would have done it without blinking. Wishful thinking: Vader was too powerful to attack directly.

"There is a great disturbance in the Force," the Emperor said.

"I have felt it," Vader said.

"We have a new enemy. Luke Skywalker."

Skywalker? That had been Vader's name, a long time ago. Who was this person with the same name, someone so powerful as to be worth a conversation between the Emperor and his most loathsome creation? More importantly, why had Xizor's agents not uncovered this before now? Xizor's ire was instant—but cold. No sign of his surprise or anger would show on his imperturbable features. The Falleen did not allow their emotions to burst forth as did many of the inferior species; no, the Falleen ancestry was not fur but scales, not mammalian but reptilian. Not wild but coolly calculating. Such was much better. Much safer.

"Yes, my master," Vader continued.

"He could destroy us," the Emperor said.

Xizor's attention was riveted upon the Emperor and the holographic image of Vader kneeling on the deck of a ship far away. Here was interesting news indeed. Something the Emperor perceived as a danger to himself? Something the Emperor feared?

"He's just a boy," Vader said. "Obi-Wan can no longer help him."

Obi-Wan. That name Xizor knew. He was among the last of the Jedi Knights, a general. But he'd been dead for decades, hadn't he?

Apparently Xizor's information was wrong if Obi-Wan had been helping someone who was still a boy. His agents were going to be sorry.

Even as Xizor took in the distant image of Vader and the nearness of the Emperor, even as he was aware of the luxury of the Emperor's private and protected chamber at the core of the giant pyramidal palace, he was also able to make a mental note to himself: Somebody's head would roll for the failure to make him aware of all this. Knowledge was power; lack of knowledge was weakness. This was something he could not permit.

The Emperor continued. "The Force is strong with him. The son of Skywalker must not become a Jedi."

Son of Skywalker?

Vader's son! Amazing!

"If he could be turned he would become a powerful ally," Vader said.

There was something in Vader's voice when he said this, something Xizor could not quite put his finger on. Longing? Worry? Hope?

"Yes . . . yes. He would be a great asset," the Emperor said. "Can it be done?"

There was the briefest of pauses. "He will join us or die, master."

Xizor felt the smile, though he did not allow it to show any more than he had allowed his anger play. Ah. Vader wanted Skywalker alive, *that* was what had been in his tone. Yes, he had said that the boy would join them or die, but this latter part was obviously meant only to placate the Emperor. Vader had no intention of killing Skywalker, his own son; that was obvious to one as skilled in reading voices as was Xizor. He had not gotten to be the Dark Prince, Underlord of Black Sun, the largest criminal organization in the galaxy, merely on his formidable good looks. Xizor didn't truly understand the Force that sustained the Emperor and made him and Vader so powerful, save to know that it certainly worked somehow. But he did know that it was something the extinct Jedi had supposedly mastered. And now, apparently, this new player had tapped into it. Vader wanted Skywalker alive, had practically promised the Emperor that he would deliver him alive—and converted.

This was most interesting.

Most interesting indeed.

The Emperor finished his communication and turned back to face him. "Now, where were we, Prince Xizor?"

The Dark Prince smiled. He would attend to the business at hand, but he would not forget the name of Luke Skywalker.

THE TRUCE AT BAKURA by Kathy Tyers
Setting: Immediately after *Return of the Jedi*

The day after his climactic battle with Emperor Palpatine and the sacrifice of his father, Darth Vader, who died saving his life, Luke Skywalker helps recover an Imperial drone ship bearing a startling message intended for the Emperor. It is a distress signal from the far-off Imperial outpost of Bakura, which is under attack by an alien invasion force, the Ssi-ruuk. Leia sees a rescue mission as an opportunity to achieve a diplomatic victory for the Rebel Alliance, even if it means fighting alongside former Imperials. But Luke receives a vision from Obi-Wan Kenobi revealing that the stakes are even higher: the invasion at Bakura threatens everything the Rebels have won at such great cost.

STAR WARS: X-WING:
by Michael A. Stackpole
ROGUE SQUADRON
WEDGE'S GAMBLE
THE KRYTOS TRAP
THE BACTA WAR
by Aaron Allston
WRAITH SQUADRON
Setting: Three years after *Return of the Jedi*

Inspired by X-wing, the bestselling computer game from LucasArts Entertainment Co., this exciting series chronicles the further adventures of the most feared and fearless fighting force in the galaxy. A new generation of X-wing pilots, led by Commander Wedge Antilles, is combating the remnants of the Empire still left after the events of the STAR WARS movies. Here are novels full of explosive space action, nonstop adventure, and the special brand of wonder known as STAR WARS.

In this very early scene, young Corellian pilot Corran Horn

faces a tough challenge fast enough to get his heart pounding—

and this is only a simulation! [P.S.: "Whistler" is Corran's R2 astromech droid]:

The Corellian brought his proton torpedo targeting program up and locked on to the TIE. It tried to break the lock, but turbolaser fire from the *Korolev* boxed it in. Corran's heads-up display went red and he triggered the torpedo. "Scratch one eyeball."

The missile shot straight in at the fighter, but the pilot broke hard to port and away, causing the missile to overshoot the target. *Nice flying!* Corran brought his X-wing over and started down to loop in behind the TIE, but as he did so, the TIE vanished from his forward screen and reappeared in his aft arc. Yanking the stick hard to the right and pulling it back, Corran wrestled the X-wing up and to starboard, then inverted and rolled out to the left.

A laser shot jolted a tremor through the simulator's couch. *Lucky thing I had all shields aft!* Corran reinforced them with energy from his lasers, then evened them out fore and aft. Jinking the fighter right and left, he avoided laser shots coming in from behind, but they all came in far closer than he liked.

He knew Jace had been in the bomber, and Jace was the only pilot in the unit who could have stayed with him. *Except for our leader.* Corran smiled broadly. *Coming to see how good I really am, Commander Antilles? Let me give you a clinic.* "Make sure you're in there solid, Whistler, because we're going for a little ride."

Corran refused to let the R2's moan slow him down. A snap-roll brought the X-wing up on its port wing. Pulling back on the stick yanked the fighter's nose up away from the original line of flight. The TIE stayed with him, then tightened up on the arc to close distance. Corran then rolled another ninety degrees and continued the turn into a dive. Throttling back, Corran hung in the dive for three seconds, then hauled back hard on the stick and cruised up into the TIE fighter's aft.

The X-wing's laser fire missed wide to the right as the TIE cut to the left. Corran kicked his speed up to full and broke with the TIE. He let the X-wing rise above the plane of the break, then put the fighter through a twisting roll that ate up enough time to bring him again into the TIE's rear. The TIE snapped to the right and Corran looped out left.

He watched the tracking display as the distance between them grew to be a kilometer and a half, then slowed. *Fine, you want to go nose to nose? I've got shields and you don't.* If Commander Antilles wanted to commit virtual suicide, Corran was happy to oblige him. He tugged the stick back to his sternum and rolled out in an inversion loop. *Coming at you!*

The two starfighters closed swiftly. Corran centered his foe in the crosshairs and waited for a dead shot. Without shields the TIE fighter would die with one burst, and Corran wanted the kill to be clean. His HUD flicked green as the TIE juked in and out of the center, then locked green as they closed.

The TIE started firing at maximum range and scored hits. At that distance the lasers did no real damage against the shields, prompting Corran to wonder why Wedge was wasting the energy. Then, as the HUD's green color started to flicker, realization dawned. *The bright bursts on the shields are a distraction to my targeting! I better kill him* now!

Corran tightened down on the trigger button, sending red laser needles stabbing out at the closing TIE fighter. He couldn't tell if he had hit anything. Lights flashed in the cockpit and Whistler started screeching furiously. Corran's main monitor went black, his shields were down, and his weapons controls were dead.

The pilot looked left and right. "Where is he, Whistler?"

The monitor in front of him flickered to life and a diagnostic report began to scroll by. Bloodred bordered the damage reports. "Scanners, out; lasers, out; shields, out; engine, out! I'm a wallowing Hutt just hanging here in space."

THE COURTSHIP OF PRINCESS LEIA
by Dave Wolverton
Setting: Four years after *Return of the Jedi*

One of the most interesting developments in Bantam's STAR WARS novels is that in their storyline, Han Solo and Princess Leia start a family. This tale reveals how the couple originally got together. Wishing to strengthen the fledgling New Republic by bringing in powerful allies, Leia opens talks with the Hapes consortium of more than sixty worlds. But the consortium is ruled by the Queen Mother, who, to Han's dismay, wants Leia to marry her son, Prince Isolder. Before this action-packed story is over, Luke will join forces with Isolder against a group of Force-trained "witches" and face a deadly foe.

The Empire Trilogy:
HEIR TO THE EMPIRE
DARK FORCE RISING
THE LAST COMMAND
by Timothy Zahn
Setting: Five years after *Return of the Jedi*

This #1 bestselling trilogy introduces two legendary forces of evil into the STAR WARS literary pantheon. Grand Admiral Thrawn has taken control of the Imperial fleet in the years since the destruction of the Death Star, and the mysterious Joruus C'baoth is a fearsome Jedi Master who has been seduced by the dark side. Han and Leia have now been married for about a year, and as the story begins, she is pregnant with twins. Thrawn's plan is to crush the Rebellion and resurrect the Empire's New Order with C'baoth's help—and in return, the Dark Master will get Han and Leia's Jedi children to mold as he wishes. For as readers of this magnificent trilogy will see, Luke Skywalker is not the last of the old Jedi. He is the first of the new.

The Jedi Academy Trilogy:
JEDI SEARCH
DARK APPRENTICE
CHAMPIONS OF THE FORCE
by Kevin J. Anderson
Setting: Seven years after *Return of the Jedi*

In order to assure the continuation of the Jedi Knights, Luke Skywalker has decided to start a training facility: a Jedi Academy. He will gather Force-sensitive students who show potential as prospective Jedi and serve as their mentor, as Jedi Masters Obi-Wan Kenobi and Yoda did for him. Han and Leia's twins are now toddlers, and there is a third Jedi child: the infant Anakin, named after Luke and Leia's father. In this trilogy, we discover the existence of a powerful Imperial doomsday weapon, the horrifying Sun Crusher—which will soon become the centrepiece of a titanic struggle between Luke Skywalker and his most brilliant Jedi Academy student, who is delving dangerously into the dark side.

CHILDREN OF THE JEDI
by Barbara Hambly
Setting: Eight years after *Return of the Jedi*

The STAR WARS characters face a menace from the glory days of the Empire when a thirty-year-old automated Imperial Dreadnaught comes to life and begins its grim mission: to gather forces and annihilate a long-forgotten stronghold of Jedi children. When Luke is whisked onboard, he begins to communicate with the brave Jedi Knight who paralyzed the ship decades ago, and gave her life in the process. Now she is part of the vessel, existing in its artificial intelligence core, and guiding Luke through one of the most unusual adventures he has ever had.

DARKSABER by Kevin J. Anderson
Setting: Immediately thereafter

Not long after Children of the Jedi, *Luke and Han learn that evil Hutts are building a reconstruction of the original Death Star— and that the Empire is still alive, in the form of Daala, who has joined forces with Pellaeon, former second in command to the feared Grand Admiral Thrawn. In this early scene, Luke has returned to the home of Obi-Wan Kenobi on Tatooine to try and consult a long-gone mentor:*

He stood anxious and alone, feeling like a prodigal son outside the ramshackle, collapsed hut that had once been the home of Obi-Wan Kenobi.

Luke swallowed and stepped forward, his footsteps crunching in the silence. He had not been here in many years. The door had fallen off its hinges; part of the clay front wall had fallen in. Boulders and crumbled adobe jammed the entrance. A pair of small, screeching desert rodents snapped at him and fled for cover; Luke ignored them.

Gingerly, he ducked low and stepped into the home of his first mentor.

Luke stood in the middle of the room breathing deeply, turning around, trying to sense the presence he desperately needed to see. This was the place where Obi-Wan Kenobi had told Luke of the Force. Here, the old man had first given Luke his lightsaber and hinted at the truth about his father, "from a certain point of view," dispelling the diversionary story that Uncle Owen had told, at the same time planting seeds of his own deceptions.

"Ben," he said and closed his eyes, calling out with his mind as well as his voice. He tried to penetrate the invisible walls of the Force and reach to the luminous being of Obi-Wan Kenobi who had visited him numerous times, before saying he could never speak with Luke again.

"Ben, I need you," Luke said. Circumstances had changed. He could think of no other way past the obstacles he faced. Obi-Wan had to answer. It wouldn't take long, but it could give him the key he needed with all his heart.

Luke paused and listened and sensed—

But felt nothing. If he could not summon Obi-Wan's spirit here in the empty dwelling where the old man had lived in exile for so many years, Luke didn't believe he could find his former teacher ever again.

He echoed the words Leia had used more than a decade earlier, beseeching him, "Help me, Obi-Wan Kenobi," Luke whispered, "you're my only hope."

PLANET OF TWILIGHT
by Barbara Hambly
Setting: Nine years after *Return of the Jedi*

Concluding the epic tale begun in her own novel Children of the Jedi *and continued by Kevin Anderson in* Darksaber, *Barbara Hambly tells the story of a ruthless enemy of the New Republic operating out of a backwater world with vast mineral deposits. The first step in his campaign is to kidnap Princess Leia. Meanwhile, as Luke Skywalker searches the planet for his long-lost love Callista, the planet begins to reveal its unspeakable secret—a secret that threatens the New Republic, the Empire, and the entire galaxy.*

The first to die was a midshipman named Koth Barak. One of his fellow crewmembers on the New Republic escort cruiser *Adamantine* found him slumped across the table in the deck-nine break room where he'd repaired half an hour previously for a cup of coffeine. Twenty minutes after Barak should have been back to post, Gunnery Sergeant Gallie Wover went looking for him.

When she entered the deck-nine break room, Sergeant Wover's first sight was of the palely flickering blue on blue of the infolog screen. "Blast it, Koth, I told you . . ."

Then she saw the young man stretched unmoving on the far side of the screen, head on the break table, eyes shut. Even at a distance of three meters Wover didn't like the way he was breathing.

"Koth!" She rounded the table in two strides, sending the other chairs clattering into a corner. She thought his eyelids moved a little when she yelled his name. "Koth!"

Wover hit the emergency call almost without conscious decision. In the few minutes before the med droids arrived she sniffed the coffeine in the gray plastene cup a few minutes from his limp fingers. It wasn't even cold.

Behind her the break room door *swoshed* open. She glanced over her shoulder to see a couple of Two-Onebees enter with a table, which was already unfurling scanners and life-support lines like a monster in a bad holovid. They shifted Barak onto the table and hooked him up. Every line of the readouts plunged, and soft, tinny alarms began to sound.

Barak's face had gone a waxen gray. The table was already pumping stimulants and antishock into the boy's veins. Wover could see the initial diagnostic lines on the screen that ringed the antigrav personnel transport unit's sides.

No virus. No bacteria. No Poison.

No foreign material in Koth Barak's body at all.

The lines dipped steadily towards zero, then went flat.

THE CRYSTAL STAR
by Vonda N. McIntyre
Setting: Ten years after *Return of the Jedi*

Leia's three children have been kidnapped. That horrible fact is made worse by Leia's realization that she can no longer sense her children through the Force! While she, Artoo-Detoo, and Chewbacca trail the kidnappers, Luke and Han discover a planet that is suffering strange quantum effects from a nearby star. Slowly freezing into a perfect crystal and disrupting the Force, the star is blunting Luke's power and crippling the Millennium Falcon. *These strands converge in an apocalyptic threat not only to the fate of the New Republic, but to the universe itself.*

The Black Fleet Crisis Trilogy:
BEFORE THE STORM
SHIELD OF LIES
TYRANT'S TEST
by Michael P. Kube-McDowell
Setting: Twelve years after *Return of the Jedi*

Long after setting up the hard-won New Republic, yesterday's Rebels have become today's administrators and diplomats. But the peace is not to last for long. A restless Luke must journey to his mother's homeworld in a desperate quest to find her people; Lando seizes a mysterious spacecraft with unimaginable weapons of destruction; and waiting in the wings is a horrific battle fleet under the control of a ruthless leader bent on a genocidal war.

Here is an opening scene from Before the Storm:

In the pristine silence of space, the Fifth Battle Group of the New Republic Defense Fleet blossomed over the planet Bessimir like a beautiful, deadly flower.

The formation of capital ships sprang into view with startling suddenness, trailing fire-white wakes of twisted space and bristling with weapons. Angular Star Destroyers guarded fat-hulled fleet carriers, while the assault cruisers, their mirror finishes gleaming, took the point.

A halo of smaller ships appeared at the same time. The fighters among them quickly deployed in a spherical defensive screen. As the Star Destroyers firmed up their formation, their flight decks quickly spawned scores of additional fighters.

At the same time, the carriers and cruisers began to disgorge the bombers, transports, and gunboats they had ferried to the battle. There was no reason to risk the loss of one fully loaded—a lesson the Republic had learned in pain. At Orinda, the commander of the fleet carrier *Endurance* had kept his pilots waiting in the launch bays, to protect the smaller craft from Imperial fire as long as possible. They were still there when *Endurance* took the brunt of a Super Star Destroyer attack and vanished in a ball of metal fire.

Before long, more than two hundred warships, large and small, were bearing down on Bessimir and its twin moons. But the terrible, restless power of the armada could be heard and felt only by the ships' crews. The silence of the approach was broken only on the fleet comm channels, which had crackled to life in the first moments with encoded bursts of noise and cryptic ship-to-ship chatter.

At the center of the formation of great vessels was the flagship of the Fifth Battle Group, the fleet carrier *Intrepid*. She was so new from the yards at Hakassi that her corridors still reeked of sealing compound and cleaning solvent. Her huge realspace thruster engines still sang with the high-pitched squeal that the engine crews called "the baby's cry."

It would take more than a year for the mingled scents of the crew to displace the chemical smells from the first impressions of visitors. But after a hundred more hours under way, her engines' vibrations would drop two octaves, to the reassuring thrum of a seasoned thruster bank.

On *Intrepid*'s bridge, a tall Dornean in general's uniform paced along an arc of command stations equipped with large monitors. His eye-folds were swollen and fanned by an unconscious Dornean defensive reflex, and his leathery face was flushed purple by concern. Before the deployment was even a minute old, Etahn A'baht's first command had been bloodied.

The fleet tender *Ahazi* had overshot its jump, coming out of hyperspace too close to Bessimir and too late for its crew to recover from the error. Etahn A'baht watched the bright flare of light in the upper atmosphere from *Intrepid*'s forward viewstation, knowing that it meant six young men were dead.

THE NEW REBELLION
by Kristine Kathryn Rusch
Setting: Thirteen years after *Return of the Jedi*

Victorious though the New Republic may be, there is still no end to the threats to its continuing existence—this novel explores the price of keeping the peace. First, somewhere in the galaxy, millions suddenly perish in a blinding instant of pain. Then, as Leia prepares to address the Senate on Coruscant, a horrifying event changes the governmental equation in a flash.

Here is that latter calamity, in an early scene from The New Rebellion:

An explosion rocked the Chamber, flinging Leia into the air. She flew backward and slammed onto a desk, her entire body shuddering with the power of her hit. Blood and shrapnel rained around her. Smoke and dust rose, filling the room with a grainy darkness. She could hear nothing. With a shaking hand, she touched the side of her face. Warmth stained her cheeks and her earlobes. The ringing would start soon. The explosion was loud enough to affect her eardrums.

Emergency glow panels seared the gloom. She could feel rather than hear pieces of the crystal ceiling fall to the ground. A guard had landed beside her, his head tilted at an unnatural angle. She grabbed his blaster. She had to get out. She wasn't certain if the attack had come from within or from without. Wherever it had come from, she had to make certain no other bombs would go off.

The force of the explosion had affected her balance. She crawled over bodies, some still moving, as she made her way to the stairs. The slightest movement made her dizzy and nauseous, but she ignored the feelings. She had to.

A face loomed before hers. Streaked with dirt and blood, helmet askew, she recognized him as one of the guards who had been with her since Alderaan. *Your Highness*, he mouthed, and she couldn't read the rest. She shook her head at him, gasping at the increased dizziness, and kept going.

Finally she reached the stairs. She used the remains of a desk to get to her feet. Her gown was soaked in blood, sticky, and clinging to her legs. She held the blaster in front of her, wishing that she could hear. If she could hear, she could defend herself.

A hand reached out of the rubble beside her. She whirled, faced it, watched as Meido pulled himself out. His slender features were covered with dirt, but he appeared unharmed. He saw her blaster and cringed. She nodded once to acknowledge him, and kept moving. The guard was flanking her.

More rubble dropped from the ceiling. She crouched, hands over her head to protect herself. Small pebbles pelted her, and the floor shivered as large chunks of tile fell. Dust rose, choking her. She coughed, feeling it, but not able to hear it. Within an instant, the Hall had gone from a place of ceremonial comfort to a place of death.

The image of the death's-head mask rose in front of her again, this time from memory. She had known this was going to happen. Somewhere, from some part of her Force-sensitive brain, she had seen this. Luke said that Jedi were sometimes able to see the future. But she had never completed her training. She wasn't a Jedi.

But she was close enough.

The Corellian Trilogy:
AMBUSH AT CORELLIA
ASSAULT AT SELONIA
SHOWDOWN AT CENTERPOINT
by Roger MacBride Allen
Setting: Fourteen years after *Return of the Jedi*

This trilogy takes us to Corellia, Han Solo's homeworld, which Han has not visited in quite some time. A trade summit brings Han, Leia, and the children—now developing their own clear personalities and instinctively learning more about their innate skills in the Force—into the middle of a situation that most closely resembles a burning fuse. The Corellian system is on the brink of civil war, there are New Republic intelligence agents on a mysterious mission which even Han does not understand, and worst of all, a fanatical rebel leader has his hands on a superweapon of unimaginable power—and just wait until you find out who that leader is!

A SELECTION OF STAR WARS TITLES
AVAILABLE FROM BANTAM BOOKS

THE PRICES SHOWN BELOW WERE CORRECT AT THE TIME OF GOING
TO PRESS. HOWEVER TRANSWORLD PUBLISHERS RESERVE THE RIGHT
TO SHOW NEW RETAIL PRICES ON COVERS WHICH MAY DIFFER FROM
THOSE PREVIOUSLY ADVERTISED IN THE TEXT OR ELSEWHERE.